GUMSHOE

Also by Rob Leininger

GUMSHOE

A Mortimer Angel Novel

ROB LEININGER

Oceanview Publishing
Longboat Key, Florida

ISBN: 978-1-60809-163-8

Published in the United States of America by Oceanview Publishing
Longboat Key, Florida
www.oceanviewpub.com

10 9 8 7 6 5 4 3 2 1

PRINTED IN THE UNITED STATES OF AMERICA

For my wife, Pat, as always.

GUMSHOE

CHAPTER ONE

FOUR HOURS INTO my new career as a private eye—a gumshoe—I found Reno's missing mayor. Me, Harold Angel's son, as unlikely as that was to all those who know me. Mayor Jonnie Sjorgen had been missing for ten days. By the time he'd been gone a week, he was national news, so my locating him was a major coup that got me well-deserved but unwanted media attention. More about that later. First, there were the two gorgeous women who came into my life.

* * *

I was sitting at the bar when the first girl wandered into the Green Room at 10:56 p.m. and looked around. Other than two middle-aged ladies drinking mai tais at the farthest table from the entrance, and, of course, me, the place was empty.

An old *Star Trek* rerun was winding up on the TV over the bar, the real deal from before my time with Kirk and Spock, old funky bad-ass Klingons in bad costumes.

Tucked into a corner of Reno's Golden Goose Casino, the Green Room was a dim, unlikely watering hole overlooked by many of the locals. It was also too tucked or too dim to attract the attention of folks from out of town, which made it a good place to get a quiet buzz on or get loaded to the gills.

Pretty damn fine evening, it was, too. I had sole possession of the bar's remote, and I was about to start a whole new career in the morning as a PI, Reno's very own Sam Spade, when this finely tuned *Penthouse* creature appeared at the entrance and looked around with nothing promising on the horizon except me.

Which shows how much looks can be deceiving.

After giving the place a quick scan, she sauntered over and eased onto the stool next to mine at the otherwise empty bar. This was, of course, a sizeable mistake on her part, but how was she to know? And what were her options? I gave her a quick scan of my own. By some clever, possibly industrial, process, she had been poured into a slinky black dress that had responded by filling out more than adequately in all the customary places. Or maybe she'd been dipped in liquid silk and inflated.

But enough about her. In my personal experience, and in the court of public opinion, IRS agents rank somewhere below that of politicians or prostitutes. As a result, my place in society for the past sixteen years had been fixed somewhere beneath the rock you'd look under to find a Sunset Boulevard hooker or the politician atop her.

Sixteen interminable years. It was time for a change. First week in July I finally made it. Told the IRS to shove it and took three weeks off—a well-deserved mini-vacation before embarking on my new career. I figured this change in my life, as radical and irresponsible as it was, was going to be a snap, exactly what I needed as I approached the midlife-crisis years. As it turned out, I was wrong about the snap, but that was anything but new.

It's said that a change of careers is stressful, but I didn't see it that way. Why would I? I was going from one of the world's worst jobs to one of the best. My equanimity was also due in part to the large number of Pete's Wicked Ales I'd downed that evening, elbows planted on the bar's oddly colored green leatherwork, awash in dim green lighting as Scotty fixed the Enterprise's busted warp drive for the umpteenth time. Warp drives in the future, I decided, were like the Xerox machines of today—a promising and useful technology, but buggy.

I took a sidelong look at my newly acquired drinking partner. It wouldn't be long before she hit on me. That she would was pretty much guaranteed, practically a requirement of my upcoming position as a private investigator, which would begin—I glanced at my watch, not a Rolex or even a knockoff—in about ten hours. The girl showing up at this pivotal moment in my life was predictable, written in the stars as they say, my way of getting a jump on what I knew was destined to become routine.

She was a looker, all right. Slender, frizzy blond hair, long legs, perfect curves, sleek as an otter. I took another hit of Pete's from a longneck as I awaited the inevitable. I'd read the books. I knew the drill. No doubt there's an entire chapter on gorgeous gals in the PI's manual. I gave the guy in the mirror behind the bar a fatuous wink, and he winked back at me, right on cue. Turns out both of us were drinking Wicked Ale. I liked that.

During my years as a field agent for the IRS, I could count true friends on the fingers of one hand, with a few fingers left over. Reno's phone book was a roster of potential enemies. After finally dumping the whole mess—all those years, including a percentage of what had metastasized into an almost attractive pension that I couldn't touch for another twenty years—I told people I'd quit because of the grim silences that resulted at parties when I was asked what I did for a living and, due to a well-exercised lack of judgment, I let on that I was a field agent for the IRS. I might as well have announced that I had a virulent form of airborne rabies. On the surface, therefore, my reasons for leaving the IRS sounded more or less plausible. Who the hell invites Internal Revenue goons to parties in the first place? Social climbers with a death wish? What kind of a life was I leading as a wallet wringer for Uncle Sam? The pay wasn't bad, but did I want to endure another two decades of forced smiles and paranoid glances?

My ex, Dallas, shook her head when I ran that sorry pile of excuses past her. Her explanation charted a very different course: according to her, I was forty-one going on eighteen. I might argue that second number with her, but I couldn't fault her logic.

My name is Mort. Mort Angel. Not Mortimer—although that mistake made its way onto my birth certificate all those years ago. My mother's idea of a joke, no doubt. It would be just like her, but she says the name comes from a long-dead favorite uncle on her father's side, and a bona fide war hero to boot—Guadalcanal— "so you oughta be proud of the name, kiddo." Knowing mom, and not trusting her as far as I could spit a lug nut, I checked. There is no such uncle on her father's side, which means there's no Guadalcanal war hero, which in turn suggests the name Mortimer is, in fact, her idea of a joke. Someday I'll have to get her drunk and ask her about it again. Sober, she would laugh and give me the finger, or pay someone else to give me the finger. She's that rich.

So there I was, Sunday evening, not entirely sober at 10:58 p.m., TV remote in hand, a girl right out of wetxxxdreams.com all set to proposition me, and me as eager as a teenager to start my new adult life at my nephew's firm, Carson & Rudd Investigative Services.

I was going to be a PI, the next Mike Hammer or Magnum, but not Hercule Poirot, which I've always thought sounded like a guy who might wear lace undies, which I don't. I was transitioning from a man universally reviled to a man about to become steeped in dark mysteries—although I might've played the part better wearing a trench coat at a rundown, rathole bar over on Fourth, east of Virginia Street. A dark and dangerous place like Waley's Tavern. I thought noir suited me. But I liked the electric air of the casino, too, the tension, the incessant money jangle and kinetic activity, the half-assed James Bond atmosphere—what would've been closer to a 007 atmosphere if not for the moronic siren song of the slots that have taken over—a slap-happy, nerve-shredding noise right out of Sesame Street.

The girl set a sparkly black purse the size of a gerbil on the bar in front of her, made herself more comfortable on the green leather stool with a dexterous wiggle, removed a Cricket lighter from her purse and casually placed it in the neutral zone between us, just within my reach. She tapped a cigarette out of a pack of Camel 99's and held it absently between her fingers, unlit, not looking at me, sitting there as if momentarily distracted, waiting for me to pick up the lighter and act every inch the gentleman so she could act surprised, smile, and get on with the business at hand.

All of which shows how little she knew. I took another pull on my Wicked Ale, then hit a button on the remote to change channels, thinking I'd catch the news on Reno's NBC affiliate, see if anything new had popped up about Jonnie and Dave, respectively our missing mayor and district attorney. Missing, to be clear, as in gone without a trace.

The girl sighed at my density, lit up, inhaled a lungful of carcinogens, God only knows how in that dress, then blew a smoke ring—a conversation piece. No comment from me even though it was a nice green-hued ring in the track lighting. She gave it another ten seconds, then turned and hit me with a smile so spontaneous and dazzling it had to have been rehearsed in a mirror on a daily basis.

"Buy a girl a drink?"

I *knew* she'd do that. Or something like it. I'd seen her around. A high-end hooker, she'd been working the Goose for a month or two. But, "Buy a girl a drink?" C'mon. She should've been able to do better than that even if she thought it wasn't strictly necessary. A few hookers have class, but most don't. Sleek or not, this one probably lived in a single-wide trailer out in the redneck wasteland of Sun Valley north of Reno, not because she didn't have enough money but because she wouldn't know any better.

Hookers can be fun if you don't take them seriously, which I don't. And I'd downed enough beer in the past three hours to fully appreciate the lighter side of life.

"Nope," I said, just warming up.

She gave me a pout, something done entirely with her lips, but a calculating look never left her eyes as she continued to assess her chances. She crossed her legs slowly, revealing an interesting length of expensively tanned, aerobicized thigh. I figured her for twenty-one, twenty-two tops, still fairly new at the game, especially at the casino level, and cheating like a sonofabitch on her federal income taxes. Her tip income for services rendered was probably over a hundred fifty grand a year, maybe two hundred. If I'd still had my IRS badge, I could've stopped her heart.

So call it a hundred eighty thousand. Roughly three times what I'd been making as an enforcer for our nation's Gestapo. Which begs the question, which of us was the smarter? Who was more successful? Then again, I didn't have a twenty-four-inch waist and I wasn't straining a C-cup, so it could be argued that she had a natural advantage, very likely enhanced by a few unnatural procedures, not that I was complaining.

She blew another perfect ring.

"Knew a girl once who could blow square rings," I said.

"Yeah?" Her eyes got wider.

"Uh-huh. Down in El Paso. Cute little Mexican gal. Something she did with her tongue."

"Her tongue? Sounds fun," the girl cooed, turning a little more in my direction. "You got a name?"

"Damn right. And yours is...?"

"Uh, Holiday," she said, timing thrown off by my non-response. "Holiday Breeze."

"You're kidding."

"No, really. Breeze really is my last name."

"What about Holiday?"

"My very own." She looked around, lowered her voice. "We could be friends, hon."

"Yes, we could, Holiday. You could buy me another beer." I swirled my bottle. "This one's pretty much done."

She pursed her lips again. "Tough guy, huh?"

Hell, yes. Come the dawn I would be a full-fledged PI, or close enough. Beautiful girls were going to flock to me like pigeons to a statue. I could take my pick. My previously humdrum life was about to do a great big one-eighty.

Little did I know.

She smiled. "You here on...holiday, or what?"

Oh, man, this kid.

O'Roarke sidled over, eyes glittering in amusement at the two of us. Patrick O'Roarke was six-five, a lean whipcord of a guy an inch taller than me, balding, with a bushy red mustache. Great bartender. At two-twenty-eight, I outweighed him by the better part of fifty pounds. We're about the same age. I'd hate to try to outrun him, and he'd hate to have to wrestle me. No one's the best at everything.

The girl ordered a Tequila Sunrise, then went back to work on me. "So, good-lookin', what's up with you, huh, you won't buy me a drink?"

"Good-lookin'" almost sprayed a mouthful of beer past those sturdy round globes into the depths of that slinky black dress. Last person who'd said I was good looking was my mother, back when I was still in middle school, and she was lying through her teeth, as mothers are prone to do—mine in particular. When I was ten years old I'd run a skateboard into the side of a car that was doing thirty miles an hour, broken my nose, acquired two dangerous-looking facial scars which had eventually helped during field audits with the IRS, and it'd been all downhill ever since.

But I shouldn't have been surprised. Holiday was a hooker. Hookers say dumb things. They lie. They'll tell you things like their name is Holiday. They tell you what they think you want to hear. To her, every schmoo with a wallet was "Good lookin'," even guys with a face like Wilford Brimley or Edgar G. I decided it was time to spin her around a time or two.

"I've got this side mirror on my car, Holiday," I said, running a finger around a damp ring on the bar's faux walnut surface.

"Yeah?" A wary note crept into her voice, so maybe she wasn't so dumb after all. No way was the side mirror of my car going to lead to anything she wanted to hear, conversation-wise.

"Yeah. The freakin' thing howls, up around sixty miles an hour."

"Lucky you." Her jaw worked, trying to decide if I was for real. She ground her cigarette out in an ashtray and stashed her smoking paraphernalia into her purse, preparing to bail in case this business with the mirror took a turn for the worse. Which it did.

"You oughta hear it," I said with oblivious, cheerful abandon. "Sonofabitchin' thing howls like a banshee."

"Fascinating." Her eyes darted toward the exit, then one final thought crept in. "What kinda car?"

"Toyota Tercel. Nineteen ninety-four. Still got its original paint, too. Yellow."

She snatched her purse off the bar. "Serves you the fuck right, bozo," she snarled, then stormed away.

Bozo. Good one, Holiday. I grinned, watching her go.

O'Roarke came over with her drink and the two of us stared with unbridled piggish male admiration at the sight of her marching away, ramrod straight, taut hips swiveling angrily. She disappeared into the video-game jangle of slot machines and the metallic din of dollar tokens tumbling into stainless steel bins.

"I've lost her," I said.

"Howling mirrors. Every girl's secret dream, good-lookin'."

I stared at him. "Christ, you must have ears like a radio telescope."

"Comes with the job, laddie. And I wish you wouldn't chase 'em off before they've paid for their drinks."

"Maybe next time." The eleven o'clock news started up on TV. I hit the remote, jacking up the volume for the latest on Jonnie and Dave.

For two days they'd been national news. Another day or two and the story might get international exposure. Jonnie Sjorgen and Dave Milliken, Reno's mayor and district attorney, had been missing for nine days, since Friday before last. Two of Reno's most visible public figures, gone without a trace. Twenty-four hours would have been a long time. Nine days was an eternity.

In truth, the story was in danger of growing stale locally. People lose interest when the news is no longer new, or when its interest quotient dips below the public's attention span. It wouldn't take much to stoke that fire again, but for the moment the story was like an old comet disappearing into the cosmos, leaving behind a glowing trail of dust. National attention had given it a much-needed boost. It was as if the pair had been sucked into a black hole. Of course, the lack of anything new in the case was itself news, but that only works for a while.

I wouldn't have followed the story quite so closely, except that my one-and-only ex, Dallas, had been living on and off with Jonnie Sjorgen for the past two years. Mostly on, which had made the gossip columns of the *Reno Gazette-Journal*, which was hinting that the two of them were hinting at marriage.

Tonight, however, Channel 4 delivered the same old tired rehash which meant it was time for me to hit the road. I had to go to work in the morning. Looking forward to it, too, for the first time in a decade.

"See ya," I said to O'Roarke, dropping a few extra dollars on the bar, relinquishing my grip on the remote.

O'Roarke jerked a thumb at the TV, at clips of Jonnie and Dave and a voice-over by Ginger Haley droning on, speculating furiously, trying desperately to keep it all fresh and alive. "Find those two," he said. "Make a big name for yourself."

"Hah."

He sucked his teeth, grinning mischievously. "Then do it for Dallas, Great Gumshoe."

"Double hah."

I drained the last of the beer and headed for the door.

* * *

Great Gumshoe, hell. I was starting to wish I hadn't told him about the change of jobs. I'd made the mistake earlier of telling him about my upcoming career change and of course he'd laughed at what was nothing less than my one-and-only future, the jerk, which didn't surprise me in the least—O'Roarke and I go way back. I would've done the same for him if he'd told me he was going to raise llamas or start designing women's dresses.

I went out the Virginia Street exit into a muggy July night. This is desert, but half a dozen times a year Reno confuses itself with

New Orleans or Miami. At 11:06 p.m. the sky was overcast, clouds tinged muddy orange by the city's lights, temperature in the eighties. Heat lightning flickering in the mountains to the east. Despite the humidity, the night had a pleasant muzzy whirl to it—about six beers' worth. Or eight. I'd lost count. Didn't matter.

I was about to walk up north toward my home in the hills, not far from the university, when something caught my eye, or a lack of something—darkness, a hole, an emptiness punched like someone's fist through the garish casino glare. Maybe it was the Sjorgen thing, the constant media pressure, but I found myself staring at the three-story Victorian mansion across Virginia Street known locally as Sjorgen House—or Woolley House, depending on how one viewed its ownership, legally or historically.

The place had been one of Reno's finest in 1898, about the time of the Spanish-American war. It had become an island in the midst of Reno's unbridled growth, an anachronism overrun by neon, protected by the local historical society, squatting darkly amid shaggy elms beneath the Golden Goose's eerie green bulk. But for a lone yellow light in an attic window, the house was dark. Edna Woolley had lived in the place for forty years, but the house still belonged to Jonnie.

I turned away. Sjorgen's name came up a lot in Reno. It was something you got used to. Mayor Jonnie owned all or part of half a dozen businesses and three or four rental properties in the city.

Having left the wailing Tercel at home in the garage, I began the half-mile trek home, not entirely steady on my feet. Jonnie was still floating around in my mind—just what I didn't want or need, but there it was. Jonnie Hayes Sjorgen, fifty-seven years old, was a shoo-in for reelection next time around. Or would be if he turned up again. He'd vanished minutes after delivering a speech at a fundraiser for battered women. Reno's D.A., Milliken, was last seen leaving his office two hours before that. By the following afternoon, the media got wind of it, and the circus had been in full swing ever since. By now everyone knew the two of them had gone to high school together right here in Reno. They'd graduated the same year. Jonnie had been class president his senior year and six foot six Milliken had been an all star on the Reno High basketball team. They had been friends, still were, and both were gone. The story, with its connections to the past, was a sex boutique for journalists.

In spite of a tendency to use the word "proactive" in speeches, Jonnie had been a popular mayor for six-plus years. He'd been voted Reno's most eligible bachelor five years running. Women's groups adored him, swooned in his presence—that year-round tan, curly silver-black hair, boyish grin, capped teeth, dark green Jaguar. He was rich. He was a guy I loved to hate, especially after he'd made a move on Dallas.

Adding another layer of melodrama to an already unlikely story, Jonnie's father, Wendell Sjorgen, had been murdered outside a saloon on Wells Avenue twenty years earlier, a tidbit whose effect on Nielsen ratings was not lost on the networks.

So far, not a single ray of light had been shed on what might have happened to Jonnie and Dave. The dominant theory, rumor had it, was that they were somewhere in the vicinity of Great Abaco or Nassau, laughing their heads off on a pristine beach with topless giggling nut-brown girls in attendance providing rum drinks with little umbrellas in them, and that a big chunk of city money would turn up missing any day now, if only the accountants could find it. It didn't hurt that theory one bit that Jonnie's Jaguar and Milliken's Jeep Cherokee had been found the day after they'd vanished, parked side by side at the Airport Plaza Hotel on Terminal Way, directly across from Reno-Tahoe International

Airport, even though it had been determined that the pair hadn't flown anywhere, at least not using their own names. Nor had security tapes shown them to be in the airport on or around the first critical twenty-four hours of their disappearance.

Dallas had kept my name, which figured. She would die before calling herself Dallas Frick again. There were times when I thought the only reason she'd married me was for the name—Dallas Angel has an undeniable ring to it—but I knew that wasn't fair and wasn't true. We'd simply been too young. Nineteen. I knew now that my primary reason for saying "I do" back then had been simple lust and a kid's unshakable belief that lust was all it took, that love and lust were in fact the same thing, and a perfectly reasonable basis for a lifetime of forever. But at nineteen, what else is there? Testosterone is one hell of a drug, and Dallas had been an absolute knockout. She still is. Truth was, I still loved her more than ever, but sometimes you have to let go, and I'd learned that, too.

Dallas and I were on good terms, and not for the sake of the kid either. The "kid," Nicole, was no longer a kid, a fact to which I was having trouble adjusting. Twenty years old, over two thousand miles away, taking dance and theater classes at Ithaca College in New York. She wasn't the reason Dallas and I weren't at each other's throats. Hatred and grudge-holding, I've found, aren't inevitable by-products of divorce. Dallas and I have always been friends. She had no reason to hate me, before, during, or after the divorce. It wasn't my fault that the football career hadn't panned out, years ago. It hadn't been much of a career—it hadn't been any *sort* of a career, in fact—just a will-o'-the-wisp dream of a kid too wet behind the ears to have a clue. What's great in high school is second-string in college is nothing at all to the NFL. So Dallas and I were still friends. And, as I kidded her a month after the divorce was final, she might not have wanted any trouble with the IRS. The comment earned me a punch on the arm that still bothers me on rainy days.

I paused under a streetlamp to check my watch. In nine hours forty minutes I was going to report to Carson & Rudd Investigative Services, to my nephew, Gregory Rudd, my sister Ellen's oldest, age twenty-eight, and as dull and as staid as they come, as if he'd been born in the wrong century, but a good kid nonetheless, especially if vanilla's your flavor. I'd once changed his diapers, back when I was fourteen. Emergency situation. I told him about it two months ago. Now he was about to become my employer—an unsettling reversal of roles, fortune, or some combination thereof, but one I'd brought upon myself. I could've toughed it out with the IRS. Maybe I should have. But...no way. Some things in life are unspeakable. I have a soul. Sometimes I can even feel it down there plugging away.

I trudged through pools of light spilling from streetlamps, not quite as drunk as I thought I'd be when I'd hiked down to the Goose earlier that evening, but the world had a nice glow all the same. Its edges had softened. Drinking wasn't my strong suit—damned if I knew what was—and I didn't want to show up at Greg's smelling like a brewery, even if Gregory was likely, due to the diaper incident, to forgive his old uncle an occasional weakness.

Sleuthing, I figured, would require a clear head and razor-sharp reflexes.

CHAPTER TWO

FROM ACROSS INTERSTATE 80 in the hills north of downtown, the casinos rose up in a gaudy roar of light. The city's rough edges and dirt lay hidden beneath this high-rise blaze of neon. I faced it for a moment, sensing the magic in Reno's lights, its surreal, improbable beauty. Like rectangular crystals, casinos erupted from the dark desert earth. A hundred years ago there was nothing like it on the planet. In another hundred years there might not be again, if one was a cynic about such things, which I tend to be. In a geologic blink we will return the Jurassic swamps and dinosaurs to carbon dioxide and water, leaving behind a brief burst of light and UHF that will blow past the Andromeda galaxy in one and a half million years. If they have TV, and better cable than we do, maybe they can snag *I Love Lucy*, then, fifty years later, *Fear Factor*—dimwits drinking blended rats in Times Square. Entertainment for the masses. No doubt they'll be impressed by the progress we've made.

The neighborhood was quiet on Ralston Street, north of the freeway, half a mile west of the UNR campus, between Eleventh and Twelfth. I didn't see any vans parked near my house. No media types skulking about, hoping to peel a nice, controversial sound bite out of me. The skulking had gone on for a few days, but had tapered off. Maybe they'd given up on me—reporters, hoping to dig up inside dirt on Jonnie via Dallas, thinking the ex-husband of the girlfriend of the missing mayor might be happy to sing.

Being the ex, and the wronged party, if one views divorce as a contest of right and wrong, I even had something of a motive for making Jonnie disappear, if his disappearance was seen as a possible crime, which more and more people were doing, one way or another. I'd even been questioned by a pair of detectives who showed up on my doorstep Tuesday evening, five days ago. I told them what I told the media rabble: I don't know shit about this thing with Jonnie, but how'd your 1040 turn out last April?

The subject of tax forms, I've found, has a pretty much universal effect—roughly the same as a narc lurking in a corner of the room taking notes and photos at a frat party.

I went up the walk, unlocked the deadbolt, then the door, and went inside.

Years ago, the house belonged to my parents. I'd grown up in it. It held a host of childhood memories, most of them good. My father died nine years ago in what was loosely said to be a golfing accident, and my mother, Dori Angel, is in Hawaii now, Maui, sharing a multimillion-dollar condo-mansion with two other widows and having the time of her life. Her hair is dyed a phosphorescent shade of red and she drinks a lot of gimlets, Green Dragons, and other gin-based drinks. I see her every year or two, when it suits her, and every time she turns up she has a new boyfriend.

The last one was blond, tan, Nautilus-muscled, and predictably slow of wit—a pretty boy thirty-three years old. My mother was sixty-four at the time, but cradle-robbing seems to suit her. I tried not to picture him poolside at her condo in a man-thong. I got him drunk on straight shots of tequila down at Waley's Tavern, a down-and-dirty bar on East Fourth where the owner, a rough-looking forty-something guy with a black belt in several different martial arts, unplugs the juke at about two in the morning and plays classical music, of all things, until closing time at four.

We left about the time Mozart started up, Pretty Boy unable to stagger effectively, testosterone level flatlined. In the wee hours, arms folded across an ample chest, my mom informed us that we were both jerks, utterly *useless* jerks, which seemed reasonably accurate to me. At least boyfriend Stevie wasn't going to be of any use to her *that* night. Three weeks later she phoned from her aerie in Hawaii to tell me, pointedly, that she had a new "friend," thirty-*one* years old, Queens-Italian, and a hunk like I wouldn't believe. I asked if this one no longer wet the bed, which I knew wasn't fair since she was entitled to do with her life as she saw fit, and she said no, he still does, giving me one of the most ribald laughs I'd ever heard in my life. I couldn't keep up with her.

The house was all mine now, including its second mortgage. I'd rented it out when Mom left, then moved in after my divorce, after the former tenants had trashed the place. Six panels of sheet rock, a few gallons of paint, two new doors, new carpet, new cabinets, new toilet, and it was at least habitable again. It took three years for the smell of cigarette smoke to leach out of the walls enough that I was no longer smelling Marlboros. I'd burn the sonofabitch to the ground before I'd rent it out again.

Without turning on lights, I made my way down a short hall-way and into my bedroom, hit the switch on the wall inside the door, and spotted the girl in my bed right off.

I stared. Goggled, actually. Out of reflex I reached for the gun at my hip. Would've pulled it too, if I'd been carrying.

I gripped the doorframe, unable to conjure up a coherent thought for several seconds. Another girl, another blond. It was turning into one of those red-banner nights.

A sense of having been violated eased into my brain. My space was *my* space, my priceless few square feet where I kept my stuff, and in which I could do as I damn well pleased. This girl, this *unknown* girl, had invaded that cherished space, crawled into my bed, *my* bed, and put herself to sleep. On my sheets. *Mine.*

At least I *thought* it was a girl, hoped it was. These days, well, suffice it to say you can't always tell. I tiptoed over for a closer look. Yep, female, no doubt about it, and ordinarily I wouldn't have viewed a girl in my bed as an insurmountable problem, but, tonight...

I sucked in a lungful of air with which to let out a mighty yell, to catapult her out of my bed with a bellow of outrage, but a note on the nightstand caught my eye, next to a half-full glass of water. I exhaled, then picked up the note. In an untidy scrawl it read:

Tired. Explain later. K.

I dropped the note back on the table, trying to think.

K. I didn't know a "K." More specifically, I didn't know *this* K, I was sure of it. Mid to late twenties, out cold, lying on her side. Pert nose, pretty face partly hidden by tangled, still-damp honey-blond curls that didn't reach her shoulders. And one naked shoulder, which I found more than a little intriguing. No sign of clothing on the little I could see of her, which caused my mind to ramble off in an entirely new direction for several beer-enhanced seconds.

"Hey!" I said. Not the swiftest opening gambit, but I couldn't think of anything swifter and I didn't think another minute was likely to change that.

The girl snored softly.

I sucked in another lungful and yelled, "*HEY!*"—but got no more response than the first time. I poked her shoulder, twice, then gave it a good shake.

Still nothing. But at least she wasn't cold or stiff. Rigor hadn't set in, wasn't likely to.

I shook her, figuring about Richter six, and kept it up, rocking her pretty good, finally eliciting a moan of protest so far down in the abyss of unconsciousness that it might've been her last. But it was a response nonetheless, and I stopped abusing her, the better to start up a conversation. K promptly began to snore again, louder than before.

I blinked. Tired didn't begin to describe the condition of this gal.

Or maybe not tired. I looked around, starting to think overdose. No empty pill container, no syringe. Nothing but the glass of water by the bed.

I poked my head out the door into the hallway. A damp, soapy smell lingered in the air, wafting from the vicinity of the bathroom. I went down there to have a look.

The shower stall was wet. Damp towels slung on the rack, a puddle on the floor. All of which made me wonder what she would've done if I'd walked in and caught her covered in suds and singing, "I'm gonna wash that man right outta my hair." Hell, I wondered what *I* would've done.

Pursuing the overdose angle, I peered into the medicine cabinet. I didn't keep a supply of arsenic, rat poison, or barbiturates on hand, but a person can end it all with garden-variety aspirin. All it takes is a deeper level of determination and a bigger glass of water.

The Bayer was full, never opened. The ibuprofen wasn't as conclusive, but it appeared to be untouched. One bottle was turned the wrong way, however, label side in. I made a point of facing the labels out. Not that I'm compulsive; it just makes more sense to read than to grope. So, ah-hah! K had moved that bottle.

I took it off the shelf, knowing this private-eye thing tomorrow at Greg's was going to work out great. The bottle held valerian root, a mild herbal sedative, the nearest thing I had to sleeping pills. The stuff smells abominable, like vomit in a capsule, but Dallas swears by it. She'd put me onto it. It seems to work, not in a big way, but enough.

I opened it. Last time I looked there'd been a dozen tablets left, give or take. Now there were five. Unless I'd had a parade through the house, not something I could readily discount, K had taken about half a dozen. Not enough to harm a medium-sized cat, but enough to put her under farther than normal, whatever that was for her.

It also meant she knew her herbs, which put her somewhere in Dallas's league. I wondered if that also implied homemade bread, StairMastering, crosswords, mid-level Sudoku, yoga, meditation, aromatherapy, and mega doses of antioxidants as well.

As I put the bottle back, I realized that curiosity had edged out my anger. I even caught a glimpse of myself in the mirror with a silly half-grin on my face. The old PI charm was already in high gear, even before day one on the job.

My toothbrush was damp. *Sonofabitch!* For a moment I stared at it, anger returning full force. Like clockwork, I put that thing in my mouth every morning and night. That, by God, was *mine*, if nothing else on this sorry, intrusive planet.

Now I felt violated.

Then the thought dawned—and at this point my moral compass did a three-sixty and then some—that K might be hurt. How would I know? She was warm, but under those covers she might be slowly bleeding to death, might have a knife stuck in her back, might be any number of things requiring a more or less immediate response from someone, presumably me.

Having showered, brushed her teeth, swallowed a large but nowhere near lethal dose of valerian, and tucked herself into bed?

Not likely, but...how would I *know*?

Which hinted at my next move, which I thought I might be able to justify if it ever came to that. I returned to the bedroom, then paused in the doorway...figuring, with all this brain power at my disposal, that, come tomorrow at nine, I would make a damned fine gumshoe. I would make my bland young nephew enormously proud of his Uncle Mort.

Still, I hesitated. K had turned my bed into *her* bed. As I saw it, people have an inalienable right to privacy.

Usually. In their *own* goddamn beds, yeah.

I stormed over to the bed and threw back the covers, *all* the way back.

She wasn't bleeding or bludgeoned. She wasn't missing any body parts, and I consider myself an expert. She wasn't hurt in any way that I could see. But as I'd hoped and feared, she was certainly naked, right down to those last few critical square inches that told me this wasn't any bottle blond, but the real thing.

I stared for a full second longer than necessary, maybe two—okay, five, but who's counting? Some sights just take hold. Whoever this K was, she was a very healthy girl, every ounce of her as work-hardened as a gymnast or ice skater. If I hadn't been distracted I could've counted ribs. At least she wasn't underage. Finally I lowered the covers and stood there, mulling over an assortment of half-assed facts and conclusions.

Fact: Girls do not crawl into strange beds, no matter how tired they are. Not mine, not anyone's. It simply doesn't happen.

Ergo: I knew her, or she knew me. And since I didn't have a clue, I assumed she did, or would once she regained consciousness.

Fact: Since I didn't know her, she couldn't know me very well. At best, she was the most distant sort of an acquaintance.

Ergo: She was a bold one, possibly even dangerous. Not that the two are mutually exclusive.

Fact: In about nine hours I was going to begin a new career as a private investigator.

Ergo: In fewer than those same nine hours I had to figure out who K was, or at least wake her up and ask, or lose all credibility as a budding shamus.

Fact: The beers weren't helping.

Ergo: I ought to go to bed and puzzle it out in the morning with a clear head. Or ask her then, when she woke up.

Fact: I no longer had a bed to go to.

* * *

Of the fifty or so guys I've known well enough over the years, at least forty-nine would dispute that last. They'd be in bed with K like the Flash. She was there, and she'd put *herself* there. It wasn't likely she'd made some fantastic mistake. She couldn't expect to remain alone in there. After all, the bed was mine, at least in theory. There was no possible conflict, right? No moral dilemma.

Well, in theory.

But all the Wicked Ales I'd downed that evening couldn't take me that far, which was too bad, so I set about rustling up clues.

Like...who *was* this girl? How did she get into my house?

The first I couldn't answer, try as I might. I found a wad of stinky clothes in a corner of the room, right where I would have thrown them if they'd been mine. White slacks, button-up-the-front shirt, pale-blue string bikini undies, a matching bra. And as I said, stinky, which probably meant she'd been wearing them for some time. No ID of any kind anywhere in the pile, but at least the ripeness of the garments explained K's shower.

No purse, and I looked all through the house, in closets, cabinets, under the bed. I even looked in the garbage and groped beneath the mattress, lifting K an inch or two in the process, guessing her weight at about one-twenty.

My worry intensified.

I found no sign of forced entry. No broken window. No jimmied jamb. That threw me. I'd engaged the deadbolt before leaving and I'd unlocked both it and the door lock when I'd come home. The back door was also locked. It wasn't possible she'd just wandered in off the street. A terrible thought occurred to me: Was *I* in the wrong house? Could I have had that much to drink? Had my key fit the door of a stranger's house purely by chance? A moment of panic gripped me, a surreal surge of something like the opposite of déjà vu.

But, no, my things were in every room. The dirty shirts, jockey shorts, jeans, and socks piled in a corner of the bedroom closet were mine. Without a doubt, this was my castle.

I stared at the girl again. She was remarkably beautiful, crashed in my bed, out like a bulb with blown filaments. I toyed with the idea of calling 911 and having her removed, possibly in a gurney, but all things considered, that felt like an overreaction to the situation.

As did crawling into bed with her, even if it was queen-sized and rightfully mine. I'm an honest, simple-minded sonofabitch, and a poor replacement for Mike Hammer, not to mention the aforementioned Magnum. I might've had more in common with Hercule Poirot than I cared to admit.

So...what else? I went into the living room and made up the couch.

CHAPTER THREE

THE HOUSE WAS eighty years old. A few original windows were single paned. You can't buy single-pane these days. Two bedrooms, one bath. I'd turned the second bedroom into storage and an office. When my daughter Nicole came to Reno, she stayed with Dallas. On those rare occasions that she stayed with me, she took the couch in the living room. Her choice, but, tonight, after two minutes on the miserable sonofabitch, I understood her preference for staying at her mother's place. The couch, which had belonged to my parents, was lumpy, short, and still exuded the smell of bulldog, Brutus, even after all these years. God only knows how long that beast had used it as his own personal bed.

I didn't get to sleep for an hour, and then I didn't sleep worth a damn. I kept hearing noises—sly footsteps, slender manicured fingers gliding through my wallet, doors opening and closing, papers rustling. All phantom sounds, of course. I checked in on K several times during the night and she was out cold every time. She hadn't even turned over. Her gentle snore never lost its tempo, like a kind of slow surf.

Nor did the gun beneath my pillow help my peace of mind, partly because I'd never kept it there before. It wasn't a joke or a toy. It was a featherweight S&W .357 Magnum, fourteen ounces empty, with a titanium cylinder, scandium-aluminum alloy frame. It could punch holes big enough in a person that it kept me up half the night worrying about that fact. One bad dream and who knows who or what I might've blown those holes in.

* * *

I was up at the first gray light of dawn, eager to solve my own personal at-home mystery before going out and taking on whatever Greg intended to throw my way.

K was still out. I gave her a shake, testing, but she didn't stir. I took her pulse. Fifty-two, strong and steady, about what I'd expect of a woman in her physical condition. And I checked her left hand. No ring or ring mark, which made me feel marginally better.

I ran my toothbrush under hot water for half a minute to kill whatever unknown cooties might be clinging to it, then brushed my teeth. Pete's Wicked Ale the morning after isn't half as tasty as the night before.

I risked a quick shower. Not that I'm a prude, far from it, I like to think, but visions of the movie *Psycho* kept intruding, even if my new roomie bore little resemblance to Anthony Perkins and I bore even less to Janet Leigh.

I gathered up clothing and dressed in the living room, then brewed a pot of coffee to put a spark of life into my body. I had a bowl of cornflakes, hoping the crunching would wake her. It didn't.

By seven I was ready for work, two hours early. I used the time to prowl around in stocking feet, snooping around my own place, hunting for clues. I didn't find a blessed one. Not a laundry mark or gasoline receipt, postcard or movie stub. Nothing. Just K and her wad of smelly clothes.

I looked at that pretty head a lot. I didn't peek under the covers again, although the thought crossed my mind every minute or two. I might've missed something the night before. And it was possible she had a tattoo that would've told me something useful, you never know.

At 8:50 I had to leave. As a parting shot, I shook the hell out of her, managing to get something that sounded like, "Unn-ug-uhhh-Iyuhnn-neh." It might've been Urdu, or possibly a remote dialect of Ethiopia, I had no way of knowing.

I scribbled a note. Basically, "Who the hell are you and what are you doing in my house?" then I got in the Toyota and took off.

* * *

Carson & Rudd Investigative Services was in a blond brick building a few blocks south of downtown, on Sierra Street near the old courthouse, right about where you'd expect to find a detective agency if you were looking for one. I parked around back. I had on jeans and a short-sleeve striped shirt, no tie. I had a suit carrier over my shoulder with the good stuff in it, just in case. But if by chance I was going to end up in a dark alley at night—something I hoped would happen—I wanted the jogging shoes, jeans, and the expendable shirt. I also wore a windbreaker, unzipped, to hide the gun at my hip.

I'm licensed to carry. All IRS field agents are. Nor did the license depend on my being an active agent. It wouldn't expire until April, year after next, and I fully intended to renew it. I put in enough hours on a firing range four times a year that I can joke about the weapon, after a fashion, but I would never pull it in a "situation" unless I was prepared to use it.

I went through a glass door and up a dingy flight of stairs to an equally dingy hallway with threadbare, curling carpet that ran the length of the office building. Past a tax consultant I'd had a few run-ins with and didn't much like—a slippery, sleazy bastard who I might have do my taxes next year if I happen to strike it rich—past a firm that refurbished laser printer cartridges, past a dealers school, the usual blackjack and craps—and on to Carson & Rudd.

Before going in, I stood outside for a few seconds, allowing this pivotal moment in my life to sink in. Even though I didn't have any idea who K was, I was now a private investigator, at least in training. I'd thought about calling the police and having K frog-marched away in cuffs, but something told me I shouldn't do that. She didn't look like the type to murder anyone in their sleep or steal the silverware. She'd had her chance and hadn't taken it, but I'd given her a lot of thought that morning before leaving.

Mystery girl in your bed? You don't gloss over that kind of weird-ness. You don't ignore it. It makes you think. Maybe it was kar-ma—a cosmic reward for a good deed I'd done in a previous life.

I hoped so, anyway.

* * *

I walked in at 9:06, late. Best to set the tone early, I always say. It's easier to rise from lowered expectations. Gregory's secretary, Dale, was at her desk, whaling away at a computer. She's a secretary-re-ceptionist-PI-Gal Friday. Probably runs the place when Greg's not looking. Five foot nine, slender and leggy, better-than-av-erage face, reasonably good to look at, thirty years old, and as proper and stiff as a chunk of kiln-dried hickory, which, I figured, is why Mrs. Gregory Rudd—Libby—puts up with her, and Libby doesn't put up with much. Gregory and Dale could pool their collective imaginations and still not have what it takes to throw the lock on the door and use their mold-green vinyl couch for extracurricular activities. Of course, Libby wasn't a bad-looking woman herself. Then again, she has a bitchy streak that goes up one side and down the other. I guess the bottom line is, not all guys are pigs or creeps, and Greg was anything but either.

Regarding Dale's lack of imagination, the half-slice of plain gag-it-down bagel sitting on a napkin by her computer pretty much told the story. She wore earphones, transcribing like mad, or something equally exciting. At least she was efficient.

I stood there, looking around. This outer room had a colorless, aseptic, institutional flavor, cross between a Social Security waiting room and something even less enticing. Dale's desk, the green couch, two folding chairs, a desktop copier on a gray steel cart, no windows and nothing on the walls. I'd been inside my nephew's office several times in the four years he'd been a private investigator and knew it wasn't any livelier, except for a single grimy east-facing window. His office wasn't too bad, if you like gray in different shades. Part of the problem was that Gregory was colorblind. To him, a standard fuchsia and a chunk of Romaine lettuce are the same shade, and—knowing Ellen's boy—the same species. By that I don't mean to imply he isn't bright. He is. He has gaps in his knowledge, but then, don't we all? What I don't know about calculus is used as filler in entire textbooks.

Dale hadn't spotted me yet. Greg wasn't in sight. His door was closed, but I could hear a murmur in there, above the muted roar of Dale's keyboarding.

Gregory—not Greg, except that *I* call him Greg—was what some people refer to as tight-assed. Anal retentive if you're into psychobabble and think those fancy high-dollar words mean anything substantive. To me, anal retentive means constipated, something you could fix with any number of over-the-counter remedies.

Maxwell Rudd, my sister's lesser half, came from an improbably long line of New England stockbrokers and lawyers stretching back to Thomas Paine and the Tea Party and beyond, as tight-assed a clan as you'd ever want to meet. Ellen and I come from a line of office managers, CPAs, and failed bankers that go back to guys who leapt to their deaths in the Crash of '29, or should have. For a while I'd thought there was hope for the family when Greg cut loose and became a private investigator, the first sign that maybe we weren't all doomed, like lemmings, to a preordained end—a waist-deep, Bataan-like march through paperwork to the grave. But in the end, breeding won out. By all accounts, Greg had managed to turn gumshoeing into as dull an enterprise as filling potholes. Or worse—auditing the construction firm that filled the potholes.

That, in effect, was what he'd told me a little over a month ago when I asked if he might consider having a partner, or an assistant.

But that *couldn't* be right, I'd thought back then, and still did, watching Dale hammer ninety-plus words a minute into that computer, working on her repetitive stress disorder. How could you possibly get pictures of Mr. X plowing Mrs. Y's south forty and not at least run a moderate risk of bullets whizzing past your ears when the flash went off? How could sleuthing, which is es-sentially glorified sneaking around performed by so-called adults, be boring?

I was about to find out.

Dale glanced up. "Oh, Mr. Angel." She pulled an earphone off one ear and throttled back to about forty WPM. "I mean, Mortimer."

"Mort," I said, wincing. I drew back a flap of my windbreaker, exposing the flyweight .357. "Should I check this thing at the door, or are you expecting trouble?"

Dale's face turned white. Her typing stopped altogether.

"Just kidding," I assured her, concealing the weapon again. In fact, there was a point to my showing her the gun, other than yanking her chain a little, which I'm prone to do. If I was going to work for her and Greg, they might as well know I intended to carry, because I've done so for a long time and wasn't about to quit now, about the time things might finally get interesting, with car chases, bullets flying around in the dark, and all that.

"Greg in?" I asked.

She pointed toward his door. "He's with a client."

"Uh-huh. Want I should take any dirty photos?"

Her eyes widened. *"What?"*

"Someone cheating on their significant other, maybe? I can bust down a door like nothing you ever saw."

She was aghast. "We...we don't take those kinds of cases, Mr. Angel."

I shrugged. "Mort. So, here I am. Guess you've been expecting me, right?"

"Yes, of course."

"Great." I looked around. "Now what?"

She pulled a paper-clipped wad of papers from a desk drawer. "I gathered these up for you on Friday. If you could fill them out..."

I sifted through them. Federally mandated health insurance form, request for PI trainee status, a bond questionnaire, 401(k) plan.

And a W-4 withholding form. I held it up, waved it at her. "This one's unconstitutional, sweetheart."

She gawked at me. Not sure if it was the sweetheart or the form, but the gawk was pure Dale.

"I oughta know," I informed her. "Government can't take one dime of my money before I know how the hell much I'm gonna make during the year. I mean, what if I lost my job, or changed jobs and started making less? Which I am, by the way."

"I...I...but, you've *got* to..."

"Just kidding. Where do I fill these out?"

She sat me on the couch with a ballpoint pen and a clipboard, and I did my civic duty, adding to the paperwork mill that's choking the life out of this country.

When I finished up, Greg was still in there with the client. Dale's phone rang once. Wrong number, but I was impressed. Carson & Rudd was doing a land-office business, or might at any moment. Tom Carson of Carson & Rudd had been dead for eight months—liver failure at age fifty-eight—which is why I'd thought Greg might be in a position to hire another PI. All this turmoil and stress had probably driven Carson to drink and other forms of excess, God rest him.

In fact, the excitement of my new job was beginning to stiffen my joints, so for all I knew I might be headed for the same untimely end. Back home, I had a naked girl in my bed, the dream-stuff of every 24-carat, bonded PI in America, and here I was with W-4's and 401(k)s in my lap.

"Done," I said. Dale was Xeroxing stuff that had whirred out of a laser printer. "What's next?"

She shrugged. "Gregory'll be out soon."

"Am I getting paid for all this sitting around?"

"Well...yes. You're hourly, at least for the time being."

I sat back. "Pretty easy work. Easier than slamming tax dodgers upside down against a wall and picking up nickels."

Finally she smiled. At least I think it was a smile.

"I'm serious," I said.

Her smile, if that's what it was, faltered.

"Kidding," I said, putting her on an emotional roller coaster. "We never picked up anything smaller than dimes."

The inner door creaked open. Greg held it for a fiftyish woman the size of a minivan.

"Don't worry, Mrs. Newman," he said. "I'm sure we'll hear something in a day or two." He gave her a smile. She smiled back, lifting pounds of flesh to do so, then glanced at me with dead gray eyes as she went out the door.

"Hear what in a day or two?" I asked.

"Missing person," Greg said. He was an inch under six feet tall, a shrimp. Skinny but tough. Wiry. He ran marathons. Nice suit, though. He looked good. I, on the other hand, looked more like a potential client. "Her son," he added.

"Now we're talking. What's his name? Want me to go track him down?"

Gregory's lips quivered, as if he didn't know whether to laugh, smile, or cry. "She thinks he's somewhere in Wisconsin or Michigan. I'll contact an agency out there, have them look into it. It'll cost her less in the long run. Local firms know the territory, have their own connections."

"Terrific. There's money in handing the work to someone else, is there?"

"She pays us, we pay them and keep 20 percent."

"So you're...we're, what, middlemen?"

"Sometimes. Not that often, but it happens."

"Uh-huh. Pretty heart-stopping stuff."

His look told me he didn't get it. He was a literal kind of guy. "I told you about that, Uncle Mortimer. Investigative work isn't anything like what you seem to—"

"Mort. So...got anything for me?"

He rubbed his hands together. I couldn't believe it. I mean, it was something his great-great-grandfather might've done. He looked eighty years old, like Scrooge, but it wasn't in anticipation of firing anyone or ripping a drumstick out of their mouth. This, then, whatever it was, was what passed for high drama in my nephew's life.

"I've got just the thing," he said. "Came in last week. Thursday afternoon. We've been saving it for you. It's right up your alley."

I pulled my gun and swung the cylinder out, checked its load and peered down the barrel. No obstructions. Good.

"Uncle *Morti*mer—"

"Mort." Four gleaming rounds, one empty chamber under the hammer. Perfect. If you can't get the job done with four bullets, that fifth bullet isn't likely to matter. Yanking Greg's chain was part of the point—okay, a big part—and now he was aware I was carrying, in case he'd forgotten. It wasn't as if he hadn't seen the gun before.

"Uncle...Mort." His voice was strangled, half an octave high. "You are *not* going to need that."

I swung the cylinder in, shoved the gun into its holster and let the windbreaker fall back in place. "You never know. What's the job?"

* * *

If I'd known before I put the gun away, I might've...okay, lucky for him, I realized I would've had to clean the gun. I'm picky about that. A dirty gun is an unreliable gun. Of course I could have pistol-whipped him. There's more than one way to use a gun. But after hearing about the job I left the revolver at Greg's. Just as well, considering how the afternoon went.

By ten twenty I was in the Toyota, northbound on Kietzke Lane, headed for Skulstad Meat Co., a wholesaler in the city of Sparks. Sparks is to Reno what a person's left buttock is to their right. The two towns started up four or five miles apart, grew, finally slammed up against each other until they became RenoSparks, and there's not much more to say about that. Happens all the time now, all across the country. Pretty soon it'll be wall to wall from coast to coast, one big fun place, like the mess around L.A. I could hardly wait.

As mayor, Jonnie Sjorgen had been doing his part to make it happen as soon as possible, backroom deals and kickbacks under the table, slippery damn folks scratching each other's backs, which is one reason I'd never voted for the guy, even before he started running around with Dallas. What voters want doesn't mean shit to politicians once they get in office. They lie as effortlessly as they breathe.

Two years ago, when Tom Carson was still at the helm, Skulstad Meats had been a client of Carson & Rudd. Pilferage. Now they had an accounting problem. Normally that wouldn't be PI work at all, but Humphrey Skulstad, now in his seventies, had consulted with Greg and, lucky me, Greg had told old man Skulstad he had just the guy for the job, a veritable accounting genius.

I wondered...is it homicide if it's your own kin, or is there a lesser charge?

It wasn't entirely my fault I ended up an IRS agent—or auditor, if you prefer. Goon is also popular. Working for the IRS was almost certainly the result of the same genetic accident that had produced much of the Angel family and its unremarkable offshoots, the least auspicious of which was the Angel/Rudd union nearly thirty years ago that had given the world Gregory Rudd.

IRS auditing is the world's most boring work and, relative to plumbing which is its metaphorical equivalent—unplugging drains to get things flowing—it doesn't pay for shit. You get an accounting degree and think that's it, you've got it made. Then, somehow, instead of turning right toward the golden glow of money, you turn left and enter this long dark tunnel. Strangely enough, it looks okay at first, you're doing good work, it's necessary, you're needed, or so you're told—then one day you wake up and find you're in too deep. You've learned too much to turn back. The tax code, in all its shifting, side-stepping glory, becomes your life. Twenty thousand La-Brea-Tar-Pit pages of it. A horse couldn't eat the *index* of that son of a bitch in a week. You can't think past that kind of thing, past noncompliant and frivolous returns, tax delinquent accounts and "nonfilers." There is a phrase, "Tax Professional," but we on the inside know there's no such thing. No one knows the tax code in its entirety. It isn't possible. Phone the IRS with a simple question and there's a fifty-fifty chance they'll get it right. Make it a hard question and you're on your own—just don't get it wrong or you'll need a lawyer, and good luck finding one who has a clue regarding the pride and joy of the IRS: the Federal Tax Code. So, numb and blind and part of a bureaucratic system that would've made Stalin weep with joy, you find yourself slogging waist deep through the archeology of people's lives, dust flying off old ledgers, a confetti of receipts kept in random order in shoeboxes, bored out of your skull, lunging at trivia like a Black Lab at chicken bones.

But there's an element of danger in it, too, wondering if this or that John Doe has finally reached the end of his rope and is going to whip a shotgun out of a nearby closet and start blasting. Field audits are stressful times, hence the license to carry. You sit with your back to the wall and check people's eyes, looking for that final, murderous spark. That might have been all that kept me going during my sixteen years with the IRS, that sweet hint of danger, but in the end it wasn't enough.

I pulled up in front of Skulstad Meats and left my Toyota—faded to an indecisive shade of yellow—to broil in the sun.

Humphrey Skulstad met me at the door and whisked me into his office before I could give his secretary my phone number. A nameplate on her desk said Rachel Cabrera. Thirty-five, give or take, beautiful, nicely filling out a knee-length summer dress. No ring on her finger. And she'd given me a wink. Several winks, in fact. Either that, or she had something in her eye the size of a number two pencil. Skulstad hauled me into his office before I could determine which.

The place reeked of hamburger, animal fat, and cheese—the anteroom, Humphrey's office, all of it. The aroma at Skulstad's was part of the job.

"We don't have a lot of time," he said, pale-blue eyes darting between his office door and my face. He looked well-scrubbed, pink-faced and tidy, even in shirt sleeves.

"We don't?"

"You're my newest employee."

"I am?"

He stopped and stared at me, growing wary. "You *are* from... ah...that is..."

I could tell he wanted me to say it first. Or get the hell out of his office. "Carson & Rudd," I said.

He relaxed slightly, but kept up a squint. "Mr. Rudd told me he'd have a man out here this morning about this time. When you came in the door, I assumed it was you."

"It is. Didn't Dale phone?"

"His secretary? Yeah, but to be honest, I thought you'd be better informed."

"I know our mayor and district attorney are missing," I said. "I know every local issue on the upcoming ballot, I get the newspaper, and my subscription to the *Wall Street Journal* is good for another six months."

Bless him, he smiled.

"And I know you've got an accounting problem," I said, showing off a little. I sat down in a leather chair, facing him.

"That I do, Mister, ah...?" He started rummaging on his desk for something.

"Angel. Mort Angel."

He sat back. "Right, good, Mr. Angel."

"Mort."

"Right. Mort. I shouldn't keep you here too long. Wouldn't look right. Besides, there's not an awful lot I can tell you. You'll be posing as a new employee. In accounting."

"Bottom-line problem, huh?"

He nodded. "Five, six months ago my gross dropped .6 percent. Like a rock. Doesn't sound like much, I know, but—"

"But .6 percent of"—I did a quickie calculation, based on what I'd seen so far, and experience, which was considerable and might prove useful even if I didn't want to admit it—"say, five million five, is...thirty-three thousand a year."

"Close. Five million eight."

"So, thirty-four eight. Are you sure it's not a normal fluctuation?"

"I've been rock steady the past two years, percentage-wise, adjusted for the season. Then it dropped, stayed dropped. No reason for it that I could see."

"So you think someone's cooking the books?"

"It took me a while to come to that, but...yeah, that would be my guess." He looked unhappy.

"But, you've got no proof?"

"No, just the sudden drop in gross."

Which, as a small-business owner, would eventually find its way into Skulstad's take-home pay. "Have you hired any new accountants lately?" I asked.

"Nope, although I lost one eight months back. Retired. Mike Anderson, head of the department. Good man. I didn't replace him."

Which might have opened a door of sorts.

"Now I've got three bean counters," Skulstad went on. "All of 'em have been with me more than three years."

"Thirty-five thousand is a fair amount of beans."

He nodded, then ran fingers through graying hair. "You got that right. My margin on gross here is only three and a half, four percent. Point six percent is a lot."

"So...which one of them is doing it?"

He gaped at me. "That's what I want *you* to find out."

"It wasn't a legal question, Mr. Skulstad. It's just between you and me. If you had to guess, which one would it be?"

"Well, Phil Galloway, if I had to pick one. But I wouldn't want that to get out of this office."

"It won't. Which one of them is driving a new car?"

He gaped again, then smiled slowly. "Iris. Iris Kacsmaryk. Now, why didn't I think of that?" He gave me a look that told me I was one damn fine detective. I didn't tell him about K in my bed.

"Might not mean anything at all," I said. "It's just another place to look."

He checked his watch, then stood. "I take it you know all about ledgers, computer spreadsheets, that kind of thing?"

"Christ, do I. I've seen goddamn quadruple books."

"Well, I don't. I'm into the buying end of it. And quality. Means I do a lot of traveling and evaluating. I have to trust my staff. The money end...Mike used to handle that. I can't do it all. But I'm not a fool, Mr. Angel. Someone's got their hand in my pocket here. Or maybe I'm getting old."

"So I'm the new accountant?"

"If you want to work it that way. I didn't know how you'd want to do it. I've been telling 'em I was thinking about hiring another person, just in case. Betty is the department head now. She's been with me going on twenty years."

I shrugged. "We can do it that way, sure. No problem. But if I ask for time off, I'll want it, no questions asked, even from this Betty. I might need to do some outside surveillance, and I can't do it sitting at a desk. I want to be all set to go when your people get off work."

"I understand," Skulstad said. "I'll let Betty know you might need personal time off for a while, until you get settled in." He put a hand on the doorknob, then paused. "I don't want to fire anyone, Mr. Angel. I only want it to stop."

"It's like one big happy family here, huh?"

He smiled. "You understand, then?"

I didn't, but I nodded anyway. Some families need a dose of tough love now and then.

Skulstad opened the door and ushered me into the anteroom, into Rachel's presence again. For her benefit, he shook my hand and said, "Rachel will take care of you, Mr. Angel. It's good to have you on the team." He went back into his office and closed the door.

I smiled at Rachel. "Take care of me."

She handed me a sheaf of papers. "Fill these out, please."

Another sonofabitching set of W-4s, 401(k), insurance. I couldn't believe it. "You've gotta be kidding," I said.

She stared at me. "What's wrong?"

"Christ, not again." I glared at the paperwork.

"Again?" she echoed.

Okay, so that wasn't terribly swift of me. It's just that I saw my future flash before my eyes, and it was an entire vaudeville act of filling out W-4s and 401(k) shit, no offense to Greg.

"Nothing," I said.

"You can fill them out in there." She aimed a wine-colored nail at an empty room.

I went, emerged twenty minutes later a tiny bit angrier than when I went in. Rachel smiled as I handed back the paperwork that's killing this country, so I returned the smile and said, "How would you like to have dinner?"

"I almost always have dinner, thanks."

Sharp. "I mean, with me."

"No, thank you."

"Wine? Reno's finest pasta?"

"And where might that be?"

"Olive Garden?"

"Not even close."

"Pasta Maniacs?"

"They closed ten years ago. I see you're right on top of things, pasta-wise. And, my 'no' was generic, Mr. Angel."

"Mort. So, okay then, what'd you have in your eye?"

She gave me a startled look. "What?"

"Forget it. Where do the bean counters count the beans around here?"

She stood up. And up and up. Man, was she ever leggy. "This way." She headed down a short hallway, past a lunchroom, toward a big back office space. She had a nice walk, very distracting, and I took full advantage of it.

Back there in the depths of the building, the smell of meat grew stronger. Rachel handed me off to a woman with an artificial mass of flaming red hair, the kind of thing you could use to stuff a mattress. Reminded me of my mother, which was eerie.

"This is Mr. Angel, Betty."

"Mort," I said.

Rachel walked away.

"We've been expecting you, Mr. Angel," Betty said, giving me a guarded smile and limp, damp fingertips to either grab or shake, it was hard to tell which.

Yes, they had. Betty Pope. Phil Galloway. Iris Kacsmaryk. All of them were staring at me. Every hand in the place turned out to be limp and damp except mine, so, no clue there if I thought I was going to act as a mobile lie detector.

After "hi's," vague smiles, "gladt'meetcha's," Phil and Iris went back to their screens. These days, computers count the beans and bean counters oversee the counting. And maybe one of them jiggles a number or two in a spreadsheet that modifies the end result ever so slightly—say, to the tune of 0.6 percent. Just greedy enough to be stupid. Skulstad might not have noticed 0.2 percent.

Betty was in her fifties. She looked like a former Soviet shot-putter by the name of Tamara Press. Phil was roughly my age, lank blond hair, the freckles no longer boyish. I had him by seventy pounds and half a foot. He didn't look overjoyed to see me. Iris was in her mid- to late-twenties, pale, thin, pretty in an overly delicate way that reminded me of a not-yet-filled-out Mia Farrow. With the IRS, I'd once had a paperweight—a bronze bust of Nixon with "I am not a crook" inscribed on the base—that might've outweighed Iris Kacsmaryk. If a gust came through, I could maybe slam her down on my desk to keep the loose stuff in place.

Nothing overtly unfriendly. Iris, in fact, had given me a glimmer of a smile. But bean counters are a naturally serious lot. *Numbers* are serious, not to be trifled with. They aren't subjective, except on Wall Street, in and around Washington, in the hands of tobac-co-company statisticians and lobbyists, and out of the mouths of pathological liars—if you can tell the difference between any of those groups.

But they can be juggled, if one is adroit enough and has the inclination.

I was given a squeaky chair and a desk facing Iris, or, more accurately, the top of her head with its pale-white part right down the middle. She was currently plowing through a stack of well-thumbed, slightly greasy tally sheets from the warehouse, from whence, I assumed, issued the heady aroma of meat.

I began to take stock of my surroundings.

I had a computer and a nineteen-inch Samsung flat-screen monitor, all my own, and what looked like coffee stains on the keyboard.

I had a phone. Ext. 41—my age, what a stroke of luck. With it, I could probably get hold of Rachel in an instant. Maybe Zozo's Ristorante would do the trick. She'd caught me off guard with that bit about Pasta Maniacs having gone out of business. I oughta get out more.

I had a framed picture of a cat on my faux ash, sheet-metal desk, and a brownish water stain on the desk itself that looked remarkably like a portrait of Lenin. Or Marx. Or maybe Engels. I can never keep those guys straight, but they'd been a dour-looking bunch.

Twenty seconds later, I had a three-ring "procedures" binder full of tabs that explained certain company policies and outlined what I was supposed to be doing there, courtesy of Betty Pope.

My phone rang.

I stared at it. Everyone else did too, waiting for me to pick up. New guy gets a call. Right away, things are getting interesting.

Figuring Rachel, I caught it midway through the second ring. "Hello?"

"Mort?" A woman. I knew that voice.

"Yeah."

"It's Dallas."

The ex-wife, being hassled and harried by the media even more than I, now that our beloved mayor, Jonnie, had flown the coop. I had a choice of responses, a few of which might blow the lid off my cover, things like: "How'd you find me here?" So I said, "What's up, kiddo?" Kiddo to throw off the ears in the room, but I call her that from time to time to keep her loose.

"Who's the girl?"

"What girl?" I asked.

Iris's head hitched up half an inch. Both Phil and Betty's fingers slowed on their keyboards.

"The girl at your house."

"Uh, K."

"Kay?"

"Yeah, K."

"Not especially bright, is she?"

"Why do you say that?"

"It was a bit like talking to a fence post."

"At least you got through."

"What's that supposed to mean?"

"She's kind of tired."

"Oh? Did you wear her out? If I remember correctly, you have a way of—"

"Is there a point to any of this, Dal?" Ears twitched at the name. No one looked up, however.

"I have a flat."

"Yeah? You looking to rent it out or sell it?"

That stopped her. "A flat *tire*," she expounded.

"Flat all the way around or only on the bottom?"

"For God's sake, Mort..."

"Exactly what do you want me to *do*, Dal?"

"I...What are you doing at...at that place? Skulstad Meats? I spoke with Gregory."

"Then you *know*," I said. Iris flicked her eyes up at me, then down.

"Oh. Sorry. Private investigation stuff, right?" A hint of irony in her voice. "You can't talk right now, can you?"

"Now you're cookin', kid."

"Well, I was hoping...maybe if you could get off for an hour, like for lunch?"

"That depends. Are you buying?"

"To change my *tire*, Mort." She was starting to sound weary. Jonnie's absence was probably getting to her. That and the media, going through her bank account, underwear drawer, crawling through her life like a bunch of roaches in the name of truth and the public's Right To Know, which, as sheer luck would have it, coincides with ratings, market share, advertising revenue, and end-of-year bonuses.

"What happened to your Triple-A?" I asked.

"I, uh, sort of let it lapse."

"Good move. Where are you now?"

"Macy's. Meadowood."

Macy's. Of course. Where else? What kind of a gumshoe was I? "Where at?"

"The east side. North of the Sears extension."

"I'll get there soon as I can. Say, fifteen, twenty minutes?"

"Great. Thanks, Mort."

I hung up. Three pairs of eyes looked up, then down. The chair squawked as I got to my feet, announcing my departure.

"Family emergency," I said to Betty. "Try to keep me on the payroll, okay?"

She didn't smile as I left, but I thought Phil looked hopeful that maybe I'd blown it and wouldn't be back.

* * *

The Toyota was hot enough to broil salmon when I opened the door. I let it cool a little before getting in. It's too small for me, but on IRS wages, and with a double mortgage, and stashing the maximum allowable into a Roth IRA, it was all I could reasonably afford. Well, okay, I can be cheap. Perhaps it was one of those final straws, the reason Dallas finally split—me buying that car, used, already scarred by battle. Once she got the name Angel and figured out where I was headed, how far I was likely to go, and Nicole was in her freshman year of high school, there wasn't much to hold her. I couldn't blame her. Turns out there wasn't much to hold me either, once I'd hit forty and saw that long empty stretch of road ahead. It had just taken me longer to figure it out, or at least to do something about it.

Dallas was standing beside her Mercedes when I pulled up. No TV crews were hanging around filming the event, which made me think Jonnie's disappearance was winding down even more than I'd thought. Later she told me she'd raced through an almost-red light somewhere on South Virginia Street to give two news vans the slip.

She looked good. Dallas always looks good. At the breakfast table, asleep, mucking in the garden, sweating on a StairMaster, Dallas looked terrific. She would look good mud wrestling Tommy Lasorda. Hell, she would make *Lasorda* look good, not a mean trick.

She had on a green skirt, a sleeveless pearl-colored blouse, gold necklace, gold bangles. Even in all that clothing you could sense the Playmate body underneath. *I* could, at least.

"Nice outfit," I said, squeezing out of the Toyota like a circus clown. "I can see why you didn't want to change the tire yourself."

She beamed at me.

"What I can't understand is why you don't have a line out here," I added, looking around. The lot was about half full this close to the building. Farther out it was empty, rippling with heat waves. The asphalt felt slightly squishy under my shoes.

"A line?"

"Of drooling hopefuls, fighting over who gets to change the tire and impress the gorgeous lady."

"Oh, Mort."

Oh, Mort, *what*? She thought I wasn't serious? I crouched by the tire. She didn't have to tell me which one, sleuth that I am. Left rear. It was one flat sonofabitch. I even spotted the gash where the knife blade had gone in.

I stood up quickly and looked around. I didn't see anyone staring in our direction, but someone knew where Dallas was. Either that or it was one of those random things. Some people don't like Mercedes, or Mercedes owners. Maybe she should've been driving a Smart Car, or a Zapino. Something that would fit in her purse.

"Got a spare?" I asked.

She shrugged, handed me a set of keys, singling out the one for the trunk.

She stood a few feet away as I popped the lid and looked in, my eyes goggling and double taking at the sight of Jonnie Sjorgen's head staring milky eyed up at me, blackish tongue protruding. Just his head. Nothing else.

Dallas screamed. I caught her a quarter second before she fell.

CHAPTER FOUR

THE NEXT FEW hours went by in something of a blur. At least we got a free lunch out of it. Well, I did. Dallas barely touched her salad.

Two patrol cars were at the scene two minutes after I called it in. Twenty minutes later I counted ten RPD cruisers, four sheriff's cars, one paramedic van, a fire truck, three carloads of unsmiling RPD plainclothes detectives, a coroner's wagon, and a particularly ugly gray-green sedan full of blue-suited, stiff-legged, serious-looking FBI agents who must've broken every speed law on the books hauling ass over from their Booth Street offices. Everyone with a scanner, a siren and a so-called need-to-know had hot footed it over, and a few more besides. I was the only former representative of the IRS, which would no doubt make my previous colleagues green with envy. I didn't see any border agents, but the day was young. The number of flashing blue-and-red lights was enough to cause skin cancer. The huge turnout of law enforcement personnel was too late to help Mayor Jonnie when he'd really needed it, but it was impressive all the same.

Like locusts, the media descended—an almost biblical plague. Television crews from each of the four local network affiliates were crawling over each other like Twister contestants, practically rioting in an attempt to out-scoop everyone else. Given the situation, that was a physical impossibility, as any eight-year-old could've told them, but apparently they didn't know that. The word had gotten out and they were trying to get a shot of Sjorgen's head for the six o'clock news, just in time for dinner. But with the banners of crime scene tape and the burly officers backing it up, neither they nor the print newshounds were having any luck.

Reno Police Chief Paul Menteer was nosing around, staying out of the way while trying to appear in charge, looking solemn, no doubt sizing up the political angle. The decapitation was already general knowledge, no way to put that genie back in the bottle, keep the story from going international. The British love a good bit of gossip, as did much of the rest of Europe and parts of Asia. The French in particular would eat this mess up.

Reporters shouted questions at Dallas and me across the barrier of yellow police tape, which encompassed her Mercedes, four squad cars, and my Toyota. Their questions were beyond idiotic—coarse, vapid, vulgar, predictable. Tabloid TV questions, geared to appeal to the dimmest of wits who might tune in. And they got paid to do it. Is this a great country or what? Forget education or class. All you need is an eighty-dollar haircut, two hundred if you're a woman, and a mouth unfettered by sensitivity or intelligence.

Chief Menteer was keeping us well away from them, but video cameras intruded, lenses set on full zoom, glinting in the sunlight. Dallas was photogenic as hell, I was her ex, and Jonnie's head, his *head* for Christ's sake, had been found by the aforementioned ex in the trunk of her car. The word "Scandal," with a capital "S," hovered over us like a neon cloud. An erupting volcano in that parking lot couldn't have drawn as big a crowd or incited as frenzied a feeding.

Through the predictable law enforcement whirl, preliminary forensic busywork, and the sheer noise, excitement, and strangeness of it, I focused on Dallas—keeping an eye on a pair of RPD detectives Menteer was in the process of assigning to work her over. And me, of course. Dallas was still weeping softly, mascara running.

"Don't say anything," I told her as the two detectives drew near.

"Who the hell're you?" the male of the team asked me, a guy in his forties who bore an uncanny resemblance to Buddy Hackett back in the day.

"My husband," Dallas answered, an automatic response that made my day. "I...I mean...my—"

"Mortimer Angel, the ex," said the other detective, Shannon Neely, a woman in an attractive blue-gray skirted suit, evidently more up on current events than her partner. My face had been on television too, briefly, one small sideshow in the media circus.

Hackett, whose day-to-day name was Russell Fairchild, said, "Oh, yeah, him," catching up like a greyhound. "We'll get to you in a minute, big guy."

"You won't get to either one of us out here," I informed him in my best IRS-like voice.

"Say what?"

I nodded at the burgeoning horde of *paparazzi*, backed up by a growing throng of onlookers. "Not here, not with them out there. It's too hot and I was promised lunch."

In fact I wasn't, not that they would care. I was only promised the fun of changing a flat in the sun as the temperature approached a hundred, but I could tell that would have to wait for calmer times. I have a sense about these things.

Russell glanced at his partner and shrugged. I had him pegged as a man who liked the word *lunch*. He was paunch-bellied and round-shouldered. His polyester tie was pulled loose at the collar.

Shannon returned his shrug. "It *is* awfully hot, Russ."

Out of hearing, Dallas's and mine, they got the okay from

Chief Menteer. One look at the TV crews convinced him. After he'd asked a few "how and why" questions for show, which I answered, the four of us took off in a marked unit, Russ driving, Shannon up front with him, Dallas and I in back where the door handles don't work. Two RPD cruisers ran interference for us, cutting off half a dozen news vans as we got the hell out of there. I put an arm around Dallas's shoulders. She didn't look well, and I hoped for her sake that whatever ordeal lay in store wouldn't drag out.

Russ headed for a yellow light, went through on red with the siren wailing. The two cruisers stayed with us. Menteer wasn't about to hand over two prime murder suspects to Russ and Shannon without rolling backup as escort.

"So, how about Rapscallion?" I said to Russ. "I hear they've got a pretty good luncheon menu."

"Seafood. You got it." He grinned at Shannon, happy to be the guy in charge of the scamp who might have killed and beheaded his beloved mayor. Rapscallion, on Wells Avenue, is arguably the best mostly fish place in Reno. But Russ, the idiot, made a wrong turn and we ended up downtown at RPD headquarters on Second Street instead, south of the river in one of the least attractive buildings in all of Reno, butted up against the municipal courthouse.

Dallas and I were taken to separate rooms. Mine had chairs bolted conveniently to the floor and a plain wooden table, stained and gouged by countless suspects, who, from the looks of it, had been allowed to keep their knives. Dallas went off with Shannon, and I was left with Russ and a taciturn blue-uniformed officer by the name of Clifford Day. Day was noticeably bigger than me. Six-six, three hundred-plus pounds. The word on me must've gone out. God only knows why—the most violent thing I've done in the past few years is occasionally laugh out loud watching episodes of *Breaking Bad*, but I guess these guys weren't taking chances.

No rubber hose, but they Miranda'ed the hell out of me. I waived my right to shut up and/or have my attorney give them a hard time for $400 an hour, not an expense I cared to take on, which is the Catch-22 in that arrangement, and they set up a recorder and began asking questions.

Before switching on the recorder, Russ gave the door a glance and said, "So, that's your ex, huh?"

"Yep."

He shook his head. "Man, I wouldn'ta let that one off the hook." Out of his bed, he meant. Dallas would've been thrilled to the point of speechlessness by his interest.

"She threw me back," I said.

"Weren't big enough, huh?" He punched Day on the shoulder, happy that he'd made a joke. Day grinned. Two good ol' boys, one nearly twice the size of the other in spite of Russ's paunch.

"Why don't you ask her?" I said. Dallas would've ripped him a brand-spanking new asshole before the entire sentence was out of his mouth.

Then they went to work. They were almost cordial before they learned I was Reno's newest private investigator, or might be in the future. Before that moment, Fairchild even managed to find me a tuna sandwich. "Seafood," he said, tossing it on the table in front of me. It landed with an appropriately dead plop, one day past its expiration date, having stewed in a vending machine for the last three days. And, I learned later, Shannon got salads for both her and Dallas from somewhere, although Dallas just picked at hers.

When Russ asked what I'd done before I joined the firm of Carson & Rudd, both he and Officer Day got a little more serious, a bit less smug. IRS agents live in a world of forced smiles and artificial goodwill. I suspected the two of them of having been creative with their 1040s a few months back. When it comes to taxes, almost everyone's an artist, including cops. *Especially* cops, I'd learned early on in my career. They never report bribes as tip income.

My questioning didn't take as long as I'd thought it would. Five minutes of scintillating background stuff, then we went through Dallas's phone call, my trip to Meadowood and the subsequent discovery of the body—or head, corpse—twice in maybe another ten. The story was simplicity itself. The second time around was a carbon of the first, not so much as a change of syllables, same during the third go-around, so after consulting with someone in another part of the building, getting my story one last useless time and instructing me not to leave town in the next few days without notifying RPD, Fairchild and Day cut me loose. Total time, one hour twenty minutes.

Later, armed with forensics data and pathology reports they might haul me in again and dig into things farther back in time, like motive and opportunity, alibi—if they could pinpoint time of death, which I didn't think likely. Jonnie's last known body temperature was up around a hundred forty degrees. Without a *body* or the actual murder scene, which the trunk of Dallas's car was not, I didn't think they'd come up with a time of death, much less a murder weapon or any of that stuff that so impresses juries. And it wasn't lost on them that the district attorney, David Milliken, was still missing or at large—*unaccounted for* was the current, politically correct term—not that his absence necessarily had anything to do with Jonnie's even if it had looked that way right from the start. Nor was it clear how Dallas or I were connected to Milliken, even to detectives eager to solve a case and look like heroes before a bug-eyed public now holding its col-lective breath. Indictments were a long way off and they knew it, evidenced by all the long faces I saw, everywhere I turned.

I hung around, waiting for Dallas in a room that hadn't been cleaned anytime that week. It had vending machines, worn-out chairs and tables, a bulletin board for the cops to buy things from each other, and wire-reinforced windows that looked out on a dingy hallway with green linoleum tiles on the floor.

Shannon and a burly cop, Mary, took a lot longer with Dallas. All the way from when she'd last opened the trunk of her car: *yesterday afternoon*. And was Jonnie's head in there at that time: *no, she was certain she would've noticed*. Where, if anywhere, she'd gone the night before: *nowhere*. When she'd gotten up that morning: *6:20 a.m.* Where she kept the car at night: *in her garage*. And was the garage locked: *yes*. Had she heard anything unusual the night before: *no*. When she'd had breakfast, showered, dressed, and left the house. Every stop she'd made before ending up at Meadowood Mall: *none*. Did anyone else have keys to her car: *Jonnie, but chances are he hadn't used them to put himself in the trunk*. And why, exactly, had she phoned her ex-hubby for help and not Triple-A or any other person or organization? Later, according to Dallas, there'd been a lot of that ex-husband kind of thing. Evidently they liked the idea of a big guy with a possible motive—jealousy—right there on the scene when Jonnie had finally turned up.

After I'd cooled my heels for an hour she came out, looking pale and drained. The damage to her mascara had been repaired, however. Women understand the importance of such things. I asked Russ for a ride back to my car. Dallas's, too.

He shook his head. "Been impounded. Might get it back in two, three days. Maybe four."

"What? Both of 'em?"

"Nope. Just hers."

He led Dallas and me out a back door. The temperature was 102 degrees. My Tercel was baking in the heat in a parking lot with its windows up. "All yours," he said, handing me my keys. "We've been through it already. Nice rig, by the way."

"Hey, thanks for rolling up those windows nice and tight," I said.

"Don't mention it. You wouldn't believe the amount of crime in this neighborhood."

Wrong. The lowest 10 percent of IQs in society are responsible for 90 percent of the break-and-enter and violent crime. Average prison inmate intelligence quotients are in the low- to mid-eighties. At such lofty levels of cogitation and analysis, the police station itself would be viewed as a Grade-A burglary opportunity, all the computers they've got in there, not to mention boxes of paper clips, hole punches, pencil sharpeners, things like that.

"You remind me of someone," I said to Russ, just to spin him around a little.

"Clinton?"

"No...someone in the movies."

"Charlton Heston, probably. I get that a lot."

"Nah. *I* remind people of Heston."

"Don't you wish."

We left it at that. He went back into the station. I opened the Tercel door, hoping the influx of oxygen wouldn't cause an explosion or fire. It didn't. I don't know why not. Dallas stared at the car in distaste. Its laboratory-specimen color had always been a point of contention between us. That and the cushions, which I'd purchased in a slightly pre-torn condition and covered in heavily matted sheepskin.

"Hop in," I said.

"My God. This thing still runs?" She sounded disappointed.

"Does it ever. You oughta hear it at sixty. Mirror sounds like Madonna."

"I don't suppose you've got air conditioning?"

"I sweat, sure."

She stared at me.

"It's not about the *car*, doll," I said, lowering my voice half an octave. "It's about the handsome brute inside it."

At last her mouth twitched, but she still didn't say anything.

I said, "You want it cool, we'll roll the windows down and go real fast. You can take off your top if you think that'll help."

She gave me one of her looks, the one that meant she was sorry for me, that I was never going to grow up, never going to make it past this stalled adolescence. Well, I'd already topped forty, so she was probably right. If it doesn't happen in the first forty years, it's not likely to happen in the second. But at least I have fun. I've met guys so serious that a smile would crack their faces like ceramic slamming into a brick wall.

Life's too short for that kind of shit.

*   *   *

"Where to?" I asked.

"I don't know," she answered listlessly.

Her life, the she-and-Jonnie part of it, was a shambles, and every media buzzard within a thousand miles was either on a plane headed this way, on the road breaking speed limits, or already in Reno, trying to photograph or videotape the wreckage for the benefit of an information-starved nation.

"Want to get something to eat?" I asked.

"No."

Neither did I. I'd eaten half that tuna sandwich, hoping it wasn't lethal.

"How about I take you to your place?" The suggestion wasn't overly bright, but I wasn't tracking a hundred percent.

She shrugged, not yet up to making decisions.

I took off, headed south and west into the hills that overlook the city. My excuse was that it was hot and my brain was addled.

Dallas was rich before I came along, and she was rich after. Good accountants and rock-solid investments, much of it in mutual funds that hadn't tanked immediately after Enron hit the fan. Before the full extent of corporate greed had been discovered, she'd cashed out and put the whole thing into T-bills and, of all things, gold, which soared to new heights only a few years later, then back into a nice selection of mutual funds again. Financially she was looking better than terrific. If anyone thought Dallas had done in Jonnie, they'd have to come up with a motive other than money. And figure out how a person who faints at the sight of blood could cut off a person's head, which has got to be a god-awful grisly chore.

But Jonnie had had money too, so money might be a motive for someone. His father, Wendell, had made a fortune in the restaurant supply business and a title company, put some of it into real estate, some into other local businesses, and built himself a modest empire on the fringe of Reno's gambling community, enough to get a street named after him in the northwest part of town. Jonnie, an only child, had never hurt for money, and had inherited the whole shebang when Wendell died. When you get that silver spoon, you eat caviar, amazed that others aren't doing the same. I'd always thought of Sjorgen as a self-absorbed, out-of-touch so-and-so, not good, just lucky, and not big into rocket science, as thinkers go. All tanned skin and too-white teeth, nothing of significance up there in the attic, but maybe that was sour grapes.

The house belonged to Jonnie, but Dallas had been living there with him for much of the past two years. Two point eight million at the height of the real estate balloon in '05-'06, maybe one point seven mil now—stucco, gray slate and river rock, big plate glass windows with a terrific nighttime view of the city. Why two people needed sixty-two hundred square feet is beyond me. I couldn't have afforded the vacuuming bill. Great place for parties, though. I'd been to a few of them as Dallas's guest, which had been interesting given my status as her ex. No one put on a party like our mayor Jonnie. All the city's movers were there, and a few of its shakers as well. And me.

I turned onto Jonnie's street and pulled over to the curb, fast, aware of my mistake.

Three squad cars and two sedans were parked in the drive and on the street. The front door of the house was open. Crime scene tape was strung all over, like bunting.

Jonnie had no relatives in the immediate area, so the cops had gone in with a hastily signed search warrant to go through the place, hunt for bloodstains. A news van lurked across the street, parabolic antenna on the roof, Channel 8 logo on the side, guys and gals with video cameras hanging around, using binoculars, hoping to get lucky. I was surprised they didn't have a helicopter in the air overhead. A car was parked behind the van. *Gazette-Journal,* with a pair of women inside, waiting, cameras no doubt ready, probably praying to some obscure god of newsprint for a chance at that elusive Pulitzer.

"Want to be waylaid by the press?" I asked.

"Oh, God, no."

"Want to flee the scene?"

She stared at me. "What do you think?"

"Police are going through the house. Probably your stuff, too."

"Let them. I don't care."

So we fled. Dallas put her head back, eyes closed. Her headache pose. The afternoon heat wasn't helping—or the Toyota's lack of air conditioning or anything resembling an amenity or dealer upgrade, including variable-speed wipers, which I would've liked.

"How about your house?" I asked. Dallas hadn't yet sold her own place, maybe waiting to see how this thing with Jonnie panned out.

"I don't think so."

I didn't think so, either. Police were probably over there, too. I drove her straight to the Grand Sierra Resort, a hotel casino a few hundred yards off U.S. 395, formerly known as the MGM, Bally's, and the Reno Hilton.

I toyed with the idea of taking her to my place, but the news hordes were probably camped out there by now—and K might still be there, which could be more than a little awkward. I'd screwed up once already, and like my car, my house didn't have air conditioning, so I went to a neutral zone: big, anonymous, and chilled.

The Grand Sierra was the biggest hotel casino in Reno. White, monolithic, twenty-five stories tall with copper-tinted windows. It has two thousand rooms. A lake at the south side, formerly a gravel pit, had been turned into a driving range where folks in funny hats could whack golf balls at islands covered in Astroturf and fake palm trees.

We went inside, into the ever-present jangle of slots and money. I guided Dallas toward the hotel desk, which was the length of four shuffleboards set end to end along the west wall.

"Stay with me," she said.

"Huh?"

"Tonight." She stopped and looked at me. Her arms were folded across her chest as if she were cold. "I...I don't want to be, you know..."

"Alone." I was picking up speed.

"Yes."

She wasn't offering anything. She was taking, not giving. I knew that, and she knew I knew. That kind of understanding doesn't grow on trees. IRS or not, she never should have divorced me. I wondered if Jonnie had known her a tenth as well, or cared a tenth as much. He'd always struck me as the kind of guy who couldn't pass a mirror without giving it a wink and a loving smile.

"Sure. If you want," I said.

"I want."

Suited me. I didn't have a house or a bed I could call my own, though what I did have was intriguing. But—*c'est la vie*. I signed us in as Mr. and Mrs. James Davis from Bakersfield while Dallas hung back, concealing her face as much as possible.

I got the key and we took an elevator to the eleventh floor, Room 1122, and managed to get inside without drawing a crowd.

Dallas napped, or tried to. I gazed out the window for a while, then risked a trip down to the mall in the building—a miniature city in its own right—bought us a change of underwear, toothbrushes, toothpaste, and *Mad River*, a John Sandford paperback, and hightailed it back to safety.

Dallas finally slept. Stress and pain left her face, and she looked younger, even more beautiful. I covered her with a light bedspread, then settled into a chair. I read, finally looking up when I realized it was getting dark out. I'd lost track of time. Sandford does that to me.

Thoughts of K drifted through. I imagined my possessions being carried out the door to a van, the most valuable of which was a six-year-old VCR with a drive mechanism that eats tapes on occasion. I was thinking about upgrading to DVD, but then what would I do with all those tapes in my closet?

I left Dallas a note telling her I'd be back soon, hung a *Do Not Disturb* sign on the door and locked up, elevatored down to the first floor, and strolled out to the Toyota. The sky was a dozen shades of fading rose and burgundy, the clouds dark gray, lined in gold and scarlet. It was warm out, but no longer stifling. Traffic whisked by on 395, west of the hotel.

I drove over to Ralston, eased down from the north and stopped a block and a half from my house. For a while I watched the street. No news vans, police, or cars with shadows shifting in them, but a few vehicles were parked along the street and there's nothing more devious or patient than a serial killer or a hungry reporter.

The sky lost all color and went dark. City lights tinted the clouds a murky orange. I watched the street a while longer, then drove closer, parking two houses up from my place. I watched a few more minutes, then got bored. Hell with it. If a media ghoul got close enough, I'd bring up a bunch of obscure IRS regs, see if he or she had complied with laws most IRS agents have never heard of.

I got out and walked to the house. The lights were out, door locked. I opened up and went in.

"K?" I called.

Nothing. Dead air.

I turned on lights and looked around. No sign of her, but the bed was made. On the spread was a pile of clean clothes, neatly folded. My clothes. Jeans and underwear, T-shirts, socks. Gone was my pile of dirty laundry in the closet, and K's clothing. And K.

A note lay atop my clothing. This time the writing was some-what neater. It read:

We need 1% milk, bread, fresh fruit, toothpaste.
Could you spare a little money? K.

She'd finished it off with a dumb-ass smiley face.

CHAPTER FIVE

WE NEED. I liked that. It showed a fair amount of spunk. I left her forty dollars and a note asking her to do the windows, then drove back to the Grand Sierra Resort.

Dallas was wallowing in the tub, awash in bubbles when I walked in. The tub was black with gold fixtures, big enough to include me and a sorority party. The air was humid and smelled of lilac.

I didn't go near the bathroom until she called, and then I stood in the doorway, trying not to stare, at least in an obvious way.

"Do you love her?" she asked. "Is this a serious thing or what?"

"Love who?"

"Kay, silly."

"Who said anything about K?"

"Your note. I read between the lines. Where else would you have gone, Mort?"

I shrugged. Greg should've hired her, not me.

"So, how was she?" Dallas asked. The bubbles hid much of her. Not all, but what did it matter? I'd already memorized her, years ago. It was amazing how much time had changed me, but not her. I was a month younger than Dallas, but I looked five years older. Maybe the divorce was a good thing, for both of us. In another twenty years she might've been mistaken for my daughter, then where would we be?

"Gone," I replied.

"Gone?" She lifted a glass of white wine with a racquetball-sized strawberry in it and took a sip.

"Missing. Vamoosed. But I think she'll be back." I indicated the wine. "Any more where that came from?"

"Out there." She waved a hand. "Vamoosed?"

"She asked for money. That's a sign, isn't it?"

"Of what?"

"That she'll be back."

Her lips moued into a disapproving frown. "Or possibly that you owe her for something. I wonder what that could be?"

"Yeah, me too."

"So, how long have you known this person, Mort?"

"I still don't know her."

She struggled to keep up. "How long have you *not* known her, then?"

I had to think. Time had dilated recently. "About twenty-two hours, give or take."

"Twenty-two...oh, Mort..."

I used to get a lot of Oh, Mort's when we were married. Three or four a day. I went off in search of the wine, came back with a glass in hand, no fruit.

"Hungry?" I asked her.

"Yugoslavia."

She could slam them back pretty hard. I grinned. "You've still got a great backhand, Dal."

She held out her glass, looked me straight in the eye. "Fill me up?" I managed not to say anything stupid by not saying anything at all.

I got the bottle and refloated her strawberry. "You ought to eat something," I said. "We could have something sent up."

"Go ahead and order. Surprise me. Just make it something light."

I found a menu, ordered her what they called the sunburst platter, cut fruit and banana nut bread with yogurt. It sounded like Dallas. I knew it was light because I wouldn't have eaten it on a bet. I ordered the prime rib. I was ravenous. I hadn't had anything to eat since risking my life at the police station on Russ's sandwich.

Back in the bathroom—or spa, whatever it was—the bubbles were starting to thin out. Okay by me.

"Might want to think about getting out of there," I said. "Food'll be up in a few."

"This Kay, does she have a last name, or is she a one-namer like Cher or Beyoncé?"

"Who knows?"

"You're being uncharacteristically close-mouthed about this one, Mort."

"Uh-huh."

"She must be something special."

"She is that."

"And in only twenty-two hours," Dallas marveled. "No telling where you'll be by the end of the week."

"Truer words were never spoken."

She was fishing. I didn't have anything to give her so she reeled in an empty hook, stood up and headed for the shower to rinse off the suds. I went back to the living room to slow my racing heart—there's something about a wet, naked woman covered in bubbles—and read another paragraph of Sandford, over and over and over. It wouldn't go in and stick.

The rift between Dallas and me, such as it was, was partly cultural in nature. There was a time when she would drag me off to symphonies by the Reno Philharmonic. I have nothing in particular against Schubert, Beethoven, any of those guys, other than that I don't enjoy their music, but I balk at the idea of conductors, which Dallas finds amusing. I once saw Victor Borge in one of his memorable skits that proved what I'd long suspected: the conductor isn't necessary. He or she waves a stick, but doesn't play so much as a tin whistle. As a conductor, Borge did everything wrong—hilariously, I must admit—and the orchestra played on... in spite of him. They knew what they were doing. Right then I decided a conductor could wave a pair of black panties to the beat of "Light My Fire" and the oboes and violins wouldn't miss a beat.

Dallas, of course, disagrees.

A knock sounded at the door as she came out in a Grand Sierra robe and a towel turban. I gave the kid a ten for his tuition—he looked about that age—and said "*Voilà!*" as I whipped the lid off Dallas's sunburst platter.

"Looks lovely, but...I don't know. I don't think I can eat," she said. In spite of her words she was eyeing the food like a wolf eyes a rabbit. After all, life goes on.

"How 'bout I cram it down you, kiddo?" I said.

"Well, since you put it that way."

* * *

News at eleven. Jonnie Sjorgen's startling reappearance got top billing, of course. We'd missed the five o'clock coverage and the six o'clock repeat, but the furor and suppressed journalistic joy of the late-night rehash was a page taken straight out of the O.J. romp of yesteryear.

Dallas looked great on camera. I looked like a poorly trained ape. We didn't have any lines, so all we got was an insinuating voice-over identifying us as the grieving girlfriend and her non-grieving ex, the two of us, *lo!*, finding a critical body part of Reno's long-lost mayor in the boot of her $110,000 automobile. The incriminating shot of the two of us being packed into a police car and whisked away was a nice touch. Police Chief Menteer gave an interview, answering brain-dead questions with predictable, off-the-rack answers.

As the nearest living relative of the deceased, Jonnie's daughter, Rosalyn Sjorgen, got a fifteen-second honorable mention. There was a shot of her two-story maple-dappled clapboard house in Ithaca. I'd never met her, but she was a dance instructor at Ithaca College, which is why my daughter, Nicole, was out there in New York, nearly three thousand miles away. Nicole's dreams and Rosalyn's profession were a match. Once Dallas tied up with Jonnie, Nicole's choice of colleges was a foregone conclusion. Rosalyn wasn't available for comment. No one had seen her in almost a week, and the media was making hay out of that, too, unearthing mysteries and disappearances every time they turned around.

"We are in the eye of the storm," I said. "You and I."

Dallas stared at the television, numb. I picked up the remote. "Want me to turn it off?"

"It's okay."

"That's not what I asked."

"No." She took a deep breath. "That wouldn't make it go away. Let's see what we're up against."

So we watched. All twelve rollicking minutes of it. I don't know about Dallas, but it passed over me like a dream, watching it unfold, seeing the two of us as the world would see us and judge us. By the time it was over, we'd used up 80 percent of our allotted fifteen minutes of Warhol's infamous fame in one short evening, and I had the feeling we were going to get a whole lot more than our fair share by the time all was said and done.

Wendell Sjorgen's stabbing death in an alley behind a Wells Avenue bar twenty years ago was once again a hot topic. Jonnie's dad had received forty-six knife wounds, all in the torso, and his wallet was found on his body, containing over three hundred dollars. No suspects had ever been picked up, no motive put forth, no murder weapon found.

I turned it off when a bit came on about the latest gang shooting on Neil Road. News that wasn't news. Half the crime in Reno could be ended by cordoning off Neil Road one night and plowing it under, then waking up to a bright new day.

Dallas said, "How did he...it...get in there?"

I knew what she meant. Jonnie's head. And I knew she wasn't up to par yet because the "how" was obvious. Only the who, when, where and why were unknown. She probably hadn't given it a lot of thought, but I didn't blame her for that. You don't dwell on the details of a day like the one we'd just been through.

"Jonnie had a set of keys to your car, didn't he?" I said.

"Oh. Yes."

"Now someone else does, Dal."

Which meant if she kept the car she'd have to have the locks changed, but knowing Dallas she'd get rid of it and buy another. What's a measly hundred ten thou, minus a $70,000 trade-in—maybe more since the car was now world famous. A thought I kept to myself.

"A key to your house, too?" I added, because that might not have occurred to her. I made it a question. I didn't know if Jonnie had had access to her place—which she'd kept and used only infrequently—but it seemed likely.

She nodded yes.

And that was that. No more talk of heads or bodies or trunks. Dallas told me she'd got another letter from Nicole, who was off in the French Pyrenees with Edward Kiehl, same boyfriend as last year, so this one was looking serious. At twenty, Nikki was doing what she wanted now with no interference from mom and pop, which both pleased me and scared the hell out of me. She was a bright girl but a bit on the giddy, innocent, overly trusting side, and the world was full of human vampires and other hellish critters, like Bundy and Dahmer and others to be named later.

I took a cool shower, scrubbed off the day, and at midnight Dallas turned on the TV to a late-night movie—*Father Goose*, with Cary Grant and Leslie Caron.

She turned the sound low as I crawled into the other bed—the suite came with two king-size beds. I lay awake for a while amid the soothing burble and flicker of the television as the day unreeled: K unconscious in my bed, Dale and Gregory, Skulstad's bean counters and his voluptuous secretary, Rachel Cabrera. And Jonnie in the trunk of Dallas's car, hair mussed in his usual boyish way—but, now that the day had slowed to this contemplative crawl, I saw the deep slash mark on his left cheek an inch below his eye, and a thin ring of dried blood encircling his scalp above his forehead, barely visible through his dark Mediterranean curls.

* * *

I awoke from a tangled knot of dreams when Dallas slid into bed beside me. It was one of those razor-edged moments you play by ear. I made no assumptions, didn't reach for her. I just lay there and, like a good gumshoe, awaited clues.

First, I discovered she wasn't wearing a thing. But Dallas has always slept in the nude, summer, winter, and every season in between, so that was less a clue than an ordinary, garden-variety fact. Not an unpleasant one, however.

Second, she snuggled up to me. But I more or less anticipated that as well. It's hard to give comfort across the acreage of a king-size bed, and I figured that comfort was what she was after, nothing else.

Third, she said, "Hold me, Mort."

When a woman says she wants to be held, you have a whole slew of ways to make either a fool or a swine of yourself. She probably does want to be held, but a naked woman, unless she's an idiot, has to know that her presence can have a certain predictable effect on a man's physiology—unless that man is possessed of iron control, and few women want to be found resistible enough to witness that iron control. But then, some do. A few say what they mean, and then mean it, which can be very confusing. You could go crazy sifting through it all, trying to puzzle it out, especially right there on the spot, in real time. She'd said, "Hold me, Mort." So, what else?...I held her. And I liked holding her. I always have. Given the quagmire of motive and counter-motive that fills our lives, you can only do what you do, be who you are, play as few games as possible—so I pulled her into my arms and held her and felt her tears on my chest. They landed hot, then turned cool on my skin.

After maybe ten minutes she said, in a whispery voice, "We were going to be married. Next May. We weren't going to say anything until the first of the year."

"I'm...sorry, Dal." Okay, *not*.

"But—I was scared, too." She stirred against me, and I looked into her eyes. They were dark, made even larger than usual by the dim city light that filtered into the room.

"Of what?" I asked.

"Him."

"*Jonnie*? How come? He ever hit you?" A sudden protective urge rose up in me even though he was dead.

"No, nothing like that. It was...I don't know, maybe scared is too strong a word. I just felt there was a part of him I didn't know. That he wouldn't *let* me know."

"Everyone has parts no one else'll ever know."

"Maybe."

She didn't sound convinced. She didn't follow up with more, either, so I didn't press her. Whatever it was, it had been between her and Jonnie. And it was over and done with now, so what did it matter? Which shows how little I knew.

I started to nod off again.

Dallas thumbed the waistband of my Jockeys. "Are these necessary, Mort?"

"Probably not."

"Then why are you wearing them?"

"That could take a while to explain."

"It's that damned chivalry thing, isn't it?"

"I'd throw a cloak across a puddle for you," I said, and I meant it, but if I were ever caught wearing a cloak I'd throw it in front of her just to get rid of it, which is another matter entirely.

"Well, don't, okay?"

So, hell, I took the Jockeys off. Because Dallas was not resistible, and I was still in love.

* * *

When she came, she muffled her cry by pressing her mouth tightly against mine. I felt her climax right down to my toes.

Same old Dallas.

But even then I knew I didn't have her back. She wasn't mine again. Nor was I a mere convenience to her, a throwaway. It was more complicated than that, reaching back in time, but I didn't want to destroy it by picking it apart, separating the good from the bad, even if it wasn't going to last beyond the dawn.

Sometimes love isn't all there is. Sometimes it isn't enough.

* * *

I hadn't made love to Dallas in over three years. I hadn't made love to anyone for ten months, in fact. Working for the IRS is like having visible body lice when it comes to meeting women. They find out what you do, think it over for two seconds, three if they're drunk, and that's the end of it. I felt a nice glow that morning. I was probably smiling too much, foolishly no doubt, but Dallas was too much a lady to mention it although her mouth was twitching.

"I want to hire you, Mort," she said over breakfast. For her, that was half a grapefruit for $3.75 and two slices of toast for $2.80. I was working my way through a double stack of blueberry pancakes, a side of scrambled, an English muffin with strawberry jam, and orange juice, for which I would've had to get a weekend job at a 7-Eleven if I were picking up the tab.

"I was that good, huh?" I asked.

She gave me the look she'd given me the other day. I told her I was sorry.

"No, don't apologize. You can't help it."

"Hire me how?"

"As a private investigator."

"Yeah?"

"You *are* an investigator now, aren't you?"

And a damn fine one, I thought. In all this great nation, in all the world, in fact, I was the one who'd found Jonnie Sjorgen. "What do you want me to do, Dal?"

"Find out who killed Jonnie."

I shook my head. "It's an active case. *Real* active, in case you hadn't noticed. I'd be bumping into RPD detectives all day long. And probably FBI. My no-fault insurance would skyrocket, kiddo. I'd have to sell the screaming Toyota."

"I'm serious, Mort."

"So'm I."

She pushed her lower lip into a pout. "With your vast experience as a PI, I can see why you'd be reluctant."

"Christ, Dal—"

"Okay, fine. If you don't want the job—"

"I don't want the job."

"—I'll hire someone who does."

"C'mon, Dallas. Let the police do what they do."

"I thought you worked for Gregory."

"Gregory Westergaard Rudd. Maybe. I'm not sure. I haven't checked with him since yesterday."

"I would think he'd have some say about what cases you do or don't take, since it's his business."

I relaxed a notch. This wasn't Greg's kind of deal. He wouldn't touch this gremlin with rubber gloves, wearing a hazmat suit. Which gave me my next brilliant idea. I phoned him.

Dale answered with, "Carson & Rudd Investigative Services. Dale Larkin speaking."

Stiff, very stiff. She sounded recorded. "It's Mort. Greg in yet?"

"Uh, yes. Hold on." Sound came through Dale's palm for a few seconds, then Greg came on the line. "Uncle *Morti*mer..."

He made it that far, then ran out of steam. I figured he'd caught our act on TV, Dallas's and mine. Who in this hemisphere hadn't?

"Yeah," I said. "How's business, kid?"

"Mr. Skulstad phoned—"

Hell. Three little bean counters had also caught our act. I was busted. "What'd he want?"

"He let us go." Greg sounded wounded. "He wants his retainer back. Dale's cutting a check for him right now. For God's sake, Uncle Mortimer, you were on every TV station in Reno—"

"Exposure like that costs a bundle. You oughta do a whale of a business now that Carson & Rudd is on the map. Not sure about the name, though. Angel & Rudd might be more—"

"Your cover's been blown—"

"Call Skulstad back, tell him I'll fix it. How much was the retainer?"

"Five…five hundred. Didn't you hear what I *said*? We've been fired, terminated."

"I told you, I'll handle it."

"How?"

"*Call* him, Gregory."

Something in my voice got through. Or maybe he remembered I'd once changed his diapers and was afraid I might remind him of that fact. "Okay," he said.

"Good news," I told him. "I've got us a job offer." I glanced over at Dallas. She smiled back at me.

"Oh?"

"Hot stuff. Dallas wants us—your firm, that is—to try to find out who killed Jonnie."

Dead air. I tried not to smile. The effort made my face feel waxen. I could see him there, staring at the phone in disbelief.

"Well…yeah," my idiot nephew said. "Okay."

"What!"

"I've been thinking about tackling new things. Bigger projects. This might be, you know, a kind of breakthrough, interesting."

Oh, you simple, simple twit. Interesting? "You gotta be shittin' me."

"No. I mean, why shouldn't we—?"

"I hope you've got an airbag glued to your chest, kid." I didn't look at Dallas. Her smug look would've killed me.

"What do you mean?"

"If you're gonna play bumper cars with the media and the police and tabloid slime and the FBI and maybe Interpol, you've gotta wear an airbag. It's a state law. Look it up."

"Well...is Dallas there?"

"Yeah." He hadn't asked where "there" was, so how good a private dick could he be?

"Could you put her on, please?" he asked.

I handed her the phone. Dallas said, "Hello," and, "That's right, Gregory," and, after a half minute or so, not looking at me, "Two thousand's fine."

I closed my eyes. Gregory Rudd, a card-carrying wet blanket for every occasion, was on the case, and I was a monkey's uncle.

* * *

On my way over to Skulstad Meats I could still see that look of satisfaction on Dallas's face. She didn't rub it in, but in the next hour or so I was, in effect, going to be working for her.

But, first things first.

I walked in and smiled at Rachel Cabrera. She was looking very good, very healthy. As leggy as ever. Her legs might've even grown half an inch overnight.

"Oh...Mr. Angel," she said, startled. I could tell by the look on her face that she'd caught my recent stunning success on TV.

"Call me Mort," I said. "How about that dinner? Think it over, huh? Zozo's?"

Without waiting for a reply, I marched back to the bullpen where Skulstad kept the sharpies who kept his books. Unless you're a gang member, fear isn't normally a gratifying thing to see in people's eyes, but I'd seen it with the IRS which has definite ganglike qualities, and I was counting on it now.

Nor was I disappointed. All the media insinuation had made it seem possible, even likely, that I was capable of murder most foul. And at six-four, two hundred thirty pounds after a big meal, who, here, was going to stop me if I suddenly ran amok?

I perched on the edge of Betty Pope's desk since she was head of accounting. I swung a leg. If one wants to intimidate, a little disrespect goes a long way. No one knows where it'll stop.

I had their undivided attention without saying a word. Jonnie and I had probably been the subject of much conversation over coffee and doughnuts that morning. They'd all narrowly escaped with their lives the other day, and here I was again, like an enduring Egyptian curse.

"Someone here isn't playin' by the rules," I said.

Tomblike silence.

"Someone—or maybe more than one—knows *exactly* what I'm talking about."

Betty, Phil, and Iris stared at me with huge eyes, Betty eyeing a pair of scissors, Phil blinking a mile a minute, Iris ready to pass out or run. I leaned a few inches closer to the lot of them. Invading space is a useful intimidation technique—IRS manual, Eighth Edition, page 915.

"Whoever that someone is, or someones," I said ominously, "I want it to stop, *now*."

No one said a word.

"So let's call the game even. Whoever knows what I'm talking about, I want you to give ten thousand dollars to Mr. Skulstad. Put it in an envelope, deliver it to him anonymously. Today is Tuesday. Do it by, say, quitting time Thursday, or I'll be back." Hell, the line worked for Schwarzenegger. I figured it'd work for me.

"If that *doesn't* happen," I added, smiling significantly, "heads will roll."

I gave each of them a final look and walked out. That last line might've been over the top given yesterday's events, but I couldn't resist, so I guess Dallas is right about me.

I poked my head into Skulstad's office. "I'll phone later in the week, maybe Friday." He looked up and stared. I ducked back out, then wrote my phone number on a fluorescent lavender Post-it on Rachel's desk and stuck it to her monitor screen.

"In case you get hungry," I said.

She gawked at me, open-mouthed. I strolled out, got back in my portable Japanese hibachi, and drove over to my place on Ralston Street.

The forty dollars was gone. "*Thanks. K,*" her latest note read. Fresh fruit was in a bowl on the kitchen counter, milk and bread in the fridge, a new tube of toothpaste in the bathroom and a brand-new hot-pink toothbrush upright in the holder. K, of course, was gone.

Sonofabitch.

I grabbed an apple, left another twenty dollars and a reminder for her to do the windows, then went back to the Grand Sierra.

By now the dame was into me for sixty bucks. Spade would've called her a dame, so that's what I did. First chance I got I was gonna call her kiddo, right to her pretty face.

* * *

I walked into the room at 10:15. Dallas had the crossword done and was dressed, ready to go. Dazzling, even in the wilted outfit she'd worn the other day. She was going to stay at least one more night there, maybe more, but she wanted to get clothes and a few

other things from her place—Jonnie's house, that is. I pointed
out the obvious risks, and the fact that she could bop on over to
Macy's and have a ball shopping for new things, one of her favorite pastimes, but she didn't want to do that. The media trolls
might have abandoned Jonnie's place. She had clothes in drawers
there, washed and folded. And she wanted me to tag along, just
in case.

"That mean I'm on the payroll now?" I asked.

"I don't know. I don't know how it works."

"Neither do I."

On the way over to Jonnie's in the Toyota, she turned to me
and said, "About last night, Mort."

Uh-oh. "Yeah?"

"Well, with you and Kay. I know it's a little late to be saying
this, but I didn't mean to get in her way." She hesitated a moment,
then said, "If."

"No problemo."

"I mean, if things are serious between the two of you."

Still fishing. Women. "They're not."

She smiled. "You haven't set a date yet?"

"We're still a ways out from that."

"Oh? How far out?"

"There's this place, Oort's Cloud, somewhere out beyond Pluto,
sort of a hatching ground for comets—"

"Therapy might help, but I wouldn't count on it."

We turned onto her street. The lack of activity had finally got
to the hordes, or maybe it was the heat. Only one news van was
parked on the street. No police cars, not even banners of crime
scene tape since the place hadn't checked out as a crime scene. The
house looked like it always had. The van was local, Channel 25, so
we'd caught the network guys and gals napping.

I pulled into the driveway too quickly for the crew in the van to react. They were scrambling out as Dallas and I jogged up the walk to the door. She got it open before they were able to aim their minicams. Dallas darted through first and I yanked it shut behind me. Channel 25 might have got a shot of the front door closing. Explosive stuff, although we still had to get back out.

Dallas screamed.

I turned, caught her as she fell, and lowered her gently to the cool foyer tiles as I looked around, reaching for the gun I still wasn't carrying.

On a rosewood table against one wall, two lacquered vases in matching Chinese designs flanked Milliken's head. His *head*... goddamn. Like Jonnie, the D.A.'s tongue protruded dark and horrible through bloated lips. His eyes were empty milky orbs.

I didn't have any idea who K was, but in only twenty-four short hours I'd maybe solved Skulstad's problem, and I'd been locating missing persons right and left. This PI thing was really panning out.

CHAPTER SIX

BACK TO THE station we went. Before they got started on me, I said to Russ Fairchild, "You guys didn't by any chance overlook anything at Sjorgen's place when you were poking around over there yesterday, did you?"

This did not appear to amuse him. Nor did it get a chuckle out of Clifford Day, who looked ready to Mirandize me with a rubber hose if only Russ would give him the nod. But now, more than a decade into an enlightened twenty-first century, they no longer do that. They just think it and wish for the good old days.

Cliff was quiet, giving me a hard stare. He was a real behemoth. I doubted that he could get over the obstacle course wall in less than a long afternoon, but he might've knocked it over in two seconds flat, and I'd have bet a ten-spot he could wrangle a drunk to the sidewalk with the best of Reno's finest.

"Finished?" Fairchild said. "Anything more you want to say?"

I nodded toward the see-through mirror. "How's the view from in there? Good?"

"Damned ugly, most of the time. Only thing you can see from in there is in here, if that gives you any idea, but the coffee's a lot better. Anything else, Angel? I wouldn't want you to bottle any of that shit up, herniate your brain, then try to sue the department."

I smiled. Fact is, I was starting to like this guy. "Call me Mort, Russ. And I don't make heads. All I do is find 'em, which is more than I can say for the RPD."

At that, Day moved an inch closer, like a glacier with intent.

"You and your ex," Russ said. He gave me a sour look, then lit a stinking Joe Camel, waved out the match. Guess he wasn't a Bic or Cricket man.

"I wish you wouldn't," I said. "Air's not all that wonderful in here to begin with."

He blew smoke in my direction, and I found it harder to like him. He'd been so much friendlier about this time yesterday. His eyes were red-rimmed, suit rumpled. I doubted that he'd slept much that night, if at all.

"You want to smoke," I said, folding my arms like the locking of a vault, "I want my lawyer. Joe Needham. We'll see whose Joe is more annoying to whom, your Camel or my Needham."

Cops don't like lawyers any more than they like IRS agents. He glared at me, took another drag, then stubbed out the butt.

This time we went through it five, maybe six times. After the third time I lost count. On occasion, when the interrogation room door opened, I could see a glare of lights in the hallway and hear the voices of media buzzards. It's a distinctive sound, like human bark strippers. Dallas and I were truly in the eye of the hurricane this time.

My story was no more complicated this time than last. There wasn't much to tell, so we went over and over what Dallas and I had done the night before, which certainly hinted at who they thought might have killed Milliken. Dallas and I didn't have much in the way of alibis except each other, which didn't overly impress the men in blue. I was glad I'd tipped that grad student the ten. He remembered me, but couldn't vouch for our whereabouts from the critical hours of midnight to six when it was thought that Milliken's head was placed in Sjorgen's foyer—an unmarked car had been outside until midnight and the Channel 25 van had pulled in at six that morning and neither one had seen anything.

None of which was the least bit conclusive, but without anything more substantial than putting us at the top of their wish list, the police couldn't hold either one of us. By two thirty Dallas and I were back on the street, this time taking corners sharply in the Toyota and timing traffic lights to lose a collection of network vans behind us.

"Now what?" Dallas asked. She looked pale and drained. I had the car rolling down Kietzke, fast enough to make the mirror howl.

"How 'bout Tahiti?"

She closed her eyes. "I would, but we were told not to leave town, or maybe the county. Or the state, I don't remember which."

I was told the same thing.

Dallas was quiet for a moment, then she said, "They asked me about Jonnie's penis, Mort."

The Toyota swerved a foot. "Say what?"

She wouldn't look at me. "His penis. They asked me if it had any distinguishing marks or anything." She sounded beyond exhausted.

I didn't know what to say. It wasn't a topic I wanted to pursue in any depth. The question, "Did it?" bubbled around in my head, but I managed to suppress it without difficulty.

"Do you think that means they found...it?" Dallas asked.

"I'm sure I wouldn't know." But I hadn't searched the trunk of her car the morning we'd found him. Maybe something else had been rolling around in there.

"What the hell is going on, Mort?"

I shrugged, slowing for Plumb Lane. "Maybe someone doesn't like Reno's elected officials all of a sudden. If I were on the city council, I'd think about an extended leave of absence, beginning day before yesterday."

She stared at me. "You think *that's* it? Politics?"

"Could be. The mayor, the D.A. Both were up for reelection. Now...I wouldn't give much for their chances, Dal. What do you think is going on?"

"I don't have any idea. I just want it to end."

With both Jonnie and Milliken located and about as dead as people ordinarily get, I thought it *had* ended. Again, that showed how little I knew.

"Did Jonnie have any enemies you know about?" I asked.

"Scads."

"That's helpful."

"He was the *mayor*, Mort. Mayors have lots of friends and lots of enemies, that's how it works. For every person who wants to shake your hand, ten others want to stick a knife in your back."

"I was hoping you'd come up with a place to start."

She shut her eyes again. "That's your job. You're the big PI."

Touché, baby.

One thing was certain, we couldn't drive around all day ducking news vans. My Toyota was becoming too well known. We couldn't go back to Sjorgen's. That would be a three-ring circus, now that it was a genuine crime scene. I thought about my place, but I wasn't up to it, not with K there and Dallas having a fairly cruddy day so far.

We would probably have to go back to the Grand Sierra, but first I drove over to the office of my latest employer. Dallas and I hiked up the back stairs and down the hallway to Greg's office.

Dale was filing papers with her back to us, bent at the waist, legs straight. Great pose. Dallas rammed an elbow into my ribs, so I guess I was noticing too much how great it was.

At the sound of bone on beef, Dale turned. "Oh, Mr. Angel."

"Mort. Greg in?"

"No, he's out somewhere." She hesitated, then said, "The police were here earlier. They wanted to know if you work here, and for how long, things like that."

"Uh-huh."

"It was regarding, you know...Mr. Milliken."

"Uh-huh."

"They said you found him." Her eyes briefly met mine, then dropped away uneasily.

"Uh-huh. By the way, do I get a finder's fee for that? Some sort of a bonus?"

"And Mr. Sjorgen, yesterday. They asked about him, too," she said, completely ignoring my bonus. Maybe she would mention it to Greg later.

"You oughta send me to Wisconsin," I told her. "I'd have that lady's kid back in no time. I've got a knack. So where is Greg?" I got my gun out of the back of a filing cabinet where I'd stashed it and the windbreaker the other day. Seemed like a good idea to have it around again. I threaded the holster back onto my belt.

"I'm not sure, exactly." Dale stared at the gun until it disappeared behind the windbreaker. She glanced at Dallas. "Gregory was going to check around. About Mr. Sjorgen. Go around to his businesses, and, well, places like that."

For what Dallas was paying, Greg would do it right, too, if stiffly, by the book, without a gram of imagination. The sad thing was, with all those strikes against him, he still knew vastly more about how to go about it than I did. I was lost.

"He leave any instructions or anything for me?" I asked.

"Just this." She looked around, found a slip of paper on her desk. It read: *Uncle Mortimer: I'll talk to you later. We'll figure out an approach of some kind. Gregory.*

I felt my wheels churning up sand. We were getting nowhere fast. Dallas had sunk down on the couch. She sat with shoulders slumped, staring at the floor.

"Back to the Grand Sierra?" I asked.

She looked up at me. "Please."

"Uh—" Dale said, a hint of color rising into her cheeks.

"Yes?" I lifted an eyebrow at her.

"Gregory was wondering if...that is..." Her eyes darted toward Dallas.

"A retainer?" Dallas said.

Dale nodded, relieved. Before we left, Dallas wrote a check to Carson & Rudd for two thousand dollars, something I couldn't've managed without a home equity loan.

I drove Dallas to the Grand Sierra, escorted her up to the room, then took off again, back home. Jonnie and Dave were dead. It was likely they'd keep another hour or two. I didn't have anything specific to do for Greg right then, and I had my own little mystery to look into.

A news van was pulling away from the curb as I crept down Ralston from the north. Channel 6, out of Sacramento. Goddamn things were starting to get to me, like roaches with wheels.

I opened the front door and went in. A whiff of ammonia hit me. The room seemed brighter. It took me a moment to figure out why. Damned if K hadn't done the windows! They hadn't been cleaned since Clinton was in office, maybe years before. That alone was worth the sixty bucks I'd left her. I may even have smiled.

About that time I became aware of the sound of running water. The shower. K was home—*my* home, not hers, I almost had to remind myself. She was awake, almost certainly naked and wet. Things were looking up.

Five steps past my bedroom, the bathroom door was ajar, which allowed me to peek inside without feeling too guilty about it.

K was showering away. Flesh tones rippled behind pebbled glass giving me a general sense of the girl, which was all I needed because it brought back crisp memories from Sunday night.

"Hey!" I called.

K stopped moving. She looked in my direction. "Mortimer?"

Goddamn, she knew my name. Either that or she'd been through my mail. "Mort," I said.

"I'll be out in a few minutes."

I liked the sound of her voice, low, sexy, even playful—not the least bit worried that I'd found her where I'd found her. "Take your time, kiddo."

A moment of silence. Then, "Kiddo?"

"A promise I made to myself. Nice work on the windows, by the way."

"I've never seen anything like them. Have they *ever* been cleaned, Mort?"

Mort. At last. She wasn't shy or backward, this one. "Not by me," I said. "Maybe about the time Bush was first elected."

"Which Bush?"

"Which one you think?"

"I'd hate to guess. It took me practically all morning. I didn't get the front very well, though. A news van pulled up before I got done. I had to duck back inside."

"Yeah? I was here earlier this morning."

"What time? You must've just missed me. I had to go out for window cleaner."

"You wouldn't want to tell me your name, would you? And what the hell you're doing here?"

She popped the door open, stuck her head out and smiled at me. A very pretty head, even sopping. I caught a glimpse of her shoulder, part of a thigh, calf, foot, all foamy and glistening and nicely tanned. "In a minute, okay?"

I'd waited this long. I could wait another minute. She ducked back in and shut the door.

The doorbell rang, twice.

I thought about drawing my gun. If a network bloodhound was at the door I might persuade him or her to respect the privacy of private citizens with a casual display of Second Amendment rights.

But, no...I left the gun concealed at my hip.

Just as well. Fairchild and Day were outside, Cliff in straining blues, Russell in his rumpled suit.

"You're in," Russ said, surprised.

"Now I know how you made detective, Detective."

"What we'd like to do is have you come up to Mr. Sjorgen's place, show us exactly what you did when you and Mrs. Angel went in. Reenact the scene, so to speak." He looked past me into the house. "By the way, you wouldn't happen to know where she is at the moment, would you? Your ex?"

From inside, K called out, "Mort? You there?"

"That's not her," I said to Fairchild.

Russ lifted an eyebrow. "That right?"

"That's right. Dallas is at the Grand Sierra. Room 1122."

"Yeah?"

"Yeah. Don't tell the media."

"And you spent the entire night with her last night?"

"That's right."

He looked past me again, then over his shoulder at Clifford Day, who'd evidently been assigned bodyguard or general intimidation duty, it was hard to say which. "I'll be damned. Mickey Spillane ain't dead, only buried."

"Mickey only wrote 'em," I said. "Mike Hammer had all the fun."

Russ shook his head. "I'm in the wrong job. So, about Sjorgen's place? How about we go on over? The chief is there now. Bunch of forensic guys, too."

"A party," I said.

"Right."

"You got some of those little hats, balloons?"

"Not yet. They're on order."

"We did this already, remember? This morning at Sjorgen's, then again at the station? You guys oughta take better notes."

"Yeah, but we could maybe do it one more time, just for fun."

"If it'd make you happy."

"It would." Russ tried to look past me into the house, then he nodded at the interior. "What about her?"

"She'll keep." I didn't tell him how long she'd kept already. "She's not part of this." And I had no intention of dragging her into it, either, at least until I figured out who she was, which was looking like a project akin to quarrying rock for Khufu's Pyramid, dragging it miles through the Sahara, then hauling it three hundred feet up the side of Khufu's to set it in place. About like that.

Russ shrugged. "Your call. What's her name?"

"K."

"Kay?"

"Yep."

"Kay who?"

"Just K."

"Yeah? Like Cher, huh? Doesn't ring a bell. Maybe she could alibi you?"

Nice try, Russ. "I was with Dallas. All night long, Detective. K doesn't know anything about any of this."

I could tell he wanted to pursue this K angle further, but he didn't. I closed the door in his face, shed the windbreaker, and stashed the gun under a couch cushion. No sense making waves. I went out, locked up, and got in my hotbox to follow Russ and Clifford up to Sjorgen's place.

I hadn't told K I was leaving. It was my turn to pull a vanishing act, and I have to admit I got a little kick out of that.

* * *

When they don't have proof, motive, or even a murder weapon or murder site, they rarely come right out and tell you you're a suspect, but you know. It's in their eyes. It hides in their words, or in what they don't say. I could feel the pressure of my status as the number one suspect in the room. The entire world was watching, and Chief Menteer's head was on the block, which wasn't the best metaphor under the circumstances. For the next few days he would be in the limelight with Dallas and me, until America found a newer, brighter diversion, like another Rodney King, or, if God smiled on us all, another O.J. But for now, like Tonya Harding and Joey Buttafuoco years and years ago, we were the national pastime, even if no one remembers good ol' Joey.

And somewhere, behind this hubbub and the roar of conjecture, *someone* knew what was going on, someone with a sharp knife or a hacksaw and the will to use it in a most ungodly fashion.

I tried to think about that someone, what kind of a person it might be, but came up with nothing. I saw rage, lots of rage, but little else. I figured, though, if you polled every psychologist in the country then took an average, you'd come up with an amorphous pile of nothing. Plus here and minus there multiplied by thirty thousand equals exactly zero. No one can agree on anything these days. It's even worse on the witness stand: one paid psychologist whore contradicting the other side's whore. All I knew is, it wasn't Dallas and it wasn't me, RPD's two prime suspects.

At Jonnie's place, news crews had set their cameras on full zoom from 150 feet away. The police were keeping them at bay behind patrol cars and a stringer of yellow tape that fluttered in a hot breeze. Their lenses followed us along the walkway and through the front door. If they were feeding live, untold millions of inquiring minds might be tracking us into Sjorgen's house that very moment, calculating the odds of my being marched back out in cuffs based on yellow journalistic gibberish and 2 percent actual fact.

Inside, the house was teeming. A party indeed. Two serious-faced women were dusting everything they could find in the living room for fingerprints. Two men were discussing something with Chief Menteer. A man was vacuuming, using an odd-looking forensics Hoover. That would brighten Dallas's day. The place would be spotless when she got back. Except it wasn't her house, and I figured she'd soon be back in her own.

In the backyard, a young guy was tiptoeing through flower beds, checking windowsills for signs of forced entry. A woman was photographing rooms from every conceivable angle. Two forensics guys were in the foyer going over the table that had held Milliken's head. They had spray bottles, an ultraviolet light, tape, calipers, a steel ruler, and something that looked like a tool a dentist would use to probe for cavities, which was one of the few tests they might be able to perform on Milliken the last time I'd seen him.

Menteer came over and we all stood in the foyer and went over it a few more times, those ten seconds between the time Dallas and I got inside, shut the door, she screamed and I kept her from falling, then I stared at Milliken's head—gone now. No matter how they ran it past me, or how I ran it past them, there wasn't any more to it, not even when I acted it out, step by painful step.

Simply put, they got nothing. I, on the other hand, kept my eyes and ears open and picked up a few tidbits I hadn't had before.

There was no sign of forced entry anywhere, so Jonnie's keys were still at large, or so it seemed. That was enough to put Dallas squarely in RPD's sights, if not one Mortimer Angel.

Jonnie's and Milliken's bodies hadn't been found yet. All the police had were heads. I caught a few squirrelly looks regarding that, but couldn't make anything of it. I stared back blankly and they gave up, reluctantly, whatever they were looking for.

The cops hadn't set Jonnie's burglar alarm when they closed the place up yesterday night. I had the impression they were sorry about that now, but it was too late for sorry. The front and back doors used the same key. Medeco locks, about as good as locks get, which made it damned unlikely that anyone had picked their way in. Nor was there any sign that anyone had tried. Again, that hinted at either Dallas or yours truly, people with ready access to a key.

"Which door'd this guy use to get in?" I asked, rustling up more clues on Dallas's behalf.

Fairchild said, "You tell me."

"Very funny."

That was as close as anyone got to trying to wring a confession out of me. Couldn't say as I blamed them any.

I toyed with the idea of telling them not to worry, that Gregory and I were on the case—call it professional backup—but I restrained myself. No one seemed in the mood for news that good.

They turned me loose at 4:45, without an escort. There was a general riot by the media and a scramble for their vehicles when I came out alone and squeezed into my car. Fairchild stood outside and watched them come after me. As I rounded a corner, I saw him wave. I caught a glint of teeth as he smiled. Bastard.

* * *

I lost the last one, a station wagon out of Los Angeles, at 4:58. Tenacious sonsofbitches. This one had a driver like Andretti behind the wheel, except it was a young, fierce-eyed woman with a mane of frazzled blond hair. These days you can't beat gals in the eighteen- to twenty-five range for daring and raw speed. With testosterone levels like bulls, it's a wonder they don't grow beards. Her arrogance, however, was her undoing. She was ten feet behind me, tailgating after running a red light to keep up. I put the Toyota up on two wheels turning left off Sierra into an alley, and she overshot, then spun out. Not even testosterone gives you traction.

I drove past my house. Two crews had the place staked out. They knew I'd been cut loose. One of them came after me, a kid of maybe twenty-two driving, a woman riding shotgun, holding a video camera. I sped up, lost him in the maze of streets west of UNR. Poor guy didn't stand a chance. All he had was testicles, wasn't driven by rage.

I motored around aimlessly for ten minutes.

I could have gone home and fullbacked my way through the carrion feeders that had either stayed behind or fluttered in to roost in the ten minutes I'd been gone—if I'd wanted to see my-self on the news again, looking like a sure thing for county jail in the next few days, and then, of course, lethal injection. I decided, no way. If K was still there, she was on her own and good luck.

So I was adrift. In other circumstances that wouldn't have been unpleasant. I can amuse myself. I do okay alone. Bump up against too many people in too short a time and I feel a primal urge to hole up, be by myself for a while, and I'd pretty much had my fill in the last two days. Not of Dallas, never of Dallas, but the weight of humanity was starting to wear me down, especially those with cameras and asinine questions.

I wondered, though, how I must look to all those good folks in Iowa, Indiana, Ohio, Illinois, any of those Midwestern vowel states. Guilty as sin, no question. Big lumbering guy like me could lop off a head in no time.

So...now what? Go solve the case or cases? Fat chance, in spite of Dallas's hopes. Troops of Reno's finest were on the job, crawling all over it. I had no hope of win, place, or show.

But a job was a job. Dallas had only said try. To her, a couple thousand was blow-off change. Greg and I had no chance of find-ing Jonnie's killer, but Dallas might have felt obligated for some reason. Or maybe she needed to feel more in control.

But...where to start?

Truth was, I was worn out, exhausted. I'd been a private eye for only two days, and I'd already found Jonnie Sjorgen, Milliken, and maybe fixed things over at Skulstad's. Gregory was dead wrong. This gumshoe business definitely had its heart-pounding moments.

Except that I could see him now, going door to door, business to business, trying to get a line on Jonnie that no one else was getting. Shoe leather grunt work. Hopeless, I thought. He'd go over to Sjorgen Fence Company out on East Sixth, or to the Silver Strike Motel, of which Jonnie had been part owner. What the hell could he ask? I couldn't even imagine. "Hey, guys, any of you see anyone threaten Jonnie's life around here in the past month or two?"

Like I said, hopeless. If anything like that had happened, the police would've had it days ago.

I was lost. I had no idea where to start. I still didn't know who K was. Maybe I wasn't cut out for this private eye thing after all.

K, I found, was really starting to rankle.

In the meantime, I was hungry. I also had a memorable face and size, had been on TV too much of late, was due for a serious bath, and I'd lost my house, my kitchen, shower, bed, and every last shred of privacy I hadn't realized I valued so highly until it was gone. And my formerly nondescript Toyota was becoming the White Ford Bronco of Reno.

So—I drove it on back to Dallas.

CHAPTER SEVEN

THAT NIGHT WAS not one of fun and games. Nor had I expected it. I hadn't expected it the night before, either. But Dallas came straight from the shower into my bed, and I held her until we both fell asleep. That was nice. Sometimes nice is more than enough.

I dreamed that a pack of dogs was chasing me—or wolves. When I looked back, they were one faceless, silent-running man, wielding a machete, and his eyes were as blank as silver dollars.

* * *

Early the next morning in the Grand Sierra's parking lot, I found that the media had discovered my Toyota. They hadn't gathered in an obvious way, not like a British soccer riot, but from the top of the stairs overlooking the southeast lot I saw half a dozen vans scattered around. Reporters and cameramen were out stretching their legs, drinking coffee from Styrofoam cups. They were a wiry looking pack, fleet of foot, ready to spring into action.

I had two choices: back off, or get on TV in Bangkok, Paris, Rangoon, everywhere on the planet where they had electric power and free time on their hands. I didn't give a damn what they thought about me in Rangoon, but Hawaii was another matter. What would Mom think?

I hadn't given any thought to that. By now, Dori Angel had to have heard about the stunning successes of her one and only son in his new career. It was possible she'd been on TV in Maui, telling them God only knew what about me. Next chance I got, I would have to ask K if Mom had phoned with her congratulations.

I retreated, caught a De Luxe cab under the Grand Sierra portico.

"Court Street," I said to Ralph Lockett—none of this Rasheed Abdul stuff you get in New York City. Ralph was a hundred pounds overweight, finishing a jelly-center donut with powdered sugar on it, drinking coffee from an ancient Thermos. A fine dusting of sugar trailed down the front of his shirt. He took one look at me and almost spewed Maxwell House over the windshield.

"Jesus, you're that heads guy, huh?"

"Heads?" I gave him a blank look. "Tractor parts convention. Got in from Iowa last night."

He peered at me in the rearview mirror. "Then you better get yourself a hat, fella. Guy here in town looks just like you, probably been cutting off people's heads."

"No shit? *That* guy? Wow. Heard about it on the news, way over there in Des Moines. They haven't caught him yet, huh?"

"Not yet. He's pretty smart. But they'll get 'im, don't you worry."

Straight from Joe America. Mortimer Angel was one dangerous sonofabitch. Smart, too. I sorta liked that.

Ralph cruised down the ramp, headed for Glendale Avenue. He glanced back at me again and shook his head before making the turn. "I'd buy me a fake moustache, too, I was you."

* * *

Twenty-five minutes later, sporting a porkpie hat and a bristly, Scottish-looking moustache from a place called Life-Like Hair for Men, I climbed the back stairs of Gregory's office building. Damn if that Ralph fella didn't have a good head on his shoulders.

I got there at 8:53, before Dale or Gregory showed up and had to wait in the hallway. No one had thought to give me a set of keys. I nodded to two young women who opened the gaming school, feeling idiotic, touching the moustache every couple of seconds to make sure it hadn't slipped out of place.

Dale arrived. She stared at me.

"Mr. Angel?"

"Nope. Judd Perkins, tractor parts. Iowa."

"Why are you...oh."

"Yeah, oh."

"It's, uh, getting pretty bad, isn't it?"

"Bad is relative. It's been worse for Jonnie and Dave. How about opening up so I can get this pretty face out of the hallway."

"Oh. Of course."

"And maybe you could get me a key so I don't have to do this again."

"Yes, certainly."

She unlocked the door. I darted in ahead of her. "When's Greg usually get in?" I asked.

"Well...most days he's here before me. This is unusual."

"Kid's a regular ball of fire, huh?"

"It's all the paperwork. He likes it when it's quiet. He's usually in by seven thirty." She looked around again, as if she might've missed him somehow on the first pass.

Greg was late. Very late.

I didn't like that. For a creature of habit and very little else, his absence kindled a spark of worry in me.

I ambled over to his door, opened it, and stared at his head, perched on his desk on the blotter in a small black pool of blood, staring approximately over my left shoulder, tongue lolling.

Son...of...a...*bitch*.

* * *

Back at the station I thought they were going to hook me up to a transformer, plug it into an outlet, and announce my sudden demise right there—close all three cases and end the carnage with one-and-a-half cents' worth of Sierra Pacific power. Like Ruby blowing away Oswald, it would be one of those wild, unexpected things that end up saving the taxpayers untold millions.

Dallas was in another interrogation room, Dale in another. A search warrant had been issued to go through my house, so I figured I'd at least get an ID on K out of it, if they didn't indict me right here and run me straight up to the jail on Parr Boulevard. Finding out who she was wasn't worth Gregory's life, but at least it was something.

"Know what tiny little common denominator keeps popping up in all of this?" Russ asked me, puffing furiously on a Camel, *fuck your lawyer* glowing in his eyes.

"Tell me."

"You, hotshot. You, coming across heads."

"He was my *nephew*, Fairchild."

"Guess who's most likely to commit murder?"

I didn't answer.

"Family member," he said in a tough-guy voice. "Goddamn family. The people who know you best. Maybe there's a message in that. What do you think?"

To Jonnie, Dallas was something like family. And his daughter, Rosalyn. Who else? His first wife, Jean, now living in Memphis?

His second wife, Anne, up in Seattle? Both of them had been on the tube lately. Rosalyn was still AWOL.

I said, "Far as I know, I'm not related to either Jonnie Sjorgen or Dave Milliken, but you never know. You might want to swing up into my family tree and look into that."

That slowed him down for a moment, invoking the tricky concept of a common *motive* to all three murders, but it didn't take him long to build up another head of steam.

"You are squarely in the thick of this," he said, billowing carcinogens.

"Lucky me."

"Why do I get the feeling if I lock you up, lives will be saved?"

"I love rhetorical questions. You want a rhetorical answer?"

He glared daggers.

"If I'm hacking these guys up," I said, "why am I calling them in?"

"Boy, you got me there, hotshot. Maybe we ought to get us a psychologist in here and track that down."

"If you lock me up, you won't find them as fast, that's all. I've got a knack." I returned the stare he was giving me. "You've got a hell of a problem in this town, like a serial killer. I'm not it."

"Yeah? We'll see."

He got down to it. Maybe he'd got plenty of sleep the night before, because he came at me from every angle he could think of, some of which I'd never considered before. He was good. My respect for Reno's finest went up a notch. Trouble was, he didn't get a confession and he didn't get one micron closer to solving the murders of Sjorgen, Milliken, and Rudd. But anger like his is the stuff of legend. I'll bet he left contrails in the hallways, a smoking ring on the toilet seat.

I was feeling sorry for myself, too, doomed to stumble across one new head each morning, doomed to spend too much of every day in this ugly, airless cubicle, trapped with Fairchild, Day, half a dozen others drifting in and out, and Smokin' Joe Camel. I had a vision: that this or something like it is what God has in store for agents and former agents of the IRS in the afterlife. Call it karma. Hope that brightens your day.

Russ put a foot up on a chair and stared down at me. "Who's Kay?"

"I give up."

Like a mountain shifting in an earthquake, Officer Day stirred, anticipating action. Russ's eyes narrowed. "Now is not the time," he warned me.

"I have no idea who she is. Ask her."

"We would, but she's not there, Mr. Angel. There is blond hair in the shower and in your bed, but Kay is not in, and I'm starting to wonder who she is and what she is in all of this."

"She's not anything in this."

"Says the man who finds heads."

"Trust me, it's not that much fun."

"One last time, hotshot. Who's Kay? And if you don't know, how is it you're so sure she's not anything in all of this, as you say?"

So, reluctantly, I told them the saga of K, as well as I could piece it together myself. It was a murky, unlikely tale, even to me, but I think the truth of it finally got through, after a fashion. Who could invent something like that? What kind of a PI would admit to it? Fairchild's eyes grew fractionally less fierce, or so I imagined.

"K?" he said. "Just the letter?"

"Just the letter."

He nodded. "We found the notes." He took a drag, blew a cloud of smoke toward the ceiling that disappeared reluctantly into an air vent. "No idea who she is, huh?"

"None."

"Or even how she gets in?"

"I figure she got hold of a key somehow."

"You figure."

I shrugged. "How else? There's no trail of soot leading from the chimney."

Russ aimed a grin at Day. "Private dick, huh? Cracker Jack prizes are better than when I was a kid."

I said, "You find out who she is, let me know. Until then, you and I are dead even."

"Jesus H. Christ." He ran fingers through his hair. "Okay, let's go over it again. Start with that station wagon you almost made that news lady roll on Sierra Street. I kinda like that part."

*   *   *

In spite of my probable danger to society, I was back on the street by four p.m. My stints at police headquarters were getting longer, however. Not a good sign. One day they would roll over into the next and that would be that. Perpetual interrogation, case closed. Until the next head was found, that is, but that might take a while with me out of action.

Dallas was back at the Grand Sierra. She'd known nothing about Greg's death or how we'd found him. All she gave them was background information, how Greg and I were related, how long she'd known him, how well he and I appeared to get along, that sort of thing. Dale had been sprung earlier too, sometime around noon. I had no idea where she was.

The police had picked up my Toyota at the Grand Sierra and gone over it with tweezers, a vacuum, and, I imagined, a portable electron microscope. They found nothing. It was waiting in the inferno of the back lot of the station for me, windows rolled up nice and tight like before.

Maybe Russ was feeling sorry for me, because he had a car run interference as I left, jamming up a battalion of news vans and wagons from all over the West Coast, and one from the *Fort Worth Star-Telegram*. The story wasn't getting any less interesting with time. I expected to see a *Tass* van any moment now. No doubt Muscovites enjoyed a circus as much as anyone.

Going home was out of the question. Dropping by the office didn't seem like a swift idea either. I didn't know if there *was* an office, as such, anymore, or if I was still employed, or if Dale, who had an investigator's license, whereas I didn't, could or would keep the place open. All told, I didn't know shit, which was par.

My jaundice-yellow Toyota was becoming a liability, however. If I kept circling around, I'd draw a following of media trolls.

I pulled into the Circus Circus parking garage and stuck the car in a dark slot way up on the fifth floor, put on my moustache and hat and hiked over to the Green Room at the Golden Goose where the relative lack of lighting might give me a few hours' peace and quiet. And where, with luck, I might get a decent buzz on. This whole thing was going too damn fast. Alcohol has a tendency to slow things down, or bring it to a complete halt. Either way, I figured I'd come out ahead.

With all that figuring, however, I hadn't counted on O'Roarke.

"Nice goin', spitfire," he said. The laconic son of a bitch.

"Stuff it."

He slid a bottle of Pete's Wicked Ale across the bar toward me. "On the house, Sherlock."

"Can it."

"Real nice moustache, that."

I touched it. "Yeah? How 'bout the hat?"

"That's nice too. Porkpie, right?"

"Right."

"Nice. Wish I had one."

Goddamn if that girl from the other night didn't pop in and sit down next to me. Holiday. She looked fresh, just starting out, still sleek as an otter, size six, small waist, nice everything. Still hooking, God love her. At least she still had a job.

She shot me a smile. "Hi, there, good-lookin'."

"Hi, yourself, kiddo." I took off the hat and stuck my moustache on a jar of beer nuts. "About that howling mirror—"

"Oh, shit," she yelped. "You!" She leapt up. "Glue a fuckin' *rat* to the sonofabitch!" She left.

Glue a rat to the sonofabitch. To the mirror, presumably. Which, obviously, would alter the air flow. Why hadn't I thought of that? Sometimes the simplest solutions are the most elusive. I looked over at O'Roarke. "She's a rocket scientist, not a hooker."

"There's no such thing as rocket scientists," he said. "Engineers design rockets. And put the fuzz back on. You're scaring customers." He nodded toward two elderly ladies off to my right who were staring nervously in my direction.

"Ever have one of those weeks?" I jammed the moustache to my upper lip again and gave the ladies a reassuring smile.

"What's the problem?" he said. "You're a celebrity, Great Gumshoe. You found our missing mayor and district attorney. You're a household name all across the Land of the Free."

"Yeah?" I said. "So's Ty-D-Bol."

* * *

When I'd had enough beers to be only slightly less coherent than usual, I dug out my cell phone and dialed my sister, Ellen, Greg's mother. Like it or not, it was something I had to do. The call went to voice mail. Ellen is a certified public accountant. I'd forgotten that she was out of town, in Denver at what had to be the world's most boring convention—three hundred CPAs droning about the latest in spreadsheet techniques. I dialed her house number and spoke for a long minute with Maxwell Rudd, my brother-in-law, which in times past has been like holding a conversation with a computerized insurance salesman.

Like me, Gregory's father was under the influence, a state in which I'd never seen him. I liked him better for that wordless display of emotion. He hadn't told Ellen yet, but he was working himself up to it. He would have to do it soon or she'd hear about it on TV. I commiserated, told him I'd try to phone Ellen later, then hung up, had another beer, then another, then blissfully lost count, like those savages who have no words for numbers greater than three.

It was dark when I left and hiked up to my place in Reno's eternal twilight, leaving the Toyota ensconced in the Circus Circus parking garage. Hiking wasn't quite the right word for it, but I thought reeling sounded overwrought. Sailboaters call it tacking, and they do it intentionally. Lights smeared across my vision as I turned my head. All my aches were gone, faint pains that creep up on you, so much a part of age that you hardly notice them on a day-to-day basis.

I tacked past my house at ten fifteen. Six news vans were parked along the street. *Six* of the bastards. I kept the porkpie pulled down over my brow, moustache in place. I faked a limp, keeping to the shadows, a modern-day Quasimodo in the dark.

I made it. No one leapt out to interview me even though I was a possible neighbor of the infamous Mortimer Angel. Fooled 'em all, I chortled darkly, but they had my house covered like a whore giving freebies.

Okay, maybe I was more sozzled than I thought. Even so, I knew I was going to have to make a nonstandard approach to my house, or make headlines again.

I circled the block, then ambled down Mrs. Knapp's driveway and through her backyard, looking at the ground to avoid obstacles...and clotheslined myself on a strand of wire I'd put up for her last summer. Velma Knapp wouldn't own an electric dryer if you gave her a new Maytag, right out of the box. She's four foot ten, eighty-five years old, and what was a stretch for her was precisely neck high to me. The things you forget when you've had one too many brewskis.

I spent a minute on my back on the grass, which needed cutting, collected my thoughts, such as they were, then stumbled to the fence between my property and hers, lofted myself up and over and onto my back again on the other side, spent another minute getting my lungs to process air again, then wended my way to the house.

After a lengthy attempt to open the back door with my key upside down, I righted it, went in, and called out, "K," but got no response.

I went through the house. She was gone.

I left the lights off to avoid causing an uproar out front, stripped and showered, washing off the day, then crawled into bed.

My bed.

Alone. At last. It felt good.

I figured I'd fall asleep right away, but no such luck. I smelled K, a fresh, perfumy scent, and I saw Greg on his desk, and I composed rambling speeches of apology or condolence to Ellen, and to his wife, Libby. And I worried about Dallas, how close she was to all of this, whatever *it* was, hoping it wouldn't reach out and find her. I thought I should have been with her right then, every minute, until the guy or ghost or bogeyman in charge of hell in Reno was caught. But I'd phoned her from the Goose after talking with Maxwell and she'd told me she'd be fine over there at the Grand Sierra, that she wanted to sleep. Alone, Mort.

Okay, I could understand that.

But...*what was going on?*

I didn't have a clue, not even a guess. Finding Jonnie Sjorgen and David Milliken had taken about as much expertise as a suicide stepping off the roof of a building and hitting concrete.

Great Gumshoe, hah.

* * *

A glance at my bedside clock told me *The Tonight Show* was about to come on. I risked the light from the TV and caught Leno's monologue. Damned if I wasn't part of it. Two jokes. Now *that* was a spooky feeling. You know you're getting somewhere when you're on Leno's list, right up there with Clinton, Bush One or Two, Obama, Enron, either of the merry Bobbitts, any of that fun stuff of yesteryear.

The phone on my nightstand rang.

I stared at it. My number's unlisted. IRS agents don't encourage the public to call and harass. Finally I picked it up, knowing it would be a media scuzzball. Bribery had finally shaken my number loose and this was the first salvo. I said, "The number you have dialed is not in service—"

"Guess what, Mort? You were on TV, your name, I mean. Jay Leno mentioned you."

A woman's voice, but it wasn't Dallas. "I saw it. Is this K?"

"No, it's...oh. Yes. I guess. Is that what you've been calling me?"

"What else? The Mystery Blond in my Bed? Which I've had to resort to lately, come to think of it. It's been more than a little embarrassing."

"I'm sorry. Things are, well...*weird* right now, that's all."

"Tell me about it. The windows look sensational, kid. Or did I tell you that already?"

She paused. "Have you been drinking?"

"Now that you mention it, I had a drop or two, yes."

"I...I heard about your nephew, Mort."

"Who on this hungry little planet hasn't?"

"I'm so sorry. I just wanted you to know."

"Thanks."

"And...well, that I'm okay, in case you...Anyway, I'm in a no-name motel out on East Fourth. The media outside your place was getting to be too much. And, I, uh, used the rest of the money you gave me for the room."

"S'all right."

"I'll pay you back. I don't know when that'll be, but I will."

"It's not necessary. How'd you get out of the house without the hordes bringing you down like cheetahs and gathering around to feed?"

"I went over the back fence."

Lot of traffic over that fence in recent hours. As I'd guessed, K was an athletic lady. Probably hadn't landed on her back, either, with the wind knocked out of her. "What time?"

"About five this afternoon. I came back earlier, about three, but the police were all over the place so I couldn't go in. I watched for a while then came back later. Then there was a guy skulking around in your side yard, one of those reporters, trying to peek in the windows. I thought he might've spotted me, so I took off right after he left. Your neighbor's really sweet, though."

Great. I could imagine Velma watching K drop over our mutual fence into her backyard. "That would be Velma. Knapp."

"Yes, I know," K said. "She introduced herself. We had tea. She was weeding a vegetable garden and I practically landed on top of her. She thought you and I were having a deliciously torrid affair."

"You set her straight about that, of course."

"Well, no. I *couldn't*. I mean, she was so delighted. And I got the impression she hasn't heard anything about...well, Mr. Sjorgen or Mr. Milliken, so why *else* would I be climbing over your back fence? I had to have a reason, right? I hope you don't mind."

Velma would be more than delighted, of course. Her eyes would glow in the dark for days, like a cat or vampire. Next time I saw her she would pump me for information like bilge pumps on a battleship.

I said, "I've never been on the phone this long with anyone whose name I didn't know. Wouldn't care to enlighten me, would you?"

"Later, okay? I better go. I'm pretty sure this place charges phone calls by the minute. I might have to sneak out in the morning, early. I'll be in touch."

"If you say." If she was getting as low on cash as it sounded, I thought it wouldn't be too long before she was back for a refill.

"You—you're a private investigator now, aren't you? It was on TV."

In fact, it was the thrust of both of Leno's jokes.

"There's some debate about that," I said. "Even though I've got the best missing persons record in all of North America."

She gave a somber little laugh. "Gotta go. Bye."

"Yeah, see you."

I hung up. Goddamn if I wasn't starting to like this woman. I liked her voice. And the way she'd looked in my bed hadn't put me off any, either. I just didn't want to find her head anywhere, which is a skill I've developed recently.

* * *

I stared up at the ceiling. My watch on the nightstand let out a quiet double chirp, announcing midnight. And again at one o'clock. I was still awake, proof that I hadn't had nearly enough to drink.

Jonnie, you son of a bitch. What were you into? Or was it Milliken? Or was it both of you? Who got you guys?

And Gregory, you dumb shit, what did *you* stumble across?

Something.

I sat up partway in bed. *That* was something, right there, a great *big* something and I'd missed it. Greg had been out beating the bushes, checking out Sjorgen's various properties or whatever and had come across the killer. Must have. Decapitations aren't that common.

Where one went, I thought, another could follow.

Right. And what killed one could kill another.

I sank back down on the mattress. Truth was, I wasn't in any position to assess how good a sleuth Greg was, or his ability at self-defense, but he'd run into something lethal and hadn't had the wit, strength, or perceptiveness to survive, so he hadn't been good enough.

And I was an ex-IRS auditor, not a goddamn PI, so where did that leave me?

Great Gumshoe, hell. I couldn't find a *lake* up in Wisconsin, much less some lady's kid.

Suddenly I sat up again, blinking.

Greg hadn't gone to Wisconsin, either. He'd farmed the case out to someone out there who knew the territory.

Right then I knew what I had to do if I was going to stay in the game, since I wasn't an IRS agent *or* a PI—since I wasn't anything at all now—except, maybe—a middleman.

Come the dawn, I had to go out and hire myself a private investigator.

CHAPTER EIGHT

I DIDN'T FALL asleep quickly, and when I did, I didn't sleep worth a damn. The way Greg had looked on his desk kept me up past two that morning. For all his stuffiness, he'd been a darn good kid.

When morning came, it came hard. Sunlight blasted through my window like a searchlight. I felt an almost biblical punishment in the brain-searing glare that lit up my eyelids. I never should've asked K to clean the windows. I hadn't appreciated the value of dirt.

That was it, I vowed. I'd had it with beer, anything with alcohol in it, including cold remedies. I turned away from the light, finding myself sore in places I couldn't account for until I remembered Velma's clothesline and the six-foot freefall onto my back lawn.

I peeked out a window that faced the street, careful not to move the curtains quickly or let my face show in the window. As I'd feared, news hounds were still out there. K was right about one thing: they were getting to be a bit much.

It seemed as good a time as any to do something about that. What with the change of careers and the recent turmoil in my life, I hadn't been out for a jog in several days. Somewhere I'd heard a good run does wonders for a hangover, if you can stand the jarring. And if you like to eat, as I do, it helps keep the waistline under control and the cholesterol down. Normally I try to get out three or four times a week for at least five miles, sometimes more. I was due.

And, as a bonus, I thought today's outing could be made fairly entertaining as well.

To test that theory, I came out the front door at seven fifteen wearing lightweight sweat pants and an old T-shirt. Without a glance at the news vans and wagons, I took off at a lope, headed downtown. Shouts erupted behind me and engines roared to life. About then, I may have smiled.

I pounded along faster than usual, which hurt more than usual. It didn't take the first van long to pull up alongside, weaving slightly. I hadn't made it two blocks, and this long-haired kid was leaning out a window, squinting into a viewfinder while shouting inane questions. I doubled back abruptly, a quarter of the way down the block. The van's brakes squealed, followed by a satisfying crunch, the sound of a van and an SUV mating. Channel 2, Reno, and 7 out of Las Vegas, crossbreeding.

After observing more close calls and indecisive maneuvers at the intersection, I trotted east. Within half a block, a pale-blue station wagon pulled up alongside. Recognizing the female Rambo at the wheel from the other day, I cut down an alley behind a row of houses and lost her, same trick as the day before, except on foot. A van out of Sacramento turned into the alley and kept pace on my heels.

"Yo, Mr. Angel, when'd you first—?"

Vans don't double back worth a shit, especially in narrow alleys, so I made another U-turn. The alley plugged up with two vans, an SUV, and a barking golden retriever.

That threw them. Engines roared as other vehicles circled the block. Chaos reigned as they tried to sort themselves out and get a bead on me. I was in the clear for two blessedly quiet blocks. By then I'd reached Sierra Street and was chugging downhill toward Circus Circus and the garage where I'd left my car the night before.

A van pulled up and idled along with me, video camera aimed out a window. I gave them a view of a damn fine gumshoe out for his morning run before going off to find another head. It was a great morning. The sky was blue, the air cool. I'd never had an escort on a run before. Maybe I could get used to it, though if I'd had my gun I might've fired a round into the air to see what effect it had.

I glanced back, ignoring questions being shouted from the van. There was an entire unruly cortege of them, weaving, tailgating each other, jockeying for position. I counted eight. Somehow, I'd picked up two more. Ever since I'd found Jonnie, Reno was bursting at the seams with them.

Across the I-80 overpass, across Sixth Street against the light. I jogged into the entrance of the Circus Circus parking garage as the light changed. On they came, roaring into the garage, tires squealing on oily concrete as I trotted up the ramp between rows of parked cars, most of them with out-of-state plates.

I led them up three levels, then ducked down a flight of stairs, embarrassed for our great nation and its so-called education system. Apparently high school doesn't teach critical-thinking skills. I could hear more squealing tires, curses echoing off naked concrete. If the video cameras were still rolling, most of this was going to end up on the editing room floor, figuratively speaking.

Out a door at street level. A local van was hugging a curb, engine idling. A Channel 4 crew. I hadn't fooled them, but then they knew the territory. I led it east on Fifth, then south on Virginia, past Fourth. Ramboette in the blue station wagon got in front of Channel 4, then edged right and hit the brakes, forcing Channel 4 back until Lady Rambo was opposite me. It was a ballsy maneuver. I thought it should be rewarded. Three vehicles were now behind me with more on the way. Under the Reno city arch, embossed with the words *"Biggest Little City In The World,"* past Harrah's Club and a bunch of touristy gift shops. Early morning pedestrians stared as we went by. A lazy right turn down a service alley halfway down the block to give everyone a chance to follow, one block west through the alley, then a sudden turn north on Sierra—wrong way up the one-way street.

An abrupt squeal of brakes, then an even louder and therefore more satisfying crunch of metal and glass. I looked back. Lady Rambo had met a Citifare bus head on. Ouch. Expensive way to start the day. I saw steam rising. I saw her hop out and glare up the street at me. I saw her give me the finger in a highly dexterous manner.

I slowed, trotted back to Virginia Street, across to Center, and looked around. I'd lost them. Hard work, but worth every lungful.

I jogged up Lake Street to the university, across the campus, around the track twelve times, then back home on various side streets, feeling better than I had in days.

I did eighty sit-ups, lifted forty-pound dumbbells, and spent a few extra minutes in the shower, lathering up and singing old Beatles tunes, including "Yellow Submarine."

All traces of my hangover were gone. I thought I might publish the cure in JAMA one day. If I did, I'd be sure to send a copy to the Rambo gal. I was sure I could get her name and address from RPD's traffic division, especially now that I had friends on the force. Russell Fairchild and I were getting to be pretty good pals.

* * *

I left my gun at home, still under the cushion of the couch. This time I went through the fence, not over. I found a loose plank near the northwest corner of my yard, pried it off, and the one next to it, and squeezed through.

And came face to face with Velma, who had a fistful of chopped honeysuckle in one hand, shears in the other, a glint in her eye. We stood in the shade of a leafy plum, serenaded by sparrows.

"She still over there?" Velma asked.

Ah, my big chance. "Who?"

"That girl."

"What girl?"

"Don't you play dumb with me, Mortimer." She shook the shears at me. She was all gray hair and wrinkles, wore a hearing aid and weighed no more than eighty-two pounds. She had on shorts and a Grateful Dead T-shirt covered in silvery cobwebs and bits of minced honeysuckle.

She peered closer at me. "When on earth did you grow *that* horrible thing?"

I touched the moustache. "Something I've been working on."

"Horrible. Just horrible. And that *hat*!"

"What's wrong with it?"

"Doesn't suit you a-tall."

"I was thinking about getting rid of it. You wouldn't happen to know her name, would you?" I pulled the boards back in place. They were behind a good-sized pine tree in my yard. From the street no one would notice they were loose. I hoped.

"Her plane?"

"Her name, *name*."

Velma peered at me through one eye. "You don't have to shout. *Whose* name? Not your lady friend, I hope?"

"Yeah. Her."

"You mean to tell me *you* don't know?" Her look darkened.

"It, uh, slipped my mind."

"I would *think*, Mortimer..." she said in an admonishing tone.

"Yeah?"

"*You* know." She frowned at me, then at the fence. "Why you two think you've got to go through this fence is beyond me." Her look became faintly pugnacious, challenging me to explain.

"It's a long story."

"I bet it's a doozy."

"It is. So, you don't know her name, huh?"

Her eyes dropped away. "It was something like Kelso, or Callie, or...or, you know, Mortimer, I believe she said one thing, then another. So I asked, and I swear she came up with another—Kelly."

It sounded as if Velma's hearing aid needed new batteries. Either that, or K was intentionally muddying the waters.

"What're you two doing?" she asked. "You duckin' her husband or something?" The gleam returned. Her voice lowered, becoming conspiratorial. "You kin tell me."

"You're too sharp for us, Velma."

"I knew it, I *knew* it!" she said joyfully. Then she cut that off and pursed her lips. "That's an awful risky business, boy."

"Don't I know it."

Her bony shoulders lifted in a shrug. "Well, you kin use my yard, I reckon. Anyone asks, I don't know nothin' 'bout nothin'. "

"Thanks. I appreciate it."

"Fact is, a feller came nosing around yesterday, long about dusk, asking about you."

"What'd you tell him?"

"I already *tole* you." She waved an arm, slinging around bits of honeysuckle. "*Nothin'.*"

"Thanks. It'd probably be best if you kept it that way." I edged past her shears, then bent down and kissed her cheek. "I've gotta get going."

Velma nodded toward my place. "She in there?"

"Not right now."

"She's a beauty. I can see how she turned your head, Mortimer."
Her look became wistful. "There was a day when...well, if I see
her, I'll show her the boards you got loose here. Pretty girl like
that shouldn't be hiking herself over fences."

"You do that." I went around the side of her house to the street,
then walked downtown in my disguise, keeping an eye out for
roving vans.

*   *   *

Give up or go on? Floating for the moment on one of life's cusps,
I found myself faced with a choice. Nothing said I had to pursue Jonnie's death. I could bail out any time I wanted. And, I
thought...I *would*. My stride slowed. By God, I would do exactly
that. For one glorious second a dozen paths opened up ahead.
Fifty. Light shone down. I felt illuminated. I could do whatever I
damn well pleased. I was free. I came to a stop right there on the
sidewalk. Free.

"Do it for Dallas, Great Gumshoe"—the idiotic words of the
bartender, Patrick O'Roarke, rattled around in the perfect vacuum of my skull.

Hell.

Love is a trap.

And, I admitted, if I quit now that would be the end of it. The
spark would go out. I would go back to being an IRS agent. The
tax code would bubble up past my eyes and blot out the sun. I
would get a paunch, turn gray, end up on a porch fussing with my
medications, yelling at kids as they whizzed by on skateboards,
calling them whippersnappers or something equally demented.

In an instant the light winked out and all those paths ahead
disappeared. Except one.

So much for cusps. I kept on walking.

The Yellow Pages had listed fifteen detective agencies, including Carson & Rudd, the status of which was in grave doubt now that both Carson and Rudd were dead. I'd gone through the remaining fourteen and picked one within walking distance that sounded like more than a one-horse operation: Rix & Associates, Inc.

Rix was on Arlington in a low, stone-and-glass building next to the Arlington Tower. I removed the porkpie and the moustache as I pushed through a glass door and went in.

A young woman was talking on a cordless headset while making coffee. She was hassling with whomever about a delinquent account and the terms of a revised payment schedule. She was slender, pretty, nicely dressed, curvy, and I figured those attributes were minimum requirements for working as either a PI or a PI's secretary.

The place looked profitable. The outer office had more pizazz than Gregory's—not that it mattered, now. Potted plants, magazines on a table, framed prints on the walls, pleasant mint-green wall-to-wall carpeting, even an old-fashioned water cooler, complete with a stack of four-ounce paper cups in a holder that gave the place a nice retro look.

The girl looked at me. Her eyes widened, and she doubletaked, or doubletook, whatever, then terminated the call with a quick, "Gotta go. Call ya back. Bye."

She stared at me. "You...you're..."

"Yep."

"...that guy...I mean... "

"Your ad in the Yellow Pages said discreet. Your sign, too, right there on the door. This place *is* discreet, isn't it? Confidential?"

"Why, yes, of course." An offended note crept into her voice in spite of being face to face with the most successful locator of missing persons in all of North America. Of course, some people might think that didn't count since I was most likely the one who'd caused them to go missing in the first place.

"Then I was never here," I told her. "And I'm not even who I am, so you don't have to keep staring at me like that, right?"

My words broke her paralysis. She pressed a button on her desk, twice. A moment later, a door opened and a man in a hundred-dollar haircut came out, power tie loosened, shirtsleeves.

Mike Grissom. One look at me and he waved me inside without a word and shut the door. In his office, which overlooked Arlington and a gaggle of workmen, one of whom was jack hammering a hole in the street, I explained what I wanted.

He grinned at me from across a cluttered desk. "You're shittin' me. One PI hiring another."

"Nope. Happens all the time," I said with some authority. But maybe not in the same city, I didn't bother to say. "And I expect full confidentiality." I nodded toward the outer office. "From her, too."

He shrugged that off. "Beyond these walls, we don't discuss our clients' business, ever." He leaned back and put his hands up behind his head. "Damn if I don't wish I could help you, too, but I gotta fly to L.A. this afternoon and we're backed up three weeks around here, minimum. A month if you're looking to bag a cheating spouse."

"How many investigators work out of this office?"

"Five, including me. All of us booked solid. 'Tis the season for infidelity and runaways, not to mention the ongoing problem of delinquent dads, and moms, and what the courts hand us, which I've got to tell you has priority. That's bread and butter, and they want what they want pretty much the day before they ask for it. District Court alone keeps two or more of us running full time, and we serve a lot of defense lawyers around town."

I sank back in the chair. "So...got any suggestions?"

He shrugged. "DiFrazzia might have time for it." He gave me a first name: "Jerry."

DiFrazzia. The name rang a bell from my recent perusal of the phone book, but I'd rejected it as a one-man operation. It hadn't said "& Associates."

Mike grinned. "It's close. Office is a few blocks west of here, on Washington, between First and Second."

* * *

The place was a house, or had been. Good-sized one, too. Two stories, peeling pale-yellow paint with cream trim, a section of gutter held up with wire. Next door was a nest of lawyers in what had once been a modest riverfront mansion. The street was shaded by elms and maples. Sidewalks were buckled, grass growing in the cracks. No traffic going by on the street at the moment. Quiet neighborhood.

I went in blind, but what else is new? The sign on the door read *DiFrazzia Investigations*, so how was I to know?

The gal at the desk was shorter than any I'd spoken with recently, five-three. But she was a looker, in a solid, Mediterranean, outdoorsy way. And, like Dale, she could type a mile a minute, so that was also a requirement of the job.

A dozen prisms dangled in a window on fishing line, catching sunlight and shooting rainbows throughout the room—a large, open, humid place. It was a jungle, twenty potted plants, including a rubber tree and two enormous palmetto things eight feet tall. The pegged wooden floor creaked as I crossed the room.

"Help you?" the woman asked, looking up from her terminal. She had on a comfortably baggy brick-red cotton shirt and black sultan pants. I guessed her age at about twenty-eight, give or take.

"I'd like to talk to Mr. DiFrazzia."

"You're assuming something."

"Huh?"

She smiled. "I'm DiFrazzia." She paused a moment, then said, "Okay, now you're staring. Is it the outfit? Not businesslike enough for you?"

"You're DiFrazzia?"

"Yep. Geraldine, but everyone calls me Jeri, including my dad."

I didn't know what to say. Jeri, not Jerry. A vision of Jonnie's head came back, his fogged stare, a maniac out there somewhere, gliding through the darkest of Reno's shadows.

"You were expecting a man," Jeri said, pushing herself away from her computer. She had short dark hair with feather bangs, full of deep-red highlights, cut in a carefully tousled way. Her eyes were direct, unwavering, right on mine.

"Sort of." Okay, yes. I wanted a man the size and disposition of Officer Day, say three hundred twenty pounds, naturally suspicious of all humanity and sporting an Uzi he could field-strip in the dark, with a neck you couldn't chainsaw through in a weekend. What I didn't want was a fluffball who located missing dogs. Again, this shows how little I knew. Given all that, it's amazing I've gotten this far in life without succumbing to some tremendous, avoidable accident, but, give me credit, something like that could still happen.

"Investigator-wise, I'm it, Mr. Angel. At least in this office."

Christ, she practically knew my name. "Mort. At least you're up on current events."

"Everywhere one turns, there's Mortimer and Dallas Angel. The two of you have been impossible to miss."

"Not by choice. And the name's Mort."

"What you're looking for, let me take a wild guess here—it's got something to do with the Sjorgen and Milliken murders."

"Jeez, you're good."

"Better than you know."

I edged half a step toward the door. "Uh, no offense, but this is a pretty rough deal." The floor squawked under my foot as I transferred weight.

Jeri leaned forward. "I can handle rough. Sit down. Let's talk."

"It's more than rough. You heard about Gregory Rudd?"

"Your nephew, sure."

"Then you know. This thing reaches out and grabs people, Ms. DiFrazzia."

She made a face. "Jeri, please. And, yeah, I know. All the world knows. They found Mr. Rudd's car this morning. Why don't you sit down?"

I stared at her. "They found Greg's car?"

"It was on the news," she said, giving me a look.

While I'd been out busting vans and busses. Jeri was more on top of things than I was. The look she gave me wasn't precisely one of scorn, but I knew she was wondering what planet I was from.

"Where'd they find it?" I asked.

"Parking lot at the Peppermill."

Two miles south of his office. I had no idea what he might've been doing down there.

"Sit," Jeri said.

"Really, I don't think this is a good idea. I probably oughta can the whole idea. Might be best if you forgot I ever came in."

"Sit *down*, Mr. Angel."

I paused. "Mort."

She pointed. "In the chair, Mort."

There was only one parked in front of her desk. So, to be polite, I sat. I wasn't about to hire her, but I couldn't just walk out. She looked like she'd weigh in at about one-fifteen, soaking wet.

I could see her walking into whatever Greg had come across. Goddamn if I wanted to find her head lying around anywhere.

"Exactly what're you looking for?" she asked.

"Is the money clock running?"

"Not until I take the case. Which I haven't yet." She made an impatient "come-on" gesture with a hand tipped with short, bright red nails, about what I'd expect of a finder of lost mutts.

So, what the hell, I laid it out. Hired by my ex, Dallas, Gregory Rudd had gone out to check out Sjorgen's properties and businesses and had been decapitated. The top portion of said decapitation had been returned to the desk in his office. A grim tale, but not lengthy or overly complicated.

Jeri held my gaze. "And you want to follow up, try to find who did it."

I nodded. "That, and who killed Jonnie and Dave."

"Find one, you'll find them all."

"Probably."

"You don't trust the police to do their job?"

"I do, yes. Absolutely. Dallas doesn't, though, and it's her money, her call."

"So here you are."

"You wanted the story, there it is."

"So, not being a, uh, qualified investigator yourself, you want to hire one." In the depths of her eyes I detected a hidden spark of amusement. Not hidden enough.

"No. What I want is to get out of here." I got to my feet.

"Sit."

I sat. Voice like that, she would've made a terrific drill instructor or IRS field agent.

"You need an investigator," she repeated.

I nodded reluctantly.

"And you'd prefer that investigator to be a man?" Her eyes bored into mine.

"It's not that," I said, forced into an outright lie. "It's just...you know, whatever Greg ran into—"

"You're still assuming things, Mort."

"What?"

"That I can't handle it. Or myself." The look she gave me was neutral, except for a flickery little light way down deep, something you had to look for.

"I didn't say that."

"Great. So, I've got the job, right? At least on a trial basis. Say, for a couple of days to start?"

"I didn't say that, either."

She gazed at me for a moment. "Okay, what *do* you say?"

"I think...this isn't a real good idea, that's all."

"Suppose I were six-six and weighed two-eighty?"

A little on the light side, but she had the right idea. "C'mon, Jeri."

"What *if*?"

"I'd say your chances of meeting a guy and having kids would go down quite a bit."

Her eyes narrowed. "That's a pretty damn sexist remark. Who said I want to meet a guy?"

Just what I needed: a pissing match with one Miss Geraldine DiFrazzia at—what?—10:47 in the morning.

I was assuming the Miss, of course. She didn't have a ring on her left hand. Or her right. No earrings or bracelets. In fact, other than her attire and the color of her nails, she looked reasonably ready for action, find a missing pooch by noon.

But Greg had run marathons, and he was dead.

"Look, Jeri, I'm real sorry, but—"

"But I'm a woman and there's no way I could dump a big huge guy like you on your butt, right?"

"Aw, jeez—" The day was turning into one of those. Best thing was, just throw a switch and pop straight into tomorrow or back to yesterday, then turn north instead of south.

"Right?" she asked.

"What? Me?"

"Right on your butt, Mort."

"Christ, Jeri. What d'you weigh?" And *that*, by the way, wasn't the swiftest thing I'd said all week, either. Women never give you a straight answer when you ask.

She stood up. "Get up."

Aw, shit.

"Up," she said. "On your feet, Mort. Let's go."

"What the *hell*...?"

She opened one of two doors that led to the back of the house. So, I had a choice: quick out the front, now, or into the back with her. Oversized macho jerk that I am, I went into the back.

Why? Who knows? It might've been curiosity. Maybe I wanted to see how far women's lib has taken them. Maybe I wanted to show her a thing or two, something that might save her life if she ever ran into real trouble. Maybe I wanted a tour of the house. It looked like an interesting place.

We went down a short hallway and into a good-sized room with a padded floor, free weights in a corner, jump rope, chin-up bar, rowing machine, expensive treadmill, heavy punching bag, a faint smell of sweat. A private gym, good equipment—which should have told me a lot more than it did, but my forte was missing persons, not common sense or straightforward deduction given relevant facts.

Jeri headed for another door. "Wait there," she said. "And take off your shoes. You might want to warm up a little while you're at it."

She left. I stood there, feeling dumb, out of place, then I untied my laces and pulled off my Nikes. I jogged in place for about five seconds, then stopped, feeling moronic, like a big awkward kid, first day in gym class. I looked down at my sneakers. I could've picked them up and been out the door in three seconds flat, maybe two.

"This isn't necessary," I called out, eyeing my shoes.

Boy, was it ever not. But how was I, an ex-football player of sorts who still clung to that dead historical fact, supposed to slink out now? Things had gone too far for that. Male pride was at stake. Lots of it.

"Yes, it is," she yelled back, voice muffled by the door.

"How 'bout I take your word for it?"

"Not hardly."

She popped back into the room. Gone was the Baghdad Nights outfit. She'd changed into a navy-blue sports bra and black jogging shorts, bare feet.

I stared at her. First at the bra, because I'm like that, then at the rest of her.

She touched her ankles. Okay, I could almost do that. Then her toes. I couldn't. *Then* she plopped the palms of her hands down flat on the mat, knees locked, then bent her elbows, finally touching her forehead to her knees. I shivered slightly. If I'd done that, my spine would've torn out leaving a bloody groove from butt to shoulder blades.

"Ready?" she asked after a few minutes of stretches that would have put me in the hospital, jogging in place as she rolled her neck and shoulders.

Best I can describe her, she looked like a clever steel framework covered with the finest imaginable latex. Her stomach was flat, hard with muscle. I was glad she hadn't told me to take off my shirt. I revised my estimate of her weight upward to one-thirty, maybe more. A lot for a gal her height, but I didn't see anything that wasn't lean and hard. The loose shirt and sultan pants had hidden a multitude of secrets. Too late now, but I should have looked at her forearms.

"Weights?" I asked her.

"Powerlifting. I took fourth in my weight class last year."

"Yeah? Here in Reno?"

She grinned. "In the U.S." She came closer. Either she had a nice tan or her skin was naturally dark. She looked good. I didn't see any tan lines, so I was looking at her Italian heritage or at someone with a very high backyard fence. I thought it best not to ask which.

"Ready, Mr. Angel?"

I edged away. "Mort. What're you going to do? Press me?"

She grinned. "Why don't you try to push me over?"

"That wouldn't be polite."

"As of this moment, you're excused for any and all perceived impoliteness or ungentlemanly behavior."

"I was afraid of that."

She was an extraordinary sight, muscles flexing in her thighs, calves, arms. She looked vaguely like a pit bull—a remarkably pretty pit bull, however, which was maybe the last purely sexist thing I ever thought about her.

"Push me," she said.

So—I pushed. Her shoulders.

She rocked backward an inch, didn't lose her footing at all.

"What was that supposed to be?" she asked. I didn't like her smile.

"Warm-up push," I said.

"That wouldn't have spun a revolving door. Push me *over*. Right on my butt. I promise I won't break."

So, what the hell—I shoved her, *hard*, because the floor was padded, and because powerlifting or no I still outweighed her by a good ninety pounds, and because she was starting to piss me off. She popped back two or three feet, but stayed up, perfectly balanced, steady as a damn rock.

"One more try?" she asked. "I'm still on my feet. I expect you to put me right on my ass, great big moose like you, poofy little gal like me."

Poofy, shit. I lunged, put her right on her very solid rear, or tried to. But the world spun, flipped end over end, and I was on my back on the floor staring up at her, lungs not quite working up to par. Part of my hangover had returned. Felt like it, or like I'd gone over my back fence in the dark again.

She smiled down at me, hands on her knees. "What I want you to do now is keep me from doing that again."

Inspired, I sucked in enough air to say, "Who says I'm gonna try?"

"Me. Do it. You want revenge, don't you?"

I did, but found that getting to my feet was a slower and more involved process than I would've liked.

"How about I buy you brunch over at the Gold Dust and we call it a tie?" I asked.

"Shove me."

Okay, she asked for it. I gave her a sudden straight-armed shove, crouching slightly to lower my center of gravity and anchor myself. Old football hero's trick.

She picked me up. Goddamn if she didn't, or levered me off my feet somehow with a little grunt, took my full weight for two seconds, then slammed me down on my back again, more or less. I think she broke my fall, and that hurt, too. The ceiling had a crack in it. Pretty big one. I hadn't noticed it before, but from this angle it was fairly obvious. In an appraisal it would've cost her four hundred bucks. Settling damage, looked like.

"Shit," I breathed. I closed my eyes.

"Again?"

"No, thanks." I looked up at her. "What do you do if someone tries to put a fist in your face?"

"Care to try it and find out?"

"Secondhand knowledge works for me."

"Just as well. Fists are different. That'd cost you a kneecap or a rib, maybe an elbow joint, something that'd hurt, slow you down a lot, and take a month or three to heal. You know, with pins and hardware, physical rehab, therapists."

I believed her. I felt slow enough as it was.

"You look disgruntled," she said, hands on her knees, looking down at me.

"Not at all. I'm always a bit cranky before noon. And I should've had more coffee."

"You wouldn't happen to think coffee would help or that I got lucky, would you?"

"If I say yes, will you visit me in the hospital?"

She smiled. "Thing is, I *might've* been lucky. You could give it one more try, find out."

"No, thanks."

Though I toyed with the idea of mentioning that I wasn't up to my usual, what with my lack of sleep the night before and a mild recurring hangover. Then I decided not to push my luck. She might slam me around again—if not then, then some other time.

I rolled onto my side, pushed myself to my knees, then got to my feet. My lungs were working at maybe 60 percent, barely enough to keep me going.

"So, do I get the job?" Her hands were on her hips, eyes on mine. If she had a faint sheen of perspiration on her, I couldn't see it.

"Maybe I can't afford you."

"I'll give you a nice discount."

"What's the bottom line?"

"Say, one-sixty a day. And expenses."

"I dunno, sounds high."

"Rockford was two hundred a day and expenses back in the seventies, Mort."

"That was TV."

"And a reasonable price, even then. Go check around. One-sixty is absolute bargain basement. So, how 'bout it?"

"If you don't tell anyone how badly I kicked your butt here today. I wouldn't want anyone to know I was picking on a woman half my size."

"Done."

"One day only, Jeri. And only if Dallas okays it. If it works out, we'll look at something longer term tomorrow."

She pursed her lips. "Okay..."

"And, I get to tag along, pick up a few tips."

She frowned, looking unaccountably hesitant for a gal who'd just bounced a prospective client around her workout room. "Up to you. Just..."

"What?"

"If you come along...I don't want you to get any ideas about that."

"What kind of ideas?"

"About...us."

I stared at her. "Now look who's being sexist."

"It's not sexist. I just want it perfectly clear, right up front."

I rubbed my rear. She must've bounced me off that, too. "I'm not the only one making unwarranted assumptions, Jeri."

"Okay, fine." Her jaw jutted belligerently. "I won't mention it again. Just remember, I'm not part of the deal."

I shrugged. "Never thought you were."

CHAPTER NINE

WHY SHE FELT she had to get that on the record, I didn't know. Maybe she'd had trouble with clients in the past. I could see how that might happen. She was gorgeous, stunning.

But a roll in the hay with Jeri might be like a trip through a threshing machine. Was I missing anything, her laying down the law like that? And who said I had "ideas" about her? Not I. She was attractive, in a lean, powerlifting way, model beautiful, but all I could see was that jagged line in her ceiling. Maybe her house wasn't settling. She might have caused the damage herself, slamming ex-football players around.

We ended up in her car, a 2013 flame-red Porsche 968 Cabriolet with the top down, me in my moustache, one hand holding onto my dumb-ass porkpie hat as she laid a nice strip of rubber. As Porsches go it wasn't top of the line, but it had my Toyota beat to hell and gone.

Oh, the inequity: Jeri's Porsche, Dallas's Mercedes, my yodeling Toyota—now on its third transmission. A depressing look at what it was like to be stalled on life's tracks, but at least Jeri's car wasn't known to the press, and it was a less embarrassing species were I to suddenly find myself on television again. Which could happen at any moment.

As we roared down First Street, I marveled at all the changes seventy-two hours had wrought in my life. With the IRS, I'd never done fifty in a twenty-five zone, and nameless blondes hadn't passed out naked in my bed or soaped up in my shower. I'd never found heads before, not one, and women half my size hadn't slammed me around without breaking a sweat. Greg had been wrong about the PI life—dead wrong, if you must know.

"Where to?" I asked. "Want to talk to Dallas?" It was my first real stab at conversation since Jeri had gone into a back room and changed into black jeans and a dove-gray sleeveless shirt, then led me out a back door to her car. Off we'd gone. I was still having trouble getting enough air.

"Coroner's office," she replied. "Might as well. It's on the way. We'll see if we can get autopsy reports."

"Jonnie's?" I asked, lighting up like a hundred-watt bulb.

She nodded. "And Milliken's."

"What for?"

"You never know till you ask. It's called gathering information, Mort."

At least we were still on a first-name basis. "You mean clues?"

"You could say. Kinda melodramatic, though. Very Perry."

"How would you put it?"

"What I said. Gathering information. You *are* new at this, aren't you?"

"Yeah, but you oughta see me in action when people turn up missing. It's a sight."

She gave me a look like the ones Dallas gives me, then turned her attention back to the road. She jinked around a drifting taxi like a fighter pilot, tore through the tail end of a long yellow light, powered into a right turn, and raced down to Mill Street in time to catch the light there too, making me feel old and out of touch, knowing I wouldn't drive like that even if I had the car.

I sank back in the leather, aware of the bite that something had taken out of my hide a year ago in May, the day I turned forty. And today in Jeri's gym, if you must know. Maybe that was what this unexpected funk was all about.

Funny, though, how Dallas had avoided all that, the entire age-angst thing, while every year, like clockwork, I got one year older.

Driving one-handed, still jinking, Jeri handed me a penny from a cup holder that held loose change.

I gave her a questioning look.

"For those deep, deep thoughts, Mortimer."

Mortimer. I pushed the penny back at her. "You don't want to know, Geraldine." I was going to let it go at that, then my big mouth added, all on its own, "It's a forties thing." It just came out. Saying it was practically an out-of-body experience, watching some other fool spill his guts to what amounted to a virtual stranger.

She maneuvered around a wallowing UPS truck, then said, "I've put great big guys in their twenties on their backs, Mort. It wasn't you."

"Yeah? It sure *felt* like me."

She chirped the tires braking for the light at Wells Avenue, then looked over at me and smiled. "Hey, you look good for forty, fella. Most men've lost it by then, only look good in Italian suits, and only if they're rich."

"Yeah, thanks." I thought her comment harbored a fair amount of that sexism she'd gone to such lengths to quash in me.

"And, I've got a black belt in judo. Fourth degree. Third degree in Aikido. And I know a lot of back-alley stuff."

"Huh?" I said. "You—?"

The light changed and the coroner's office was only a few blocks away on Kirman Avenue, one block north of Mill. She barely got it up to fifty-five and back down again before we were there.

But even in that short space of time the fog was lifting. I wasn't all that old yet, and, hell, if Paul Newman could do it, maybe *I* could drive like Jeri. Only two days ago, in a Toyota giving off palpable rust vapor, I'd left that pre-yuppie news gal in the dust.

I smiled, remembering her spinout. The doldrums might come a little more often these days, but they don't last long, thank God.

* * *

Jeri told me to stay in the car. She ducked inside. Judo? Hell, I didn't know that stuff was still around, thought it had died in the seventies, done in by tae kwon do and Ninja Turtles, Jean-Claude Van Damme. No one used judo anymore. Judo was cheating. And she'd mentioned back-alley stuff, which was cheating on steroids.

The coroner's office was a red-brick, squat, gritty-looking thing. Institutional. I oughta know, I can smell institutional. Its steel-framed windows were filmed with dirt. Washoe Medical Center was a block south and east, a rambling, discordant, crammed-to-gether collage of styles from old crumbly red brick to hyper-modern antiseptic high-rise topped with partly hidden cooling towers.

Traffic rolled by on Kirman, rattling over potholes. From all around I heard the drone of air conditioners. The temperature was already north of ninety-five and climbing.

Jeri stuck her head out a door and waved to me. I waved back. Annoyed, she waved me in.

To avoid any misunderstanding that might result in bodily harm, I removed the moustache and the hat, got out of the Porsche, and ambled over to the door to see what was up.

She yanked me inside. The sensation was like getting an arm caught in a dredging winch. "I thought you wanted to *learn*," she said.

"Learn what? Maybe you forgot, but I've seen these two guys already." I blinked, trying to adjust to the gloom. After a moment I saw a figure standing in deeper shadow.

Jeri ignored me, pulled me closer. "Mort, this's Ben Ragland."

I took stock of the kid, mid-twenties, limp brown hair, wearing a white smock over blue jeans. He was trying not to gawk at me or drool over Jeri, but he wasn't having much luck with either.

He took my hand and pumped it. "It's an honor to meet you, sir," he said, grinning foolishly.

An honor? Me? Sir? It took all I had not to laugh. Then I got it. In America we honor our celebrities, even if they're technically mass murderers and/or cannibals—anyone in the throes of Warhol's fifteen minutes. Ben hadn't had his moment yet, so he was honored.

"Mort," I said, knowing the gesture was hopeless. I was too big a celebrity. Ragland wouldn't call me Mort after twenty years together on a desert island.

"How much time do we have?" Jeri asked him.

Ben lowered his voice. "Not much. Mr. Carroll's due back in like ten or fifteen minutes." He licked his lips, suddenly more nervous than awed.

"Then let's get rockin'," Jeri said.

Boyce Carroll was the coroner. New guy. He'd held the position for less than a year. The most I'd seen of him was on TV the past couple of days. He was barrel chested and flinty eyed, smoked cigars, sounded like he knew what he was doing and wouldn't put up with nonsense, including dumb questions by mindless press corps drones coiffed to within an inch of their pampered lives. I got the impression he wouldn't approve of one Mortimer Angel darting in for a gander at the former heads of state, so to speak. Or Ms. DiFrazzia, PI, either.

We rode an elevator down one floor to the basement, then Ben led us along an echoey corridor, through double steel-lined doors with gurney marks scuffed onto them at waist level and into a sickly smell of chemicals and ill-concealed death.

On a table with stainless steel gutters, a body lay under a sheet with its feet hanging out, a tag on the right big toe, flesh white as Styrofoam. The floor was damp tile, giving off a stink of ammonia and industrial-strength Lysol. A mop was jammed into a bucket of sudsy liquid, giving me a fair idea of what Ben Ragland did here at the facility. How this special-purpose janitor was supposed to help us, I didn't know. Maybe Jeri just wanted a look at Mayor Jonnie.

Which we then did.

Ben yanked the latch of a drawer and rolled Jonnie Sjorgen out in a gust of sterile, refrigerated air and a puff of condensation.

"Hell," Jeri muttered. She turned away, then swiveled back and looked at him.

He wasn't frosty, as I'd expected. They didn't freeze them, which I supposed would play hell with the forensics. He had gauze patches over his eyes, held in place with tape. A plastic collar around his neck kept him upright. A strip of adhesive held his mouth shut. He had a deep slash wound on his cheek an inch or so below his left eye that I vaguely remembered seeing when he was in the trunk of Dallas's car. All I can say is it was a god-awful lousy way to end up.

But as near as I could tell, this was a dead end, pure sideshow. Staring at his head, I didn't feel one bit closer to figuring out who'd killed him.

"Look," said Ben, and a glow of conspiracy filled his eyes. He lifted the hair on top of Jonnie's head. It came away, a circular patch of hair and scalp and bone, exposing the terrible dark hollow of his now-empty skull. I felt a shudder right down to the soles of my feet.

"We don't have his brain," Ben said, looking from Jeri to me, back to Jeri.

Jeri appeared not to be breathing. Her eyes were locked on that portal to Jonnie's vacant skull. "Who does?" she asked at last.

Ben shrugged. He put the lid back on Jonnie's dome. "Whoever killed him, I guess. He was like this when he came in, except the top was sutured in place." Like a pumpkin, he didn't add, but the thought occurred to me, I'm sorry to say.

"They removed his *brain*?" Jeri said, incredulous.

He grinned. Working in this place, he'd been transformed into someone who could grin at things that would turn the average person green. I figured he'd come a long way since high school. "Yep," he said. "Guess what they put there in its place?"

Immediately, I didn't want to know.

"His dick, uh, penis," Ben said, coloring nicely, unable to meet Jeri's eyes. "And his balls."

"And if you mention one goddamned word of that outside this office, I'll have you thrown in jail," said the coroner, Mr. Boyce Carroll, glaring at us from a doorway.

* * *

A skeleton hung in Carroll's office, the kind of thing that might have been found in a doctor's office fifty or sixty years ago.

"Name's Bony Maronie," Carroll said, raising an eyebrow at me. "After the song, which came out in nineteen fifty-seven, if that makes you feel old as dirt. I was one year old."

And I wasn't even a twinkle, though I had trouble imagining dad facing my mother with anything resembling a twinkle in his eye.

"She was a woman," Carroll went on. "Died a hundred and ten years ago in New Orleans. Belonged to my dad—the skeleton, I mean. Nowadays, it's hard to get anything but plastic, but it's not the same. Plastic lacks the detail of the real thing, the authenticity. Like learning anatomy from a goddamn Revell model."

In spite of his conversational tone, his eyes were hard. I figured he was going to get down to bedrock with us momentarily, but all in good time. He'd phoned the police. Now, he had a few minutes to kill.

"You want to do science a favor," he said, staring at me, "donate your skeleton to research."

"I'm not through with it yet," I replied.

He smiled. "That thing you just learned about Mayor Sjorgen," he said with much portent, "is *not* for public consumption."

"I had no intention."

Carroll shifted his gaze to Jeri.

"Nor I," she said, tongue pushing out her upper lip, giving him a defiant stare.

"Best we can make stick, I think," Carroll mused, "is some kind of a trespassing charge."

"I don't think so," I countered. "We were invited in by an employee of this office."

"Who was fired as of five minutes ago. And I think I can make the trespassing charge at least damnably irritating, Mr. Angel. Even haunting, like a case of herpes."

I shook my head. Carroll wasn't thinking clearly, while I, for once, was.

"No?" He gave me a half-amused, half-quizzical look.

"The ears of a hungry nation await my every word."

That stopped him in his tracks. He lifted a shaggy eyebrow at me, waiting for elaboration on the theme.

"I'll make you a deal," I went on. "A round-robin thing that includes you, us, and the police department. Ms. DiFrazzia and I don't say a word to anyone. In return, you keep Ben on the payroll and tell us everything you've learned about Jonnie."

"You're asking too much."

"Think about it. It'll grow on you."

To his credit, he did. He opened a desk drawer and dug out a cigar in a glass tube, cut the seal with a penknife, removed the stogie and sniffed it, then said, "I give Ragland a week off without pay."

"How much does he make?" I asked.

"Ten twenty-five an hour."

"Four ten a week," I said. Numbers just pop out. I'm a human abacus. The IRS does that to a person. Women find it annoying, particularly in malls. "Three days off and," I glanced at Jeri, "we'll cover it. Two forty-six." Jeri pursed her lips at me, then shrugged. Ben had been her idea. She owed him.

"Don't worry. Dallas'll make it up," I told her.

I looked at Carroll. "How's that? Ben's a good kid. You send a message, no one gets seriously hurt." I would've bet Dallas had two hundred fifty dollars clattering around in her change purse. I had no problem spending her money, especially since she's the one who started this ball rolling.

Carroll leaned back in his chair. "Why in hell am I haggling with you, Mr. Angel?"

"Mort. Because an army of news crews is out there on the streets aching to talk to me, and America is one big inquiring mind. And if I'm locked up, I get that one phone call that is my legal right. And, since I can't afford a lawyer I wouldn't bother phoning one, whereas NBC or CNN might cut me a sweet deal for an exclusive, buy me an O.J.-lawyer to run everyone's tits here through a wringer."

He smiled. He stood up and pumped my hand, something he hadn't done earlier. "You are a complete asshole," he said, plopping back down in his chair.

"I used to make my living in that capacity."

"So I've heard."

"Any trouble filling out that 1040 this year?"

"None whatsoever." He smiled again. "Filled it out myself. I even filed it on time."

"Filled it out yourself, huh? Taking into account imputed interest and the de minimus rule?"

His smile faltered. People get nervous around rules they've never heard before, especially IRS rules, and the IRS has thousands of them. You can't beat the IRS for raw intimidation. The IRS can bust anyone it wants, anytime it wants. "So...about Jonnie Sjorgen, Mr. Carroll."

Slowly, the tension went out of his shoulders.

"Might's well call me Boyce, Mort." He finally lit the cigar. I smelled sulfur, but it was his office. He could smoke camel dung if he wanted. "Jonnie Sjorgen had roughly a four-point-two-inch diameter hole cut in the top of his skull. Best we can determine, it was done freehand with a sabre saw. High speed, fine teeth. We got pretty much the same result using a dog's skull and a Sears Craftsman. Not exactly a Stryker saw, but it got the job done."

To her credit, Jeri didn't even blink. I'm not sure I could say the same about myself.

"Sjorgen's brain was missing," Boyce went on. "More or less scraped out like a pumpkin."

Like a pumpkin. Just as I'd thought. When this was over, Boyce and I might become drinking buddies.

Boyce puffed his cigar. "His penis and testicles were inside, all in one piece. The skin of the cap, or whatever you want to call it, was sewn back to the rest of his scalp. Neat job of suturing, too.

Whoever did it used a curved needle, like something you'd use on sailcloth. Needle like that isn't hard to find. Get one at Walmart. But the sewing took 'em a fair amount of time and effort."

I didn't think I'd be reporting any of this to Dallas. I hoped she would never find out.

"And Milliken?" I asked.

"Same. Suturing wasn't as good. He was probably done first. Whoever did it had gained a little skill by the time they got around to Mr. Sjorgen."

"How about Gregory? Mr. Rudd." I had to ask.

"Nope. His was just a head."

Just a head. How far we'd come in only a few short minutes.

"Their necks were severed between the fourth and fifth cervical vertebrae. Ligaments, cartilage. My impression is that whoever did it took their time. Not in any big hurry."

I exchanged a glance with Jeri.

"Their heads had been refrigerated but not frozen," Boyce went on. "Hard to tell for how long, or at precisely what temperature, so time of death is unknown. All the charts for decomposition rates are screwed up—autolysis, putrefaction. If I had to guess, I'd say Sjorgen died between three and eight days before we got him."

And he'd been missing for ten.

Beside me, Jeri stirred. "Potassium," she said.

Boyce's smile turned plastic. "Come again?"

"Potassium in the eye fluid. Doesn't depend on temperature. Surely you checked that?"

Boyce gave me a look. I shrugged and said, "You did, surely?"

He sank back in his chair, eyes on mine, not Jeri's. Finally he said, "Where'd you dig *her* up?"

Maybe that was coroner humor. I watched Jeri carefully for signs of activity, prepared to tackle her if she tried to leap across the desk and deadlift him, or pass him through the nearest available knothole.

His look swiveled to Jeri. "You know a lot."

"One can never know too much."

He continued to gaze at her for a while. Finally he said, "Not a word of this beyond these walls, but Mr. Sjorgen died seven days ago, give or take approximately an eight-hour window. Mr. Milliken died one day before that."

"Thank you," Jeri said. "Was the penis in Mr. Sjorgen's head his own?"

I stared at her. I wouldn't have thought to ask that in two years. But that thing about potassium levels had been right on the tip of my tongue. Wish she hadn't beat me to it.

"Far as we can tell," Boyce said, leaking smoke. "The lab work won't be in for a while, but we've got something of a preliminary ID on the organ."

That would be Dallas's statement. Things were coming together. Not in any useful way, but parts of the police end of it were falling into place.

Speaking of which, Fairchild, Officer Day, and a policewoman with a .45 Glock 20 on her hip and a neck like a Steelers lineman barged into Carroll's office.

"You," Fairchild said, face red, staring at me.

"I," I replied.

"You've really done it this time, Angel."

I got to my feet. Carroll had been warning the detective off with his eyes, but Fairchild was on a tear, wasn't picking up on it. Guess he didn't know we were pals, yet.

I stretched my back, felt a vertebra pop back into place. Heard it, too. It felt good, best I'd felt since leaving Jeri's gym. I turned to Jeri. "Whose turn is it to buy lunch, kiddo?"

"Yours," she said, standing up.

"Figures."

Fairchild spun in place, trying to keep up. He wasn't used to being ignored. "Huh? What?"

"Take a seat," Carroll said, huffing smoke in Fairchild's face.

* * *

"Kiddo?" Jeri gave me a look as we headed for her car.

"Feel honored," I said.

"If you say so, Tonto."

Okay, this was going to take some work. I don't think Spade or Hammer had this much trouble with the word, or the dames.

Fairchild, Day, and the lady cop came outside as we were getting into the Porsche. Fairchild scurried over, lighter on his feet than I would've thought. Day lumbered. I wondered how he would fare against Jeri the giant-killer. Ninety minutes ago I would've said no contest. Now I would have flipped a coin.

"Not one word, Mort, okay?" Russ said, forcing his lips into something resembling a smile. He was making nice. Carroll had set him straight. As I'd realized, the penis thing was the ultimate lever. If that got out, no one at RPD would know a moment's peace.

I made a silly zipping motion across my mouth, just to yank his chain.

"And you." Fairchild turned his gaze on Jeri. "Uh, who *are* you, by the way?"

"Private citizen," I told him.

"Yeah? How 'bout you introduce us." He swept his eyes over the car, coveting it or memorizing it, I couldn't tell which.

I smiled. "Maybe later. We're kinda busy right now. You know, lunch?"

"She's a dick," Day said.

"Huh?" Fairchild stared at him, then at me.

"Private eye," Day said. "Name's DiFrazzia."

I was impressed. The behemoth had a brain, retentive qualities. He wasn't just another pretty face.

Russell grinned. "That right?" I thought he'd pursue it, but he was still trying to smooth the waters. All he said was, "Next time you go out for a jog, how about notifying Traffic Division first."

"Oh? Was there a problem?"

"About twenty-six thousand dollars' worth, all told."

"My, that's a shame."

"Thought you'd think so."

Jeri sensed the moment, fired up the engine, backed out, and headed for the street. Fairchild, Day, and the lady cop stood in the parking lot and watched us go.

"You did good," Jeri said, gunning it up north, past Kuenzli and across the Truckee River.

"Thanks."

"I mean it. You scored points."

"With whom?"

She shrugged. "Me. Life. You show promise, Mort. For a while there I thought we were in for a booking, just for the hassle value."

"No one knows hassle like the IRS."

She laughed, a nice genuine feminine sound. A gorgeous lady, strong as hell, but I sensed that there was breakable stuff in there too. She'd put up walls to hide the crystal.

* * *

We were barreling along Sixth Street, headed west. I sensed that Jeri didn't have a plan. We were putting distance between us and Fairchild. "What do you make of it?" I asked her.

"Of what?" she said, downshifting hard.

Momentum shoved me forward against the seat belt. "Jonnie. Wanger stuffed in his skull like that. What's the message?"

"You think it was a message?"

"Probably. Most likely."

"You tell me."

I shrugged. "Someone was calling him a dickhead?"

Jeri grimaced. "Or maybe that he thought with his cock instead of his brains. Or maybe there's no message, Mort. It might be one of those sicko Columbian necktie things."

"It's sicko, all right. But a Columbian ascot is also a message."

She shrugged with her lips. "Could be. Or maybe it's your basic psycho's idea of fun."

We circled around, aimlessly at first, as if motion alone might get us somewhere. I didn't want to see Dallas for a while, not while the image of what we'd learned at the coroner's office was still so fresh. The world didn't need another monster, another Dahmer or Gacy.

Finally I suggested we head over to Carson & Rudd. I'd toyed with the idea of having her cruise past my house, see if the media was still camped outside, but I let it go. It didn't matter. Let them sweat it out. Let them rot. It was their choice. I wanted to find out if I still had a job, and I wanted to see how Dale was holding up, if she'd managed to make it into the office that day.

When we went in, she was packing. One solitary cardboard box, half full of personal things from her desk. Her eyes were bright, glistening with unshed tears. She had on paint-spattered jeans and a faded UNR sweatshirt. This wasn't work. This was goodbye.

I didn't know what to say. Words had suddenly left me.

"I'm so sorry, Dale," Jeri said.

Dale burst into tears. Jeri held her. Turns out they knew each other. In many ways, Reno is a small town. The two of them had had professional contact on occasion.

In an empty voice, Dale told me the police had impounded Gregory's case files dating back two years, and that the courts were going to have to sort out what could be done with them before the police could dig in, given the confidentiality factor inherent in his work. Which I knew would turn up nothing. Greg had been eaten by the same spider that had eaten Sjorgen and Milliken, but that had nothing to do with his past work. The police probably knew that, but they had a job to do, scores of dead ends to chase down in order to make the paperwork look good. They had to work all the legal angles, too, which would lower their efficiency to less than 5 percent.

"What'll happen to the business?" I asked her, once her tears had subsided.

"It belongs to his wife now, such as it is," Dale said. "I imagine she'll clear everything out in the next day or two. There's eight hundred forty dollars in the account, six fifty due in rent on the first. And the phone. Building owner pays the power bill. I don't think your wife's check has cleared yet. I guess when that shows up, it'll have to be refunded."

"Where to now?" I asked, groping for words.

"Montpelier, New Hampshire." Her eyes looked a thousand years old. "I have a sister there." She placed a set of keys in the middle of her empty desk.

Where did all of this leave me?

I couldn't bring myself to care. Maybe Libby was my employer since she owned the agency now, or maybe Dallas was, or maybe I was unemployed and could go apply at the nearest Home Depot, help people find plumbing connections.

Dale picked up her box and took one last look around the office. Then she looked me right in the eye and said, "He was going to leave his wife...Libby. We were going to be married."

Then she was gone.

CHAPTER TEN

HISTORICALLY SPEAKING, IN the long line of Angels, Rudds, and others of that ilk roosting in the limbs of our staid family trees, life expectancy of the men runs to about ninety years. Other than my dad—who was so far off the charts he didn't count—no one had had the imagination to die of anything remotely exciting, once the last Angel plunged to his death on Wall Street way back when. Like Maytags, we simply wore out. During a tepid existence of shuffling paper and managing other people's money by way of low-risk and no-risk investments, that took a considerable length of time.

Gregory Rudd had had more zip in him than anyone had known, except for Dale. That zip had eventually killed him. He should've listened to the centuries-old calling of his genes.

I felt bad for Dale. In her final confession I sensed that Greg was all she'd had, all she thought she ever would have. Statistically, he should have lived another sixty years. And she'd seen him in his final hour, perched on his desk after having run, with blinders on, into that unknown black force moving through Reno's streets. She shouldn't have seen that.

And I, in my own unaccountable way, had helped contribute to his death. I felt lousy about that, too.

* * *

God knows why, but I figured Dallas would hate Jeri on sight, or vice versa. It would be a natural, mutual, instantaneous thing. Two gorgeous women, not enough of me to go around. Why wouldn't they hate each other?

When I'm wrong, I do it up right.

We arrived at Dallas's suite at the Grand Sierra. I introduced them, stuck around long enough to determine there wouldn't be any immediate bloodshed, then went down to the casino's gift shop to wear my silly moustache, buy Dallas a magazine, get myself the kind of shapeless, colorless hat you see on golf courses on the heads of men thirty years my senior—old guys who have given up all pretense of style and just want shade—and give the gals upstairs time to get acquainted, figure out which of them was going to be the alpha dog.

When I got back they were discussing 10K runs, racing tips, and their favorite jogging shoes, having already exchanged several low-fat recipes and a few priceless snippets about me, one of which may have included Jeri's workout room.

I felt left out. I roamed the room, peeking out windows. From time to time, feminine laughter erupted. Finally I wandered over and stood over them. Dallas looked up, startled, as if she'd forgotten I was there.

"Am I still on the case?" I asked her, surprising myself as much as anyone. Greg's death and Dale's pain had done something to me that I hadn't been aware of until that moment. I no longer wanted out of this mess, even if I had no idea what I could do to help clear it up or get retribution.

"I don't know," Dallas said. "You don't have a PI firm to work out of anymore, do you?"

"You always did ask tough questions, Dal."

"Maybe you should phone Libby and find out."

Technically, according to Dale, ownership of Carson & Rudd had passed into Libby's hands. I didn't see how she was going to be able to keep it going. It occurred to me—for the first time, which was revealing—that I still hadn't phoned Libby about Greg. Okay, not all that revealing. Simply put, I'd never cared for Elizabeth Capehart Rudd. We'd never bonded, not even close. At times I wondered if she and Greg had, since they were childless and had never shown the slightest bit of affection in public, though that might've been a trait of the Rudds, part of their DNA. I didn't want to phone her now, but decided I had no choice.

The grieving widow answered on the fifth ring. "Hello?"

"Libby?" Music in the background. It wasn't a dirge, either. I recognized Roger Miller's "Chug-A-Lug," of all the lunatic songs.

"Mort? That you?"

"Yeah."

A muted voice, Libby's, then the music clicked off. "Uh, Mort. It's so nice of you to call."

"I'm real sorry, Libby. About Greg."

"Yes, well, thank you."

She didn't sound devastated. If she had, I might've had an idea where to go with the conversation. As it was, I didn't have a clue. An awkward silence dragged out. Should I plunge into the subject of the future of Carson & Rudd or console her in a time of deep emotional crisis?

"Was there anything else, Mort?" Impatiently.

Wait around long enough, all your questions will be answered.

"Well, yeah, come to think of it. I was wondering about Greg's business, what you're thinking of doing with it." Dallas and Jeri were watching me, ears perked.

"I haven't given it much thought." More whispery voices in the background, then, "Maybe you should know I had the account frozen. This morning."

"What account?"

"Greg's. You know, with the bank."

"Carson & Rudd's business account?"

"That's right."

Blood in the water, that's what does it. Drives 'em nuts. They'll snap at anything, even eat their own tails. In fact, my sister had hated Libby, the way Libby had slid in and taken over during Greg's second year of college. Libby was a looker, but her body temperature, I'd always felt, derived from her immediate surroundings.

"Why'd you do that?" I asked.

"Just...security, a precaution. Until everything can be sorted out. You know."

I *did* know. "How much was in the account?" I asked, feeling a hollowness in my gut.

More voices. Then, "I have no idea why that would be any of your business, Mortimer." Her voice was calculated sweetness.

"Okay. Your call, Lib."

"You caught me at a bad time. I wonder if we might talk about this later?"

"Sure, kid. Why don't you call me?"

She hung up. I figured there were moving vans in front of her house that very moment. Roger Miller would segue into "King of the Road" and Libby, and whoever she was with, would be off in a cloud of champagne bubbles.

"Call your bank," I said to Dallas, handing her the phone. "Stop payment on that check."

"She wasn't sobbing in your ear?"

"Hard to tell. I couldn't hear over all the tap dancing."

Dallas got through. The check hadn't cleared yet. She stopped payment. Once Libby found out, she would be the very essence of fury. I wished I could be a fly on the wall.

I got a four-dollar can of Coke from the room's refrigerator and sat on the couch with it. "Carson & Rudd is gone. It's been deboned and eaten."

"It was gone regardless," Jeri said. "With your nephew and Dale gone and you without an investigator's license."

"Which means what, exactly?" Dallas asked her.

"No access, for one." Jeri turned to me. "A license gives you certain privileges. Without it, you either do a quasi-legal maverick thing with desperate quasi-clients, or go into another line of business."

Dallas lifted an eyebrow at me.

"I'm through with the IRS," I said. "No way I'm going back to that god-awful scutwork mill again, grubbing for pennies."

Dallas shrugged. "Well, maybe you could work for Jeri."

Some bombshells explode in slow motion. This was one of those. Shrapnel tore through the room at a snail's pace, ignoring gravity and logic.

Jeri stared at me. Then Dallas stared at me. I quit breathing. Then I quit smiling. I saw problems piling up like nuclear waste. I saw Jeri start to grin.

"No way," I said.

Dallas tossed that day's newspaper in my lap. "Then you're in luck. Casino workers are in demand. You can deal blackjack, stand over a crap table, run the chuck-a-luck."

I would kill myself first. I looked at Jeri.

"You might do," she said thoughtfully. "You kept us out of jail today. That's a marketable skill."

I wanted to say something. Words scrambled around in my head like drunken rats. Trouble was, I didn't have the slightest idea which ones of them to use or how to string them together. While I was doing that, Dallas took out her checkbook. "I've got to pay somebody. I imagine that would be you." She was looking at Jeri, not me.

"Mmm," Jeri said.

"Three thousand okay for now? Expenses and all that? You can let me know when it's used up."

"That'd be fine."

Dallas wrote out the check and handed it to her. "What about Mr. Angel here?" she said.

Jeri gave me a slow, contemplative look. "I'll have to think about that. Could you drop by my office tomorrow, Mort? Say, ten-ish? I'll let you know."

Throwing my words back at me.

The day had started out okay. Best I've had since Monday. I'd managed to cause two well-deserved fender benders and hadn't come across more heads. Now, suddenly, I was Jeri's employee, or might be. She had her own private dojo. She might want a judo dummy to keep her skills up.

Shows how fast any given day can go downhill.

*   *   *

On our way downtown, Jeri and I passed Sjorgen & Howard Title Company, Jonnie's closest foray into the murky world of law. S&H Title was reputed to be his most successful business venture, the cash cow from which all else had sprung. In fact, to give credit where credit is due, it was Wendell Sjorgen's cash cow, not Jonnie's, started in 1958 when Wendell was two years out of Harvard Law. Be that as it may, Jonnie hadn't managed to run the business into the ground after his father's death, which either meant Jonnie had a head for business, or enough sense to leave well enough alone and let others run the place. Probably the Howard of Sjorgen & Howard.

Jeri parked on Mill, half a block from the title company.

"You up for a little sleuthing?" she asked.

"Oh? Am I invited?"

"I asked, didn't I?" She got out. "Consider this an employment interview."

I was still miffed about being bandied about, unemployed and vulnerable, at least until tomorrow, say around "ten-ish." She hadn't said more about that, only that she couldn't give me the final okay without looking into a few things first.

Well, maybe she did. Maybe I would've, too. It still felt like a hazing stunt, watching me squirm on the hook, dangling over the water.

I took off the golf hat and left it in the car. It was starting to make me feel like a gigantic leprechaun.

"Christ, Mort. Ditch the moustache, too," Jeri said.

I peeled it off as we approached the two-story building, stuck it in my shirt pocket, opened the door for her.

As she went through, I said, "Think I'll need my gun?"

She chucked me in a rib with an elbow as neatly as Jackie Chan as she passed by. Which reminded me, I still hadn't asked her about that judo or Aikido stuff.

I held my side as we approached a secretary wearing a headset phone, tucked behind a three-quarter circle of blue Formica. She greeted us with a toss of glossy, black ringlets and a tremendous smile. The smile congealed into an uneven grimace when she saw who I was. Blood drained out of her face, an interesting thing to observe.

Jeri said, "I'd like to speak to the most senior person here, please."

Heather—according to the nameplate on the countertop—gave me a nervous look, then tried to make sense of Jeri's request. "What?"

Jeri ran it past her again. Heather said, "Uh, that would be Mr. Howard."

Not the original, from what I'd picked up on the news, one of those fast-flying tidbits on the periphery of the case. Jefferson Howard would be about a hundred ten years old if he were alive today, which he wasn't. The Howard Heather was offering us was almost certainly not even Jefferson's son. His grandson, maybe.

Heather hit two numbers on a console and spun partway around in her chair for privacy. I took a quick look around. Dark-blue carpet, small waiting room with faux Period wing chairs in gold damask, Max Warner lithographs on the walls: geese flying into pastel sunsets. The phrase "cash cow" went through my mind again. Heather hung up. "He'll be out in a minute."

All through the office, people were staring.

At me. Work had come to a standstill at Sjorgen & Howard as everyone gawked at the genius who'd located their missing boss.

I turned to Heather. "I don't suppose a Mr. Rudd stopped by the other day? Tuesday?"

She looked at me, eyes wide. "Yes, he did." Her voice was airless and breathy. "He also spoke with Mr. Howard."

Of course she remembered him. He'd made the six o' clock news. And, having watched the news, she remembered what had happened to him. And there *she* was, trapped behind a desk—

Jeri bumped me with a shoulder as a man in his late twenties, five foot eight, wearing a three-piece tailored suit, emerged from a hallway and approached the reception desk. He wasn't smiling. "I'm Peter Howard," he said. "Come with me, please."

Jeri followed him. I followed Jeri. "Right to the top man," I said *sotto voce*. "That was easy." And the top man was a boy, abrupt, and a tight-assed little priss, from the look of him.

"It was my smile," she whispered over her shoulder.

"Might've been mine." I glanced back at Heather.

"Not in a million, Mortimer."

We went down the hall and up a flight of stairs to where the carpet was spongy and plush, russet gold, the walls paneled in walnut, the lighting indirect and expensive. Past a desk where a young, gifted pneumatic doll of a girl named Amyee was filing her nails, not papers, and into an office. Peter shut the door. Much of one wall was a tinted plate glass view of the traffic and ruined asphalt on Mill Street, a Laundromat, and a graffiti-covered corner store across the street that probably did a land office business in specialty condoms, wine, and nudie mags. There may have been a time when this had been a prime location, but that time was long gone.

We all sat down, Peter behind his desk, Jeri and I facing it. The surface of the desk was almost bare, so I figured the secretaries and actual title agents ran the business—except for Amyee, who didn't look as if she could load a dishwasher, though she might have had other skills. In this place, it was likely that Peter was nothing but an annoying figurehead who needed appeasing at frequent intervals. In a corner of the room I saw an electric putt returner, and a putter leaning half out of sight against a mahogany bookcase that held golf trophies. Man-child Pete was twenty-some pounds overweight, with pudgy fingers and longish brown hair. He probably had a handicap of two, whereas mine was unknown, but likely to be into three digits.

"Know why I agreed to see you two?" he said. Neither Jeri nor I answered, but we exchanged looks. It seemed like a trick question.

"Because of you." Peter Howard stared straight at me.

"*My* smile," I said to Jeri.

"You were disrupting the staff," Peter remarked sourly. He wasn't even remotely afraid of me. Too bad.

"Oh? Were there complaints?" I asked.

Jeri shot me a warning look.

"What do you *want*?" Peter asked, eyes shifting between Jeri and me.

"We're investigating Mr. Sjorgen's death," Jeri said.

"I thought the police were doing that."

"It's a free country."

He pursed his lips. "I don't know anything at all. I have no idea how I could be the slightest help to you." His tone was stiff and flat, indicating he was already bored with us, wanting to get back to his putter, make the PGA tour.

"Gregory Rudd was in here yesterday," I said.

Peter Howard looked at me as ten seconds went by in silence. Finally he said, "I wasn't any help to him either."

"Really?"

"Yes, really." His look hardened. Not easy, with his smooth, baby face, chubby cheeks, and pale-blue eyes, but he tried. It made him look like a pouty kid who wasn't getting a toy he wanted, *that* kind of hard. A big spoiled kid, used to getting his way.

I looked around. A diploma hung on a wall. Peter had an MBA, purchased from Yale. He'd been to the ball, and the next morning the glass slipper had fit, lucky him. I doubted that he knew the first thing about title companies. If Peter Howard drove anything less than a top-of-the-line Audi, I would eat an adobe brick. He looked like the Audi Quattro type, sitting there in a $1500 suit, class ring on one finger. I thought the horsepower-to-weight ratio of a Porsche 911 would scare the lad spitless.

"Are you his grandson?" I asked. "Jefferson's, I mean."

"Great-grandson." He must have figured that Jeri was the senior partner because he looked at her and said, "I don't have time for this. The police already asked their questions." He shrugged and added, "I didn't have anything useful to tell them, either."

"Yeah?" I said. "Why do you say that?"

He stared at me, frustrated. "What would *I* know? Jonnie had an office here. He came in every two or three weeks. He's been the firm's senior partner for the past four years, ever since my dad retired. As far as I can tell, that has nothing to do with anything."

Probably. If it were true. No reason for it not to be, but I was feeling antagonistic toward the guy. I didn't like him. Too smooth, eyes too close together, who knows? Maybe bad chemistry. That or I sensed he wasn't a carbon-based life form.

"You want to see his office?" Peter said. Hoping to get rid of us, no doubt.

"How long was Mr. Rudd here?" Jeri asked.

"No more than five minutes."

"Did you see him leave?"

"Not personally, no. The girls out front would have."

The girls who did all the work, I thought churlishly. Like a true capitalist, Peter Howard was getting rich off the labors of others. But of course, that's how it's done. That's what makes this country great. Soviet-style communism was the most visible political flop of the previous century.

"About Jonnie's office," Peter prompted.

"Sure," Jeri said, standing. "Let's go have a look."

We trooped out past Amyee and down a short hall to an office twice the size of Peter's, but without a secretary posted out front. Better view, too. A huge west-facing window showed casinos rising against the Sierras. At night it would be quite a sight, impressive. I was surprised Peter hadn't moved in yet.

"Mr. Sjorgen didn't have a secretary?" I asked.

"He had no need for one," Peter said. "At least not here."

"But you do?" I glanced back down the hall to where Amyee was busy with her manicuring chores.

"Of course. I'm here every day."

"She looks like a whiz with a computer," I said. Jeri kicked me in the ankle then spun me around to face the room. My employment interview wasn't going well. Come tomorrow, after ten o'clock, I was likely to find myself in a county government building somewhere, filling out unemployment forms.

Jonnie's desk was a big important slab of polished rosewood. It probably weighed four hundred pounds, even more than the behemoth, Officer Day.

"Anything in that?" I asked.

"The police went through it," Peter said, yellowish teeth gnawing at his lower lip. "They took some stuff, logged everything they took." He leaned against a wall. "I'll have the rest of it boxed up for his daughter when I get a chance."

"You should put Amyee on that," I said, moving out of range of Jeri's feet.

Peter remained silent.

Jonnie's daughter, Rosalyn Sjorgen—Nicole's dance instructor at Ithaca, New York. Floating out there on the far edge of this uproar. Which was hardly her fault. It sunk in then, standing there in Jonnie's office, that one way or another, guilty or innocent, Rosalyn Sjorgen wasn't that far out on the edge. She was Jonnie's daughter, his closest relative. His *only* relative, in fact, since Jonnie had no siblings and hadn't gotten around to marrying my wife. Okay, ex-wife. Rosalyn stood to inherit everything, every last dime. Maybe even this corner office, and the desk. A better motive than mine. I ought to run that past Russell Fairchild.

Family. Family member. Rosalyn was his family. I wondered if that might mean anything, given Fairchild's pearl of wisdom the other day: *The ones who know you best...*

I wondered if she'd locked her doors in Ithaca, disconnected her phone, burrowed in to wait out the storm. Or if she was aware that he was dead. Like my daughter Nicole, she might be in Europe, roping her way up a craggy Alp. She might be in India, passing out alms.

Jonnie's house alone was worth a bundle. I wondered how much equity he had in it, how much his estate was worth, all told—

"Mort?"

I popped out of my reverie. Jeri was seated at Jonnie's desk, giving me a questioning look. "Huh?" I said sluggishly.

"I said, let's go through this thing, okay?"

"What, the desk?"

"That's what I said."

"The police already did that."

"Now it's our turn. C'mon."

She was in his chair. Thing probably cost eight hundred bucks. I crouched down next to her and opened a drawer on the right while she opened the one in the middle. Peter watched for a moment, then said, "Hey, if you need anything."

"Yeah, thanks," Jeri mumbled without looking up.

Peter shrugged, went out.

The drawer I'd opened contained a bunch of Sjorgen & Howard business forms, letterhead, general office memos, some of which were five years old. Jeri was into paperclips and old pens, a staple remover, rubber bands, scissors, seventeen cents in change.

A photograph on the desk caught my eye. Walnut frame, glass. Jonnie, twenty years ago, squinting into the sun on a beach somewhere. With him was a bony girl twelve or thirteen years old with Jonnie's black hair, wearing a droopy green bikini, glasses, braces on her teeth. Rosalyn again. Had to be.

I'd never met her, but it was hard to imagine that gawky kid as Nicole's dance instructor. The picture was probably taken about the time Nicole was born. Time marches on, carrying kids along with it into adulthood, adults into various kinds of oblivion.

"Find something?" Jeri asked.

"Nope."

"Then keep looking."

"That mean I'm on the payroll?"

"Keep looking, Mort."

I made a show of it, but in my heart I knew it was hopeless. The desk had been sterilized. No way was it going to harbor a packet of death threats from a psycho written in a childlike scrawl, with inky fingerprints, DNA-laden drool, and a return address.

In time, even Jeri called it quits. Ignoring Amyee's squawk of protest, I stuck my head into Peter Howard's office unannounced and told him we were leaving. Having missed a putt, he wasn't thrilled to see me, but he was elated to have us out of his building and out of his life. Me, especially. He might've put up with Jeri, one on one.

Outside, walking toward the car, Jeri said, "You're like a rhino in a china shop, Mort."

"You mean bull, don't you?"

"No. Rhino suits you. You need to lighten up. Peter Howard *might* have told us something."

"Yeah, well, he started it with that get-outta-here-and-don't-bother-me attitude of his."

"Oh, say, *that's* an enormous help."

"I didn't like the look in his eyes, Jeri." I had to hurry to keep up with her. Women and aerobics will be the death of tens of thousands of men in the U.S. in the coming years. In droves, we will have heart attacks trying to keep up.

"What *look*?" she demanded.

"Something squinty. Sneaky."

"So, based on that, you think what? That he killed and be-headed Jonnie? And worse, used a sabre saw on him? *That* wimp?"

"I didn't say that. I doubt if the useless prick knows what a sabre saw is. I think we ought to give him another look, that's all."

She stopped at the car and faced me, talking across the width of her Porsche. "Motive, Mort."

"He wanted Jonnie's office."

"Try to get a grip."

"In L.A. they'll murder you for jogging shoes. An office with a view is better than shoes, especially if you think it would impress little Amyee darlings."

"I said, try to get a grip. She'd be impressed with gum." She got in behind the wheel.

I flung my hands in the air. "Motive? How would I know? Maybe Peter Howard's got illegal land deals coming out his ass, and Jonnie found out and was about to blow the whistle. Or mus-cle in. We don't know what's going on in that place. And we don't know how the business is set up, either. With Jonnie out of the picture, maybe it'll just be Howard Title Company now."

"Terrific, now work our dead district attorney into this surreal little theory of yours."

I stared at her for several seconds. "It's not a theory, it's a possibility."

"Technically, that would make it a hypothesis, and a weak one at that. Now get in. Or do you want to go back and paw through Jonnie's desk for another hour or two?"

"Not on your life." I hopped in, wedged into the seat like a two-hundred-pound woman into size seven panties, then stuck the moustache back on again.

Jeri fired up the engine and took off, looked over at me. "Offhand, I don't see any compelling reason to uproot Sjorgen &

Howard, Mort. We need a helluva lot more than squinty eyes and darling Amyee. Unless what you really want is her phone number."

"Maybe I do. Gum's a cheap date."

She laughed, then snapped my head back shifting the Porsche into third.

CHAPTER ELEVEN

JERI DROPPED ME off downtown at the corner of First and Virginia and sped away. I watched her go. I still hadn't asked her about the judo, not that it mattered. I pretty much had the gist. She turned a corner, gone, and I headed up north on foot, through the heart of Reno's gaming district.

The golf hat didn't suit me, so I shoved it in a pocket and bought a cheap black cowboy hat at a tourist ripoff joint on the corner of Second and Virginia. Reno's transient and tourist population is eclectic enough that you can get away with that wild west, drugstore cowboy look without drawing stares, even if this wild west is one of used car salesmen, crack dealers, fast food, and massage parlors.

It was nearing three o'clock when I got to the Golden Goose. O'Roarke was just coming on shift, tying on an apron. He stared wordlessly at the hat. I took it off, knowing by his smirk that buying it had been one more mistake in a long line. I set it on the stool next to mine, ordered a plain Coke.

"How 'bout a sarsaparilla, pardner?" he drawled. "Cuts trail dust like nothin' you ever saw."

"Aaaaand, there goes your tip, smart ass." I stuck my moustache on a jar of beer nuts again. Made it look like Groucho, or Hitler.

"You haven't tipped me in two years, Angel." He slid a Coke in front of me.

"Not true. February I told you tomato paste gets out skunk odor."

He went to the other end of the bar and waited on three elderly ladies who were waving drink coupons at him. He didn't return for ten minutes. So much for giving him cool tips.

I sat there in the gloom, thinking about this deal with Jeri, letting the week's events wash over me.

K.

Three people dead.

And me, right in the thick of it, with no more idea of what was going on than your average teenager knows about Kurds in Iraq or border tensions between Mexico and Guatemala.

How close was the danger? More to the point, how close was it to Dallas? Or to K, or Jeri? Or even Dale, though she was probably safe now, on her way to New Hampshire.

Questions without answers. The danger might already be past. It could have been a transitory horror that had swept Greg up in one final blaze of glory and was over now.

I closed my eyes and...saw rage. At a gut level, penises hacked off and stuffed into holes cut into skulls equates to rage, hatred of an astronomical order.

Or not. Colombians in the drug trade might do that on a whim, a warning to the competition, or as a way to amuse themselves on a slow night, but I didn't see Colombians anywhere near this. Or drugs. Nothing like that.

Fact is, I didn't see much of anything in it. Nothing added up. Milliken might have been the initial target and Jonnie and Greg had somehow ended up on the tracks when the train went by. The enemies of Reno's D.A. would number in the hundreds. An imaginative psychopath might've been sprung from the state prison down in Carson and come north to settle a score. Things like that happen. If so, it was strictly a police matter. I wouldn't have a hope in hell of finding a lunatic with prison tattoos and a smoldering grudge who might already be off in the Great Smokies of Tennessee working as a dishwasher in a rowdy little no-name roadhouse.

And, was I fooling myself?

Was I a gumshoe, or just an early middle-aged ex-IRS agent on a barstool fooling himself, headed down one more dark road to an unknown destination?

Some questions don't have easy answers.

* * *

Four Cokes and four hours later, I left, regretting the choice of drinks. Coke doesn't have the ongoing appeal of beer. It doesn't cloud the mind, so you can't even fool yourself into thinking you're getting somewhere. The only diversion of note was the national news on TV at five thirty, in which one bulky and almost certainly dangerous Mortimer Angel—unquestionably a household name by this time—out for his morning jog, had led news vans into a parking garage, jogged downstairs to an exit, and, minutes later, was more or less responsible for the collision of an L.A. news wagon and a Citifare bus—to which O'Roarke, still smirking, said, "And to think I knew you when." The jerk.

By seven fifteen I was on the sidewalk, facing east. The day was cooling but still hot, still in the nineties, bright sunlight slanting in from the west. A stink of exhaust overlay Virginia Street. The tourists had a worn, glazed look. Even normally alert panhandlers were lethargic.

Across the street, Sjorgen House was a grayish-brown hulk rising into the shadows of overhanging elms. Light glinted off a rickety TV antenna on the roof, near a canted, copper-green cupola topped by a weathervane.

Sjorgen House.

Or Woolley House, depending. A dark, haunted-looking thing of old gables and cornices, dormer windows, square columns supporting an empty porch that ran the full width of the front. The place should have been painted New England white. It would've transformed it.

Whose was it now? What was its legal status, and what would happen to it and to Edna Woolley now that Jonnie was gone? Would the Huns of Progress bribe someone on the historical society and a few council members, raze the mansion and the rest of the block, and put up another gleaming six-hundred-million-dollar casino or a new parking garage?

A dormer window was open on the third floor, a yellow curtain hanging limp over the sill. The yard was deserted, the grass dry and gone to patches of bare earth and weeds. Thick shrubs grew along both sides of the house, and a climbing rose had reached the second floor, putting out bright explosions of yellow.

I jaywalked over, cowboy hat tilted at a jaunty angle. The front yard was unprotected by a fence. Cigarette butts and gum wrappers were ground into the dirt near the sidewalk like the aftermath of a double-A baseball game.

I remembered seeing Edna Woolley on television a few years ago, during her ninety-sixth birthday. By now she would be nearing a hundred.

How had she come to live in Sjorgen House? I had a rough idea of when, but didn't know any of the particulars. Either I hadn't paid enough attention to the news of late, or the subject hadn't been brought up. Wendell and Jane Sjorgen—Jonnie's parents— had vacated the place, and Edna moved in. I *did* know that Jane

Sjorgen divorced Wendell a few months after that, which carried the scent of scandal, but there wasn't a hint that a scandal or anything like it had occurred.

Now, I was or wasn't a private detective. If I wasn't, I could turn in my badge, symbolically speaking, go home, shower, circle job openings in the paper, catch another of Leno's Mortimer Angel jokes, crawl into bed and dream sweet dreams. If, on the other hand, I still had dreams of another kind, I could go nose around Jonnie's holdings, shake the trees, see if anything interesting fell out. And I was standing in front of one of his holdings right now.

So, Great Gumshoe, what's it gonna be?

I strolled up a concrete walk toward the house, hands in my pockets, not yet committed to anything. Who knows? I might've been an encyclopedia salesman in a cowboy hat. Come to think of it, that might be in my future, or going door to door with Electroluxes.

For forty years Edna had lived here. Last I'd heard, she had a live-in housekeeper or nurse taking care of her, something like that.

I climbed four warped treads to the front porch and came face to face with a recently written note on a three-by-five card that read: *No solicitors, no interviews, no reporters. Do NOT Ring the Bell! This means you!* It was thumbtacked to the wood above the doorbell.

Evidently the Sjorgen-Milliken saga had also reached this place and the occupants were fed up with it. I knew how they felt.

Roadblocks, decisions. I turned and looked back at the street, fifty feet away. What would a real gumshoe do at a time like this?

Ring the bell, of course, see who answers, try to strike up a conversation, apologize if necessary, wing it, backpedal if anyone pulled a gun, pretend to be a Mormon, hand out tracts.

Or maybe come back at two in the morning, climb in through a window and skulk around. A real gumshoe might do that.

I compromised. I knocked.

Waited half a minute, knocked again. Waited a full minute, then rang the damn bell. Nothing. I listened to the dead quiet of the house, stared at the blank, empty gaze of its windows.

So much for Plan A. Plan B, skulking in the wee hours of the morning, didn't have much appeal. If a Plan C were in the works, I'd have to invent it.

I stepped off the porch, went around the side of the house and looked down toward the back. High above, the attic window still stood open, curtain across the sill as if a gust of wind had blown it there. A sound of jazz floated on the air, as faint as a memory.

Toward the back, a separate garage sat in the backyard, also in a state of disrepair, low and shadowy beneath the leafy elms. Along the outer wall of the main house, a phone line dangled from loose, rusty staples and disappeared through a badly puttied hole. I looked up. The siding was stained where water had leaked from a damaged gutter. Big discoveries, these.

Between the shrubbery, whatever foundation the house had was partly hidden by latticework, two-inch-wide cedar strips crisscrossing in diagonals, forming diamonds beyond which lay blackness, exuding a cool moist odor of dark earth and worms.

The first-story windows were eight feet off the ground, too high to peek inside, so I stepped between two bushes and crouched down, peered through the latticework into the darkness beneath the house. At first I saw concrete piers, supporting the house. Then I jerked my head back sharply. Inside, six inches from my eye, was a glistening black widow spider, fat as a plum. I'd never seen one so big, hanging there upside down in the gloom, waiting for meat, for flies that sought that rank, undisturbed coolness beneath the house.

Bright red hourglass, so shiny it looked freshly painted. My skin crawled. I don't care for alien critters: spiders, scorpions, centipedes, earwigs, potato bugs, but there's nothing worse than black widows. Things can move fast as hell. I was glad they didn't have wings. I glanced to one side and saw another, then another. A dozen of them—

"Hey, you."

I turned, looked up. Not four feet away stood a gorgeous girl with straight black hair hanging to the small of her back, pale-green nylon jogging shorts and an off-white crop top with a ragged lower edge, as if she'd hacked off a sleeveless T-shirt with scissors. She was a real beauty, twenty years old, maybe only eighteen. Hard to tell when they're that young. The bottom edge of her top was cut off high, too high. The fabric stood well out from her body, riding the swell of her breasts. From that angle I could see two inches of sweet curving undersides, where a woman's skin is softest.

The nudity was jarring. Pale rounded globes, as unexpected as ghosts. The thought darted through my mind that there'd been a lot of this kind of thing in my life lately. Greg's fate notwithstanding, this PI gig was still right on track.

The girl's feet were planted well apart. No shoes. Her stomach was flat. Cute little pierced bellybutton sporting a silver ring that held a green stone. She was slender, approaching skinny, ribs so prominent I could have counted them, if I'd been so inclined.

"You rang the bell," she said accusingly.

"Guilty as charged."

"Can't you read?"

"Read what?" When in doubt, feign ignorance. For me, that's never a stretch.

She frowned. "What're you doin' down there?"

"Pest control," I stayed in a crouch and waved a hand toward the latticework, took another peek at her breasts even if she was way too young for an old codger like me.

She smiled, pushed her chest out another quarter inch and said, "So, sport, what d'you think?"

Any number of things, an entire murky galaxy of things, none of which seemed right for the moment, so what I chose to say was, "Be sure to get your oil changed every three thousand miles."

She blinked. Finally she said, "You're an idiot."

Okay, she didn't fool easily.

Another woman came up beside her. Older, but they looked enough alike to be sisters, or mother and daughter. "That's no way to talk, Winter, honey," she said.

Winter. A chilly name, but appropriate. I got slowly to my feet. The women were the same height, about five foot five. Winter had an incredibly tiny twenty-three inch waist. I guessed her weight at a hundred pounds, if that, but she looked wiry enough. Her stomach was flat, hard with muscle.

"John Wayne here is checking out bugs, Mom," she said, still looking at me.

John Wayne? Swiftly—or maybe not so swiftly—I removed the hat.

"And here I thought you were a private investigator, Mr. Angel," the older woman said. She was a looker, too, mid-thirties, wearing blue denim shorts and a yellow shirt with bits of redwood bark or mulch clinging to them. A two-way radio was attached to her belt.

"You've been watching television," I said. My moustache, now that I thought of it, was still stuck to that jar of beer nuts in the lounge across the street. I might've fooled her with that.

"They'd recognize you in Atlanta. Or Miami, Chicago, you name it. You're quite the celebrity, Mr. Angel."

"Mort. Guess you got me," I said, catching an eerie little smile on Winter's face, in her eyes.

"So...bugs?" Winter's mother asked.

"Spiders." I shrugged. "Black widows. There's a bunch of them under the house."

Winter's eyes widened. She took a step back. "Oh, ugh."

"Pretty damn big ones, too," I said, trying to give the kid's chain a little extra yank, now that I'd found a chain.

"But," the older woman said, "are they any concern of yours?"

"Only if one bit me."

She ignored that. "Nor did they bring you here, onto our private property, all the way to the side of our house."

Our property, our house. Did I see a hint of Edna Woolley in this woman's face, or was I only imagining it? "Uh, no."

"Mr. Sjorgen's death *did*, however." A question filled her eyes, but it was a question whose answer she already knew. Might've meant she was a lawyer.

"Sort of."

"More than *sort* of," she pressed, in pursuit of a confession, truth, possibly even justice. It was hard to tell.

"Yeah, okay."

"And right now you're wondering who *we* are." She put an arm around Winter's shoulders.

"The thought crossed my mind."

"I'm Victoria, Edna's granddaughter. And this is my daughter, Winter."

Something filled Winter's eyes, like amusement. If it was, it was very chilly humor. Strange kid. I didn't much care for her, I have to admit. And yet, I was aware that if I were to crouch down to tie a shoelace I'd have an interesting view if I wanted one. She would let me look. She wanted me to. She knew she looked good. Her arms and legs were hard. Not like Jeri's, though. Winter was more the slender type, more like a dancer, someone into ballet.

"Nice to meet you," I said.

"Now," Victoria said, "go away."

As abrupt and as hard as a slap in the face. Winter stared at me, registering nothing.

Get pushed though, and sometimes you push back. Suddenly I wasn't ready to go. "I was hoping to have a word with Edna."

"You and everyone else. You're the last person on earth I'd let see her right now," Victoria said.

"Is that your call to make?"

"Mine alone, Mr. Angel."

I thought about that and decided it was time to fold the hand. She was right, I had no business there, or at least no legitimate way to get past the Minotaurs guarding the portal. And, what was the point?

"Who is it, Victoria?" an elderly voice called down from above.

I looked up. Edna Woolley was peering down at us from that third-floor dormer. Her eyeglasses reflected light, turning her eyes into shiny disks.

"No one, Grandma," Victoria said loudly, still looking at me.

"Send him up."

"It's no one. Just an exterminator."

"Send him up. He wants to see me. You never send anyone up." Her voice had a thready complaining quality, but it wasn't as frail as I'd imagined it would be.

I looked at Victoria. "Is that right? Is there a reason you never send anyone up?"

She studied me, then in a surprise move she stepped back and indicated the way with a sweep of her hand. "Go right ahead, Mr. Mortimer Angel. Be my guest."

"Mo-o-o-m," Winter said, her voice suddenly that of a typical whiny teenager.

"Let him." Victoria's eyes bored into mine. "Go. Have a nice visit. She'll like that. Just don't mention Jonathan."

"Jonathan?"

"Jonathan *Sjorgen*." Victoria's nose wrinkled in distaste. "Jonnie, as everyone seems to call him. Grandma doesn't know anything about what's happened. It would only upset her to find out. If you do..."

She let the thought hang. Still, just like that, I was in.

Like Thomas Magnum, like Hammer.

Well, almost.

CHAPTER TWELVE

I WAS IN, but I had no plan, no idea where to go from there. What could Edna tell me? Ten minutes ago I'd been on the street, brain idling in neutral, no prospects, a gumshoe only in my overwrought imagination. Why I thought I'd gained ground since then I couldn't say.

A chandelier that hadn't been cleaned in thirty years hung over the entryway. The foyer led off in four directions, left, right, straight ahead into the back, and up. Parlor, living room, hallway, stairs. The interior of the house absorbed light, paneled and trimmed in walnut and mahogany. The air was stale with disuse, pregnant with age. The floor creaked.

I went up, cowboy hat in hand. Halfway to the floor above, I looked back. The gals were at the foot of the stairs, watching me, Victoria with one hand on the newel post. I'd expected them to dog my steps, Victoria, if not Winter. But maybe there was a trapdoor at the top of the stairs that would land me in the basement on a bed of spikes. Or maybe Victoria was hoping I'd go up, get lost, never find my way back.

Which seemed likely, I thought, once I'd reached the second floor. The house rambled off in several directions and there was no sign of the stairs to the third floor or attic, whatever Edna was in. That Victoria was allowing me to roam around at will meant I wasn't going to find anything worth finding, but now that I was here

I was damned if I was going to just go away. The two of them had acted snotty so I intended to make a nuisance of myself. And Edna wanted company, as so many old folks do. How could I deny her the pleasure of that scintillating conversation that so amuses Dallas?

The walnut railing showed signs of age and use, but was layered in dust. Expensive antique wallpaper—blood-red velvet roses on a pink background—was peeling away from the wall up near the ceiling and along the seams. A blue flowery runway carpet lay over oak strip flooring. As on the first floor, the boards creaked underfoot. The halls were dark, lit only by distant dirty windows. I caught a faint whiff of mold or rot. Brass fixtures held glass candles. I found a switch, threw it, and the candles flickered to life, illuminating nothing. They were mostly ornamental. The effect was tawdry, something you'd expect to find in a low-budget whorehouse.

I poked my head in one door and saw a toilet, a clawfoot tub, pedestal sink, a hair dryer that would've blown fuses in the house in 1920. In another room I saw red lace curtains, a four-poster covered by a jet-black comforter and matching pillows, women's clothing draped on a chair, including a black bra and thong. Crossed swords were on the wall above the bed, which looked hazardous in the event of an earthquake. A fencing mask had been hung in the lower part of the X, centered, completing the effect. All in all, lace and foils, the room looked very French.

Another room. More female things. Doors had been left ajar and I was alone, which made snooping easy work.

I stuck my head in one empty room, then another. Dusty cobwebs hung between a lamp shade and a bookshelf, grayish-gold strands waving gently in a feeble ray of sunlight. I guessed the room wasn't Winter's favorite hangout. Or anyone's for that matter.

I found a flight of Dickensian stairs at the end of a hallway so dark it made me wish for a flashlight. Floating down from above was that ethereal sound of jazz I'd heard earlier, outside the house.

I went up, then along a short hallway, and knocked on a door where the music was loudest.

"Come in, come in," said a voice. I turned the knob, one of those cut crystal things I hadn't seen since I was in the house of a great aunt when I was a kid, and went in.

Edna Woolley wasn't what I'd expected, but then, people rarely are. I recognized her from that time on television a number of years ago, but the T-shirt with a purple pirouetting hippo on it was a surprise, as were the green Bermuda shorts and the Air Nikes. The shoes looked enormous on her feet. She'd put on a helmet-shaped strawberry-blond wig that made her face seem even smaller, and her eyes, now that I could see them behind the wire-rim glasses, were made up poorly with liner and a hint of pinkish-orange color. Her lipstick was bright red, applied with approximately the skill of a six-year-old. She weighed all of eighty pounds. She'd probably lost six full inches of height since she was a young adult.

Thirties jazz issued softly from a CD player sitting on a wooden table, hand carved in an Oriental design.

"Oh, my," she said, dismay written on her face. "I've forgotten your name." She stood in the middle of the room, a cluttered, place with an overstuffed couch and matching armchair, their arms and backs covered with yellowed lace. The ceiling was all slopes and angles under the gabled roof. The area in front of the dormer window was free of furniture, making it easy for her to see out. Old oil paintings crowded the few walls that were vertical, and photographs in small, tarnished silver frames appeared every-where, like geometric mushrooms.

One small section of a wall held nothing but a single crucifix, a beautiful thing made of silver, fourteen inches high. If it was solid, it was worth a small fortune.

"Mortimer Angel, ma'am."

"Mortimer. That's a fine name." She smiled, then grappled with her hair, trying to get it straight. A pure-white strand leaked out from under the helmet by her left ear.

"Thank you, ma'am."

She gave me a disapproving squint. "You should call me Edna, dear. Family, you know."

"Okay...Edna." That bit about family threw me, but not for long.

"Do sit, dear," she said.

We sat. I sank into the couch and she perched on the edge of a century-old armchair close to my left elbow, touching my hand with dry, skeletal fingers.

"Now then, how is dear old Charlie?" she asked.

"Charlie?"

"Your father. How is he?" Before I could figure out a suitable response, she went on, "I don't believe I've seen him in...since..." She pursed her lips then pressed a finger to the side of her cheek. "Well, since my Herman passed on, but...of course..." She looked at me, apologetic and flustered. "I'm afraid my memory isn't what it used to be."

"Mine either."

She smiled. "Charlie. Goodness, but didn't he and my Herman raise Cain in Chicago, growing up? Those two! Oh, the stories! Herman was two years older, of course, or"—she frowned—"was it three?"

"Two," I said helpfully. I doubted that it would matter.

"Thank you, dear." She patted my hand. "Your father Charlie was best man at our wedding. But of course you would know all about that, wouldn't you?"

"I'm Charlie's grandson." I didn't know if she would pick up on the improbability of my being the son of a man about a hundred years old, but I didn't want to take the chance.

"You look so much like him, too," Edna said, beaming at me, eyes bright.

Like who? I wondered. Did Charlie even have a grandson? I sat tight.

"Did you know Jacoba?" Edna asked, leaning toward me.

"I, ah...don't think so."

"Such a pity. She was so lovely, so very beautiful." Slowly, like a wilting flower, Edna's face grew sad—a gradual transformation, powered by a deeply rooted, forlorn memory, lost in time.

I glanced at several photos on a nearby table. People I didn't know. All the pictures were faded, a few of them sepia toned. In one, a woman in her forties was in a rose garden, holding a baby wrapped in blankets, smiling happily.

"Would you care for some tea, Douglas?"

Suddenly I was Douglas, whoever that was. I didn't try to correct her. It didn't matter. Not all of Edna Woolley was there, and that didn't matter either. Her past was a montage of images—years and decades blending into one another, faces, names, events. We are all headed in that direction.

"Tea would be nice," I said. "If it wouldn't be too much trouble." In fact, I might not drink tea while dying of thirst in the Sahara, but I would sip a cup if it made Edna happy.

Edna picked up a walkie talkie, a twin to the one I'd seen on Victoria's belt and said, "Ruthie, dear."

Not three seconds passed before Victoria's voice came back. "What is it, Grandma?"

"Could I trouble you for tea? Charlie has come to visit."

"In a few minutes, Grandma. I'll have to boil the water." Her voice was patient, solicitous.

So I had tea with Edna Woolley. I was alternately Douglas, Charlie, Albert, and someone named Rupert. I was never again Mortimer to her. The tea was wickedly awful, Victoria's revenge, no doubt, though Edna seemed to like it. Winter delivered it wearing white jeans and a conservative shirt, sandals. And a smile I couldn't read, but it was meant for me, and I didn't much care for it.

When she was gone Edna looked at the door and said, "Isn't she the loveliest child, Albert?"

"She certainly is."

"So much like my precious Jacoba." Then the sadness descended again, lifting only after minutes had gone by. Evidently the memory of Jacoba had its dark moments.

Shadows crept up the walls. Sunlight on the window frame became golden, then turned burgundy and gray. Clouds went pink, dulled, lost all color. I found myself stifling yawns. Three hours of sleep the night before was beginning to catch up, and it had been a full day. I almost nodded off several times, gagging down swallows of now-cold tea the color of olive brine to rouse myself. The rest of it went out the attic window where it most likely killed a few plants. Finally I said, "Do you know the Sjorgens, Edna?"

Edna's eyes cleared, brightened, filled with a harder light. "This is *his* house," she said.

"Whose?"

"Wendell's, of course." Her lips pressed together in disapproval. "He never visits any more, you know."

Jonnie's dad. She got the name right, which surprised me. I couldn't tell if she knew he'd been stabbed to death in an alley some two decades ago. Perhaps she'd never known, or had, years ago, but had long since forgotten.

"I thought the house was Jonnie's." I didn't know how far to go in that direction, but just mentioning his name seemed safe enough.

"Jonnie. *That* boy." Her cup rattled on its saucer and her face grew agitated.

"Mr. Angel," Victoria's voice came over the radio, crisp and hard.

I picked it up. "Yes."

"Your time is up."

"Just about to leave." I set the radio down. I hadn't known it was two-way, like a cell phone, a kind of monitoring device, always on. "Time for me to go, Edna."

"Oh, and we were having *such* a lovely visit, too, Albert," she said, disappointed.

"Yes, I know. I'm very sorry."

She looked around, perplexed. "Now where on earth do you suppose Sparky's got to?"

"Sparky?"

"My kitty. He was here only a moment ago."

The attic window was open. Had been all day. Sparky probably kept his own hours. I'd been there nearly two hours, so a moment in Edna's life was an indeterminate amount of time.

Her hands fluttered helplessly. "Do tell Charlie I miss him so, won't you, dear?"

"Yes. I certainly will."

"Will you come back?" Her eyes seemed to tug at mine, wanting company.

"I'll try."

I hugged her as if she were my own grandmother. She stood in the middle of the room where I'd first seen her, watching as I let myself out.

Into a dark passage. Dim light came from the far end, through a north-facing window with a view of an almost-black sky through a canopy of elms.

I felt blind. I missed my gun. I groped to the stairs, found a switch that turned on a grimy fifteen-watt bulb that might've once belonged to T. A. Edison himself.

Down the stairs and back along a hallway lit only slightly better than the one above. Then past several doors, off to my right. Ahead, I saw the second-floor landing at the head of the stairs.

A light clicked on. "Mort?"

I turned. Six feet away, Winter was in a doorway wearing a filmy black bra and a black thong, illuminated in soft light by a frosted globe lamp on the ceiling. Her pubic hair must have been shaved off because the thong was a silk patch the size of a credit card. The bra was loose, straps off her shoulders, cups drooping at the sides as she held it to herself with a pale hand. That whorehouse feeling ratcheted upward a notch or three.

"I'm undone," she said. She turned, revealing the free ends of her bra in back, a nice expanse of bare skin, that improbably tiny waist. The thong hid nothing at all of her bottom, which was nicely rounded and well-muscled.

I stared at her. She turned and faced me again, returning my look, still holding the bra to her chest, one hip thrust out far enough to touch the frame of the door. It was a striking sight, the filmy black undergarments, the raven-haired girl, her smooth, pale skin. I could see that black comforter behind her, the crossed foils on the wall.

"Hitch me up?" she said.

"Depends," I answered. "Where's the plow?"

She struck a measured pout. "I mean, my *bra*, cowboy."

"Nope."

I headed for the stairs, started down without looking back. Under the conditions, hooking up Winter's brassiere wouldn't have been the smartest move of the day. Under any conditions I could imagine, it wouldn't have been.

The word "fucker" floated down after me, and a lilting, almost indiscernible laugh. Sweet child.

I'd almost reached the front door when Victoria appeared at the double doors to the parlor. Her face was in shadow, eyes glinting, catching stray light. How these people got around without crashing into things was beyond me, but I guessed they saved a bundle on electricity.

"I told you not to mention Jonathan," Victoria said tightly.

"You told me not to tell her he was dead. Or how."

"Get out. Don't come back."

"That's not very friendly."

"You are an extremely nosy person, Mr. Angel. Very annoying."

"So I've been told. It was a requirement of my former job."

"Out."

"No problem." I opened the door, then looked back, "You might want to try to find Sparky," I told her. "It looks like he might've gone out the window."

"As near as we've been able to determine, Sparky died in 1923, Mr. Angel. When Edna was seven years old. We don't anticipate that he'll be coming back."

"Oh."

"Good-bye."

I went outside. Before the door closed behind me, I said, "You might consider giving Winter a good spanking."

"Might *I*?"

All I could see was one of Victoria's eyes, staring at me through a two-inch gap, then the door snicked shut.

I strode down the walk to the street. At the sidewalk I looked back at the house, half expecting to see Winter standing naked at a window, peering out, wanting whatever she wanted. Other than faint yellow light emanating from Edna's window, the house was dark.

I headed home on foot again, wondering when I could safely retrieve the Toyota and start driving again.

Jonathan, Victoria had called him. No one called Jonnie that. It didn't sound right, like saying Jonathan Wayne or Robert Hope. You just don't *do* that.

*   *   *

I loosened the fence boards and slipped through, stood in my backyard gazing at the house.

All dark, all quiet.

News vans were still camped on the street in front. Persistent as mosquitoes, the sons of bitches, but there were only three of them, so maybe things were starting to cool off.

I unlocked the back door and went in, left the lights off while I toured the house to assure myself that I was alone, then took a quick shower and got dressed again in clean clothes. I made a sandwich in the dark and ate it in the backyard sitting in a lawn chair with a view of casino lights through trees to my left. I washed the sandwich down with two beers while looking up at the stars. I was dog tired, but knew I wouldn't be able to sleep for a while. I thought K might show up, but she didn't. Finally I opened a window in the bedroom for air and went to bed, caught the eleven o'clock news and, later, Leno on *The Tonight Show*.

Channel 4 ran a recap of the Sjorgen-Milliken-Rudd-Angel circus, but they had nothing new to add. I watched one last clip

of Mortimer Angel's infamous morning jog and the blonde's en-
counter with the Citifare bus, which I enjoyed very much. No
mention of Dallas or me by Leno, so I went to sleep thinking
maybe our moment in the limelight was over. With luck, this
whole thing might blow itself out, except for the lingering dregs
of an unfinished investigation. Once they caught the perpetrator
things would flare up again, but by then Dallas and I would be
out on the furthest reaches of it, barely a footnote. We were done.

Innocent babes dream the deepest, and I was innocent enough,
or dumb enough, to sink into the Valkyrian mists of a very deep
dream indeed.

And, I was tired right down to the bone.

* * *

Which explains why I didn't wake up when K crawled into my
bed, sometime during the night.

Fact is, I didn't wake up at all, didn't feel a thing. But when I got
up at three in the morning to pee, I damn near jumped out of my
skin when I encountered a warm body. I yelped, scrambled out of
bed taking the sheets and the blanket with me, and ended up on
the floor against the closet, crushing a lampshade.

For a moment I wondered where my gun was. I wasn't operat-
ing at anything like full capacity. Panic is like that.

"Mort?" K's voice came at me in the dark. It brought me back
to reality just as I'd remembered where my gun was. Lucky her.

"K?"

She groped around and turned on the other bedside light, the
one I hadn't destroyed. She sat on the newly stripped bed, naked
except for panties. Christ, she looked good. A little peeved, too,
though it wasn't easy to tell while looking at her tits. She crossed

her arms across her chest and stared at me with the lamp back-lighting her hair.

"Why'd you do *that*?" she said.

"Do what?"

"Tear the sheets and everything off me. I mean, if you wanted to look or anything you could've just asked."

It was a comment I would have to digest at my leisure, especially the "or anything."

"It wasn't intentional," I said, wired to the gills on adrenaline, heart hammering away. "I didn't know you were here. I never heard you come in. I was headed for the bathroom, and there you were. I mean, I thought I was alone."

"You flip out pretty easily." K hugged a pillow and sat with her legs crossed. A strip of blue French-cut cotton was visible at her hips. The rest was behind the pillow.

"Hell, woman, you should've nudged me or something when you came in." I stood up with the blanket in front of myself and took a deep breath, willing my heart to slow.

"I made plenty of noise. And I bounced around a little too, on purpose, but you never moved, so I figured, okay, you need your sleep. I could relate to that."

"You didn't bounce enough."

"I would've hit you with a chair if I'd known you'd act like this. You were *out*, Mort."

"There, see."

"See what?"

"Hell, I don't know." I rubbed the back of my neck, trying to think, making it look like something I don't do all that often.

She pressed her lips together. Her hair was mussed, eyes big but puffed with sleep, which made me wonder how long she'd been lying there alongside Mr. Oblivious.

I backed toward the door still holding the blanket. Sleeping in the buff had become risky of late. "Don't go anywhere," I said.

"Where on earth would I go?"

"Excellent question. God only knows, but it happens a lot with you. And kill the light before it attracts national attention."

The light winked out. I came back a few minutes later and stood beside the bed, looking down at her in the watery gloom filtering in the windows. Outside, I caught a distant glimpse of high-rise neon.

"Who are you?" I asked.

"Would you please sit?" she asked. "You look positively huge standing over me like that." She scooted over a few inches.

I sat, warily, still holding the bedclothes. She kept the pillow in place. Between Jeri, Dallas, Winter, and Victoria, not to mention Libby, Dale, Rachael, Amyee, and the hooker, Holiday, at the Golden Goose, the past few days had been full of unexpected interactions with the fair sex—although fair sex, as in *delicate*, was beginning to sound like a misnomer of the first order.

"Who are you?" I asked again.

She pursed her lips at me, then yawned. "It might be better if we discussed it in the morning. I'm awfully tired, Mort. You too."

"Oh, no," I thundered. "No one sleeps. No one closes their eyes or so much as *blinks* excessively until I find out who you are."

"Izzatso?" Her tone got huffy.

I folded my arms across my chest, blanket wadded in my lap, feeling more than a little huffy myself. "You got that right, Miss K."

She sighed. "If you insist. My name is Kayla."

Which didn't mean a thing to me, but I liked it. It suited her. "Kayla," I echoed, then followed up smartly with, "Kayla *who*? Mind telling me that?"

"Williams."

I gave her a blank look. I didn't know any Kayla Williams.

"Actually," she said, "if you want to get picky, my name is Rosalyn Kayla Williams."

I felt a chill travel up my spine on tiny feet, right to the base of my skull.

"Before Williams it was...uh, Sjorgen."

Aw, shit. She was Jonnie's kid.

CHAPTER THIRTEEN

"Jonnie's kid," I said.

A humorous light filled her eyes. "If I look like a kid to you, then yes."

"Okay, his daughter."

"You don't look awfully thrilled about that, Mort."

"Should I be?"

"I guess not. Probably not. One more person connected to Jonnie. I imagine you've had plenty of that lately." She glanced around. "You wouldn't happen to have like a nightlight or anything, would you? I can't see your face very well."

"It's not that good a face."

"And people think only women fish for compliments."

"Just stating a fact, K—*Kayla*."

"Well, if you believe it, I guess it must be true. One of those nightlight thingies? Maybe a flashlight? This is hardly the way to get acquainted."

I dug a flashlight out of a nightstand and stuck it partway under a sheet, turned it on. The room took on a dim yellowish glow, hopefully not bright enough to attract the likes of Brian Williams, Katie Couric, or Wolf Blitzer—or a ragtag gang from *Inside Edition*.

"Better," she said.

I stared at her. "Your hair was dark in a photo I saw recently."

"Must've been an old one, about the time I was in middle school. Mom let me dye it black for my birthday. But haven't you heard? Blondes have more fun."

"Do they?"

"In fact, that's a myth. I oughta know." She twirled a lock of hair. "This is my natural color. "

"I know."

Her eyes held mine. "*Do* you?"

"Got that when I was checking for bullet holes."

She thought about that for a moment, then laughed. It was a nice, musical sound, without a trace of annoyance or dismay in it.

"What're you doing here?" I asked.

"I needed a place to stay."

That wasn't an answer. "Why *here*, Kayla? Why me?"

"Why you what?"

"Was it because of Nicole?"

"Uh-huh. Indirectly, at least. She's been away in Europe for a month, as you probably know. She doesn't know I'm here."

"Neither does the rest of the world. You're a missing person, an enigma. Part of this puzzle everyone's trying to figure out."

"And I'd like to keep it that way. Dad disappeared and suddenly I was ducking reporters all over Ithaca. They were beyond persistent. It would be worse if anyone knew I was here in Reno. A *lot* worse."

"But in spite of that you came back."

"I had to."

"Understandable. He's your father."

She hugged the pillow tighter. "It wasn't that. I mean, he is, and maybe that's part of the reason I'm here, but that's not why I had to leave Ithaca."

"Yeah? Why did you?"

She shivered. "How about I explain it in the morning? It'd take too long now."

"You cold? Want me to shut the window?"

She smiled. "No. It's still pretty warm out. Muggy. I'd forgotten the desert can get like this. Which, by the way, is one reason I'm dressed the way I am."

"One reason? What's another?"

"I haven't worn clothing to bed since I was ten." She shrugged. "PJs are uncomfortable. When you turn, they twist around you like those Chinese handcuff thingies."

Dallas might've said the same thing. "How old are you, Kayla?"

"Thirty-four." She tilted her head and smiled. "Relieved?"

"More than you'll ever know."

"Maybe not. Nicole told me you were a, well...something of a stick-in-the-mud."

"She said *that*? My own kid?" That damn stockbroker heritage had surfaced again like a whale covered in old squid-sucker scars.

Kayla pursed her lips, suppressing a smile. "She didn't mean it in a bad way, Mort."

"Of course not. A stick-in-the-mud in a *good* way, what else?"

"Nicole loves you, Mort. A lot. She talks about you often. From everything she told me, I thought it would be safe to come here, you know, that first night. Then..." She shrugged. "You started finding all those heads and all hell broke loose."

All those heads. Hell of a phrase. My own head was beginning to throb. I sensed nuances in Kayla's words. I could tell I wasn't picking up on even half of them. "Jonnie was your father, Kayla," I said, trying to sound as nonjudgmental as possible.

She stared at her toes, wiggled them, then looked up at me again. "Dad and I weren't close. We hadn't been in a long time, since before I left for college. Once I left, I hardly ever came back, except for an occasional holiday. Weird, huh?"

"Maybe not. It all depends on the family."

"My father...I don't know, at times I had the feeling he wasn't a very nice man."

"Care to elaborate on that?"

"Not really. I just didn't like being around him all that much. He wasn't like a...a father. He made me uncomfortable. And... well, we didn't get along all that great, that's all."

She was fumbling. I felt she wasn't telling me the whole truth. And I was tired, suddenly feeling the need for more sleep now that the adrenaline had worn off. And I had to see Jeri at ten, find out if I was still a trainee-PI, but questions kept popping into my head. Guess it was all the gumshoe training I'd had that week. Hard to turn a thing like that off once it gets to be second nature.

"How'd you get in?" I asked. "Or do you scrub windows *and* pick locks?"

She smiled. "They do look better, don't they?"

"The neon's never been brighter, the sky's never been so deep a blue."

The look Kayla gave me was not unlike the ones Dallas gives me on occasion. She said, "Nicole told me she lived with her mom after the divorce. Your divorce, I mean. She hid a key to your house under a brick in your backyard. You'd sometimes go out of town on an audit or something, places like Elko or Hawthorne, and she'd come here with some friends and have a party."

I stared at her.

"No big deal now, right?" she said. "This was when she was sixteen or seventeen. Anyway, I got into Reno at dusk on Sunday. You weren't home so I hunted around out back and eventually found the brick and the key, so I let myself in. I wouldn't have done it...well, okay, maybe I *would* have, but at the time I didn't have a choice. I didn't have any money, just a ridiculous Citgo card. My only credit card. Good for gas, junk food, staying on the road. I guess I'll have to break down and get a real credit card sometime, even though I hate the idea of credit, owing people."

I was still way behind, miles behind, not catching up very fast, either. "Parties," I said. "In my house."

"Not *big* ones, Mort. She didn't have the junior class over. No more than six or eight kids, from what I gathered."

Six or eight kids, strangers, hormone-driven purveyors of pure mayhem—*teenagers*—here in my castle, running amok, doing God knows what. And I'd never known, Great Gumshoe to be. Jesus H. Christ.

"Mort?"

"Huh?"

"You okay?"

"Terrific, thanks."

"She was a *kid*. They do things like that, you know. It's part of growing up."

"Yeah, sure." I felt like the fat kid in gym class, the freckled donut-muncher whose glasses won't stay on, last one around the track, shoelaces flapping, everyone pointing, laughing. The kid who ends up getting locked in his own locker. *That* kid.

"I let myself in," Kayla said. "Showered, went to bed. I've never been so utterly over-the-top exhausted in my life."

"Why? What'd you do?"

"Drove out from Ithaca—straight through, the whole damn way."

"Christ, that's over two thousand miles."

"Twenty-seven hundred. I didn't have money for a motel, and... well...by the time I got to Reno not even megadoses of caffeine were having any effect, I mean four No-Doze washed down with black coffee in Lovelock. I was seeing double. Or maybe triple. I lost count. I don't know how I made it that last hundred miles, brain buzzing and dead, all at the same time. After I got in the house and had a shower, I got some valerian from your medicine cabinet."

"I noticed."

"It helped bring me down. Then...I went comatose. Guess I'd make a lousy long-distance trucker." She paused. "I owe you a lot, I know. I'll pay back every cent, I promise." She yawned expansively. "I would tell you about it now, the Ithaca thing, I mean, why I left, but I'm exhausted. I'm still feeling the effects of the drive. And I didn't get much sleep last night at that awful little motel."

"Me either. I didn't fall asleep until three last night."

"You look it."

"Thanks a bunch. You don't."

"Ah, chivalry. I love it." She grinned at me.

"I'm serious. Tell me one more thing: Why'd you call yourself K in that note? Why not let me know who you were?"

"I didn't know what you'd do. I mean, with Jonnie gone, in the news everywhere. I couldn't risk having you tell anyone I was here, not before I had a chance to explain, face to face." She smiled. "And I didn't think you'd recognize me. Or turn me in as a stray, either."

"Meaning—men don't call the cops when they find strange, beautiful women in their beds with their clothes piled on the floor."

"Well, they don't, as a rule."

"There's a rule?"

"I'm sure there must be."

"Anyway, I'm glad you found me so predictable."

"You haven't been predictable at all. I haven't done windows in I don't know how long. Could we sleep now?"

"One last question. You said your name is Williams now. Who's that?"

"Why? You worried?"

"Damn right I am. That's trouble I don't need."

"My ex. Clay. He's nothing. A mistake I haven't seen in ten years. I kept the name, that's all. It's an okay generic name, a lot easier to pronounce than Sjorgen."

I looked into her eyes. "I want you to know this's really weird, Kayla, you crawling into my bed like this, especially with me in it."

She smiled. "I know. I tried the couch first. Did you know that thing smells like a dog?"

"Uh, yeah."

"I mean it *really* stinks, Mort. It's gross. You oughta get rid of it. Or have it fumigated."

"It's an heirloom."

"The smell, too?"

"Okay, I could maybe have it cleaned."

"And, it's too short."

"Another complaint I've heard before."

She looked around the room. "So, um...maybe you've got a spare T-shirt around here I could borrow?"

She'd been sitting behind the pillow the whole time, otherwise naked from the waist up, relatively naked from the waist down too, showing no signs of embarrassment.

"Yeah, sure." I got one from my dresser, one that she'd washed. I turned my back, waiting while she pulled it on over her head.

"There," she said. "Can we sleep now?"

I turned and looked at her. "Uh-huh. Sleep tight." I got to my feet. Holding the blanket, I went into the hallway. "If you're not warm enough with the sheet, there's a spare blanket in the hall closet. This one's mine."

"Hey."

I went into the living room, flopped down on the couch which emitted a distinct doggy odor, and began to arrange the bed-clothes around me.

She came in, padding on bare feet and stood in front of me, ghostly and small in my shirt. The thing was huge on her, reaching four inches above her knees. I couldn't see her face.

"You can wear a suit of armor, if you like," she said. "You can recite the Boy Scout oath—brave, thrifty, chaste, whatever—but *no one* is going to sleep on that damn couch tonight. Or I can go back to that howling roach palace on East Fourth."

She stood there, waiting, hands on her hips. I didn't know what to say, so I didn't say anything. Finally she said, "I promise I won't touch you, Mort."

"Yeah? What if *that's* what I'm afraid of?"

I saw her teeth in the gloom, meaning she was smiling or about to bite. She yanked the blanket off me, which left me wearing nothing but the dark of night. "Come on, dope," she said. "You can't sleep there." She left, taking the blanket with her.

I got up and followed her into the bedroom. She was seven years younger than me. Seven years isn't much. She was thir-ty-four, fully grown. I didn't know where Greg had gone astray, but other than that thing he had going with Dale he'd had this PI thing all wrong.

Kayla sank down on the bed, leaving room for me. Her voice came out of the gloom. "You already got a pretty good look, right? That first night, checking for bullet holes?"

"Pretty good, yeah."

"So?"

"I didn't see any blood so I let you sleep."

"Well, nothing about me has changed since then, Boy Scout, so what's the problem? I intend to sleep, period, how 'bout you?"

"Absolutely."

"So, sleep. Put on underwear. Put on a shirt and tie if that'll help. Wear nothing if that's your usual. And here. This is *my* usual." She pulled off the T-shirt and tossed it to me, then settled in, closed her eyes.

I opened a drawer and grabbed a pair of boxers. In the morning I would find that I'd got the ones with little red hearts all over it, a lucky grab in the dark.

"Night," Kayla said, voice already drifting off.

"Night. Place had roaches, huh?"

"Bunches of 'em. Big ones. They wore nametags. Ralph told jokes."

Then she was gone.

* * *

I slept fine, oddly enough, better than I had in days, since before the week's festivities began. I didn't stir until quarter past eight. When I did, I looked over at Kayla. She was still conked, mouth slightly open, a glint of moisture on her teeth, blond hair tangled, one naked shoulder showing. I marveled that I'd managed to sleep at all, next to a creature so beautiful.

I got out of bed quietly, grabbed some clothes and went out, into the bathroom, and turned on the shower. Soap and water first, then breakfast.

I had a nice lather going when she opened the shower door and stepped in, shut it behind her with a decisive metallic click.

"Hey, hey, hey!" I yelped.

"Hey yourself."

She kissed me. I didn't have any choice but to return it. It was either that or drown.

"I'm confused," I said, once I got the chance.

"You're sweet," she said.

"What the hell does *that* mean?"

"You didn't try to touch me last night."

"Yeah? I'm still trying not to." I wasn't succeeding very well, however. The stall wasn't big enough for the two of us.

She nudged me aside and hogged the water for a moment, then said, "Do my back, huh?"

"Wait a minute, wait a minute, hold it right—"

"*Now* what?"

"You know what."

She looked into my eyes "Okay, I'm being kinda forward here and this is unexpected and you're uncomfortable because you don't know where the limits are or what to make of it, right?"

"Right. You got that exactly right."

"If we're going to share a house and a bed, why tiptoe around each other? What's the point?"

"That isn't *any* explanation at all." I was trying not to look at her breasts, which were magnificent. Finally I gave it up since it didn't seem to matter, at least not to her.

"That's because there *isn't* any. Do I *need* to explain it? Nicole said you were a nice guy and I trust her. She's a sweet kid. And I happen to think she's right. I've learned to trust my instincts. I'm not the type to get all uptight and hysterical about conventions, especially those of other people. I mean, how big a deal is this? I didn't see a bunch of religious artifacts lying around the house, no crucifix on the wall. But, hey, if you want me out of here so you can shower in peace, I'll leave you to it."

She put her hands on her hips and stared at me.

I was aware of her, *all* of her, the challenge, the playfulness, the risk she was taking, the gift and the taking, her naked body, water and steam, the scent of soap, the waiting look in her eyes.

"Three more seconds," she said, "...two...one..."

I have more than my share of slow moments, but I'm not a complete dimwit, at least not all the time. I picked up the soap, turned her halfway around and started to scrub her back.

"Good," she said. "You had me worried there for a moment."

It was a nice back, slender, full of fine muscles, nicely sculpted shoulder blades, tapered waist, trim rear end. I felt myself heat up at the silken feel of her body under my fingers.

"This still feels strange," I said. "You and me, here, like this."

"Uh-huh. Anything else?"

"It feels...good."

"Uh-huh. Anything else?"

"Better than good, okay?" I ran my hands up her sides, catching the weight of her breasts with my fingertips.

"There's hope for you yet," she said, shivering slightly.

"Okay. That's what I'll put in my report."

"You do that."

She lowered her head and sighed as I massaged her neck and shoulders. Her skin was smooth and slippery beneath the soap.

After a minute she spun suddenly and faced me. "Don't stop."

"What do you—?"

"I said don't stop, Mort."

I soaped her breasts, arms, belly. I felt her body tremble beneath my fingers. Her eyes were closed, back pressed against the warm tile wall, arms out to either side in a gesture of total surrender.

Exquisite. There was no other word for her. Years of dance had honed her, hardened her, made her sleek and smooth, alluring, erotic.

She arched her back. "There comes a magic moment," she said in a whisper, eyes still closed. That was all she said, but I thought I knew what she meant. Us, alone like this for however long we had, discovering unknown parts of ourselves in what amounted to the vastness of an improbable universe. I sensed the breathtaking awareness we had of each other, the aggression and yielding of sex, like complementary tides. All that and more.

After a while she opened her eyes and took the soap from me. "My turn."

"That might not be such a good idea, Kayla."

"Why not?...oh." She grinned. "You don't consider that a problem, do you?"

"It...it's, uh..."

"You're feeling a tiny bit obvious," she said. "Polarized."

"You might say that."

"At least you're nicely proportioned."

"Thanks a lot."

"Relax. This'll be good for you, Mort. Call it a mental health moment."

She pushed me against the wall and soaped me thoroughly from neck to toe, then concentrated her efforts, stopping two seconds short of tipping me over that final precipice.

She gave me an inquiring look. "More? Up to you."

"No," I answered breathlessly. "I'm fine."

"You sure? You don't sound like it. I'd be happy to work these suds around a while longer, get everything all spick-and-span here."

"I'm sure."

She arrowed her deep-blue eyes into my brown ones, drilling me. "Control is one of those double-edged swords, Mort. Women like it, don't like it. It might be a sign of respect, caring, something like that, but it also makes us wonder if we're not simply resistible."

"Resistible? You're absolutely intoxicating, woman."

"Nice to know." Her look told me she wasn't convinced.

"This...it's something we might share later, Kayla. If you want, I mean."

"I want."

"I wish I knew why."

"You're analyzing. That'll get you nowhere. You can't analyze white magic, pure awareness."

"White magic?"

"Sex. Ether waves. Cosmic ties. Vibrations."

I would've been a fool to try to analyze any of that. I kissed her. Her tongue darted across my teeth. "How about a rinse?" I asked.

She laughed. "Okay, Boy Scout. After I shampoo my hair, if you don't mind."

"I'll help."

"Please do."

The moment passed into a pleasant soapy interlude, a wet rambunctious sharing, visually pleasing, without the peakiness. At one point a nipple found its way into my mouth for fifteen or twenty seconds, but that was an accident. The undertow was still strong, however, still threatening. I could feel it pulling at me, wanting her. I could feel it pulling at her too, see it in her eyes. I found it utterly remarkable.

"What kind of dance do you teach?" I asked.

"Modern dance and jazz, dance composition."

"It's done wonders for you." I passed my hands along her sides, over the resilient sheath of muscle at her waist, then over the rounded swell of her hips.

"Thank you. If you keep that up I'll have to wrestle you to the floor. We might drown."

I quit, thinking I knew how to take a hint.

"You're so darned literal," she said, poking me in the belly. "Shower wrestling is a blast."

"It might lead to other things, though."

"Yeah? So?"

Back in the bedroom she crawled into bed and watched as I put on faded jeans and a short-sleeve shirt.

"Where to?" she asked, lying on her side, head propped up on an elbow.

"You wouldn't believe me if I told you."

"Try me."

I told her about Jeri, not all of it—meaning her gym and the way she bounced me around like a basketball—but enough. Kayla's eyes twinkled in amusement. "One private investigator hires another, then the whole thing gets yanked inside out. How fun."

"Dallas suggested it. Things got a little out of hand yesterday."

"How old is this Jeri person, Mort?"

"Closing in on thirty."

"She pretty?"

"Uh-huh."

"How pretty? I'm not being possessive, really."

"No?"

She made a face at me. "Nope. This morning was fun and I'm willing to do a lot more of it, but it certainly wasn't meant to tie you down. If you've got anything else, well...going."

"You're just naturally inquisitive, nothing more."

"Uh-huh."

"She's very pretty, strong as a freaking ox, and she made it clear she doesn't get involved with her clients."

"How about with her employees?"

"I got the impression her decree encompasses everyone on the planet right now."

"Mmm. Sounds like a little problem there."

"Could be. Not for me, though."

She sank back down, still looking at me. The sheet covered her to her waist. I tried not to stare, but finally gave up.

"So," she said, "where're the two of you off to this morning?"

"I haven't the slightest idea. It's Jeri's call. I could walk in and find myself unemployed."

"Her name just rolls off your tongue, Mort."

"Ms. DiFrazzia, then."

She gave me a drowsy smile. "Just kidding. You can call her Jeri. I'm not the jealous type."

* * *

Not the jealous type. Maybe. Some people are, some aren't, but few of those who are will admit it. And what did I know about Kayla? The shower was one thing, jealousy was another. And... what did it matter? Walking downhill toward Jeri's, I found myself as confused as ever about last night and this morning. I didn't know what Kayla wanted, down deep. I didn't know where we were headed, or if we were headed anywhere. I was in a wait-and-see mode, but I wasn't about to close any doors.

I'd given myself plenty of time to get to Jeri's. Too much. I arrived early, at 9:35. The front door was locked. One of those clock signs was in a window by the door, hands pointing to 10:00. I rang the bell but didn't hear anything. I waited, then went around the side. Through a half-open casement window I could see into Jeri's gym. She was there. Her back was to me. She was doing chin-ups, men's chin-ups, the hard way, palms forward, moving up and down like a tireless, infinitely clever mechanism. Every third rep she pulled the bar behind her neck, It was an uncanny sight, seeing a woman do that, back and arm muscles rippling beneath a light glaze of sweat. Pound for pound, she was a bobcat and I was an out-of-shape moose.

I counted twelve chin-ups before she finally slowed and dropped to the mat, landing as if on springs. I had no idea how many chin-ups she'd done before I started watching, but twelve of those killers was six or eight more than I could've done.

She turned, saw me, came to the window with a towel looped around her neck, smiling. "Good, you're early."

"Good?"

"Got something for you to do while I rinse off and get dressed."

"Yeah? What's that?"

"Come around front. I'll show you."

She unlocked the door and let me in. She wore a red-and-white striped exercise bra and jogging shorts, well-used sneakers. She looked good. She wasn't one of those female body builders, bulked up beyond all reason, past femininity into a nightmare of gristle and weird stringy cords. As a powerlifter, she had a weight class to maintain. Too much muscle mass would have worked against her. I supposed there was a fine line to be walked there.

"Over here," she said. She led me to her desk and handed me a job application, a 401(k) form, as if I were going to make enough to put anything away, a bond questionnaire, W-4.

"Oh, Christ, no."

"What?"

I sighed. "Nothing."

She put her hands on her hips. "I spent all yesterday afternoon rounding up that stuff, after I dropped you off."

"Aw, you shouldn't have."

"If I'm going to hire you, Mort—"

"Yeah? I'm hired?"

"Only if you fill out those damn forms. If you don't, you can go shovel snow."

"In July?"

"Not my problem." She didn't seem in the mood for humor.

"So, what's junior-level PI work pay these days?"

"Eighty bucks a day, take it or leave it."

"Great. Thirty-eight eighty more than minimum wage."

"Dallas told me you were like lightning with numbers. Don't plan on getting rich at this, Mort. It won't happen."

I shrugged. "So teach me. I'll get rich later."

"That's not likely either." She opened the door to the gym. "Try to get those filled out by the time I get back."

I sat at her desk in a swarm of rainbows. Christ, I should've Xeroxed the last batch of paperwork. It would've saved a lot of time.

She came back as I was finishing the last sonofabitching form. She had on white slacks and a sleeveless pale-yellow blouse, white sandals, coral-colored toenails, a patchwork handbag made up of swatches of pastel-colored leather cut into random shapes. She wore no makeup. Her dark hair was short and functional, still slightly damp. She was still gorgeous, still standoffish.

She glanced at the forms, shrugged, then stuffed them into a desk drawer. "I'll worry about these later," she said. "Let's go. We'll take my car."

As if we could take mine, which was still in that parking garage, maybe staked out by NBC's finest by now. "Where to?" I asked.

"Into the past, of course."

CHAPTER FOURTEEN

Well, yeah, of course.

Jeri didn't explain until we were doing fifty in a thirty zone with a red light half a block ahead. I braced myself. If Einstein was right, neither of us was aging quite as fast as the rest of the world. But then, Albert had never ridden with Jeri, so what did he know?

"What past?" I asked.

"Jonnie's and Milliken's."

"Okay," I said, still not getting it.

"The past creates the present," she said patiently. "Things don't happen in a vacuum. They happen because of things that happened before. Jonnie and Milliken died because of something that took place before they died, so that's where we look."

Okay, that made sense. It also had a Zen flavor, something to do with those rainbows floating around her office, the palmettos, the rubber tree plant, and the sultan pants she she had been wearing the day we'd met.

"They were both targets," Jeri said, decelerating fast enough that I thought the Porsche had popped a chute. I almost looked back to see. "Both of them. They disappeared within hours of each other, but at different places at different times under different circumstances. It's not as if one was attacked and the other happened to get in the way."

"That seems pretty obvious."

"Not to everyone, if you've been listening to the news this past week or to one of those dumb-ass talk shows."

I knew that, too. Theories were scurrying around like fleas on a scratching dog. You could choose from serial murder to the mafia, the IRS to Posse Comitatus to the John Birch Society. Space aliens on "Dreamland," if you were so inclined. A few people believed Jonnie and Milliken had been abducted and autopsied by creatures out of the black hole at the core of the galaxy. These people are allowed to vote, for God's sake, and their votes count as much as anyone's, which should give one pause.

"Jonnie disappeared right after speaking at a fundraiser at the Sparks Nugget," Jeri went on. "Milliken may or may not have made it home from his office that Friday night. No one knows since he's divorced and lives alone, but his face is well known and no one saw him anywhere around the Nugget that evening. All of which suggests a psycho with a specific reason for hitting them both."

"Or psychos."

She shook her head. "Don't count on it. All the world loves a conspiracy, but it's almost never true. You can't get two or more criminals to keep a secret for eight minutes. They're like lemmings. One look at a cliff and off they go."

The light changed. We whirled away with a double chirp of tires, one in first gear, another in second. "You look where the Easter bunny's most likely to have hidden the eggs," Jeri said.

"Right. Is that in the PI's manual?"

"Page two-fifteen, right next to 'If you hear hooves, think horses, not zebras.'"

"I've heard that one. It's been a big help in my life."

She stared at me. "What we've got to do is find the link between Jonnie and Milliken."

"There are probably hundreds."

"I said *the* link. The thing that got them killed."

"Which could be almost anything."

"Just about," she admitted. "It's a crazy damn world out there." She pulled a moustache the size of a clothes brush out of the glove compartment and handed it to me. "Here, put this on. I don't want to have to explain you to anyone."

* * *

She gave me a dishwater-blond wig, too—shaggy, unkempt hair, telling me it was borrowed so don't lose it. Who would want it back? I wanted to give it a bath and a name, but we spotted three news vans before we'd gone a mile, so I wore the damn thing. The moustache was the same color, entirely hiding my upper lip.

"They had screws in their nuts," Jeri said while we waited at a light at First and Sierra, engine rumbling impatiently.

"Huh?" I stared at her.

"Jonnie and Dave. I spoke with Ben last night, way off the record. He was jumpy, but happy that we'd salvaged his job for him."

"After almost losing it for him," I said. Jeri brushed the comment aside with a wave of her hand.

"What do you mean, screws?" I asked.

"Standard drywall screws. Three inch. Twisted through their scrotums, right through their cojones."

"Aw, jeez."

"According to Ben, Boyce says it was the only thing keeping their nuts in the sac."

"This's a nice, uplifting conversation."

"Maybe I should leave you in the dark where you belong."

"That sonofabitch Boyce held out on us."

The light changed. The Porsche shot forward, across Sierra. "They always hold out, Mort. It's how they are. If that surprises you, you're probably not cut out for PI work."

"I'm learning."

She looked over at me. "Maybe." She was silent for a moment. "One of Jonnie's eyes had been put out, too. The left. Before he died."

"Sounds like the mayor had a real bad day."

Our first stop was the courthouse, fictitious names department. I followed Jeri in, looking around to see if anyone was laughing hysterically at my disguise, but no one gave me a second glance.

Jeri spent several minutes chatting with a woman her own age behind a counter, ignoring me. I tried to look inconspicuous, thinking about someone putting screws through Sjorgen's balls. A mist of sweat broke out on my forehead at the thought. Jeri finally paid a pair of six-dollar fees and got printouts of local businesses in which either Sjorgen or Milliken had had an interest.

Outside, in the Porsche, she studied them for a while then handed the sheets to me. "Remember 'em," she said, firing up the engine, backing out.

I looked them over. Sjorgen & Howard Title Co. headed Jonnie's list. He also had full or partial interest in Sjorgen Fence Co., the Silver Lode Motel, Jade Motel, K&S Vending Co., River Bend Trailer Park, and Sjorgen Restaurant Supply. Milliken's only business venture was as a junior partner in W. B. Rennie Construction Company in Sparks. In fact, I'd heard all these names on TV, but now we had hard copies with filing dates, names of corporate officers where applicable, addresses, and the law firms that had set up the corporations and filed the paperwork, none of which looked useful to me. Maybe that was why I was in training.

Minutes later we ended up at the *Reno Gazette-Journal*, in the morgue where microfiche and DVDs of back issues are kept. No one recognized me in the wig, which I found amazing until I saw myself in a restroom mirror sometime later and didn't recognize myself.

"No hassles, they just let you in here?" I peered around the room. A fluorescent fixture buzzed, blinking on and off.

"A PI's license helps. But it's connections and schmoozing that does the trick in places like this. And not making trouble."

I didn't say anything to that.

"And not making trouble," she repeated, eyes locked on mine. "In case you were thinking about removing the wig. Or the 'stache."

"Yeah, schmoozing. I got that."

She sighed. "It goes with the job. You'll find out."

The morgue held an ancient microfiche reader and drawers of canisters. The microfiche reader was a relic now, inactive, a museum piece, the information having been transferred years ago to CDs, then to DVDs. Now the news was beamed daily or even hourly into electronic storage with a few clicks of a mouse—or instantly and automatically, no human intervention needed. Six computers set up to read DVDs took up one wall of the room, and dozens of drawers of DVDs, catalogued by date, going back over fifty years. A pleasant-looking Hispanic girl, Maria, twenty-five years old, pretty and plump, was nominally in charge of the place. A few people drifted in and out, unearthing little-known facts of yesteryear to plug into today's news.

"How far in the past are we digging?" I asked Jeri.

"Not far. Jonnie and Dave were abducted two weeks ago. Whatever started all this probably didn't happen much before then. Someone was pissed off. Pissed-off psychos don't usually wait very long to spring into action."

"Any idea what we're looking for?"

She shrugged. "Something a mayor and district attorney were in together? Something political? Who knows? Anything that might get someone's back up."

"That leaves the field wide open."

"Just keep an open mind, Mort."

We sat side by side at two computers in a quiet corner. The most recent stuff was on servers, immediately accessible. I started back six weeks, and Jeri went back three. "Front page local news," she said. "Any local stuff in the Nevada section, especially if it's political. And the local business pages. Don't bother with anything national and international."

"Pretty exciting work. Where's my nitro?"

The look she gave me would've done Greg proud. She might've been his twin sister. "Detective work is 99.9 percent dead flat boring, Mort. Clues aren't going to come whistling past your ears. You have to dig for 'em. If you're looking for excitement, alligator wrestling is a good bet, or flying a single-engine plane low over the White House."

Greg couldn't have said it better.

We sat in silence for a while, scanning stories, finding nothing, then an idea occurred to me. I turned to Jeri, keeping my voice low. "Greg didn't have a penis in his skull."

"Jesus, Mort. So what?"

"So maybe his killer was a copycat."

She looked at me for several seconds. "I guess that's possible. What's the point?"

"Maybe someone took advantage of the situation, knew he'd been hired to look into Jonnie and Dave's murders so they killed him the same way, but that person didn't know about the penis thing so they blew it."

"You mean like Dale."

"Not hardly. I was thinking his wife, Libby. Greg might've told her what he was up to."

"Do you have any idea how much easier it is to divorce someone in this state than to cut off their head? You're thinking zebras, Mort."

"Greg goes out, then winds up dead, but he might not've run into Jonnie's killer."

"Terrific. But the fact is we're trying to find *Jonnie's* killer, so I repeat, what's the point—other than if we follow in your nephew's footsteps it might not lead us in the right direction?"

"Well," I said, "that's the point." At least I hoped so. Sometimes I don't make points. Sometimes I ramble and, with luck, points appear.

"Which doesn't help us one bit with Jonnie and Milliken, does it? Do you have an attention-span problem, Mort? A.D.D., maybe? Can I get you coffee or a Red Bull?"

"I've tracked tax evaders through two-hundred-page forms using a sixty-pound tax code jam-packed with redundant and conflicting information."

"Good work. Try to harness that pent-up concentration, huh?"

I went back to the computer. Jeri wrote on a notepad. Cracking this thing wide open, no doubt, while I was staring at a development deal okayed by the city council in which Jonnie Sjorgen had cast the deciding vote—a subdivision in north Reno, slated for 160 homes.

I kept reading. The moustache itched like a sonofabitch. I was thinking about stuffing it up someone's ass, but that someone would probably body slam me into next week if I so much as hinted at where the moustache rightfully belonged, let alone tried it.

The subdivision developer was W. B. Rennie. Milliken was a junior partner in W.B. Rennie, Inc.

"Ah-hah."

Jeri looked up. "Ah-hah?"

I showed her the article. When she had the gist of it, I said, "Jonnie ends up okaying a deal in which his old friend Milliken has an interest. The good-old-boy network pisses off a rabid no-growther who happens to own a Craftsman sabre saw."

"Possible," Jeri said doubtfully.

At least she didn't laugh outright in my face. "What've you got?" I asked.

"Nothing yet."

We kept at it for another hour and a half, then called it quits. One item of note: Milliken's office had dropped burglary charges against one Jason Kimball, age nineteen, who happened to be the nephew of one of Reno's city council members, Janet Cushing. Earlier, I'd come across a picture of Jonnie and Janet and others at a ribbon-cutting ceremony for a newly renovated bridge across the Truckee River.

"It's thin," Jeri said. "Practically vapor."

Felt that way to me, too. But vapor isn't exactly nothing, it's just the next best thing.

We went outside, blinking in the sunlight. The temperature was up around a hundred. I walked with her across heat-softened asphalt to her car.

"Where to now?" I asked as we got in.

The top was down on the Porsche. Jeri sat there, engine off. We were chilled from the news morgue, which was kept cool to keep the computers happy. She looked at me. "I've been thinking... Jonnie and Milliken went to Reno High together."

"Yep."

"Maybe there's something in that. A connection of some kind."

"Long time ago. Forty years. It's been in the news ad nauseam. There's nothing new in that, if we're looking for something new."

"Maybe they were more than friends."

I laughed. "No way. Jonnie was about to marry my ex. The evil bastard."

"I don't mean friends like that, dummy."

"Okay. How *do* you mean?"

"You never know till you find out." She fired up the Porsche and headed out of the lot, turned left onto Kirman. "Hungry?"

"I could eat."

"I know a place. Since it's your first day on the job, I'll buy."

* * *

Here's a rule of thumb: never eat at a place that has six different tofu entrées on the menu. The Dancing Hippo on California Avenue was one of those mom-and-pop health food places, run by a hippyish couple in their sixties who'd most likely named it while in the throes of something psychedelic and illegal, like non-standard mushrooms. The Hippo serves nothing but twelve-grain breads, alfalfa sprouts, sautéed tofu and veggies, things like that. Forget beef. Forget anything substantial. Forget anything a reasonable person might call food. The work of local artists festooned the walls, for sale at prices that made my eyes bulge. The clientele was anorexic, rich, pampered, neurotic, 97 percent female, encased in silk and leather, and wearing shoes that would make a convention of podiatrists rise up en masse and sing hallelujah. At least no one in the place was smoking.

The restaurant also sold T-shirts with pirouetting hippos on the front, like the one Edna had been wearing in that attic bedroom. I kept looking around, expecting to see Victoria and Winter walk in and take a table.

I had something called a Haight-Ashbury, if that tells a story. It tasted okay, but it didn't fill me up and it wasn't fun trying to shove it past my moustache, either. I didn't tell Jeri it wasn't filling because she might've bought me some form of tofu, which is what she had. It looked like processed, bleached pond scum with a side of crabgrass.

At two forty-five we were at Reno High. School was out for the summer, but a skeleton staff was manning the admin office, admitting kids for the upcoming school year, keeping the paper-work moving. Jeri spoke to a lady in her fifties, Mrs. Nordmeyer. Rose-tinted glasses hung from her neck on a beaded chain. She was in a storeroom next door, inventorying beat-up geometry textbooks that looked as if the students had tried to get at the knowledge by grinding it between their molars, a relatively new approach that I thought might show promise.

"Yearbooks?" Mrs. Nordmeyer asked, putting down a clipboard.

Jeri smiled schmoozingly. "Yes."

"Let me guess. Forty years ago, thereabouts."

"We're not the first ones to have asked," Jeri replied.

"More like the fifth. CBS had a gal drop by. And NBC, CNN, *Associated Press*, and the police." She pursed her lips. "Which would make you the sixth, not that it matters."

"Do you keep yearbooks that far back?"

"Oh, yes. And much further, if you want them. We were the first high school in the city."

She led us into a small room off the main office, full of boxes of documents or forms, old trophies, American and Nevada flags, dust, cobwebs, and three shelves of yearbooks spanning decades.

"These'll be the ones you're interested in," she said, pulling four of them off the shelf. "Seventy-one to seventy-four, the years Jonnie Sjorgen and Dave Milliken were here." She gave us an apologetic look. "I'm sorry, but I'll have to hold a driver's license while you look at them. Mrs. Osmetti, that's the principal, she insists on it."

Jeri handed over her license, then we sat down at a table in a conference room beside the principal's office.

1974, senior pictures in faded color. Jonnie was a roguish, good-looking kid of eighteen with an easy, confident grin and a devil-may-care lock of black hair curling over his forehead. Even back then he probably spent half an hour a day getting that curl just right. Under his picture was a lengthy caption: Senior class president, varsity football, track. Honor Society, debate club, yearbook staff, theater. Nickname, "Zonker." Favorite expression: "Yo, dude." Future plans: Harvard.

Harvard. In the footsteps of his old man. "Busy boy back then," I said, "was Zonker."

Jeri made a face at the name.

David Milliken wasn't as pretty, but he had a serious face. He looked like a future district attorney. Varsity letters in basketball and tennis. Spanish club, chess club, yearbook staff, Honor Society. Nickname, "Spider," favorite expression, "groovy," an indication of how much times had changed since then. Nothing was groovy now. Future plans: Princeton.

Not a hint that these two would one day be found decapitated, or that one Mortimer Angel, who was wearing rubber pants and eating Gerber's at the time the pictures were taken, would do the finding.

"Good-looking boys," Jeri observed.

I grunted.

"Both of them were on the yearbook staff," Jeri said, "so I'll bet we'll find lots of pictures of them in here."

She flipped pages, found Jonnie grinning in the group picture on the Huskies football team. And another shot of him, obviously faked, catching a football.

"Interesting stuff," I said.

Jeri thumped the pages with a finger. "These are the people who knew Jonnie back when. A few of them are probably still in the area."

"Tracking them down sounds like a major pain-in-the-ass dead end, Jeri."

"You never know till you try. It's called investigation. You seem to be having trouble with the concept."

"It just sounds tedious and not very likely to lead anywhere."

"True. Not everyone is cut out for this line of work." She gave me a significant look, then went back to the book. She found Jonnie in the debate team photo, giving the camera another wide, over-the-top grin. His teeth looked great.

Dave Milliken on the basketball team, an all-star, making a jump shot, lanky, number thirty-three.

King Jonnie in a tux with the homecoming queen, Sarah Jean Humbolt, a willowy, radiant blond holding roses, wearing a glittering crown and a blazing smile.

Jonnie in the school play, Dicken's *A Christmas Carol*. He'd played the ghost of Christmas past. A boy named Donald Helm had been Scrooge.

Jonnie, Dave, and seventeen others in the yearbook staff photo, a horsing-around, laughing shot, eight guys, eleven girls. Jonnie was giving one of the guys a pair of rabbit ears.

Jonnie and Dave in a big varsity-sweater shot. Jonnie on the track team. Honor Society group photo on the front lawn of the school, with Jonnie and Dave, Sarah Jean, forty-odd others.

And that was the end of the book.

"Now what?" I asked.

"Now we study it," Jeri said.

"Again?"

"What do you mean again? All we did was browse. Now we get to work."

I sighed. My own yearbook lists me as a dumb-ass football player with plans for the NFL, nickname "Bullwinkle." No Honor Society. Embarrassing if I thought anyone looked at that stuff these days.

Jeri shoved the '73 yearbook at me. "Here, make yourself useful."

"What'm I looking for?"

"Names. Connections. Try to think outside the box, Mort."

"Outside the box. Gotcha."

I went through it. Jonnie and Dave's junior year. Jonnie was still prominent, but not as much. A different yearbook staff had put it together. He'd been junior class president. Debate club, theater, lettered in his sports. One stray picture, taken in a crowded hallway, showed him with an arm over the shoulders of a dark-haired girl, but it didn't give names. I found her in the junior class photos. Clair Albrecht. And I found Sarah Jean Humbolt, one year younger but still homecoming-queen beautiful.

"Clair Albrecht," I said.

"Huh?"

I showed Jeri the relevant pictures. She found Clair in the '74 yearbook. Dave and Jonnie's senior year. Nickname "Shooey." Future plans: junior college, marriage.

Marriage to whom, it didn't say. It was likely she was figuring some guy would eventually ask, at which time she would naturally say yes.

Jeri turned a few pages. "Thought so," she said, pointing to a theater photo. Jonnie, Sarah, Dave, Clair. Clair was smiling, leaning on Milliken's back. He was in a crouch. Jonnie had a possessive arm around Sarah Humbolt's waist.

Jeri turned to another page. Milliken and Clair were eating lunch together, caught wide-eyed by someone's candid camera.

"Fun years," I said.

"It tells a story, Mort," Jeri said. "Clair was Jonnie's girl-friend in '73, then it was Sarah Jean in '74. And Clair was with Milliken that year." She stared at me. "You ever swap girlfriends, Mortimer?"

"Do I look like the type?"

"When'd you graduate? Ninety, ninety-one?"

"Ninety-two."

She nodded. "Drugs rampant in the schools, like they are today. Getting up a good head of steam in Sjorgen's day, all that hippie-era stuff, especially when he was a freshman. You ever get into any of that?"

"What, tie-dye, the hippie culture, free love? All of that was way before my time."

"I mean drugs, Mort."

"Uh-uh. Football. Half a six pack of Bud on the weekends. That was about it."

"Regular Boy Scout, huh?"

Kayla had said almost the same thing. When you hear some-thing like that more than once in a decade it's like a trumpet call, time to take notice. Coming from Jeri, though, I had no idea what to make of it.

She found another photograph of Sarah Jean, this one in a gym class with a girl we identified as Meredith Boyle—nickname "Merry," what else?—even though her hair was different in the senior pictures. From their pose it looked as if they were friends. They were giving the camera peace signs with both hands. An odd echo of the Vietnam War. Hell no, we won't go. Maybe it meant something else in '74.

We accumulated names, keeping at it until nearly five o'clock when Mrs. Nordmeyer came in to tell us the school was locking its doors in a few minutes.

Jeri got her license back, thanked her, and we left. I wondered if Jeri's approach to the yearbook information had been different to that of the police, or CNN, or any of the others. No way of knowing, of course, but I felt as if we'd been knocking on old back doors, listening to whispers, catching glimpses of long-departed ghosts. On the way back to her office I said, "Think you can track down any of those people?"

"It's possible. The girls' last names have probably changed. Odds are they've changed more than once, in fact, but there are ways."

She did it via the Internet. She got into Washoe County records and pulled up marriage info from the middle seventies to the early nineties. I stuck the moustache to a potted plant when Jeri wasn't looking and hung the wig on an old-fashioned coat rack. All that hair was bugging the hell out of me. I felt like I'd spent the day wearing spiderwebs.

"Forty years ago this would've been impossible," Jeri said. "It was all tons and tons of paper, microfiche, basements and warehouses crammed full of records. Then along came computers, scanners, software that could read typewritten text. You probably did stuff like this with the IRS, right?"

"Not personally, no."

"But you *have* heard of the Internet?"

"Sort of rings a bell. Me, I was more a go-through-the-shoebox and total-up-the-receipts kind of guy. I wasn't a techno-agent. But anything that helps the IRS hunt down tax evaders is a tool. The Internet is like one big playground to the backroom boys. We had guys who did nothing but target blogs, if you can believe that. Idiots paying taxes on an income of fifty thousand dollars who brag about their seventy-foot yachts."

"So you're not completely illiterate."

"Not completely, just the next best thing."

Jeri nodded at the screen. "Thing is, they scanned all the old records, which must've been a boring-ass minimum-wage job, but there wasn't any easy way to check the results for accuracy, so now the records are full of weird errors, like Smith coming out Zmith or Smifh, things like that. Better than nothing, but it sure ain't perfect."

In less than fifteen minutes, however, she'd found Clair Albrecht, who'd said yes to a Carl Schembri one year out of high school, and Meredith Boyle, who had married Richard Young. No record of Sarah Jean Humbolt.

So many names. My stomach growled. The Haight-Ashbury was long gone. We were light-years from Jonnie's killer and speeding around in circles, chasing our tails.

"Hang it up?" I suggested.

"That's not how it's done," Jeri replied.

"You get hold of that bone and gnaw it to splinters, huh?"

"That's right. You're making hungry references. Want a sandwich or something?"

"Or something."

She nodded toward a door, not the one to her gym. "Kitchen's back that way. Go have a look."

I went. Down a hallway and into an arboretum of fruit hanging in wire baskets. Strainers and copper pans dangled from a pot rack hanging from the ceiling, wooden spoons sprouted from jars, spider plants, ivy, prayer plants. Afternoon light spilled in through windows that were as clean as the ones at my house.

Either she was a cook, or she liked the ambience.

I found sprouted wheat bread in the refrigerator, eight kinds of cheese, brie, gorgonzola, sliced turkey. I went out front and asked Jeri if she wanted anything. She shook her head, concentrating on one little dead-end cul-de-sac of the information superhighway.

I made up a three-layer Dagwood slathered with low-cal mayonnaise, Grey Poupon, a dash of oregano, and came back. Jeri stared at it, then at me.

"Clair Albrecht-Schembri divorced Carl Schembri and married Alan DeMeo back in '78," she said.

"Uh-huh. Good deal. Schembri didn't last long."

Exasperated, she said, "DeMeo's not a common name, Mort."

"Neither is Schembri."

She looked at me, amazed at the sheer length and breadth of my density. "But her name is *DeMeo*. The point is, it's not Jones or Smith or Johnson. And both times she got married here in Washoe County, so she might've stuck around."

I picked up a phone book. A few DeMeos, but no Alan, no Clair or C.

Jeri got into the DMV database. No Clair DeMeo in their records either.

"Dead end?" I asked.

"Not necessarily, but it'll take more work."

"Why bother?"

She shrugged. "You never know which lead will take you through that golden door."

"I suppose that's in the PI manual, too."

She ignored me and consulted her notes. "Now we try Meredith Young. Or Richard."

They weren't in the phone book. Jeri went back to her computer.

I picked up the phone book and looked up Schembri. And there it was, Carl and Joyce. How many Carl Schembris could there be?

I picked up the phone and dialed.

"Who're you calling?" Jeri asked.

"Carl."

"Carl—?"

I held up a hand. The phone was ringing. A man answered on the third ring. "Yeah?"

"Hello, is this Carl Schembri?"

"Yeah, who's this?"

Not the friendliest of voices. "Mortimer Angel," I said, taking what I knew was a hell of a risk. After all, I was nouveau infamous.

"You're shittin' me," he said, and then Jeri grabbed the phone out of my hand.

"Mr. Schembri, this's Ms. Jeri DiFrazzia. Yeah, no, it was...yes, really. I...look, I...okay." She handed the phone back to me. "He wants to talk to you."

I took the phone. "Mr. Schembri?"

"You kiddin'? You're Mortimer Angel?"

"Yep. Call me Mort."

"No shit. Jesus Christ, no shit. Seen you on TV about every night this week, man."

"Uh-huh." Jeri jammed her ear next to mine, trying to listen in. I caught a whiff of perfume or hairspray, something feminine, clean and flowery.

"No shit, goddamn," Schembri said. "Uh, so why're you calling me?" A hint of paranoia crept into his voice.

"It's about Clair. I'm trying to locate her."

"Clair?"

"You were married to her."

Silence. Then, "Christ, *that* Clair. That was a coon's age ago, buddy."

"Do you know where she is now?"

"Hell, yes. Down in Carson. Name's Hutson now, Mrs. Howard Hutson."

"Uh, not DeMeo?"

"A million years ago, yeah. DeMeo was her second husband. A first-class dumb shit, I'll tell you. We worked in Harrah's together. Then it was Briscoe, then Hutson. Still is, last I heard. He's a lost-cause dumb shit too, in case you're interested. You gonna go talk to her?"

"I thought I'd try."

"Better wear earmuffs, then. If she can still fire that sucker up, that is."

I didn't try to decipher that. He didn't have an address for Clair Hutson, but Jeri would have that in no time. I thanked him, hung up.

"That schlub probably thinks he's God's gift," Jeri said as she finished writing. She stared at her notepad. "Schembri, then DeMeo, then Briscoe, then Hutson."

"Tells a story, doesn't it?"

"Yeah," she said. "Men are pigs."

"Ah—a clue comes a-whistlin' on little airy feet." I tried to put the comment to iambic pentameter for her. Succeeded, too.

"Lay off, Mort." She opened the phone book.

"Clair's bouncing around like that couldn't possibly mean she's the one with the problem, huh?"

"Her problem is that she always comes back for more."

That was a door slamming if I've ever heard one. "Now what?" I said.

"Now we go talk to Clair." Jeri found Hutson in the phone book and wrote down the address. Only one Hutson lived in Carson City.

"That's thirty-plus miles," I said. "And thirty back," I added to be clear. "It's getting late. How about we go tomorrow?"

"Tomorrow I've got to work on something else. Sunday, too. I'll have to put this thing with Sjorgen and Milliken on a back burner for a few days. Let's go now."

"Wouldn't it be a lot easier to phone?"

"No. They can hang up on you. And you can't see their eyes, so it's harder to tell if they're lying." She headed for the door. "And I want to blow out the engine. You comin' or not?"

* * *

I'd figured she'd been blowing out the Porsche's engine every time a hundred yards of road opened up ahead. I was wrong. We hit a hundred thirty on that straight stretch of 395 through Washoe Valley. The Toyota couldn't do that in freefall, though I'd be willing to give it a try. Not in it, of course.

"Jesus, Jeri..."

She gave me a still-angry look, then eased it back to ninety. By then I'd gained another second of life on Einstein's clock, lost two years on the only one I care about—my own.

"What's got you so pissed off?" I asked her.

"I'm not pissed off," she said, sounding pissed off.

"If you say so."

She was silent for nearly two minutes, then she let the Porsche drift down to barely seventy. "It's not you," she said quietly.

"Yeah? Who is it?"

"Not you."

I guessed that was something of an apology. For what, I wasn't sure.

Clair Hutson lived in a sweltering, seventy-year-old ranch house that needed painting, a new roof, and about ten thousand dollars in miscellaneous outside repairs. Her face said she'd been smoking two packs a day since those halcyon days at Reno High. It was cool at eighteen, but addictive in spite of being cool. Carbon monoxide eventually catches up. She was fifty-nine, looked seventy-five. Not a trace of that long-ago girl remained. She was stringy and dry, hair lifeless, fighting a growing case of emphysema.

She didn't recognize me in the wig Jeri made me put on again, but I had the moustache jammed in a pocket like a dead rat. I'd had it with fake moustaches.

"Jonnie Sjorgen," Clair sneered. "The oh-so-great mayor." She stood in the doorway, not inviting us in. Behind her, the room was dark, shades pulled. A swamp cooler rumbled, filling the house with cool damp air. Howard Hutson stood two feet behind her holding a beer. He had a gut the size of a shoat, three chins, stubble, lots of nose hair. He stood flatfooted in grimy socks, blinking stupidly at us. If eighteen-year-old Clair had known it would come to this, she would have slit her wrists the day she walked off that stage in cap and gown.

"Did you know him well?" Jeri asked.

"Too well," Clair replied.

"What can you tell me about him?"

"You're the first to ask." For a moment something younger was in her voice. It was softer, filled with a kind of hunger. At long last, someone was giving her a little recognition. "No one else has thought to care. How'd you find me, anyhow?"

"Just ordinary detective work, Mrs. Hutson."

"It was Carl told you, wasn't it?"

"Well, yes."

"That son'vabitch. He okay?"

"He sounded okay. We just spoke with him over the phone."

Clair's eyes shifted to me, then back to Jeri. A vindictive light came into her eyes. "Jonnie raped Sarah Jean," she said in a husky smoker's rasp, enunciating each word with the utmost care. "Least he tried. Got her drunk and tried. He almost made it, too. No one called it rape or attempted rape, though. Not Wendell Sjorgen's kid. Not our class fucking president."

"When was that?"

She thought a moment. "Guess it would've been the last month or two of school. Senior year."

"How did you find out?"

"Sarah Jean told me, of course. She wasn't a liar or anything. If she said it happened, it happened. She managed to fight him off. He didn't get her so drunk she passed out, which was a damn good thing 'cause Jonnie wouldn't have had a problem with that. He was a bastard, once you got to know him, but back then he was the Prize. All the girls loved him. He was mine for a while—in my junior year. *Zonker.* God, all us girls were as dumb as fucking cows. Sarah Jean got him, senior year. Then they elected him mayor, because he's got all those faces."

"Faces?"

"Like one of those lizard things, changes color all the time. Sneaky fuck." She looked straight at me. "If he'd tried it with me, I would've ripped his balls off."

CHAPTER FIFTEEN

BUT JONNIE HADN'T tried it with Clair back then, and last month he wouldn't have touched her with tongs and rubber gloves. He wouldn't have recognized her, wouldn't have given her a second glance. He had Dallas, the woman I love.

Jeri dropped me off at the Grand Sierra and told me to be at her office at nine on Monday. "And don't horse around with this Sjorgen thing until then, okay?"

"Horse around?"

"You know what I mean. Too much can go wrong. We'll pick up where we left off."

I thanked her profusely for the vote of confidence. She gave me one last warning look, then sped away. I went up to Room 1122. I hadn't seen Dallas in a while. I wanted to make sure she was okay.

She was reading a magazine, dressed in white slacks and a teal blouse, bare feet. I love the shape of her feet, ankles, all of her. She gave me a stunned look until I remembered the wig. I took it off, tossed it on a chair. I didn't give her the blow-by-blow about the Clair Albrecht-Schembri-DeMeo-Briscoe-Hutson circus, because it was too big a mouthful, and dredging up the past for Dallas would have been stirring up ancient muck to no purpose. Nor would it have made her life better or protected her from anything. And how much did I trust anything Clair had to say? Not much.

"Getting anywhere yet?" Dallas asked. God, she looked great.

"No," I said.

"How's Jeri? She a good investigator?"

"Better than me. A little slow at finding people, though. I'll be a terrific addition to her agency."

"Would you like to stay the night, Mort?"

Yes, of course. "I can't."

She tilted her head at me. "Kay?"

I shrugged.

"Is that a yes?"

"I don't know what it is." Nor was this the time to tell her who K was. That was Kayla's call, but I wondered how often they'd met. After all, Kayla was the daughter of the guy Dallas had been thinking of marrying, a twist I found more than a little unsettling. It wasn't that Kayla wasn't old enough. I was only seven years older. It was the sum total of our tangled relationships that made my relationship with Kayla, such as it was, seem weird. Which wasn't her fault, or mine.

"If there was any hope for us, Dal..."

"It's okay, Mort, really."

Good enough. I can take a hint. She still liked me, maybe even a lot, but that was all. I flushed the moustache down the toilet, put on the wig, rode the elevator to ground level, caught the airport shuttle to Reno-Tahoe International where I caught another shuttle over to the Golden Goose. All in all, a poor man's taxi service, but...why not?

From the Goose I walked home through sulfur-yellow pools of high-pressure sodium lights. A vermilion sunset glowed through the leaves of trees. Two vans were still out front. Only two. Without new grist they were starting to back-burner the story. Even so, I went through Velma's yard and through the fence.

Kayla wasn't in. She'd left a note:

Out walking, back in a while, K.

Out walking. I didn't know if that was such a good idea. If I found her head anywhere I would go live in Bolivia and call myself Pepe. Or something. Maybe Helmut.

I pulled drapes across the windows and turned on lights. It was my house. If a media type came to the door, I was prepared to escort him or her back to the sidewalk in a highly aerobic manner. Perhaps I gave off warning vibrations, because no one knocked or rang the bell.

I took a long shower. Still no Kayla.

I read for a while, then went to bed. Still no Kayla.

She came in while Leno was ignoring me for the second straight night—fine with me. I was stretched out, covered by only a sheet in the night's heat, drowsy, about ready to pack it in.

"Hi," she said, gazing at me from the doorway.

"Hi yourself." I hit the remote, killing the TV.

"You naked?" she asked.

"If you can't tell, then I'm not."

"I mean, if I yanked that sheet off you."

"What's it to ya, kiddo?"

"Okay, don't tell me. I'll find out for myself soon enough."

"Where've you been?"

"All over. Down to Meadowood, over to Sparks. Back again. No one's looking for me, at least not here. I guess I put in about twenty miles."

"Twenty! You walked twenty miles?"

"Uh-huh, thereabouts. I'm not used to being cooped up. I have to move. You weren't around. Once the sun got low, I left."

"Twenty!"

"It's no big deal, Mort. It felt good." She gave me an expectant look. "I need a shower, though."

"Right there at the end of the hall where we left it."

"How 'bout you?"

"Took one already, thanks."

"Spoilsport. Look what I bought." She held up a paper bag.

"What'cha got there?"

"A five-watt bulb and a yard of red silk."

"Oh, jeez."

"Here." She dropped the bag on the bed. "See if you can figure what to do with this."

She left. After a minute the water came on. I unscrewed the bulb in the lamp that we hadn't destroyed the night before and put her bulb in, draped the silk over the shade. I could imagine her in there, soapy and wet. I could go in. I was invited. It would be fun. I turned on the lamp and the room glowed crimson. I lay back. The shower ended. I heard the sound of a toothbrush churning away.

She came into the room wearing a towel, hair damp and tousled. She yawned, then smiled. "Hey, you figured it out. Just look at this place."

"Yeah, look at it."

She unwound the towel and draped it over the back of a chair. For an instant I had a vision of Dallas in the shower—and Winter, slinky in her unhooked bra and lace thong panties.

"Every time I turn around," I said, "someone's either naked or darn near."

Kayla tilted her head at me. "Is that a fact?"

"Recently, yes."

"Is it becoming a problem?"

"Not so far. I think it's a PI thing."

She smiled. "A private dick thing?"

I peered at her through one eye. "Private investigator, yeah. I've been thinking it might have something to do with that."

She stared at the bed. "Which side's mine? Same as last night?"

"Take your pick."

She crawled in, lifted my right arm and put it over her shoulders, snuggled up next to me. For a while we lay like that, comfortable, neither one of us moving, then her face turned toward mine. Her eyes had what I misinterpreted as a sultry look. She said, "I've...uh, got a tiny request. If you can stand it."

"Lucky you, this is request night. And during happy hour, drinks are half price."

"You're going to absolutely strangle me."

"I doubt it. With the IRS it's blunt trauma or nothing."

She touched the tip of my nose with her finger. "Could we...do whatever we're going to do later, like in the morning? I'm pretty tired. It'd be a lot better then."

"Sure." Not sultry, Great Gumshoe, sleepy. She walked twenty miles, for chrissake.

"You don't mind?"

"No."

She got up on one elbow and gazed into my eyes. "Mean it?"

"Know what happens if you can't shake the money out of your piggy bank, so you bust it open to get at the loot?"

"I think I see where this is going."

"You get your dollar eighty-five, and a busted piggy bank. One you can never use again."

"How ineffably wise you are, sir."

"You are lovely, Kayla."

"Wise, perceptive, and, well, extremely...something."

"I mean it. You are incredible."

"Maybe sneaky," she said. "I'll have to keep that in mind." She sank back down and rested her head on my shoulder. Her hands toyed with the hair on my chest for half a minute, then went slack. A minute later she was sound asleep.

I was tired, too. I tried to sleep, but things began to putter around in my head.

Events, numbers. One number in particular. Forty. Forty years ago, according to Clair, Jonnie attempted to force sex with Sarah Jean Humbolt. Call it rape. He might have tried to get her drunk in order to accomplish it. A year after that, thirty-nine years ago—enough of a coincidence to at least give a gumshoe pause—Wendell Sjorgen had in effect turned over his house to Edna Woolley and moved out.

But why? Why would he do that?

Did he have a thing going with Edna back then? Hard to say. She would have been nearing sixty. He would have been forty-five, fifty tops. It wasn't likely. Then Edna had gotten the house, and Jane, Wendell's wife, had divorced him soon thereafter.

The answers, whatever they might be, felt as much a dead end as the merry-go-round I'd been on with Jeri all day. What did it matter?

Kayla stirred, murmured something and put a cool hand on my groin, then promptly fell asleep again, leaving my body to undergo a pleasant but not particularly useful transformation.

I didn't love Kayla, but I liked her. A lot. She was bright and sunny and warm, playful. Maybe I could love her. Probably could, and easily. I could get over Dallas, or maybe love them both. And maybe this was just one of those wonderful but temporary things. Kayla would go back to New York, Ithaca, and that would be that. There was something of the whirlwind in her being there, one of those things you have to catch up to. A woman in your bed isn't something you understand overnight, or even in a month.

Sometimes, after a lifetime, you find you still don't know the why of it. It's another kind of white magic.

I turned off the lamp and closed my eyes.

I was half asleep when another thought came tiptoeing through. Fairchild's words, which had also replayed in Jonnie's office at Sjorgen & Howard Title Company: The most likely person to commit murder is a family member of the victim.

The people who know you best.

Kayla was Jonnie's closest living relative. But, hell, no goddamn way...it couldn't be her, not this lovely creature beside me. I put it out of my mind.

* * *

I woke up at 7:25. Kayla was still out cold. I lay there for half an hour, thinking alternately of the number forty and Kayla's body, then got up quietly and dressed out in the living room when Kayla's body started to win. I was in the kitchen watching a Mr. Coffee slowly drip caffeine into a pot clouded to opacity with various minerals when she came in, barefoot, wearing only a shirt. One of my shirts, in fact, with the top three buttons undone, making it something of a negligee. It reached to mid-thigh. Two of her could have fit inside with room to spare.

"You escaped," she said.

"I was awake, you weren't."

"About last night, I'm sorry."

I offered her my arms. She came into them and gave me a hug during which I detected a number of feminine curves. "I don't have expectations, Kayla. You are a gift I don't understand."

"Didn't we have this conversation earlier? There's nothing to understand, Mort."

"How about, 'Why me?'"

She leaned back and looked at me. "Why not you? You're an attractive man."

"Trust me, I'm not getting anywhere with that."

"Okay, truth is, it's because you're a private eye and terribly mysterious, bordering on sinister and dangerous, very Bondlike, sexy as all get-out. You make my knees feel weak. My heart flutters when I'm in the same room as you. I get all dizzy just thinking about—"

"You forgot your Prozac again, right?"

She moved out of my arms, grinning. "You're hopeless."

"Want some coffee?"

She shook her head. "Milk, fruit, toast. I'll get it."

I stared openly at her barely concealed chest. "The sights in this kitchen have improved a lot since yesterday."

She looked down at herself and grinned. "Should I button up another one or two of these guys?"

"No. I think you've got it just right."

"Uh-huh. Thought so."

"How well did you know your grandfather?" I asked, giving the coffeepot a longing look, willing it to hurry the hell up.

"My grandfather?" She paused with a hand on the refrigerator door. "Which one?"

"Jonnie's dad. Wendell."

She shrugged, got out the milk. "He was gruff and overbearing, didn't have any idea how to be around kids. He'd shake my hand like I was a business acquaintance, just about crush my fingers. I was thirteen when he was murdered. That was a huge mess."

"Do you remember much of it?"

"Not a lot. Just that Dad was shook up and all kinds of legal stuff was going on afterward, him taking over his father's businesses and everything. And the funeral. Black dresses and flowers, depressing organ music, everyone somber and quiet. I guess murder is like that."

"Any idea who Wendell's lawyer was at the time?"

"Not a clue."

"Chances are, whoever it was would've become Jonnie's lawyer after Wendell's death."

Kayla pursed her lips. "I guess so. I wasn't paying any attention to that kind of thing back then. I was past Barbie dolls, somewhere around thinking boys might be more interesting than I'd thought in the past." She put bread in the toaster, pushed the lever down. "All these questions. Does this mean we're sleuthing now?"

"We?" I asked.

"Well, you might like me better if I'm mysterious and sinister too."

"I like you fine the way you are, especially dressed like that, I might add. And who the hell says you're not mysterious or sinister?"

She smiled brightly. "Think so?"

"I found you in my bed. No name. No ID. No expiration date. Even now I'm taking your word for everything you've said. What do you think?"

"Well, darn. I've been found out. My real name is Mata Hari."

"I wouldn't be surprised, except *her* real name was Gertrud Zelle and she was executed by the French during World War I, so you'd not only be older than I give you credit for, you'd be embalmed. Not my type. So—about your father's lawyer?"

"Is it important?"

"I'm wondering how Edna Woolley ended up in that house back in 1976, or thereabouts. An arrangement of some kind was made. Wendell and his family moved out, Edna moved in. She's been there ever since. I imagine lawyers were involved."

"All of which happened years before I was born, Mort."

"Your father never said anything about it?"

"No, never."

"Think you'd recognize a lawyer's name from a list if I got you one?"

"It's possible. Especially if the lawyer was one of his friends, like a golfing buddy or something. I imagine I met most of them at one time or another, or heard their names."

"Let's find out." I told her to stay put, then went out the back, through the fence, and rapped on Velma's back door.

I'd given some thought to the problem last night. Last time I'd been up in Velma's attic, helping her look for a set of china she hadn't seen in years, I'd gone through a zillion boxes. Two of them held old phone books Velma's husband Orrin had stashed up there, God knows why. I remembered seeing over a dozen of them. It had meant nothing to me at the time, but now I saw them as a window into the past. Something of yesterday must've sunk in.

Velma was awake, of course, eager for information about Kayla and me and the husband we were dodging. Was he big? Did he have a temper? Did he know anything about guns? I fended her off as best I could as I climbed a ladder into her attic and spoke to her through the opening, raising clouds of dust as I pawed through boxes.

"You gonna do the right thing by her, Mortimer?" Velma called up to me.

I sneezed explosively, which raised even more dust. "What's the right thing?"

"You know." She let fly a few bars of "Here Comes the Bride."

"You never know, Velma." I couldn't have answered yes or no. If I had, I would've been in big trouble, one way or the other.

"Divorce still only takes six weeks here in Reno," she said.

"Know that, thanks."

More of the wedding march came from below. I found a phone book for 1977, two years before Kayla was born. Good enough. With promises to tell all soon, I escaped back to my house.

I plopped the book down on the dinette, opened it to the attorney section in the yellow pages. Back then there weren't quite seven pages of lawyers—now there are fifty-five, and personal injury lawyers have monster full-page ads. Another sign of the times. Munching toast with marmalade, still wearing my partly open shirt and nothing else, Kayla perused the names of law firms, tracking downward with a finger. I drank coffee and waited. With so few pages to go through it didn't take long.

"Okay," she said, brightening. "Here. Oleson & Critchen. I don't know about Critchen, but the other one, Oleson, was my dad's lawyer. Frank Oleson."

With any luck, he'd been Wendell's lawyer, too.

Kayla peered over my shoulder as I hunted for Oleson & Critchen in the current phone book. Nothing under "O," so we started at the front. She spotted it first: Beatty, Oleson, & Myers. How many Olesons could there be? Their office was located on Liberty Street, up near the courthouse.

I took a chance and phoned, surprised when a woman answered on the second ring, giving her name as Helen. I told her I was looking for Frank Oleson.

"Frank? Stephen's father?" I heard the incredulous note in her voice. "He passed away ten years ago. Hasn't been active in the firm in over twenty years." Kayla pressed her ear next to mine to listen in, as Jeri had done the other day. I hadn't had this much girl scent in a decade. Okay, ever.

At least we'd tracked down Frank Oleson, even if he was dead. Almost like real PIs. "Could I talk to Stephen?" I asked.

For a moment she didn't say anything. Not many people had phoned that week looking for a man who'd been dead for a decade. "I could make an appointment for you," she said finally. "He won't have an opening until, let me see"—papers rustled in the background—"Wednesday at three fifteen, if that's convenient."

"He's not there now?"

"Oh, heavens no. Not on a Saturday. We only keep the office open until noon to catch up on all the paperwork."

"Fact is, I'm interested in something that took place quite a few years ago."

"Oh? Exactly what are you—?"

Kayla pressed the disconnect button, ending the call.

I stared at her. "What'd you do that for?"

"Questions like the one you were about to ask—especially over the phone—she was already nervous, Mort. After everything that's happened this week, you were going to scare her half to death. Let's go talk to her. It's a good bet this Stephen Oleson guy is Dad's lawyer now. Or was. Or might know something useful."

"Uh-huh."

"Which I suppose would probably make him mine," Kayla added thoughtfully.

"Uh-huh," I said again.

"Which would mean, Mort, that maybe that lady, Helen, will talk to us. In person."

In person. That was Jeri's argument, too. And, given who I was, it sounded like a good idea. A phone call from Mortimer Angel at this juncture in Reno's history might be like a call from the Unabomber, years ago.

"Okay," I said. I peeled a curtain back an inch to peer outside. Four vans. Hell. They were starting to regroup. Might be a sign that our school systems are improving, and with it the attention span of a nation. One van was Channel 10 out of Seattle. It was a long drive home, so they had a stake in sticking to the story like a corporate executive to an outright lie.

"Get dressed," I said. "Let's go out the back."

"But of course," Kayla said. "How else?"

Five minutes later she was ready to go. We ducked through the fence. I had Jeri's wig in one hand like a dead possum, skinned and dyed. As we crept down Velma's side yard, she poked her head out a window right above us and said, "Oh, no you don't."

"Don't what?" I asked, looking up at her.

"Not without tellin' me nothin'," she answered cryptically.

"Telling you what about what?"

"You know." She grinned at Kayla. "Da, da, da-da." Those first four notes of "Here Comes the Bride."

I dragged Kayla toward the street. She looked back at Velma and called out, "I'll let you know, Vel."

"You'd better!"

"Now you've done it," I said when we reached the street. "She will hound us to the ends of the earth."

"She's a dear."

"You just threw twenty pounds of raw hamburger to a starving grizzly, lady."

"Surely you exaggerate."

"Don't I wish. Now she'll want the whole cow."

Kayla led me to her car, a VW bug two decades older than my Tercel, five blocks away. It had been painted at least three times. A ding in the left rear fender revealed the geology: sky blue now, formerly algae green, formerly hot hippie yellow. A fender bender would've turned it into a psychedelic acid trip.

"You drove this straight through from Ithaca?" I said, amazed, walking around the thing.

"Uh-huh. Runs great. Hop in."

She started the engine. I hadn't heard that sewing-machine sound in years, at least not from the inside. We took off, headed for Liberty Street. It took us four times as long to get there as it would have taken Jeri, but we did it without whiplash.

Kayla got a purse from under her seat, which is why I hadn't found it or anything else useful the night she'd arrived.

Like many law firms in Reno, Beatty, Oleson, & Myers was in a refurbished two-story mansion. This one was blue with lavender trim, scalloped siding, plate glass windows, wooden stairs leading up to a big front door. I left the wig in the car and Kayla and I climbed the stairs and went inside.

Two women were there, filing papers. Classical music filled the room, coming from a CD player. I hung back while Kayla asked for Helen.

"I'm Helen," said the thinner and older of the two women. "May I help you?" She turned the music down to a background level.

"Uh, well, my name is Rosalyn Sjorgen. Rosalyn Williams, now."

Helen stared at her. "Oh, my."

"Oh, my?" Kayla echoed.

"We've been trying to contact you all week. Ever since Jonnie... was...since he..." Her eyes went to me, widening in sudden recognition. "You, you're..."

"Mortimer Angel, ma'am," I offered in as non-threatening a manner possible. The other woman, Teresa, chubby and dark haired, was at a filing cabinet with papers in one hand, staring at me in either horror or awe, hard to tell which.

Kayla said, "Why were you trying to find me? Is Stephen Oleson my father's lawyer now? I mean...was he?"

"Yes, of course," Helen replied nervously.

She finally asked for some form of identification and Kayla dug her driver's license out of her purse. I kept quiet, not wanting to cause a panic with any sudden moves. They talked for a while and the tension left Helen's face. Kayla introduced me as a friend, harmless, which turned out okay since I wasn't in the first stages of a murderous rampage. Helen and Teresa didn't look so much like they wished they'd phoned 911 back when Kayla and I first came in the door.

Kayla turned to me. "What was it you wanted to know, Mort?"

I looked at Helen. "Something happened, almost forty years ago."

"Oh. That was you on the phone. *Forty* years?"

"Uh-huh."

"Stephen is only forty-five himself, Mr. Angel."

"Probably doesn't matter. Most likely it'd be in your records."

"What did you want to know?"

"Just...the terms of the arrangement that has permitted Edna Woolley to live in Jonnie's house all these years."

"Oh. That. We wouldn't have information of that kind here in the office. Not after such a long time."

"Where would it be?" Kayla asked.

"Kaplan Security Services, out in Stead, if it exists at all. They maintain secure vaults for paper storage. Fireproof and all that."

"Could we get the records?"

"Not right away. They're closed weekends. I could phone on Monday, let them know I need access. If it's important," she added.

Dead end, at least for a while.

"I don't suppose you would know anything about it? I mean, personally?" Kayla asked. "Before the records were stored."

"I'm sorry, no. I never saw the documents. Although..."

"Yes?" Kayla prompted.

"Well...Emmaline Dorman, Frank Oleson's secretary back then. She trained me, years ago. I imagine she would have seen them. She's retired, though. Has been for, oh, gosh, eighteen years now."

"Do you know where she is?"

"Oh, yes. Austin."

"Austin?"

For a moment she didn't understand Kayla's confusion, then she said, "Oh, there's a Texas Austin too, isn't there? I meant the Austin here in Nevada."

In the middle of nowhere on U.S. 50. Literally in the middle, if Nevada is nowhere, which is arguable—right in the geographic center of the state that's been slated to take the nation's nuclear waste, because one look at a map and it's obvious that Nevada is the perfect place for gambling, whorehouses, and DNA-altering radioactivity.

"She had a brother there," Helen said. "But I heard he died a few years ago. Her husband too, poor thing. I've got Emmaline's address here somewhere if that'd help."

Kayla got it, then looked at me. "Want to go?"

CHAPTER SIXTEEN

TO AUSTIN? IN the heat of summer? Hell, no.

I gave Kayla a shrug.

"Okay, great," she said.

My fault. I should have known. Never send a woman a mixed message. It will be interpreted accordingly, one of the ways they seize control. On the other hand, a trip to Austin would get us out of Reno where we might get a little breathing room. The media would never track down this Austin connection, such as it was. If it gave us a day of peace, it would be worth it.

Back in the VW, Kayla said, "Do we need anything at your place before we go?"

"Got m' wig right here, ma'am," I said in John Wayne's voice, picking it up and twirling it on one finger.

She rolled her eyes. "Is that a no?"

"Yep. It's a no."

More eye rolling. "What about money? In case we end up having to spend the night."

"Now there's a thought-provoking thought."

"Uh-huh. So...what if, Mort?"

"I've got one of those things you've avoided all your life, sugar. A hated MasterCard."

"Oh, goodie. Maxed out?"

"Not a dime on it. And it's got a limit of two thousand dollars, too." Which not only shows how little I'd used it, but also showed how little the folks at MasterCard trusted me.

"Whoopee, we're rich."

* * *

We. She had an interesting way with words.

It wasn't until one thirty that we got on Interstate 80, headed east. I'd insisted on an oil change for the VW, something Kayla hadn't had done since she'd left New York. The night before, with Kayla beside me in bed, July had slipped quietly into August. This time of year Highway 50 would be an empty, sun-scorched stretch of heat mirages and misery. Boy Scout that I am, I wanted to minimize the risk of having a breakdown. That antique air-cooled engine was risk enough. Then I got hungry and we had sandwiches at Carrows, I in my wig, she in a smile as she stared at it. And I called Dallas on my cell phone, told her what I was up to. I. Me. *I* was going to Austin.

"Is K going with you?" she asked, right off.

You can't slip anything by them. They are so much smarter than we are. Making us look like we're in charge is only a game to them, something to alleviate boredom. They probably laugh their heads off when they're alone.

"Uh-huh."

"Have fun, Mort."

"This's detective work, Dal." And it was against Jeri's express orders, too, but...what the hell, all I did was work for her, after a fashion. Something that could change as easily as the weather.

"Of course it is. Call me when you get back?"

"Yeah." I shut the phone, ending the call.

We didn't get to Fallon until nearly three. Then the real Highway 50 began, two lanes of shimmering blacktop, scoped out by floating buzzards, like riding toward the end of the world. The pavement would be up around a hundred eighty degrees. You could roast a steer on it.

The Volkswagen didn't have air-conditioning. With the windows open, hot air buffeted through. Kayla had the top two buttons of her shirt undone. She told me to take the wheel, and I held it while she untucked her shirt, unbuttoned the lower two buttons, then knotted the loose ends under her breasts.

"Watch the road," she said.

"What for? The sonofabitch is naked—I mean empty."

She grinned. "Watch the road, you fool."

She took over the wheel, and I played it cool, not looking at her belly for at least two minutes, which took all my self-control. You see stomachs like that only in your dreams, and then only if you're damn good at it.

East of the junction of Route 839, two jets from the naval air station at Fallon swooped down and dropped bombs on invisible targets, white bursts of light, smoke plumes, snarls of thunder. What else would you do with a desert on a semi-permanent basis except bomb it? Whorehouses are just something to do on your way through.

We went out past Frenchman, gliding through the scent of hot alkali. The temperature was a hundred and two. Over dry mountain passes, past twenty thousand square miles of dun-colored grass and silvery-blue sage, between hot bare mountains ten thousand feet high. The air cooled as we gained altitude, but the sun's ultraviolet became harsher, seeming to burn on my skin. We passed the Reese River and finally pulled within sight of Austin, snugged into Pony Canyon in the Toiyabe Mountains, just this side of Austin Summit.

Kayla slowed the VW as we passed buildings at the west end of town. A sign, *Stokes Castle*, whipped by, pointing to a winding dirt road that led up a gentle slope and around a low nub of hill.

"Ever been here before?" I asked her.

"No. You?"

"There's a first time for everything. Until Sunday, I'd never found a stray blonde in my bed before. Not one."

"Then all hell broke loose. Poor you."

Austin lay on the old Pony Express run, which came down through the canyon before silver was discovered in 1862. That year, a retired rider found a greenish ore, which proved to be silver sulfide, and the "Rush to the Reese" was on. At one time Austin was the second biggest city in Nevada—Virginia City being first—back when Vegas was a ghost town, having once been nothing but a camping spot on the Mormon Trail, then a fort, a mission, and finally, in 1858, an abandoned mission in the soul-grinding dust and heat of the minor Mojave Desert. So much for Vegas, which had exploded into what was arguably the most artificial city in the history of the world. Nevada's real history lies farther north, in places like Austin.

Kayla drove through town at twenty-five miles an hour, which took the better part of sixty seconds. Past the Lander County courthouse where a guy had once been hanged from a second-story balcony, up to the Gridley store, built of weathered stone, and the house next door, formerly the town brothel. The tailings of old mining operations littered the surrounding hills. The desert changes slowly. The arid land is relatively unaffected by water. The tailing piles would still be visible a thousand years from now. Austin's history lurked all around in the form of its red brick buildings, churches, abandoned mines, and, Kayla and I discovered, the size of its motel rooms, which could be described as either quaint or Leavenworthian, circa 1890.

Without exchanging a word, we decided to stay the night. Our room at the Lincoln Motel was marginally bigger than your average walk-in closet, about eight by ten, much of it taken by a queen-sized bed. One of us had to sit on the bed if the other wanted to walk around it. The bed sagged in the middle, which was likely to prove interesting later on.

Kayla bounced on the bed. "It squeaks, how fun," she said, then we went outside and looked around.

"Shall we eat now, or find Emmaline Dorman?" she asked. She'd untied her shirt so as not to draw attention or cause a riot. I had my wig on in case satellite dishes we'd seen in town were operational. If they could get the Sjorgen-Milliken Spectacle in Rangoon, odds were they could get it here too, a hundred seventy miles from ground zero.

I was hungry, but said, "Mrs. Dorman."

"Work before pleasure?"

"With the IRS, the two are indistinguishable."

"Mmm, nasty."

Emmaline Dorman lived in a house on the northern slope of a hill overlooking the town, three blocks off Main Street, otherwise known as Highway 50. Kayla and I walked over through the kind of small-town quiet you have to hunt for these days, a quiet that reminded me of a time when gas stations had soda machines with heavy lids and bottles in rows that you slid out through a gate-latch mechanism—a time before my time, when small-town grocery stores had wooden floors and paddle fans circulating stale air. I had the impression that Austin was standing still in a world that was moving fast somewhere out beyond the horizon...except for those satellite dishes, and bottled water with a per-gallon cost five times that of gasoline, sold at the convenience store at the Chevron station at the west end of town.

Emmaline's yard was hot and dry. The earth was dusty yellow-gray rock. Wiry blue-green sage and cheat grass filled the yard. The roof of the house was frayed composition shingles, lifted by the heat and wind into a reddish shag.

I knocked. Moments later a woman answered, tall but stooped, wearing a loose-fitting housedress over a thin frame. Bony arms, no chest, a gaunt face dominated by watery blue-gray eyes still alive with intelligence. Cool moist air blew out past Kayla and me. I heard the airy rumble of a swamp cooler somewhere inside the house.

"Mrs. Dorman?" I asked.

"Yes?"

"I wonder if we could have a word with you, ma'am?"

Her eyes took in Kayla, then returned to me. "And who might you be?" There was no suspicion in her voice, only interest. Her life wasn't a parade of visitors, at least not by people she didn't know.

I didn't want to tell her my name. I turned to Kayla, who stepped closer and said, "My name is Rosalyn Sjorgen, Mrs. Dorman. Or was, years ago. Now it's Williams."

Emmaline's eyes brightened. "Jonnie's daughter?"

"Yes, ma'am."

"But of course. And look at how you've grown. We met, years ago, dear, when you were no more than ten or twelve." A cloud passed over her features, which finally took on a look of resignation. "Ever since this awful business with Jonnie and David...I wondered if anyone would drop by one day." Her gaze took in both of us. "But the two of you aren't here about that, are you? I mean, not directly. You're here because of Edna."

"Yes," Kayla said.

Emmaline stood to one side. "Please, come in."

We went into the coolness. The living room was small—area rugs over wood plank flooring, ordinary but for framed black-and-white photographs of old buildings and windmills, rusting tractors, mining ruins, all in magnificent lighting, dramatic shadows and perspectives, terrific clouds.

Emmaline noticed my interest. "Those were taken by my late husband, Hank. Many of them before we moved out here to Austin."

"They're very good."

"His work was published in a number of magazines. Would you like something to drink? Coffee? Tea?"

I said no, but Kayla surprised me by asking for tea, if it wasn't too much trouble. Emmaline returned a few minutes later, and we sat in the living room on overstuffed furniture that swallowed us whole. I hoped I could get up when the time came to leave. Kayla introduced me as Morrie, of all things, a friend of the Sjorgen family. I was still wearing my wig, feeling as if a cat had parked on my head.

Emmaline nodded and gave me a welcoming smile. "Now, then, what can I tell you?" she asked, pouring two cups of tea.

She knew exactly what. Her comment about Edna at the door told me that. She wanted coaxing. I said, "Anything you remember about Edna moving into the Sjorgen mansion on Virginia Street way back when, Mrs. Dorman."

"Please, call me Emmaline." She handed Kayla a cup on a saucer, then looked at her and smiled. "You are the spitting image of Jonnie, dear. He was a terribly handsome man."

"Thank you."

"Nineteen seventy-six," Emmaline said slowly. "I...well, I'm not sure what to say." She leaned back, balancing her cup, and gazed at Kayla. "What I mean, dear, is that you have the right to know if anyone does, but...the thing that happened back then, it's not a very nice story."

"Please," Kayla said.

"I would get no joy speaking ill of the dead." She gave Kayla a direct look and her tone grew sharper. "I am referring to your father, Rosalyn." She awaited a response. I sensed that what she was waiting for was permission to continue, at which time she was indeed going to speak ill of the dead.

"My father and I haven't been close for a long time," Kayla said. "Please, tell us."

Emmaline looked at Kayla a moment longer, then down at the cup in her hands. "There was a scandal. Or might have been, but it was averted by Wendell, your grandfather. And, of course, by others who were involved."

"A scandal?"

Emmaline nodded. "It was hushed up. There would be no public record of it now. Nothing at all. Are you aware that Edna had a daughter?"

"A daughter?" Kayla gave her a surprised look, then turned her head to me.

"Jacoba," I said.

Emmaline looked startled. "Why, yes, Jacoba. However did you learn that?"

I shrugged. It didn't seem my place to point out the obvious, that these two women were in the presence of one of the finest gumshoes in the hemisphere.

"Jacoba Woolley," Emmaline said slowly. "Edna and Herman's only child, her first pregnancy. She was forty-six years old. It was a very difficult birth. During labor, the child was damaged."

"Damaged?" Kayla said.

"Deprived of oxygen for too long. She survived, however, and grew into a remarkably beautiful girl, which wasn't surprising— Edna was a great beauty in her day. But Jacoba was, well...simple."

I gave her a questioning look. Edna hadn't so much as hinted at that about Jacoba.

Emmaline sipped her tea. "There are all sorts of euphemisms for it these days, but, to be blunt, Jacoba was retarded. Genetically she was fine, perfect, but mentally...at fourteen she had the capacity of a child of no more than four."

"She didn't go to school?" Kayla said.

"No. She never learned to read. She had a child's vocabulary. Oh, but Edna doted on her all the same. Even more so after Herman passed away, when Jacoba was still only a child. Outwardly, there was nothing wrong with Jacoba." Emmaline's eyes dropped again to her hands. "Far from it, in fact. She developed quite early in the physical sense. At fourteen she could have passed for seventeen. That was the summer of '76."

Which was shaping up to be a rather bad year, I thought, but I remained quiet. Emmaline stopped talking. The drone of the swamp cooler filled the room. Half a minute went by.

"College was out," Emmaline said finally. "Jonnie and David—Mr. Milliken—were home. The summer after their first year. Jonnie was back from Harvard, David from Princeton. They were bright boys, but pampered, spoiled. They didn't want for much. One day in August, Jacoba turned up missing from the yard in front of her house, three blocks from the Sjorgen place, the house Edna lives in now. It was twilight, almost dark. Edna was frantic. No one had seen Jacoba. A search was quickly mounted, but Jacoba was gone."

Emmaline paused and looked at Kayla.

"It's okay," Kayla said. "We have to know."

"A patrolman found them in Idlewild Park, a mile from Edna's house. He heard them—Jonnie and David and Jacoba—in a thicket of bushes by the river."

Again she stopped, face flushed, then she pressed on: "They were...unclothed. The boys were nineteen. Jacoba was fourteen. They had...they had been with her. You know. The police officer guessed who Jacoba was by a description he'd heard over the radio—others had been searching for her for two hours by that time. He knew her age. He arrested the boys on the spot, took them and Jacoba into custody, the boys in handcuffs. At the police station he spoke only to the chief of police, however, because the boys had told him who they were, trying to convince him to let them go.

"Edna was called to the station, and Jonnie's father, Wendell, and David's father, Victor. Charges were made but never filed. The paperwork sat idle for several months. Everything was hushed up while lawyers on both sides made proposals and counterproposals in an effort to keep the incident from going public, perhaps ruining the boys' lives. I remember it quite well because I typed up all the legal documents on Jonnie's behalf. Frank Oleson was Wendell's lawyer...but I guess you know that."

"Yes," Kayla said quietly.

"Edna was very hard on them, but what mother wouldn't be? By October, Jacoba had missed her period, which she'd been having for over a year by that time."

"Oh, God," Kayla breathed.

"She was pregnant. Back then there was no way to determine who the father was, Jonnie or David, not before the baby was born. Abortion was out of the question. Edna wouldn't hear of it. She let everyone know that the Lord's work would be done. She was quite Catholic, you know. Each of the fathers was terrified for his son's career, as you might imagine. The upshot of it all was that Victor Milliken paid Edna a hundred fifty thousand dollars to keep her from proceeding with criminal charges against his son."

"And Edna got Wendell's house," I said.

"Yes. Not the deed, but the right to live there for as long as either she or Jacoba was alive, which might as well have been the same thing as far as Wendell was concerned, since Edna came from sturdy stock and Jacoba was a mere child. It was a rather odd agreement. I always suspected that its very strangeness was Edna's idea, that it was a cunning way for her to further punish the Sjorgens, since Wendell would have no reasonable way to explain it.

"Wendell also gave Edna sixty thousand dollars. She demanded a full confession as well, signed by both Jonnie and David, witnessed by the fathers, the lawyers, and myself and several others. Edna took one of the original copies, of course. I imagine she put it someplace safe, insurance in the event that Wendell tried something underhanded once the dust had settled, which, of course, would have been entirely in keeping with his character."

For a moment Kayla and I sat there in silence. Again, Jonnie's out-of-control libido had bobbed to the surface, this time with a mentally retarded girl fourteen years old. I glanced at Kayla. She was staring out a window at the town below, at long shadows leaning eastward in the waning afternoon sun.

She turned to Emmaline. "Did Jacoba have the baby?"

"That I don't know. Once Edna accepted their terms, a cloak of silence descended over everything. It's likely Jonnie himself didn't know, or David. I never heard about a baby, not that I would have. It's always possible that Jacoba miscarried, but I simply don't know."

Kayla set her saucer on the table in front of her. "But, if she had the baby, wouldn't it be common knowledge? Wouldn't there be records?"

"I'm sure there must," Emmaline said. "In Myrtle Beach."

"Myrtle Beach? North Carolina?" Kayla said. "Or is it south?"

"South," Emmaline said. "Edna sent Jacoba away to live with her sister. I forget the sister's name, but I'm pretty sure she never married. To the best of my knowledge, Jacoba never returned to Reno."

"Even though Edna doted on her?" I said.

"Yes. Seems strange, doesn't it? Edna's revenge was that the Sjorgens would never again step foot in their own house as long as she was alive, but the agreement was that either Edna or Jacoba had to inhabit it. It couldn't be allowed to stand empty. I can only imagine that Edna went to Myrtle Beach often to visit Jacoba, but I really don't know."

Kayla got up and paced. "I suppose there's no doubt that my father and Milliken knew Jacoba was retarded," she said.

"Oh, heavens no. None whatsoever. Reno was much smaller then. Jacoba wasn't in school or anything, but she lived nearby. The boys had known her for years."

Boys, I thought. Nineteen years old. Risking it all for a moment of fun.

"And then, after all that, Jonnie and Dave simply went on with their lives," Kayla said.

"Yes. Or so it seems. It also appears to have settled the boys down. There were no further...incidents after that. Victor Milliken had no trouble raising his part of the settlement. Wendell didn't either, but he gave up the house and had to endure a great deal of speculation about him and Edna, which I'm sure pleased Edna. Certainly she did nothing to lessen it, although the terms of the agreement forbade her to mention the incident between the boys and her daughter. The entire point of the arrangements was to buy her silence. The house had been recently renovated. It was Wendell's pride, his boyhood home. To give it up like that, without any explanation…well, in the end, the whole thing simply blew the Sjorgen family apart."

"Jane divorced Wendell," I said.

"Yes."

"And then, later, we elected Jonnie mayor of Reno."

Emmaline smiled sadly. "Nothing ever slowed him down. Jonnie was always quite the charmer."

* * *

The sun was a molten gold speck in the west when we left the house. The Toiyabe Mountains were tinged pink under a pastel-blue sky full of high, thin clouds painted a gaudy rose.

"You hungry?" I asked.

"Not very."

"Maybe in a while."

"Maybe."

She was taking it hard. Jonnie was her father. We walked along the highway without speaking, then turned and took the road that led toward Stokes Castle. The road was dirt and gravel, winding not quite half a mile into the hills. As we rounded a final bend, the castle was a dark mass against a burgundy sunset. It was a square, smallish thing of hand-hewn granite, three stories tall, surprisingly ugly for a so-called castle, built over a century ago by mining baron Anson P. Stokes, one of those bizarre anomalies you find in a land settled by eccentrics. We had it all to ourselves, and to Mormon crickets, and bats flitting dark against the sky, this monument to whatever strange dreams or mad flights of grandeur Stokes once had. He'd lived in it for only a month or two in 1897, then abandoned it. It looked cold and uncomfortable. I would've abandoned it after eight hours, or less.

In silence, we watched the last vestige of daylight leave the sky. Stars came out. The moon, almost full, floated up over the Toiyabes, lighting our way back down the hill.

We ate at the International Hotel—a hotel in name only. It no longer rented rooms. During the time of the Civil War it had been dismantled board by board in Virginia City and trundled through the desert to Austin, then reassembled. They did things differently back then.

Afterward we walked the streets until the night chill drove us back to the Lincoln Motel. At an elevation of sixty-six hundred feet, the nights in Austin are cold, even in August.

The shower was too small for two. Nor was Kayla in the mood. She showered, then I did, and we went to bed.

Although the sag in the middle ensured we wouldn't drift apart, Kayla clung to me. Not with passion, however. More than anything, I felt like a life raft, keeping her afloat. I could only imagine how it felt to learn such terrible things about your father.

We left the window open an inch, allowing cold air to drift into the room. Clean mountain air, full of magic and narcolepsy.

We slept.

CHAPTER SEVENTEEN

I AWOKE, MISSING her.

She was sitting on the edge of the bed, staring out the window at the night. Moonlight was on her neck, arms, breasts, sending glints of silver through her hair. Her nipples were erect in the cold. It was a hell of a sight, but I felt like a voyeur, looking at her without her knowing.

I sat next to her, our knees almost touching the wall beneath the windowsill. The town and the valley were bathed in eldritch light.

"He was a rotten son of a bitch," Kayla breathed.

I had no answer to that.

She leaned a shoulder against mine. Her skin was cool. "When I was fourteen," she said, "he came on to one of my girlfriends. Well, *came on* isn't quite right, but...something."

She spoke to the empty night, not looking at me.

"I never told anyone. By then he was married to his second wife, Anne. I didn't like her very much. That's one reason why I didn't say anything, to her or to anyone. I didn't want to cause trouble. And, I guess, there wasn't all that much to say."

A lone pickup truck rumbled along the highway fifty feet away, taillights and engine sounds fading, then gone.

"Her name was Suzy Evans. It was just the two of us. She was my best friend. Sometimes I'd sleep over at her place, or she would sleep over at mine. Dad—Jonnie—cupped her breast in a hallway one night as they were passing, squeezed gently. She was in a nightgown. Not flannel. Something filmy, like sheer polyester. It was way late. We didn't think he was still up."

"She didn't think it was an accident?" I asked.

"No. She said he...reached out and grabbed. Squeezed her for a second, then smiled and kept going. Didn't say a word."

Another fourteen year old. "She never said anything to anyone, either?"

"Not that I ever heard. Maybe she thought no one would believe her. But she never came over again, and I never went back to her place. After that we drifted apart. I guess I didn't believe her myself, not completely. I mean, my own father. It was so...weird. If it were true, it would have been unbelievably stupid of him, and I'd never thought of him as a stupid man. Disingenuous at times, but not outright stupid."

I took her hand. Moonlight and cold night air bathed our bodies.

Kayla sighed. "I guess it was true, though. Probably was."

I still didn't tell her about Clair Hutson and the alleged attempted rape of Sarah Jean. No reason to. Kayla already knew more than she wanted to about Mayor Jonnie.

"Makes me wonder..." she murmured, letting the thought float away in a sigh.

"What?"

"Given how my father was, if...if maybe I have a half-brother or half-sister somewhere."

"Victoria," I said. It was out before I could stop it. It must have been on my mind, ever since Emmaline told us about Jacoba's rape.

"What?"

"Nothing." I closed my eyes at my stupidity. Too late. Too damned late.

"Victoria. You said Victoria."

"It's just a name."

"You say names? They just pop out? Who is Victoria, Mort?"

Maybe I had to tell her, I didn't know. Victoria had said she was Edna's granddaughter. Maybe she was. Edna only had one child, Jacoba, who had been knocked up by either Jonnie Sjorgen or Dave Milliken. Maybe Jacoba had given birth to Victoria. But if Jacoba had never returned to Reno, why would Victoria have come back? Or was she lying? Maybe she was a scam artist. I wouldn't have trusted her or her kid, Winter, with a roll of nickels.

Kayla grabbed my jaw and yanked my face toward hers. It hurt. "Who is Victoria?"

So I told her about my impromptu visit to Sjorgen House, being discovered by Winter outside, then Victoria, then my lengthy pseudo-conversation upstairs with Edna afterward.

"Victoria," Kayla breathed. She looked at me. "You know a lot about what's going on, Mr. Angel, sir."

"That's impossible, since I don't have the slightest idea what's going on."

"You knew about Jacoba. Now I find that you know this woman, Victoria. And her daughter."

"I stumble over trivia. It doesn't amount to anything. Nothing adds up."

It might have, though, if almost forty years hadn't elapsed between the rape of Jacoba and the decapitations. I'm not the swiftest pigeon in the flock, and as a private eye I might have trouble finding my hand in my pocket, but even I saw that long-ago connection between Jonnie and Dave. I could feel its energy, feel it humming somewhere out there in the dark, renewed, resurrected and alive, like Frankenstein's monster during an electrical storm. Or maybe not. It might've been my imagination that was overheated and running wild and free. It does that.

"Victoria," Kayla said, testing the name. She put an elbow on the windowsill and rested her chin on her hand, staring out at the night.

"I don't like her," I said.

"She might be my sister, Mort."

"Half-sister. It's possible," I admitted.

"I might be an aunt, too. Half-aunt."

Meaning Winter. I hadn't told her about Winter in the hallway, her attempted seduction, or whatever it was. "Or you might not," I told her. "Those two might be swinging from branches in Milliken's family tree."

"Uh-huh, but it's intriguing all the same, Mort."

"There are some things you'd be better off leaving alone."

"What are you not telling me?"

I wanted her to keep the hell away from Victoria and Winter. I wanted that very much, so I told her what Winter had done in the hallway as I was leaving.

"In bra and panties, huh?" Kayla said when I was finished.

"A thong, actually. One of those things made out of dental floss."

"Did she look good?"

"She looked dangerous, like a cobra. She wanted something."

"You, probably." Kayla rested a hand on my thigh. "Might mean she's got good taste. And you didn't answer the question. How'd she look? Pretty?"

"Like a spider, Kayla. Like she hadn't had her quota of flies for the day."

"So she hit on you. She could've done a lot worse, Mort."

"She's nineteen or twenty, for God's sake."

"So she's a little precocious."

Which rhymes with ferocious, and I could tell I wasn't getting through. How do you explain the expression you see on someone's face, in their eyes?

"Let it go, Kayla, please?"

"Just like that?"

"Yes. They're not nice people."

For a while she didn't answer. "I'll think about it."

"You do that." I lay back down, pulled the blanket over me. A moment later Kayla eased under the covers and snuggled up next to me again.

We lay like that for a while, neither of us sleeping. Outside, a coyote howled and others joined in. It sounded like mourning, a chorus of death. Kayla shivered. I felt goose bumps on my own arms.

"Why'd you leave Ithaca?" I asked.

She was silent for a while. I waited. After half a minute she said, "Someone broke into my house."

"In Ithaca?"

"Yes. I own my own place. An old, two-story clapboard under great big maples. It's very upstate New York, with creaky floors, hissing radiators, the whole bit. I love it. The mortgage isn't too bad, but I rent a room anyway—to another teacher at the college, Kristen Hawes. She's my age. Alone, the place feels too empty.

"Anyway, Kristen was gone. *Is* gone. To Arizona until college starts up again at the end of the month. She has parents in Phoenix.

"Jonnie was missing, and reporters started following me around, wanting interviews. If it had only been Jonnie maybe it would've been just one of those things, but with two of them gone, the mayor *and* the district attorney, well...it got totally crazy. I started staying indoors, dashing from school to my car to my house. Finally, I gave up going to the college. I was using the dance studio there to keep in shape and work on new routines for the fall semester. I thought about coming back to Reno, but not very seriously. It was such a long drive and what could I do there? I hadn't seen my father in three years. Then, Friday before last, I got home late. I'd gone to a movie. It was dark. The sun had been down for hours. Inside the house..."

A shudder went through her.

"What?" I asked.

"Kristen has a hamster, Rocky..."

Again she stopped. A single warm tear landed on my chest.

"She loved him. Rocky. A lot," Kayla said. "He was this bitty, innocent thing. I was taking care of him while she was gone. He was...pinned to a wall in the kitchen. With an icepick. Someone had...cut him open, disemboweled him and left him hanging there."

A chill went through me. Kayla lay in my arms, crying silently. I held her. Other than that, there wasn't anything I could do but wait.

"It was horrible," she said after a while. "Just...the thought of anyone doing something like that to a helpless little creature. I took him down. He was dead. I put him in a plastic bag. Then I heard a noise upstairs, overhead in my bedroom. Like a footstep. It might've been boards creaking like they do sometimes, I don't know, but suddenly I was terrified. I still had Rocky in the bag. I grabbed my purse and ran out to my car and took off."

"But not to the police?" I said.

"No. I mean, I started to. That was my first thought, and maybe I should have. But...I don't know, I started thinking about how this would make things even worse, there in Ithaca. My dad had become big news and now this. I pulled over in the dark beneath some trees and thought about it, finally decided I couldn't face any more of it. I was sick and tired of being followed around. It had been on my mind that I should come back to Reno, what with my father missing and all. A few reporters had asked why I didn't seem to care—as if *they* cared, the bastards. All they wanted was a story. If I'd gone to the police they would have connected me with Jonnie and that incredible mess going on in Reno. I would have been on national TV by morning. The very thought of it made me sick."

"So you headed west and drove all the way to Reno without a break."

"There were headlights," she said.

"Headlights?"

"Behind me. I looked back as I drove away from my house. I saw lights come on. They stopped when I pulled over, then started up again when I did. In a streetlamp I saw a dark van. Whoever it was followed me around Ithaca for a while until I finally lost them. But the point is, I had to lose them, Mort. The way the van kept after me, it couldn't have been an accident, two cars happening to be going the same way, through all the turns I took."

"Probably a reporter."

"Maybe. But I didn't get that impression at the time, and, well, it got worse."

"Worse?"

"I saw the van again in West Almond. That's like eighty miles west of Ithaca."

"Same one?"

"I'm sure of it. At least fairly sure. I was getting gas at a station and I saw it down the street, parked at the curb. A dark van, engine idling. I could see exhaust. When I left, it followed. Its headlights looked exactly the same, Mort. I mean, the same shape, everything."

Another chill passed through me.

"I saw it again," she said. "At least I thought I did, behind me on the freeway in Pennsylvania, maybe a quarter mile back. So I took the next exit, switched off my lights, and turned off the road behind a building. It was after one in the morning. There was no traffic at all. This dark van came down the off ramp after me, moving quickly. But then it stopped at a stop sign and waited a while, too long, as if the driver was looking around, then it took off, fast, like it was hunting me.

"I was scared to death after that," she said. "My father was missing and here was this van, following me around. I didn't think I could sleep, and I didn't have enough money for a room. All I had was twenty or twenty-five dollars and that Citgo card. So I drove the whole way, no motel—which was awful toward the end, I was so tired."

"Did you ever see the van again?"

"No. I mean, I saw lots of dark vans, but none of them stayed behind me like that. I kept thinking about it though, seeing it pulling up behind me again, as if the person inside knew exactly where I was headed. I was on Interstate 80 almost the whole way. The worst was when it got dark again, that second night, from Iowa most of the way through Wyoming. What happened to Rocky—"

I held her, imagining a faceless person in a dark van, tracking her across much of the continent. It felt surreal.

"I buried him in Indiana," Kayla said. "In a field at a rest stop."

She fell silent. Outside, another coyote howled.

I didn't say anything, and Kayla had run out of words. We lay in each other's arms in the shallow bowl of the bed, warm, away from the world, away from reporters and prying eyes, and in that silence I drifted off to sleep so smoothly that I have no sense of when it happened.

* * *

We stayed in Austin most of Sunday, leaving only when the sun was low in the west, which promised a much cooler ride through the desert back to Reno. Breakfast at the Toiyabe Cafe, green-chili-and-Swiss omelets for both of us, a late lunch at Carol's Country Kitchen. Quiet strolling amid the weathered buildings, leisurely shopping at local arts-and-crafts shops and miniature sidewalk bazaars where locals haggled with a small handful of tourists over prices. Over Kayla's objections I bought her a silver-and-turquoise necklace at Eve's Craft Shoppe, because they took MasterCard and it's only plastic, and because the thing looked great on her. I had fun. Even before putting on the necklace she turned a lot of heads, including mine.

We were in the relative coolness of the International, resting our feet and having Cokes at the bar, when the day's news came on TV. The usual wail and moan, a train derailment here, unrest and riot there, things you can do nothing about and that do not enhance your life in the slightest to know. Most of it is nothing but voyeurism in a silk suit, like the Sjorgen and Milliken murders for example, in which no progress had been made. All it got was a ten-second mention.

Then a story out of Honolulu: the University of Hawaii had hosted a North American-Asian Karate Championship. Diana Mobley from Savannah, Georgia, had won the coveted Open Division and was all smiles, raising a trophy belt over her head on the victory platform, short honey-blond hair still frazzled from her efforts. Beside her was a stone-faced Korean woman.

Jeri DiFrazzia had taken third place, and fourth place went to a French Canadian gal whose name I didn't catch because I was staring open-mouthed at Jeri.

Jeri. She'd taken third.

I pointed. "That's Jeri, there. Few inches shorter than the others."

"Jeri?"

"DiFrazzia. My boss."

Kayla stared. "Oh, my God."

Yeah. That's what I thought, too.

"She's very pretty, isn't she?" Kayla said after a few seconds. "Gorgeous, even."

Yes, she was. Sweat, disgusted frown, and all.

* * *

We didn't get back to Reno until after midnight. My house was still standing, not necessarily good news since it's insured and it could use a new roof, new carpet, better insulation. We showered together, which was great fun, held each other for a while, then slept. In spite of all the talk and all the touching and all the innuendo, we still hadn't made love.

Why? Hard to say. There might have been something in the talk and the touching that was enough. Anticipation is sexy. It charges the air, and charged air is worth a lot all on its own. Slam-bam takes the edge off before there's an edge worth taking off.

Or, maybe our timing was off. Or Aphrodite was on sabbatical. Or the image of Jonnie raping fourteen-year-old Jacoba Woolley was still a dark specter gliding through our thoughts, leaving behind a damper that would have put out a forest fire.

Lots of reasons.

CHAPTER EIGHTEEN

I GOT TO Jeri's at 8:10 Monday morning.

She was rummaging through a desk. Rainbows glided throughout the room. The vegetation gave off an interesting, musty jungle scent that made me think a rubber tree was exactly what I needed back at my place. Without looking up, she said, "You're late."

I removed the wig she'd given me and dropped it on her desk. "Dock me a dollar sixty-seven cents."

She stared at the wig. "I think I'll just work you harder."

"Too late."

"Oh?" She looked up, suddenly suspicious.

"By the way, how'd your case go this weekend?"

"Could've been better, and why am I too late?"

Time to come clean. I'd learned too much to keep it from her. I told her about Stephen Oleson's secretary, Austin, Emmaline Dorman, even the fact that Kayla had turned up. And I told her about Winter, Victoria, and my talk with Edna, but I didn't mention the scene with Winter in the gloom of that second-floor hallway. Something about that defied explanation.

I told her about going through the fence into Velma's backyard to avoid media trolls in front of my house. I thought she'd appreciate that, but evidently not because she gave me a hard look. "Kayla," she said. "Rosalyn Sjorgen, of all people. You went to Austin with her? Christ, Mort, I told you to lay off the case."

"No charge for my time."

"Oh, don't you worry. But you could've screwed something up. There's a nasty killer out there."

"I didn't, though. Screw things up."

"Is that so? Is she pretty?"

"Does it matter?"

"Not to me." Her voice was like a knife. Her head ducked down and she began pawing through the drawer again. She had on an ivory silk shirt and plum slacks, matching ivory sandals. She looked good. She wore earrings, a hint of makeup, hair nicely done up, poofed and feathery. I caught a whiff of perfume, something I hadn't noticed before. Kayla was right, she was very pretty—gorgeous, in fact, even if she sometimes doubled as a hydraulic ram.

"Lose something?" I asked.

She slammed the drawer, hard. "No, I didn't lose anything. You didn't say *anything* about a Jacoba or a Victoria, Mort. Or anything about anyone named Winter, either. Not one word."

"I sort of dropped by that day—at Sjorgen House. I didn't think it mattered."

"So, you went all the way to Austin with this Kayla person because it didn't matter."

Unfathomable anger. It's another of their tricks, one more way to keep us rotating over the coals.

"I went because of what Clair Hutson said about Jonnie trying to rape Sarah Jean," I told her. "About that time, Wendell Sjorgen gave up his house to Edna Woolley. All those events took place in roughly the same time frame. All within eighteen months."

"So you and Kayla went and saw Oleson's secretaries. Then the two of you charged off to Austin together for the weekend."

"Hey, you're quick."

She glared at me. I thought she'd take me into her back room and slam me around a while to work off her anger. Instead, she picked up the phone and got hold of Dallas, then told me to please go get her a diet Coke from her refrigerator. I thought it would be a nice gesture if I did what she asked for once. When I got back—without the Coke because there weren't any to get—Jeri was talking to a travel agent. All I got from that conversation were a bunch of "yeses," "no's," and "uh-huhs." After a few minutes of that, she hung up.

"Let's go," she said, standing, grabbing a purse.

"Where to?"

"Myrtle Beach."

* * *

I was a hunk of newspaper, caught between two whirlwinds— Kayla and Jeri.

"Myrtle Beach?"

"The plane leaves at 9:20, Mort. In forty-eight minutes. They'll be boarding before we reach security and they're probably going to strip-search you, so let's get going."

"What about Fairchild?" I asked. "What about my not leaving the city or the county, whatever?"

She grabbed my wig as she came around the desk, rammed it into my arms with almost enough force to crack a rib. "You went to Austin, didn't you? That's out of the county. You survived that. What Fairchild doesn't know won't hurt him."

I followed her, not because I wanted to but because she had a hand on my wrist and was dragging me out the door. I had no choice in the matter. Christ, she was strong.

She left twenty feet of expensive rubber in front of her house-office-gymnasium, headed in the general direction of I-80.

"Jesus, Jeri."

"We land at Dallas-Fort Worth first," she said. "Then Atlanta and a hop to Myrtle Beach. Short layovers. My travel agent's getting all that ticketing hoopla set up as we speak."

"What's the rush?"

She glanced at me. "Miss this flight, the next one's late afternoon to La Guardia, of all the hideous places. We wouldn't get to Myrtle Beach until noon tomorrow after a four-hour layover at Atlanta. Who needs that? This way we can be back tomorrow, if things work out."

"We're already booked on a return flight?"

"Not yet, but we will be by the time we reach the airport. Don't worry about it."

"I don't have a change of clothes, anything."

"Neither do I. This comes under the heading of expenses, Mort. You can buy a change of underwear somewhere. Dallas already okayed it."

She would. She always said clean underwear was important, like in the event of a plane crash. I patted my pockets. No cell phone. Backtracking through the morning, I remembered seeing it on my dresser in the bedroom, but didn't remember picking it up as I went out. "I've got to phone Kayla, Jer." I thought calling her "Jer" might loosen her up.

"If we have time." She glanced at her watch and eased off on the accelerator. "Put on the wig. You're still more recognizable than the vice president of the United States."

Which wasn't saying much. The VP could sing the National Anthem at Shea Stadium with a sign around his neck without anyone recognizing him.

We made it through security and into the plane with two minutes to spare before the doors closed and the plane backed out of its slot. No strip search by some nice TSA lady, which made my trip through security quick but bland. I sank back in my seat and closed my eyes. "Jesus Christ."

"What's the problem? We made it."

My brain, such as it was, finally started to catch up. "Why are we going to Myrtle goddamn Beach, Jeri?"

"To find Jacoba, of course. And her child. And Edna's sister, if she's still alive."

"Rooting through the past again."

"You got it. You're the one who opened that door, remember?"

"Why not phone someone out there? Turn it over to a PI firm in Myrtle Beach."

"I don't like to do that."

"Greg did, all the time."

"Well, I don't. I do my own work. Then I know it's done right, things don't get overlooked."

"How are we going to go about it? What name do we look for? Edna's sister won't be part of the Woolley clan."

"Holmquist," Jeri said. "Edna's maiden name."

"Holmquist?" First I'd heard of it. Things like that make me feel like a three-legged bulldog at a greyhound race. I'd thought I was a mile ahead of her. How'd she get ahead of me?

"I found it on the computer this morning," Jeri said. "Marriage records go back all the way to 1889. Emmaline Dorman told you she thought Edna's sister never married. We'll start there."

"We don't know the sister's first name, Jeri."

"Holmquist isn't Smith or Jones, Mort. Trust me, this'll be a no-brainer."

A no-brainer. Precisely my speed. I decided to shut up. If anyone could find Edna's sister, it wouldn't be me, but maybe I could learn something if I kept my eyes and ears open.

Jeri had the window seat. She looked outside as we taxied toward the runway. I had the impression that she'd torn me away from Kayla. Which was ridiculous, but there it was, a gut feeling that settled in and wouldn't go away. It was also a conversational gambit I wouldn't set fire to with a length of fuse and a two-hour head start.

The 737 roared down the runway and lifted off at a steep angle. Two minutes later Reno was five thousand feet below, eight miles back.

* * *

I managed to grab a few minutes of sleep on the way to Dallas-Fort Worth. Jeri stared out the window the whole way. At the airport we had twenty-five minutes to catch our Atlanta connection. I found a pay phone and called my place, but Kayla didn't pick up. She was sitting tight, not expecting a call from me. Either that or she was out walking another twenty miles. I'd avoided a loathsome answering machine in the house for as long as possible, but it was looking like the time had come.

We gained two time zones. Jeri and I boarded a 757 that lifted off at 2:25, local time. Soon, Jeri was looking more relaxed. Somewhere over the eastern edge of Texas she turned to me and said, "So, Mort, tell me about your family."

Safe enough. I couldn't think of one reason why she'd want to stuff me out the window into the slipstream if all I was talking about was family.

"What do you want to know?"

"You know. The usual. Got any brothers or sisters?"

"A sister, Ellen."

Who proved, like most Angels and Rudds, to be a nice enough person, but a flat, circular track with no distinguishing marks. That may sound cruel, but it's true. I too am a flat, circular track, or was until I became a world-famous PI. Ellen was a senior CPA for a well-known insurance company. It took a moment to explain that aspect of our plain-vanilla heritage to Jeri.

"That bad, huh? What's your dad do, or is he retired?"

"He was also an accountant. Had a brain like an adding machine. Genetically speaking, it's what he was made for."

"Was?"

"He's dead. The only Angel to have gone out with a bang."

Her smile was hesitant. It made her look younger, as if she wasn't young enough. I had slightly more than a decade on her. When they're that age, and attractive, I start getting nervous.

"A bang?" She sipped orange juice—the synthetic kind that only airlines buy. It's a distinctive, metallic flavor, one you would never mistake for actual orange juice.

"My dad was playing golf," I told her. "Part of a foursome over at Arrow Creek. Clouds had been building all afternoon. Big black numbers. It started raining, huge drops that hit on asphalt leaving splats the size of silver dollars, thunder rumbling off to the south, and one of the guys suggested they call it quits. So right there at the sixteenth hole my dad pointed his putter at the sky and said, 'Up to you, Big Guy!' or words to that effect."

"Oh, no."

"Uh-huh. He took a bolt. That might seem rather biblical, except it's not that uncommon. Dozens of people are killed by lightning every year. Most of them aren't waving pointy metallic objects at a threatening sky at the time, either."

"Jeez-us, Mort."

"That was nine years ago. Two of the others in the foursome were knocked unconscious by the hit. Both are dead now, one by suicide, the other by cirrhosis. As my mother says, it wasn't a good day for the game of golf.

"I kind of admired him for it, though. He didn't go in his sleep or facedown at his desk, like almost every other Angel has since Martin Angel stepped out a sixteenth-story window over Wall Street in '29 and landed on a milk wagon."

Jeri smiled. "And you say your family has no color."

"What? Martin's Wall Street dive?" I shrugged. "Call it color if you like."

"It's something."

"It was over in seconds, like putting an exclamation point at the end of a very dull sentence. Mystique-wise, it didn't put much of a dent in a lifetime of stockbrokering. There's absolutely nothing else to say about him, except he went to church every Sunday of his life."

"What about your mother?"

"What about her?"

"How'd she take it, your dad dying like that? By lightning, I mean."

"Like a Mack truck. Or maybe a Kenworth. Something like that." In fact, she'd taken it like a Peterbilt, but I left that conversational gambit for a future time.

Jeri pursed her lips. "Care to explain that?"

"My mother was tickled pink, in an understated way. She was the very antithesis of the Angel clan. She had ideas, dreams. My father had only a succession of paydays that was going to follow him to the grave. His death turned her loose."

"What kind of dreams?"

I told her. Doreen Thompson Angel, age fifty-six at the time of Harold Angel's tragic end, suddenly found herself moderately rich. Good old Harold had been as conservative as he was unimaginative. He'd taken out a life insurance policy on himself for $250,000. Dori had picked up double indemnity on the policy, since lightning strikes are considered accidental even if you're talking to God and waving metal clubs around at the time. I didn't know all the details of how she got in contact with Ethan Armitage—a name that sounded made up to me—or how he'd found her, but suddenly the two of them were business partners in something called PET, Inc. Pet Entertainment Teleplays, Incorporated.

Armitage was an eager-eyed old fart, all bone and gristle, with TV-evangelist hair, who could talk a mile a minute and sound almost sane. He'd had the idea of making dog and cat videos for pampered housebound pets of the rich and not-so-bright while they were at work, and was trying to rustle up investors.

I met him once, at Harrah's Steak House over dinner. The only thing I didn't get was that Mom appeared to have her eyes wide open, yet she couldn't see this disaster unfolding. Armitage was going to skip, I just knew it. Why he had consented to meet me was beyond my powers of comprehension. For what he was doing to my dear mother I might've broken his back. Once they get the money, they're gone, and by then Armitage had the entire $500,000 and an additional $25,000 of Mom's savings besides. He'd cleaned her out, all with a harebrained get-rich-quick scheme about dog videos. The sonofabitch even had the gall to ask me if I wanted in on the ground floor, which was probably the real reason he'd agreed to meet me. I turned him down, of course. It was all I could do not to haul his ass into the men's room and use his skinny body to pound porcelain fixtures off the walls.

They went national a year later. Mom octupled her $525,000 in twenty eight months, paid her taxes, reinvested in Treasury bills and mutual funds at a time when the stock market was going bonkers, and was off to Hawaii. She never looked back. Certainly not at me, who'd told her in no uncertain terms that she was throwing her money down a rat hole.

"Great judge of character, Mort," Jeri said.

"Oh, yeah. I can spot 'em, all right."

She laughed. "And now? What's your mom doing these days?"

"Enjoying herself immensely. Investing money. Spending it. She's worth around eight million. Maui suits her. Every few months there's another stud twenty or thirty years younger than she is. It's a revolving door. She brings them to Reno sometimes, mostly to flaunt them, I think."

"Studs, huh?" Jeri looked out the window.

"That's conjecture on my part, but none of 'em have been mental giants. I don't think she keeps them around as chess partners."

By then I guessed we were somewhere over Mississippi. Dark-blue sky above, clouds and haze below.

"Tell me about judo," I said, wondering if she'd mention karate championships and Hawaii.

She took another sip of synthetic orange drink. "I grew up with it," she said. "Dad's an instructor in San Francisco, fifth degree black belt in judo, fifth degree in Aikido."

"Aikido. I've heard of it, but I haven't heard it mentioned in a long time. I thought it was dead, at least here in the U.S."

"It's not as big as it once was, but it's still around. It's about self-defense, using another person's strength and weight against them."

"Someone like me."

She nodded, smiling faintly. "Aikido wouldn't be your first choice to attack someone. Until I moved to Reno, I trained a lot with my brother, Ron. He's in Sacramento. Ron is two years older than me. He placed second in the North American Judo Championships last year, eighty-six kilogram class."

"Sounds like a bad guy to jump in an alley."

She grinned. "Like you wouldn't believe. An alley would be the worst place to tangle with him. You can do things in an alley that you can't do on a mat with judges watching, and Ron knows a lot of that. A *lot*." She paused for a moment, then said, "He taught me quite a bit of it. For a martial arts guy, he's not what you would call pacifistic. He has the idea that self-defense is supposed to mean something more than defense. His philosophy is no second chances if someone attacks you. Go for the kill."

"Which means you'd be bad news in an alley too, huh?"

"Not a lot of fun, no."

"Have you ever competed?"

She stared out the window. "Women's Nationals three years ago, New Orleans. In karate. I placed sixth. Different rules. Karate's not my thing. Judo holds aren't allowed."

"Yeah? Sixth? That's great, terrific even. Anything more recent?"

She faced me. "Okay, just say it, Mort."

"Say what?"

"If you don't know what, then I'm going to listen to music."

"Just...you looked pretty darn good on TV on Sunday."

"Hell."

"Third in all of North America and Asia. That's great, more than great. I would have placed around ten or twenty millionth."

She closed her eyes. For a while she didn't say anything. Then, "I'm too short. It's my reach. Mobley's five-ten. I'm stronger, faster too, but she gets through, scores points. Even that doggone Korean girl is four inches taller than me."

"Christ, Jeri, you took third."

"Third doesn't cut it. Not with me. I'm better at powerlifting. Not body building, which is narcissistic nonsense, but pure lifting. Putting weight over my head."

"You said you took—what?—fourth in the U.S."

"That was last year. The difference between first and fourth was only twenty-two pounds total on all three lifts. I've picked up nineteen pounds since then. And that last 10 percent isn't strength, it's pure technique. By the time the Olympic trials come around, I ought to be right up there."

I said, "Only world-class thing I do is find heads."

She gave me a look, then put on headphones and kept them on for the rest of the flight.

* * *

The plane landed at Atlanta. Our connecting flight didn't leave for half an hour so I had time to phone home again. Still no answer. I didn't like that, but there wasn't a damn thing I could do about it. Jeri also phoned, different direction, and got hold of a PI firm in Myrtle Beach called Furtado Investigations. We boarded the plane at 5:52 for the last leg to Myrtle Beach, got hung up on the tarmac waiting for six or eight planes to take off ahead of us, then roared off almost due east, headed for the Atlantic seaboard.

It was a short flight, fifty-two minutes. I took the window seat. We were forty miles from the coast when I saw dark clouds to the southeast, a squall line building. Over the intercom the pilot told us it was tropical storm Beryl, still a hundred forty miles from shore and about due east of Savannah, but headed toward the Carolina coast at twelve miles an hour with sustained winds of sixty-eight MPH. Second named storm of the season, and bigger than the first, Agnes, which had wimped out.

"Might get wet later tonight," I said.

"Uh-huh."

She'd lapsed back into moody silence, staring past me out the window. I left her to her thoughts. We started losing altitude, going into a low-power effortless glide, bleeding off air speed, flaps down a notch. We banked northward, easing down over cypress and tupelo swamps, tobacco fields, pine forests, salt marshes and tidal creeks, all of it so green it was enough to make a Nevadan's eyes bleed. You get used to a world of grays and browns—low, tough vegetation that survives on seven inches of rainfall a year. If Beryl kept coming, this place might get seven inches an hour.

We passed right over Murrell's Inlet, for many years the home of Mickey Spillane, a ragtag little backwater of homes and fishing boats. Then coastal forest, swampy inlets, more cypress, a few more fields, swampland, then we were racing over asphalt and concrete. The tires touched down at 7:25, local time.

Jeri checked reservations for our return flight while I located the car rental area, still wearing my wig. In spite of Beryl, the sun was bright, temperature in the low eighties, but a breeze was up, smelling of ocean. Jeri got a midnight-blue Mustang at Hertz, a poor man's Porsche but with plenty of zip if you own a Tercel. Jeri drove. We exited the Jetport and circled around on a few loopy roads and finally ended up on Ocean Boulevard, headed north.

A wall of high-rise condos and hotels blocked much of the view of the Atlantic. Traffic was sluggish. We passed an amusement park with a wooden roller coaster, girls in bikinis on the sidewalks, kids on skateboards and rollerblades. You could smell the tropical greenery and salt in the air, catch whiffs of hot dogs, cotton candy, cocoa butter and coconut-scented suntan lotion.

We stopped at a light. Two teenage girls wearing maybe eight square inches of material between them crossed in front of our car, bobbling, showing off what nature had recently given them.

"Nice view?" Jeri asked me.

"Terrific, if you like bubble gum and low SAT scores."

She smiled at that. "You ever been here before, Mort?"

I shook my head. "Nope. You?"

"Once. It's been a while. I was sixteen. It's bigger now than I remember, more built up."

"Progress."

"Like hell."

The light changed. The Mustang shot ahead, then slowed at the tail end of a line of slow-moving cars, mostly driven by old folks in their eighties. We went about ten jerky blocks like that.

"This thing at...what's it called? Furtado's?" I said.

"Yeah. What about it?"

"I thought you said you do all the work yourself."

"I do. But local access and resources are a big help. Keeps you from thumbing through phone books in hotel lobbies."

I nodded. Fell silent again. Learning.

To the right, a gap opened up in the condos and I saw whitecaps on the ocean, a curved beach with lots of flesh still on it, lifeguard towers. To the west was an amusement park called the Pavilion, with a steel frame corkscrew roller coaster and several other wild rides. Farther north, a pier reached a thousand feet into the ocean. Overhead, a slow-moving single-engine plane trailed a banner that read: *Crazy Zach's - North Myrtle Beach.*

"Where is this Furtado's?" I asked.

"Thirty-sixth Avenue North."

We were passing Tenth. This was going to take a while. I sat back and took in the town. Like Reno, it was experiencing growing pains. Another retirement Mecca, like West Palm Beach, Orlando, Tampa, Tucson. They crowd in until the place goes to hell and the murder rate doubles, then doubles again, then again.

Those with the means to get out, do. They crowd in someplace else and repeat the cycle.

Furtado Investigations was in a squat cinder block building sandwiched between a locksmith on one side and a cut-rate appliance store on the other where everything in the place had to go! go! go!—at unbelievable, never-to-be-repeated prices.

Emilio Furtado was in his forties, dark-skinned, thirty pounds overweight, with shiny black brush-cut hair and ancient acne scars, green slacks, tassels on white shoes and half a dozen gold chains around his neck, half-hidden in a thick nest of chest hair. He smiled when he saw Jeri, still looking good in her pale silk shirt and plum pants. The smile faded when he got a second look at me.

"Rain's comin'," he said in unaccented English to her chest, where his eyes were glued at the time. He was evidently a breast man. "Got us a storm brewin' out there. I hope you got somethin' else to wear when it comes in."

"We'll manage," Jeri said.

I took off the wig and rubbed my scalp. The thing was driving me nuts. Emilio stared at the wig, then at me, then he grinned. "Hey, you're that guy from Reno, right? That heads guy—Angel."

"Give that man a giant stuffed panda," I said.

Jeri elbowed my ribs. Emilio looked at Jeri, back to me. "Hey, this about that? It is, ain't it? Man, everybody's talkin' 'bout that."

"Everybody but you," Jeri said. "We weren't here."

Emilio's grin widened. "Oh, yeah, sure. All I meant was, hey, this's great." His face changed subtly and he looked at me. "You, uh, didn't like *do* it, didja, man?"

"I have these blackouts," I said, moving away from Jeri.

His grin went lopsided, then returned slowly. "Hey, you, what a kidder, huh? You I like, big guy."

Jeri lifted an eyebrow at me and mouthed "big guy?" then she and Emilio got down to business. I watched over their shoulders, literally. Emilio fired up a computer and brought up a list of all the Holmquists in the area, which included Myrtle Beach, North Myrtle Beach, and smaller outlying communities like Conway and Surfside Beach, dozens of others.

They found three Holmquists, but eliminated all of them within minutes.

Furtado had a collection of phone books socked away in a back room, covering most of South Carolina and parts of neighboring states. Fifteen of them were of Myrtle Beach and environs, one every two or three years, reaching back to 1978. Emilio pulled the first one off the pile, three years old. He located two Holmquists, but they were ones they'd already eliminated. Jeri went straight to the oldest book and found a Jewel Holmquist with an address in Conway.

"That was back in the days a woman could put her first name in a public directory," Emilio observed slowly, miffed that he hadn't been the one to find it. "Nowadays it attracts every kinda pervert you can imagine."

"Look up Woolley," I said to Jeri.

She stared at me, then understood what I meant. In the front room she got the most recent phone book from Emilio's desk. She thumbed through the W's, then looked up, smiling. "V. Woolley."

"Victoria," I said.

"Same address as Holmquist," Jeri said. "Got 'em." She smiled at me. "Good instincts, Mort."

Emilio said, "You wanna go out there now, check the place out? Conway's out past Red Hill on 501, fifteen, eighteen miles is all."

Jeri glanced at her watch and shook her head. "It's getting late. We'll go look around tomorrow morning."

Emilio shrugged.

I picked up the phone and dialed home, direct. Jeri and Emilio could work out the details on the bill. The phone rang.

"Where's a good place to eat?" Jeri asked Emilio.

"Depends. You want HoJo burgers like you'd find in South Bend or Des Moines, or you lookin' to find something real? She-crab, bass, lobster pie—?"

"Real," I said with the phone against my ear. It was Dallas's money, and I was here under duress. Back in Reno, the phone kept on ringing. No charge, so far.

"Gullyfield's is good," Emilio said. "Up north a ways. That or Cagney's. Or you can drive up to North Myrtle. Lotsa good places up there."

I hung up. In Reno it was 4:58 p.m. The sun would still be high. Kayla might be miles from home, putting more miles on her shoes.

Jeri took down V. Woolley's address, thanked Furtado, handed him five twenties, and we went outside to the Mustang. The sun was a last golden sparkle through trees in the west. Thirty seconds later, it was gone.

"Find a place to stay first, or eat?" Jeri asked.

"Let's get a place. I don't want to sleep under a park bench to-night. Not with rain coming," I added.

We got adjoining rooms at the Meridian Plaza Hotel, tenth floor. Nice little suites which included miniscule kitchens and private balconies, but not much else in the way of excitement. If not for the view, you couldn't tell if you were in Myrtle Beach or Akron, but that suited me fine. Travel wears me out. I wasn't in the mood for a rustic little B&B with a community bathroom down the hall and a twenty-minute wait for the shower. I was tired, looking forward to some extended sack time.

From my room I had a sweeping view of the Atlantic, dimmer and grayer now, with dark clouds scudding low over the water. Pale condos and equally pale hotels rose up on either side of the Meridian, all of it looking as if it had been cloned from a single pale block of concrete. Tropical white was the color of fun.

I sloshed water on my face in the bathroom, which made me feel marginally better. My beard was beginning to scratch, though. I had a rough look, very Hammer, very PI.

Two minutes later, Jeri knocked on my door.

"C'mon, Mort. I'm starving. Let's eat."

CHAPTER NINETEEN

WE ENDED UP at the Sea Captain's House on North Ocean Boulevard. So much for Emilio's advice. At least he'd pointed us in the right direction. On our way out of the hotel Jeri had asked the desk clerk what she recommended. The woman, a cheerful redhead in her twenties, said the Sea Captain had the best food on the Strand.

A former bed and breakfast overlooking the ocean, it had a lot of rambling rooms, dark wood, heavy tables and chairs. By the time we got there the water was purple black, foaming under a sky full of rose and orchid clouds, going black. To the north and south, the condos and nightspots along the Grand Strand had come alive with lights.

I had French bread, she-crab soup, and a platter of crab cakes and bass. Jeri had the soup and baked catfish on a bed of wild rice. And we had wine, a full bottle of Mondavi Chardonnay 2007 that set the tone for everything else that took place that evening.

"To the PI's life," I said, toasting us.

"Yeah, right." She raised her glass, gave me a smile that showed perfect white teeth.

"If not to that, then to expense accounts and filthy-rich clients."

Her smile widened. "To filthy clients." She clinked my glass with hers and took another good-sized sip.

I had an excellent crème brûlée for dessert, but Jeri was in a perpetual karate-training, employee-thrashing, waist-watching mode, which apparently didn't include empty calories. She poured the last of the wine into her glass and watched while I made a pig of myself.

"One bite?" I offered. "A nibble?"

"Nope."

"Want to smell it?"

She smiled and shook her head, hair dancing, then drained the last bit of wine from her glass.

It was full dark by the time we went outside. I'd had less to drink than Jeri and outweighed her by about a hundred pounds—which hadn't meant anything when it came to shoving and judo, but meant something in terms of sobriety.

"I'll drive." Deftly, I grabbed the keys from her. It was a sign of trouble that I did it so easily, like David Carradine in *Kung Fu*, snatching pebbles from the Master's hand.

"Don't trust me, huh?" she said.

"I trust you. I'll drive anyway."

"Coward."

I nosed out onto Ocean Boulevard, prepared to turn left, back to the Meridian. "No," Jeri said. "Go right."

"What for?"

"Let's go up to North Myrtle Beach."

"What for?"

"A drink, maybe a dance. Explore."

I was going to say "What for" again but decided not to push my luck. She was still tough, not drunk enough for me to risk another rib shot. And although it was nearly ten o'clock here, it was three hours earlier in Reno. I decided I could stay awake another hour or two.

I got onto Business Route 17, drove past the Carolina Opry, then merged with freeway traffic rolling north on Highway 17.

The river of lights flowed past dark golf courses, tidal flats and lakes on one side, the Intracoastal Waterway on the other. Up past Briarcliffe Acres and the town of Atlantic Beach, then into North Myrtle Beach. We ended up at Crazy Zach's on Second Avenue near Tilghman's Pier. Zach's was a huge place surrounded by palms, featuring four different bars, each with a different kind of music, take your pick, the whole thing more or less contained under one roof.

We parked, walked through splashes of neon, ground lighting, and the laughter of kids. To me, now pulling forty rather than pushing it, kids meant men and women Jeri's age or younger, further evidence that life is not only unfair, but that the good years are too damned short. We went inside, out of a rising wind coming off the ocean, making palm fronds rattle. Somewhere out there, Beryl was on the way. I thought it would be fun if they name the "D" storm Dori or Doreen, after my mother. Mom would make a terrific hurricane.

I steered us away from "Get Ur Freak On" and into what seemed like the tamest of Zach's bars, at least for the moment. A song was playing that I didn't recognize, no surprise there, but at least it wasn't ear-shattering. And it had a modicum of musical quality to it.

When the Beatles first hit America I wasn't yet in the planning stages. I was raised on "Help!" and "Penny Lane" and "Hey Jude," which weren't quite oldies at the time, but getting there. If there was any sort of message or subtext to any of those songs, it went right by me. Of course, "Lucy in the Sky with Diamonds" referred to LSD, but I didn't pick up on that either. I was too busy spinning donuts on my hot wheels. These days, you can tune into exploitative sex, instructions regarding suicide or homicide, and encouragement to kill policemen or rape your ho. Our de facto youth guidance counselors, many of them rappers, sometimes end up in prison, which seems like a damn good idea to me. The garbage in their songs turns to shit in the real world. They hit the wall and burn. I smile and sleep better every time that happens.

Jeri and I sat at a table with a candle on it in a dark corner of the room, twenty feet from a dance floor of polished wood. The room held about forty people. I ordered a Bud Lite and Jeri got a strawberry daiquiri in a glass the size of a birdbath. It was a Monday night, quiet enough that we could talk, if we kept our heads close together. She told me more about her brother Ron, and her father, mother, and a sister, Alyson, twenty-five years old, with two out-of-control kids, a self-destructing marriage and an on-again-off-again drug habit—cocaine, a step up from marijuana. Alyson was living proof that if it was handed to you, you might still not end up with any of it, because "it" was vapor, illusion. You can't hold the hard work of others in your hands. Only you are real, who and what you are, what you make of your life. Jeri's words, not mine. Too bad, since they rang so true.

When I asked her about powerlifting, her face came alive. She told me it was her drug, that and judo, Aikido, a little tae kwon do.

"Not private eye work?" I asked.

"You kiddin'?" By then she was working on her third daiquiri, stirring the icy slush with a thin red straw. I'd dropped down to Diet Pepsi, letting the sugar high lapse. "Six years ago I weighed a hunnerd 'n' fourteen pounds. Good pounds, 'cause of the judo, but I'm one thirty-two now, you believe that? I'm twenny-eight years old, Mort, five three an' a half, and I've never felt better or more thorou'ly alive in my whole life."

She was also more than a little thorou'ly drunk, face flushed, eyes bright. I said, "You missed blood pressure, cholesterol count, waist and shoe size, and all kinds of important astrology stuff."

She stared at me for a moment, then laughed. "I just mean...I feel great."

"I'm glad."

She punched my shoulder. "You shit."

"No, I mean it. Christ, you look terrific." I rubbed my shoulder. Maybe I could get the hotel to send up an ice pack for it later.

"Yeah?"

She was pleased, I could tell. Her eyes were out of focus and her mouth looked softer, almost kissable—an unexpected thought that made me uncomfortable.

"Yeah," I said.

She sipped her drink. "I'm a Libra. I wear size seven shoes. Waist is twenny-six, an' I'm a thirty-four B."

Yep, drunk as a skunk. Otherwise that 34-B thing wouldn't have made it out of her mouth.

Ten minutes later, I was ready to call it quits. That's when she ordered her fourth daiquiri, drank a quarter of it as soon as it arrived, then hauled me out of my chair and onto the dance floor. She was limber and sinuous, alluring in a compact, well-lubricated way, eyes bright, out of focus. She moved well, with lots of nice gliding hip and waist movement that might have drawn applause in Rio. I moved like I hadn't danced since Lennon was alive, and hadn't enjoyed it then.

Men's eyes followed her across the dance floor, and more than a few women's as well. Jeri didn't notice, didn't care.

Back at the table she said, "You're stiff, Morry." Her tongue was starting to go.

"It's probably the wig."

"So...take id off."

"And cause a riot?"

"You won." She looked around. "Idz dark. No one here'd care if you kill mayors or anything."

So I took the silly thing off, stuffed it like a dead Pekingese back against the wall. I gave it a hard look and said, "Down. Stay." Jeri laughed.

A slow dance started up. Jeri dragged me back to the floor, then clung to me like a starfish to an oyster with her cheek pressed firmly against my chest, hair on her head tickling my chin.

She looked up at me with luminous eyes. "'S nice, huh?"

"Very."

I could feel her breasts. They were solid, like the rest of her, but yielding under the pressure between us. She was warm. The pressure increased, and the yielding. Her hands moved on my back. None of which computed with what she'd said that first day in Reno, the day we'd met.

Partway through her fifth daiquiri I had to hold her up on the dance floor, sort of carry her around, holding her against me.

"We oughta go soon," I said.

"Yeeowww," she murmured, almost a purr. I hadn't had much in the way of conversation out of her in the past twenty minutes.

"Let's go, Jer."

"O-yeah, les'go, uh-huh. Bag-oo da 'ot'l."

Not a good sign. I recovered the Pekingese, Jeri's purse, and guided her out the door to the car.

I got on 17 and headed south, toward the glare of lights that was Myrtle Beach, one very drunk Geraldine DiFrazzia, PI, beside me with her head resting on my shoulder.

Her face tilted up at me. "Iz Kella ver' pridye?"

"What?"

She struggled to speak. "Is Kelya ver' priddy?"

"Kayla? Yeah, she is."

"Priddyer 'n me?"

"C'mon, Jeri."

"Iz, izn' she?" Her head lolled. "You god 'er, you do'n wan' me."

I didn't know what to say. Maybe nothing would have mattered. It wasn't likely she would remember any of this in the morning. But it mattered to me.

I was formulating a half-assed reply meant to clarify the situation when she began to snore.

Just as well.

I settled back, drove the car.

* * *

I had an attendant at the Meridian park the Mustang and leave the keys at the front desk. Jeri stumbled along as I helped her into the elevator and up to our floor. The activity woke her up some. I steered her toward her room.

"No," she said suddenly. "Your room, Morry." How she was able to tell one room from another, I didn't know. I didn't think she could see walls at that point.

She wouldn't have it any other way, however, so I opened my door and half-carried her inside.

I plopped her down on the bed.

"Oof!" she said, landing on her back, then she struggled to sit up. I helped her. She started to unbutton her shirt, then gave up. "You do id," she said.

I unbuttoned it, not without misgivings. She took it off, flapping one arm to free herself, then said, "Bra," looking at me with ten-pound eyelids.

"You sure?"

"Uhdo id."

I unhooked it. It was one of those ultra-sheer numbers that offered support but didn't hide much. She shrugged it off. She had wonderful breasts, firm, capped with dark, medium-sized nipples.

She rubbed them absently, then slowly toppled onto her left side and passed out, snoring so faintly it was barely audible.

"Jeri?"

No answer.

I lifted her feet onto the bed. She was solid and muscular, but she'd lost that etched and steely look I'd seen in her gym. She was catlike, a lynx, slack now, but with an underlying readiness—a much different type than Kayla, but every bit as sexy.

I pondered my next move. She probably needed a shower. I know I did. But I was damned if I was going to give her one and have her wake up in the middle of it and rip my heart out—or wake up the next morning, see how clean she was, put two and two together, and rip my heart out, an organ I have valued highly over the years.

I removed her sandals, then stripped off her pants. She wore dark-blue bikini panties, no lace. I left those right where they were. I pulled back the covers on one side of the bed, rolled her over, then covered her. I hung up her shirt and folded her slacks over the back of a chair. I left, after rummaging in her purse for the key to her room—one of those cards with a magnetic strip.

In her room, I phoned home again. Still no answer. I didn't like that one bit, but there wasn't anything I could do about it. I took a long shower, hot then cool, toweled myself dry, then grabbed the TV remote and went to bed. I caught the last of the news—sports—and Leno's monologue. No mention of those murderous ne'er-do-wells, Mortimer or Dallas Angel. We'd fallen off the national radar screen, disappeared beneath a fresh layer of murk. Scandals, a roller-skating dog, weird medical findings, the latest problems with Obamacare, and a bungled bank robbery had eclipsed us, thank God.

I turned off the tube and settled into the sheets. Visions of Jeri in the next room toyed with the more impressionable regions of my brain, then I sank down into a deep, dreamless sleep.

* * *

The rain came at 2:05 that morning, a sudden rattling against the window that jerked me awake. It sounded like tiny stones at first, distinct hits, then a barrage, escalating to a low continuous roar of wind and water that finally lulled me back to sleep.

I woke up a few minutes past three when Jeri turned on the light by the bed and looked down at me, swaying slightly on her feet. Her hair was damp and tangly and she had a towel wrapped around her. Rain was still thundering down. I had the idiot idea that she'd been out walking in it.

"I threw ub," she said, speaking with effort, doing a pretty good job of enunciating, all things considered.

"Did you?"

"I didn' make id to the bathroom. The bed's a mess." She blinked owlishly at me.

"Why am I not surprised?"

"I toog a shower. I'm clean. Can I sleep here, Mord, wisch you?"

"That could get complicated, Jeri."

"You mean 'cause of Kelza?"

"Kayla."

"I need sleep. I'm so dizzy. I won'...try anythig, I promiz."

"Are you all through throwing up?"

"Yes."

I patted the bed next to me. She turned off the light and came around to the other side. I heard the towel drop, then she slid in beside me. I couldn't tell how she was dressed, but she'd just come from a shower and all I'd seen was that towel, so odds were she was naked, which is the kind of deductive power that separates world-class PIs from your run-of-the-mill PIs.

"How'd you get in?" I asked.

"I use the phone by the elevadors and call down an' tol' 'em I logged myself oud by assident."

"Wearing only a towel?"

"Well, I didn' tell 'em thad. A kid broad a mazzer key. Nod a big deal. I bet weirder things habben 'round here alla time. I mean, this is my room."

"A kid, huh?"

"Sorta. He was like aroun' twenny."

No doubt Jeri had made his day, or night. For a while I listened to the downpour outside. It was a soothing sound, watery, something you don't hear much in Reno.

"Mord?"

"Yeah?"

"Juss lizzen to id. All thad rain."

"It's great. Christ, I miss rain. I guess people who live here probably get sick of it, but after years of Nevada..."

"I know." For a moment we lay there, listening to it. "Mord?"

"Yeah?"

"Could I like...hold you? Juz for a while."

"Sure."

She shifted in the dark, pressed herself against my side, and put an arm across my chest. I smelled rum and wine on her breath, and toothpaste, and soap. She suddenly felt more real to me, more human. Not that iron piston I thought I knew, but a young, vulnerable woman trying to get by in a rough world. Twenty-eight years old. To me she was young, but she would see herself approaching thirty. She would be staring at the hard press of time, wondering where the last five years had gone, starting to have an idea how fast the next five would go.

I thought about Kayla. Would she care about this? Hard to say. Would she understand? Hell, did I? I decided I didn't, not entirely, but that was nothing new. I have a history of not understanding things, then having them slam into me at high speeds.

She was warm. She was wonderful. She was hard and soft and pliant and naked and everything one might hope for in a woman. This gumshoe business was definitely underrated.

I was confused as hell. I felt every breath she took. I switched off the words and listened to the rain, secure in this temporary womb, the wild din and wet of it out there beyond the windows, howling off the ocean, glad that it wasn't a full-scale hurricane.

Jeri shifted her arm, placing her hand on my chest. Her elbow ended up touching my erection.

"Oop, sorry," she said, moving her arm an inch.

"It's okay. Go to sleep."

"Not so awvly sorry, Mord."

* * *

She drifted off.

I knew what it was, of course. Pheromones, a la Mike Hammer. Spores, burst out of an unknown pod, fatally attractive to the fair sex. I had acquired it or them that Monday when I'd woken up as a private investigator, a whole new man. It had started about then, all these women.

Before Monday—year upon year before, after Dallas divorced me—I'd lived a traditional IRS life of longing and near-celibacy. God's curse, no doubt, as if sexual fulfillment was not meant for those who confiscated the piggy banks of eight year olds and spread misery throughout the land with the steamroller weight of the federal government behind them. But of course, the rationalization is that it's a lousy job and somebody has to do it. Which wouldn't be true if we had a rational tax code.

Since Monday I'd had three gorgeous women in my bed and one scantily clad beauty beckoning to me from a doorway, even if she was a scary little brat.

Greg hadn't been wrong, the cad. He'd been trying to throw me off track, wanting to keep it all to himself. But I figured it out, Greg, you twerp. Now I know. Except you didn't have to die. There was plenty of it to go around, enough for both of us.

So darn much of it.

* * *

I woke up at eight thirty. Jeri was still out cold. I slid quietly out of bed and hopped into the shower to wake up, running the water hot, then cold, like the night before. When I came out in a towel, she was standing at the window, looking out at the storm, wearing nothing but panties.

"How's your head?" I asked.

She didn't turn around. "Hurts. I'll be okay."

"What time's our flight back?"

"Not till four fifteen." Her speech had improved markedly in the past few hours.

"How's that storm looking?"

She turned her head. "Wet. Windy."

"Think we can make it? I'm worried about Kayla. She's not answering the phone."

Jeri faced the storm again. "We'll make it. If they haven't closed the airport."

* * *

We ate at a place called Aleece's. Jeri toyed with her oatmeal and toast. I had grits with butter, salt and red-eye gravy, scrambled eggs, ham, sausage, two plates of toast and strawberry jam, coffee.

"Gawd," Jeri said, staring at her oatmeal. Her skin had a pale greenish cast.

"We oughta stay another night," I said. "Go out drinkin' again. Paint the town red from one end to the other."

"Ha, ha. You're so not funny."

I leaned closer to her. "Even when you look like hell, Jeri, you look good." And I meant it, but I wasn't sure why I said it. Maybe I was trying to make her feel better.

She almost smiled. "Go fly a kite, buster."

Buster paid the tab and we went outside into a downpour that turned the whole world gray and misty. Visibility was a quarter mile. Jeri drove. She wanted to do something. I didn't object since she was steady on her feet. I wanted to get a look at the country, what little of it could be seen from inside the unruly fringe of a tropical storm.

We went west on Highway 501, past 17 and the Intracoastal Waterway, past tobacco fields, half a dozen misty golf courses, the Myrtle Beach Speedway, shaggy waterlogged cypress, tupelo and palmetto, creeks full of brown water. Rain slanted down, unending buckets of it that turned the highway into a quarter-inch-deep sheet of gray water and oily bubbles. Jeri had to keep the speed down to avoid hydroplaning.

We turned onto Business Route 501. Houses outside Conway came into view. Watery neon signs glowed in the dimness beneath a turbulent sky. Conway was a town of about twelve thousand people, a bucolic place of modest but generally well-kept

Victorian, Georgian and Federal houses, Colonial, some recent nameless junk. It looked like the kind of place a person named Jewel Holmquist would live. Spanish moss swayed in the limbs of live oaks, dripping water. Water raced down gutters and flooded street corners in dirty swirling pools, clogged with leaves.

We stopped at a small market on a corner. The place had two gas pumps and an empty bench out front, RC Cola signs, the ghost of a fading Nehi ad painted on a brick wall. A traffic light danced on a wire strung across the intersection.

We dashed inside. A morbidly obese woman in a blue housedress was behind a counter smoking a cigarette, watching a tabloid show on a small television, something about pregnant teenage hookers who'd returned home with AIDS. Educational and uplifting. Who could ask for more at ten in the morning? Jeri asked for directions while I tried to look interested in a selection of flavored potato chips, extra crunchy Cheetos, and spicy pork rinds.

Back in the Mustang, we dripped water on the seats and grinned at each other.

"Wow," she said, wiping water from her face.

"Watch out. That shirt's going see-through. The bra, too," I added unnecessarily, but included it for the sake of completeness and accuracy.

"If it bothers you, don't look."

"Doesn't bother me."

"What'd you mention it for?"

"Just so you'd know."

"Yeah, well, I know. Not much I can do about it, is there? If it bothers you, don't look." She gave me a look.

I shrugged. "Doesn't bother me in the least."

"So we're all good here, huh?"

"Uh-huh."

"Great." She backed out and took off. We went down a main street with a few traffic lights, turned left, then left again, cruising slowly through a neighborhood of older homes, mostly two-story houses with gables and clapboard, deep porches, old oaks bearded with moss in the front yards.

Jeri slowed the car, pointed. "There it is. Six eighty-eight."

It was half the size of Sjorgen House in Reno, but similar: white clapboard, a turret, gingerbread trim, two red brick chimneys, one at either end of the house. The windows were dark. Its gutters were overflowing with rainwater, and a *For Sale* sign was in the front yard, shuddering in the wind.

"C'mon," Jeri said, opening her door.

We ran to the porch. I rang the bell, water leaking down my back from my hair.

The house looked empty, felt empty.

I rang the bell again. Jeri cupped her hands and peered in through a window. She looked at me and shook her head.

I turned, looked back at the street. "Now what?"

She rang the bell eight or ten times, then knocked, hard, tried the handle. It was locked. Finally she gave up. "Now we go talk to the neighbors."

We dashed across the street to a Georgian house with a hipped roof and columns, red brick, splashing through what seemed like one continuous puddle.

A spindly woman opened the door, hair done up in a bun, eyes dark. "Yes?"

"Do you know the people who used to live over there?" Jeri asked, pointing across the street.

The woman's face went stony. She shut the door without a word.

Jeri looked at me, shrugged.

"Not what you'd call a good sign, huh?" I said.

"Not very, but it's a sign, Mort. Let it register. C'mon."

We ran down to the next house, arriving under a porch over-hang as soaked as if we'd stepped out of a shower. Jeri's shirt was all but transparent.

"You better hope a guy answers," I told her.

"You ring, okay?"

I did. A man in his seventies opened the door and looked out at us. "Hep you?" He looked past me to Jeri. He had a twenty-pound cat in his arms that might have been dead, except that it was purring like a moped with a bad muffler, peering at me with one yellow eye.

Jeri edged around me. "We were wondering if you know the folks in that house." She pointed.

"What'd you want to know?"

"Well, where they are, for one thing."

He looked at her for a moment, then at me. "Better come on in, huh? Wet out there."

We trailed him into a parlor that had been decorated by a woman, which I recognize as a sexist remark and not necessar-ily true, but the room was full of flowered sofas and chairs, lace curtains and doilies, a red velvet loveseat, ceramic and jade figu-rines, a few dolls in satin dresses. But whoever had decorated the room was long gone, or so I thought by the film of dust covering everything, and the brown plants in pots by the windows, as dry and dead as cornstalks in December. Jeri and I stood in the room, looking around.

"Holmquist," the man said. "Either a you kin?"

"No," Jeri replied.

"Know 'em pretty good, do ya?"

"Not really."

"Then why're you lookin' for 'em?"

"I'm a private investigator," Jeri said.

He looked her up and down, then grunted, evidently satisfied with the explanation. He stuck out his hand, which both Jeri and I shook. "Name's Kennedy. Kennedy Lynch." He held up the cat and grinned. "This here's Johnson, vice president. Go on, sit wherever it suits ya. Water'll dry all right."

He didn't offer Jeri a towel, so either he liked the look or it didn't occur to him.

Jeri and I sat on a couch. Kennedy and Johnson took an armchair facing us. Kennedy had on khaki slacks and a brown sweater covered in cat hair. The hair on his head looked as if he'd slept in it for several weeks since it had last seen a comb. A stale smell of bacon hovered in the air, and a powerful reek of Old Spice.

"Ask yer questions," Kennedy said when he was settled.

"Are the Holmquists gone?" Jeri asked.

"Reckon so. Place's been sittin' empty for over two months now. Realtors come and go. Housing market's not so good around here right now. Might be too hot, muggy. Be better in September."

"Do you know where they went?"

"Didn't consult me, ma'am. Though if I had to guess, I'd say Reno. Way out in Nevada."

"Please, call me Jeri."

Kennedy smiled. "Jerry. That there's a man's name." He stroked Johnson's fur, eliciting a purr as loud as a muffled paper shredder.

"Reno?" Jeri said. "Why Reno?"

"That's where they're from. They come an' they go."

"Do you know Jacoba?"

"Knew her, yep."

"Knew?"

"She died about twenty years ago. You don't know much, Miss Private Eye."

"I'm trying to find out," she said.

"Jacoba was simple. Beautiful, but about as simple as they come," Kennedy said.

"How did she die?"

"Story is, which my Olivia got over the back fence and you kin take that for what it's worth, is that she fell, slipped and hit her head in the tub."

"What about Jewel?"

"She died too, couple a years back. Near a hundred years old, she was. After that, it was just those two women."

"Victoria and Winter."

"Yep." He looked fondly down at Johnson. "I've been in this house goin' on forty-six years. Jewel Holmquist was here long before that. Wouldn't take up with no man, that lady, not that I ever tried."

We waited. Jeri took my hand. It was warm, small, as firm as a chunk of cured ham.

Kennedy went on: "Long time ago, upwards of forty years, Jacoba showed up. Came all the way from Reno. Jewel's sister sent her. I don't recollect her name, though, the sister's. Pretty as a picture, Jacoba was, but just a kid. Pregnant, which's why she come out. Just startin' to show."

"Did she have the baby?" Jeri asked.

"Yep. Jewel named 'er. Called 'er Victoria, but I s'pose you'd know that, huh?" He gave us a squinty look.

"How were they?" I asked.

"What d'you mean?"

"As a family. How did they act?"

He shrugged, running a hand over Johnson's fur. Cat was lucky to have any left. "Quiet. Kept to themselves. Jewel took 'em off to church Sundays, Jacoba and Victoria. Other than that, I didn't see 'em around much."

He frowned. "Except..."

"Except...?" Jeri prompted.

"Well, I seen 'em a few times, now and then, over the years—Jacoba and Victoria. Down at the store, around. Nothing regular. Victoria was a kid, but when she was seven or eight years old she was like a mother to Jacoba, tellin' her what to do, doin' things for her. I saw her tie Jacoba's shoes once, right out in front of the house. It didn't take no special insight to see that Victoria loved her mama, simple as Jacoba was."

"Do you remember what year Jacoba died?"

He thought about it, then started counting on his fingers, lips moving silently. Outside, the storm raged. The water sounded like birdshot against the window. It ran in sheets down the glass, causing the street to ripple wildly.

"Be about twenty years, I'd say. That was the year my grandson Ricky was born. If Olivia was alive, she'd know to the day, God rest 'er."

Twenty years. That sounded familiar. What had happened twenty years ago? Something. I could feel it clumping around in my brain, trying to get out. Things do that more now than when I was thirty, facts trapped in there like convicts serving a life sentence.

"How did Jewel and Victoria take her death?" Jeri asked.

"Jewel was okay. She took most everything like an old Marine. Nothing bothered her. I called her Rushmore, after the mountain, all those stone faces. Olivia'd shush me when I did, but Jewel had that look. Victoria took Jacoba's passing pretty doggone hard, though, way I heard it. Fourteen, fifteen years old. Olivia said she was a handful. Got that over the back fence too. Probably true, though, since Victoria went back to Reno not long after Jacoba died."

Jeri looked at me in surprise.

Kennedy stroked the cat. "I heard tell Jewel couldn't take any more. You know how kids can be."

"But then—Victoria must've come back," Jeri said. "You said she and Winter left only recently."

"Oh, yeah. Victoria came back, all right. She was only gone for a couple or three months."

"How was she?" Jeri asked. "Better?"

"All depends on your point of view. She was as pregnant as two cats, that's how she was." He smiled at the expression that bit of news put on Jeri's face.

"With Winter," I said.

He nodded. "Yep. Victoria swelled up, then by and by along came Winter. Weird doggone name, huh? Cute kid, though. Grew up beautiful, like her mama, but thin. Not enough meat on her, I always thought."

A moment of silence spun out, filled with the sound of wind and rain.

"So Victoria and Winter lived with Jewel?" Jeri asked, trying to keep Kennedy talking.

"Yep. Kinda peculiar, those two."

"What do you mean?"

"If'n you saw Victoria, you saw Winter."

"You mean they were close?"

"Close, yeah. Like each was the other's shadow. Never saw anything like it."

"Well, they were mother and daughter."

"Even so." He rubbed Johnson's ears.

A thought occurred to me. I said, "Did Winter go to school?"

"Victoria taught her. Home schooled her. All the rage, now, from what I hear. Not quite so much back then."

"She never went to a regular school?" Jeri asked.

"Not that I ever saw. Other kids'd take the bus. Stops right out there on the corner, but I never saw Winter get on with 'em. Like I said, if you saw Winter, you saw Victoria. Two of 'em was like Siamese twins."

More silence. Jeri squeezed my hand. It felt nice.

Finally, I said, "Has there been any trouble around here lately? Say in the past year or two."

"What kinda trouble?"

"Nothing specific. Just...anything serious. Something that might get the police involved."

Kennedy pursed his lips, thinking. "A kid a couple of streets over was killed. Caused a fair commotion for a day or two. Boy was only seventeen."

"How long ago?"

"Couple or three months back."

"How'd he die?"

"Gunshot, from what I heard. Drilled 'im right through the heart. Bullet went straight on through, didn't tear up much inside, so they're thinking .22 caliber. Probably the reason no one heard anything, too. Detectives come around asking everyone in the neighborhood if they saw anything, heard anything. I was sorry I couldn't hep 'em any, but..." He shrugged.

"Did they catch the killer?"

"Not that I heard."

I thought about that, couldn't make anything of it. I looked at Jeri. She shook her head at me.

"Anything else?" she asked.

A few seconds ticked by. "Was a suicide some years back. Two houses down." He nodded up the street. "Guess it'd be four years ago. Arvin Weldon lost his job, got himself fired, hung himself off his second-floor banister with a bedsheet. Didn't know him all that good. Guy was something of a loner, kept pretty much to himself. We'd talk about the weather if we ran into each other, that's about it."

I couldn't make anything of that, either.

Half a minute of silence dragged by.

Jeri squeezed my hand again and gave me a look, a little shrug with her mouth that meant she'd run out of questions. I didn't know what else to ask, either.

I started to get up, but suddenly Jeri's hand tightened on mine and she held me down. She was looking at Kennedy.

His eyes were bright, eager, waiting. There was something more, secrets floating around in that dark light in his eyes. Jeri had spotted it.

"What else?" she asked him.

Kennedy smiled mysteriously, eyes shifting between us. "That girl, Winter, turned into quite a looker, same as her mama."

I'd told Jeri as much, and Kennedy had said the same thing a few minutes ago. But there was more to it. "Yes?" Jeri prompted him.

"History," he said slowly, "has a way of repeatin' itself."

"What do you mean?"

Whatever it was, it was good. He wanted to drag it out, savor it, chew on it a while, but couldn't figure out how to go about it. At last he shrugged and said, "Four, five years ago, the two of 'em took off for a while. Month or so. When they got back, Winter was pregnant. Just like her mama, just like Jacoba. Fifteen year old, she was, an' knocked up."

I felt cold at his words. Jeri leaned forward a little.

"Had a kid, too, name of Miranda. My Olivia died that same year, September. Only way I can remember anything nowadays, seems like. Either a you want some ice tea?"

CHAPTER TWENTY

MIRANDA. LIKE THE warning, I thought.

Jacoba, Victoria, Winter, Miranda. Every fifteen or sixteen years there was another one. Children having children, generations piling up. I was hardly able to keep them all straight. If Jacoba were alive today, she'd be somewhere in her fifties and a great-grandmother.

"Miranda died about two months back," Kennedy said. "That's when they put the house up." He looked down at Johnson. "Was one curious thing, though."

"What's that?" Jeri asked. "The way she died?"

"No, not that. She had a seizure, swallowed her tongue or some such." He hesitated. "Well, maybe that was curious, but not if you knew Miranda. Thing was, she was simple, maybe even more than Jacoba had been." He gave Jeri a half-hearted smile. "Two of 'em in one family. Now, don't that beat all?"

* * *

I drove us back to Myrtle Beach, squinting to peer through the rain. Jeri was silent, lost in thought. As we crossed the Waterway, she said, "Wendell Sjorgen was murdered twenty-one years ago."

Ah, yes, that was it. My brain gave a little sigh of relief.

"What do you make of that?" I asked. "Coincidence?"

She shrugged. We went another two miles before she said, "If you're into coincidences, two of four of those women were retarded, Mort. And both of them are dead."

"Emmaline Dorman told us Jacoba had been damaged during birth. Didn't get enough oxygen."

Jeri stared at me. "You never told me that."

"I forgot."

"You forget a lot...partner."

"I never know what's important and what isn't. You think it means anything—Jacoba being brain damaged at birth that way?"

"I think it means her genes were fine. Most likely she would've given birth to a normal child. Which it appears she did. Other than that, who knows?"

We were on Highway 501, nearing Business Route 17 and North Ocean Boulevard. "Where to?" I asked.

"The beach."

"The beach?"

"Roll your window down," she said. "There's an echo in here."

"Okay, okay, the beach."

Highway 501 had become East Broadway. I turned east, then went south on Ocean. Rain swirled over the tops of the condos, and between, driven by the wind. A few people dashed from their cars into stores and buildings, but the street was mostly deserted.

"Turn there." Jeri pointed off to the left.

"What's down there?"

She stared at me.

"Oh, yeah, right," I said. "The Atlantic, full of old Nazi submarines." I turned onto Fourth Avenue.

"Okay, pull over," she said.

I steered the Mustang into a space half a block from the beach. Whitecaps were visible, dark gray clouds, rain, ocean spray.

Jeri took off her sandals and got out. "C'mon."

"Jesus, Jeri."

"Get your shoes off. Let's go."

"Go? Go where?"

"The plane doesn't leave for hours, Mort. C'mon."

She started walking toward the beach, wind tugging at her shirt, hair already soaked. I pulled off my shoes and socks and climbed out of the Mustang, hurried to catch up with her. The rain was cool but not cold—windblown lukewarm bathwater. It was the first week of August, even if it didn't look like it.

I caught up to her where the sidewalk ended and became sand. We walked onto the beach. The sand was wet and dense, glistening, the depressions holding pools of water. To the south, waves pounded against a pier that extended far out into the ocean. Half a mile to the north, another pier was all but lost in the rain.

"What're we doing?" I yelled over the rush of wind and thudding sound of surf.

"When will you get to do this again, Mort?"

That was her answer. She laughed and spun in the rain, face upturned to the downpour. Only a few blocks away, condominiums were gray rectangular ghosts.

She grabbed my hand and started to jog along the shore, past hotels and condos with empty balconies facing the surf. Her blouse clung to her, molded to her breasts like plastic wrap. She didn't care. We were the only ones out there.

We went a quarter mile, maybe more, before she slowed to a walk. "Isn't this great?"

"Super." Truth was, I meant it. I hadn't done anything like it in a long time. Too long. This was the kind of thing kids do. Grow up too far, get too serious about life, and you lose it.

Dark green-brown stringers of glistening seaweed had washed up in tangled piles on the beach. Jeri ran partway out into a foaming tongue of gray, sandy water that came surging up high on the beach, wading in to mid-calf.

I went out after her. "We have to be on the plane in three hours, Jeri. We'll never get dry."

"Then we'll fly back nude."

"We can ask, but I'm pretty sure it's not allowed."

She laughed. "Wouldn't you like to, though?"

"Yeah, sure." American Airlines would love that, a moose like me naked in an aisle seat, downing a beer, fending off hordes of eager women once they found out what I do for a living.

Jeri looked down at her shirt. "You can see right through this little number, can't you? Bra, too."

"Sure can."

Suddenly she hugged me, looked up into my eyes. "I have to tell you something."

I didn't know what to do with my hands, but I liked the warmth and the feel of her body against mine. I returned the hug awkwardly. "What?"

"Last night at that bar I told you I've never felt so alive as I have in the past few years."

"Uh-huh."

"That wasn't true, Mort. Part of me isn't, wasn't. Alive. You've felt it, haven't you?"

"I felt...something."

"More than just something. I...I want you to know why."

A cold breaker swirled up almost to our knees. Not wanting to end up in Bermuda, I drew her higher up on the beach.

She held me. "There was this guy, Beau."

"Bo?"

"B-E-A-U, Beau."

"Oh."

"I was twenty-one. We were going to be married. I got pregnant and he took off. Just disappeared. Dumb me, I thought he and I were forever. I saw everything to the end of time, Mort—love, a Golden Retriever, white picket fence. Then, poof...I never saw him again."

"Jesus, Jeri."

"I miscarried at two months. It wasn't an abortion. I wouldn't do that. It just didn't take, whatever."

"You don't have to tell me this."

She pounded a fist on my chest in what would have been a nice CPR move if I'd needed it. "Does it look like I don't want to tell you, dope?"

"Not very."

"Then shut up." She pulled my head down and kissed me. It lasted long enough to make my head spin. She drew back an inch. "I haven't had sex since," she said. "Seven years, Mort. Little more than that. I just let that part of me die."

Quicksand lay all around. I didn't say anything. Seven years. Wow. Longer than me, even.

"I wanted to be smarter next time," she said, "not some dumb kid. But I never trusted myself. All I saw was Beau again, over and over and over."

"These things happen, Jeri. You can't give up when they do, or you go nowhere. Life passes you by."

"Easy for you to say. I was looking at having a child and no husband, no job. It was horrible, the kind of nightmare that happens to other people, not to me. It almost killed me."

I looked up and down the beach. Mist, rain, and wind, pennants whipping in the gale on the roofs of nearby hotels that were indistinct gray blocks in the storm.

I shivered. "We better go back."

I turned away, but she jerked me back and looked into my eyes. "I would sleep with you." She waited a moment, then said, "If you ever asked or anything."

My heart skipped a few crucial beats, leaving me lightheaded. "Thanks."

"Hey, that's not a commitment or a trap, dummy, it's a statement of fact. I know you've got Kayla, okay? I just want you to know. It's important to me, Mort. I don't want to keep it inside. There isn't any room for it, not anymore. I just want you to know, that's all."

"Well...thanks. For telling me."

"God, you're so stiff." She smiled. Water spilled into her eyes, ran off her chin. She pulled me against her. "You can't help it, can you?"

"I'm lost, that's all. I don't know what I'm doing."

"Maybe I wouldn't either, in your shoes."

I lifted a foot. "Hey, look, no shoes."

She took my hand. "Okay, fool. Let's go."

We walked back, arms around each other's waists, as wet as if we'd swum in from England. A man, sixtyish, in pretty good shape and wearing only a blue Speedo thing not much bigger than a jock strap came jogging by with a happy Doberman. He waved as he went by. Seagulls spiraled awkwardly overhead, struggling to stay aloft.

Back in the car Jeri wrung water from her hair. "I'm sorry," she said.

"What for?"

"Putting you on the spot like that."

"It's okay."

"Not *very* sorry," she said, grinning.

"Vamp."

"Uh-huh. I feel like one. It feels good, like finally waking up."

* * *

Jeri remembered seeing what had looked like a mall, and I drove back west on 501. Jeri spotted it again, which wasn't much of a trick. Outlet Park at Waccamaw was three malls in one, the complex covering almost a square mile, including parking lots.

We went in dripping, drawing stares. I bought jeans and a shirt, socks, a three-pack of Jockey shorts, a small duffel bag, then changed in a dressing room, threading a wet belt through the loops. Jeri bought navy slacks and a cream blouse, a bra, panties.

None of it went on Dallas's tab however. "I don't charge for my own silliness," Jeri told me.

We ate lunch at another seafood place, Pier Fourteen, taking our time, watching Beryl rage on, letting an hour and a half laze by before returning the rental and taking a Hertz shuttle to the terminal.

The rain hadn't let up, but flights were still taking off. As bad as the weather was, it wasn't enough to shut things down. Yet.

We took off ten minutes late. Ten minutes into the flight we broke through the cloud cover into sunshine and high, wind-flung clouds. We kept going up, leaving Myrtle Beach and Beryl behind. In the middle of a storm, right in the thick of it, that's all there is, the mad whirl of wind and rain, but a change of perspective reveals greater truths, whole new horizons, new realities.

Storms, I thought, were a lot like love.

* * *

Suddenly I was faced with something I hadn't anticipated, hadn't seen coming. Given binoculars, CIA-quality sound equipment, and a twenty-minute head start, I probably couldn't get out of the way of a herd of stampeding elephants.

Kayla and Jeri.

Each had disavowed commitment. Each had given the other first claim on me. Each had shared my bed and clung to me. Each was gorgeous, sexy, desirable, and evidently willing.

What an incredible mess, not that I was complaining.

Mike, old buddy, where are you? What did you do at times like these?

I would have to choose between them, and soon. Or—and this seemed equally likely—I was an idiot and they would both sail out of my life as abruptly as they'd sailed in, without so much as a backward glance. I was a rock of sorts, something to cling to, but only for a while. Life could go on perfectly fine without me.

That, too, had the ring of truth.

* * *

Chasing the sun, falling gradually behind the spin of the planet, losing time in airport terminals, we landed in Reno at 10:55 p.m. Stars were out. The air was cool and dry, smelling of sage. Beryl and all that glorious tropical outrage was part of a different universe.

Jeri drove me home in silence, slowly, almost reluctantly. I could feel her wanting to say something, but she held it in.

A lone van was camped out in front of my house. Unbelievable. You can get rid of tapeworms with less trouble. I had Jeri circle the block and let me out in front of Velma's.

Jeri licked her lips and gave me a nervous smile. "You really go through the fence, huh?"

"Until this Jonnie and Dave thing blows over, yeah."

Her smile grew sadder, full of hidden longings, unspoken words. "See you tomorrow at nine?"

"Sure," I said. "What's our next step?"

"Dunno. We'll think of something."

She stared down at her hands, twisting nervously in her lap, pale green in the dashboard lights, then she looked over at me. "If she ever lets you go, Mort. Here I am."

"Okay." Stupidly, I reached for the door handle. My only other option was to kiss her, and I couldn't do that, couldn't bring myself to get everything tangled up that way.

"Could you kiss me?" she asked. "One more time."

Now what? I had to. I did. It lingered, which was at least as much my fault as hers. She tasted good, too good. Probably the only thing that had saved us at the Meridian Plaza during those early morning hours was that we hadn't kissed.

I got out, waved, walked away. Behind me, the Porsche's engine continued to idle, a bit longer than necessary, I thought, then it wound up and faded off into the night.

CHAPTER TWENTY-ONE

KAYLA WASN'T HOME. I looked in the usual places for a note, but she hadn't left one. The words "easy come, easy go" sailed through what I loosely call my mind, but then I realized that that wouldn't be her way. She was a note-leaver.

So, where was she?

Being a world-renowned gumshoe, my name on the lips of half the population of the country, I tried to rustle up clues. The bed was made. Her shampoo and toothbrush were in the bathroom. And as far as clues went, that was about it.

I wandered through the house, feeling a sense of dread build up inside me until it became unbearable.

She'd been fascinated with the idea that Victoria might be her half-sister. Winter might be her half-niece.

I stared out a window at the night.

Jacoba, Victoria, Winter, Miranda.

Perhaps Jeri and I had flown off to follow a lead that would take us nowhere because it wasn't anything. Jacoba had been raped four decades ago. Ford had replaced Tricky Dick as president. Vietnam was over, but its scars were fresh. Apple hadn't yet rolled out its first computer. No one waits forty years to get even. Hell, after forty years there's usually no one left to get even with.

It was Tuesday, approaching midnight. I hadn't spoken with Kayla since Monday morning. Foreboding crawled through me, making me feel hot. A film of perspiration popped out on my forehead, under my armpits, all over my body like a hot flash.

Victoria. Before, the name had been just a name. Now it sounded dangerous, positively sinister.

I wondered if Kayla's Volkswagen was parked where it had been several days ago. I went through the fence and jogged five blocks to look. Her car was there. I didn't like that at all.

Victoria's name glided through my brain, like a black albatross on silent wings.

I jogged home and got my gun, still buried beneath that couch cushion. I changed into black jeans and a dark-blue long-sleeve shirt, feeling idiotic, feeling scared, too. I thought about phoning the police, but that felt a little over the top. The IRS-agent-turned-PI who found heads, calling the cops on three women living in the dead mayor's house based on nothing more than a hunch—I couldn't do it. Odds were they wouldn't listen to me, wouldn't even send anyone over to have a look at the place, but they might detain me for questioning or psychiatric evaluation, and I couldn't afford to let that happen. I had to go. Now.

I got a penlight from the kitchen and checked the load in the little .357. The cylinder carried Plus-P Hydra-Shok ammunition that could do an amazing amount of damage. I snugged it into a holster at the small of my back, donned a dark windbreaker to conceal the gun, and went out the back way again.

I walked down Ralston, over the freeway overpass, down to Sixth and turned east. I didn't have a plan. I didn't have a clue. I did, however, have a feeling that Mortimer Angel was once again going to be a household name come Wednesday, and the thought was almost enough to give me an ulcer.

As usual, the Golden Goose had turned the night into day on North Virginia Street. It was just after midnight, but the sidewalk

outside the casino, across the street from Sjorgen House, was full
of touristy-looking people coming and going, on the prowl for
Lady Luck. Two high-school-aged kids tore by on beat-up skateboards, wheels tocking out a rhythm on the sidewalk. Low-slung
cars cruised by, some of them with bass rumble issuing from open
windows loud enough to cause brain damage.

I stood outside Edna's yard looking at the house, but I felt too exposed to remain there for long, too easily seen by anyone who might
be watching from behind those dark windows. If I stayed there, I
might as well wear neon and set off a siren. I headed for the front
door, then ducked around the side of the house, into the shadows.

The house rose up dark and silent, not a light on anywhere.
Now what? Was Kayla in there? If she was, she was in trouble, if
what had happened to Jonnie and Dave was any indication. If she
wasn't, then I was in trouble, because, I realized, I was going to get
inside somehow and have a look around. I didn't have a choice.

My hands trembled. When Jeri grabbed my shirt and yanked
me up against the side of the house between two thick bushes, I
nearly screamed.

"Quiet," she hissed.

"Jesus H. Christ, Jeri!"

She pulled me down into a crouch. "Shut up!"

"What the hell are you doing here?" I whispered hoarsely.

"I could ask you the same thing, sport."

"Kayla's gone."

Jeri stared at me. She had on black clothing. All I could see was a
pale blob of face and her eyes, reflecting light. "Gone?" she asked.

"Yeah."

"And you think she's here?"

"Maybe, I don't know. I've got to find out." I grabbed her arm.
"Why'd you come back?"

"I had to."

"Why, Jeri?"

"You know."

"No, I don't know. You changed clothes. What were you going to do, come in my house through a window and have a look around?"

"No."

"What then?"

"I don't know. Watch the place. See if she was still there."

"I don't want you stalking me."

"Looking isn't stalking. Well, maybe it is. It won't happen again, I promise." Her hands found my face, held me. Her voice went soft. "I mean it. I'm sorry, okay? But I had to know, Mort. I just had to know. I love you."

I sighed. "That's not helping. Not now."

"Sorry." Her hands fell away. "I saw you come out at your neighbor's place and head downtown."

"Terrific. I forgive you. Now go away, Jeri."

"Uh-uh. I'm going to help, even if it's for her."

"No. Get the fuck out of here."

"Make me."

Perfect. Just what I needed. Getting rid of Jeri by force would sound like the crash of a C-130 full of Humvee parts. Short of clipping her without warning on the jaw, I doubted I could manage it, and if I didn't clip her just right, I'd end up in the hospital, which wouldn't do Kayla any good, either.

"Jeri—"

"No, partner. I'm in."

"Je-sus, Jeri."

"You keep saying that. I said I'm in."

She meant it. Nothing would change her mind. Some things you just know.

"Now what?" she asked. "How do we get in?"

"I hadn't worked that part out yet."

"Good plan." She stood, then started to creep out from be-tween the bushes. "Let's try doors first."

I grabbed her arm again. "Go home."

"Read my lips. No."

Hell. I couldn't even see her lips. I followed her to the back of the house, into darkness. The rear door was locked. I didn't want to try the front door with all that casino light blasting over from the Golden Goose. No point anyway. It wasn't likely to be unlocked.

We crept over to the single-car garage I'd seen behind the house the other day. A quick peek through a dirt-encrusted window with the penlight disclosed a dark-blue GMC Safari van. It would look almost black at night, say around Ithaca. I didn't like that at all. Now, beyond any doubt, I was going to get inside that house, which probably meant Detective Fairchild and I would have an-other entertaining discussion sometime in the near future.

At the side of the main house, I gave Jeri a boost and she tried windows. I had to admit it was easier than testing them myself since I would have needed a stepladder. At the north side, near the front, one of them slid upward at her shove. It rasped quietly as she lifted it until it jammed tight in its frame, then I lowered her to the ground.

"I'll go in," I said. "You wait here."

"You're good, Mort. You oughta do stand-up."

"I'm serious."

"You'd sound like a water buffalo going through there first. I'll help you. Lift me up, huh?"

I did. If I hadn't, she would have chinned herself on the sill and been inside in four seconds anyway.

From inside she reached down and took my hand, then pulled. It felt like I'd caught it in a conveyer belt. She'd braced herself and was lifting at least two-thirds of my weight. I'd known she was one god-awful strong lady, but some things impress more than others.

I came over the sill and piled in as quietly as I could, which was a joke. Inside, a dim greenish glow came from the casino through lace curtains backed with some kind of fabric. We were in the parlor from which Victoria had appeared when I'd last seen her. The parlor was musty and warm, full of angled shadows. It felt like a dangerous place to be, not a good place to turn on a penlight to have a look around, and if Kayla was in the house, it wouldn't be in here. Across the room, the double doors were open. I could see into the foyer. Outside, the thumping bass rumble of some nimrod kid's car moved south, rattling windows in their frames.

I eased off the windbreaker, using the idiot-thunder outside to cover the rustle of nylon, then dropped it back out the window to the ground between two shrubs.

As I loosened the gun in its holster, Jeri pulled my head down and put her lips to my ear. "Floor's gonna creak like a son of a bitch," she whispered.

"I know. Whole house is like this."

"Slowly, Mort. Ease your weight down. If it starts to creak, pick another spot."

Skulking 101. She started off, following her own advice. I went after her. It took two minutes to cross the room to the double doors. The floor wanted to sing an aria. Like she said, it was a sonofabitch.

She stopped in the foyer. "Up, or stay down here?"

I shrugged. How would I know? "Down here, I guess."

We searched the entire ground floor, slowly. It took half an hour. I didn't hear a thing from inside except the grumble of the floor under our feet and heart-stopping settling sounds. The house didn't feel asleep to me. It felt as if it, or people in it, were watching us, waiting.

Heat in the house was oppressive. It had been a hundred degrees that day in Reno, and the house had soaked it up and kept it in. Sweat trickled down my back, drenching my shirt.

We ended up in the foyer again. Jeri looked at me and nodded at the stairs. I nodded back.

She went up first. She was better at this than I was. I placed my feet where hers had been.

It took five minutes to reach the top. My legs were trembling with the effort to move without a sound, like trying to do Swan Lake at one-fiftieth speed.

At the landing Jeri turned and headed down a hallway. I caught the back of her shirt and stopped her. "Winter's room," I breathed in her ear, pointing. "Second on the left."

Again she nodded. She started off again. It was slow, laborious, miserable work in the heat of the house, darker up here on the second floor with its dearth of windows. Kayla could be in any of these rooms—or at a movie, or at a casino catching a late dinner, or home, now, waiting for me in bed.

Jeri eased a door open. Not Winter's. I handed her the penlight and she switched it on. The light was dazzling. After the darkness it was like a World War II searchlight hunting the Luftwaffe over Great Britain. Sweat bathed my face, got in my eyes.

The light went off. Spots of color swarmed in my vision, fading slowly. Jeri came out, continued down the passageway.

I could tell this wasn't going to work. Except that I couldn't tell. Mostly it felt ridiculous, melodramatic, and illegal. But it did have a solid gumshoe feel, nothing like an IRS audit, so that was something.

Jeri crept past Winter's room, then silently checked out another. We reached the end of the passage where it turned a corner and became stairs up to the third floor and Edna's room. What else might be up there, I didn't know. I hadn't explored earlier. Now I wish I had.

I was going to tell her about Edna's room when a bolt of pain shot through my back. I let out an involuntary howl and slammed into Jeri, then into a wall. I was pinned there, held by an explosion of pure agony.

"Don't move, cowboy," Winter breathed.

* * *

A light came on, the one Winter had turned on days ago, midway down the passage. In its yellow glow, with my face and chest pressed against old dusty wallpaper by the most terrible pain I'd felt in my life, I saw Jeri scramble catlike to her feet. She turned, hands coming up, prepared to maim or kill.

"Don't," Winter commanded, and whatever Jeri saw behind me froze her. She didn't so much as twitch.

Footsteps approached, then Victoria said, "You, girl, get down on the floor now, or he's dead. You have two seconds."

The pain in my back was like a red glowing poker. I didn't know what it was, but it was irresistible. It had me completely immobilized. If I tried to move or back up a tiny fraction of an inch, the pain got worse, much worse. I saw the danger of it in Jeri's eyes, the way she shrank away.

She quickly sat on the floor.

"Lie down, girl," Victoria said. "Facedown."

Jeri did as she was told. I could hardly breathe, the pain was so enormous. Something was lodged in the meat of my back, at least an inch deep, maybe more. Another inch or two and it might find its way into a lung.

Victoria straddled Jeri and clicked handcuffs on her wrists behind her back. Another pair went around Jeri's ankles. Then she stood up and passed out of my line of sight. Moments later there came a faint whisper-whir of air and a supernova of light filled my brain. The thud of something bouncing off my skull was like an echo that followed me down into absolute blackness.

CHAPTER TWENTY-TWO

I AWOKE TO a rushing sound in my ears that went on and on, like wind howling through high-tension wires. My shoulder joints felt like they were being torn apart. I was hanging by my wrists against a concrete wall with my weight on my arms. Even though my head was hanging down, and I was staring down the length of my body, it took me half a minute to realize, or to care, that I was wearing nothing at all. My attire, or lack thereof, wasn't my top priority.

I groaned. My head pounded wickedly. Every beat of my heart echoed as a drumbeat in the back of my skull.

"Mort."

Kayla's voice, muffled as if coming through fog. I lifted my head, which hurt—a lot. It took tremendous effort, all I could muster. My eyes wouldn't focus. A blurred image of her swam in my vision. She was wearing black silk panties, nothing else. She had two heads and three breasts, then four breasts, then three again. She was directly across from me, ten feet away, tied against the opposite wall with her hands over her head, feet flat on the floor.

"Are you okay?" she asked.

I tried to answer, but couldn't. The pain in my arms and joints was incredible, searing. I put weight on my legs, lessening the tension in my arms, which helped. My legs felt wobbly, so I leaned against the wall for support. I tried to move my feet together, but couldn't. I looked down, squinting, trying to get my eyes to work properly. My ankles were thirty inches apart, lashed by nylon ropes to eye hooks screwed into concrete anchors in the wall. Like the walls, the floor was plain concrete, cool and musty. The air was chilly.

"Mort?"

"I'm...okay."

It didn't sound very convincing, even to me. I was anything but okay. The drumbeat in my head went on and on. One Kayla was superimposed over another, shifted a few inches. I tried to get them to sync together, but they wouldn't. A new pain made itself known, a throbbing in my back like a bad tooth. I remembered Winter standing behind me in the hallway.

Then...nothing. Until this.

"They got you," Kayla said in a despairing voice.

I lifted my head and looked up. Yep. They certainly had. Like Kayla's, my wrists were up over my head. Whoever tied them had looped the middle part of a nylon rope twice around one wrist, then tied a square knot behind my wrist, then a series of square knots that went up another ten inches, higher than my fingers could reach. It looked like macramé. Maybe it was. My other wrist was held the same way. After the last square knot the ends passed through a huge eye bolt screwed into a beam in the ceiling. There was no way to reach the uppermost knot of the series that began behind my wrists, which was where I would have to start if I hoped to loosen the mess. A separate length of nylon cord formed a figure eight around my wrists. The middle part of the eight was a square knot, and the ends went around my other wrist and ended in a second square knot, locking my wrists together like handcuffs. Hopeless, but I scrabbled at the knots anyway, twisted my wrists, tried to reach back, get hold of something, anything. I couldn't get the slightest bit of purchase with my fingers on any of it.

I stood there, spread-eagled. It felt nightmarish, which gave me the feeling that I wasn't yet awake, that this was a vivid dream. My head weighed a hundred pounds. It started to sag. I felt darkness rising up around me. My legs started to give way again.

"Mort!" Kayla's voice and the pain in my shoulder joints brought me back.

"Yeah." I straightened my legs an inch and tried to lift my head.

For a moment she didn't say anything, as if there was nothing to say. Where we were and the way we were tied said it all, yet it also said nothing. Finally Kayla said, "I'm sorry," then she began to cry.

My throat was dry as dust. I desperately wanted water. "What's... what're they doing, Kayla?" Not a razor-sharp question, but I wasn't at my peak.

"They're crazy, Mort. Just *crazy*."

I had no answer to that.

Tears glistened on Kayla's face in the harsh light of a sixty-watt bulb in a ceramic fixture, ten feet off the floor. A wooden door was diagonally across the room from me, several feet from Kayla. A gray-painted, scarred workbench with a big vise was against a wall to my right on my side of the room.

The room was rectangular, twelve by twenty-five feet. It had the musty smell and earthy chill of a basement. The floor sloped almost imperceptibly toward a corroded circular drain by one of the walls. I didn't like the look of that. The room could probably be cleaned out with a hose if things got messy. A wooden beam identical to the one above me ran the long way across the room opposite, forming the highest part of the wall by the ceiling over Kayla's head. The beam was wider than the wall. A three-inch overhang jutted into the room, its lower edge eight inches below the ceiling. Several big eye bolts were screwed into the overhang. Kayla was tied to one of the eye bolts as was I, wrists together, each wrist held in a double loop that rose up into a lattice of square knots that terminated at an eye bolt—half-inch steel, heavy enough to have hoisted a marine diesel, no problem.

I didn't see any weakness in the arrangement. Those two broads weren't taking any chances. I couldn't move, couldn't twist, couldn't pull myself higher by more than an inch or lower myself at all. Old woodcut images of the Salem witch trials went through my mind, a bit stuporously, I must admit. This was psychotic, medieval...crazy.

Kayla's feet had been left free. Only her wrists were tied, not that it mattered—like me, she couldn't reach the knots to free her wrists. She wasn't going anywhere.

"They killed my father," she said. Her voice was a whispery sound in the room.

I'd already guessed that. No doubt Jonnie and Milliken had been in this room not long ago. Considering the way they ended up, it was evident they'd had no better luck with the ropes than I was having.

"Where's Jeri?" I asked. My voice was thick, slurred. It sounded unfamiliar in my ears.

"Jeri?"

"She was with me. Last night."

"I don't know. I haven't seen her. I've been here...I don't know how long."

"Did you come here, to the house? On your own, I mean?"

"Yes. I...had to know. If she was my sister—half-sister. I came to the door and told her who I was. She let me in. She made coffee and—Oh, God, Mort, I'm so sorry."

I closed my eyes. I was hurting, and so tired I could barely keep my eyes open. I couldn't hear anything, no voices, traffic, nothing.

Not even bass rumble coming from the cars of cruising morons. The room had a muffled, soundproofed quality. That was ominous. I tried to keep my eyes open. A pegboard on the wall above the work-bench held a collection of tools: screwdrivers, wrenches, a hammer, electric drill, crowbar. A sabre saw dangled by a cord from a hook—maybe the saw that opened Jonnie's and Dave's skulls. Lumber was stacked in a corner, a collection of two-by-fours, warped pine shelv-ing, a few new clapboards covered in primer. A second door was to my left, not eight feet away, but it might as well have been in Norway.

"Are we still in their house?" I asked Kayla.

"Yes. The basement. They killed my father and Milliken in here." Again her voice broke. "That girl did. The young one. They showed me a video, Mort. They forced me to watch it. It was terrible."

Terrible. That didn't surprise me at all.

*   *   *

I slid back into unconsciousness. I fought it but it came over me like a shroud, an irresistible tidal wave of fatigue, or worse. Felt like something was wrong with my head. From far away Kayla called my name, but I couldn't climb back up to a place from which I could answer.

After a while, I had no way of knowing how long, I awoke to a kind of shock. Victoria was standing in front of me. My cheek was burning. She'd slapped me. Not hard, but enough to rouse me and start that drumbeat thudding in my head again. Winter stood to one side in white shorts and a T-shirt, holding a bucket. The shirt was cut off, exposing her belly, lean and tight with muscle. She set the bucket on the floor. An expectant smile played on her lips.

She was more or less in focus. My vision had improved to where I wasn't seeing double. I had no idea how long I'd been out, but my arms were on fire again. I stood up, alleviating the tension and some of the pain. I would have given a thousand dollars to be able to lower my arms to my sides.

Alone with Kayla I hadn't felt as naked as I did with Victoria and Winter in the room. I hadn't felt much of anything other than pain and a sense of hopelessness at our situation. Now I felt vulnerable, utterly defenseless, something awaiting the knife. I couldn't draw my legs together, couldn't defend myself in any way whatsoever. Now all I could think about was Jonnie's penis and testicles, stuffed into his scooped-out, brainless skull.

Had they butchered him while he was alive? The thought gave me chills.

And Kayla, topless, wearing French-cut silk panties—she had to be feeling that same terrible helplessness. She was still wearing the silver-and-turquoise necklace I'd bought her in Austin. That and her nakedness made her look somehow primitive and fresh, like a sacrificial virgin about to be hurled into a volcano.

"Who are you?" I asked Victoria. An awkward question, but somehow it felt right—a request for truth, a confession, perhaps an explanation.

"Jonnie's daughter," she said. Her smile was eerie, alive with quicksilver madness.

"How do you know?" I asked.

She tilted her head. "A riddle? How interesting."

"You might be Milliken's kid."

Her smile got wider. "You've learned a few things, how fun. No, turns out it was Jonnie who got my mother pregnant."

"How do you know?"

"I know. I went out, looked at both of them and I knew, right off. Jonathan Sjorgen was my handsome loving daddy."

"Where's Jeri?"

"Miss Fitness U.S.A.? She's around someplace."

"Is she okay?"

"Maybe not a hundred percent, but then neither are you. Are you thirsty, Mr. Angel?"

"Yes." I would have killed for water. I would have killed both Victoria and Winter for free, *paid* a bundle to do it.

Victoria nodded to Winter. Winter scooped a ladle of water from the bucket and held it to my lips. It was cold, surprisingly delicious. I drank greedily.

"Little by little," Victoria said, easing Winter's arm away. Her eyes locked on mine, and I saw devils dancing in them. "Little by little," she said again.

Her voice made my hair stand on end.

Over the next few minutes Winter gave me more water, sips only, amused by the situation. And, I felt, anticipating something. I didn't want to know what.

"Enough," Victoria said at last.

"Give her some." I nodded toward Kayla.

Victoria thought about that, then gestured to Winter, who held the ladle to Kayla's lips.

After a while, Winter took the bucket into the other room, then returned.

Victoria faced me. "Would you like to know what Winter stuck in your back upstairs?"

I didn't. I didn't want either of them to pull out anything sharp, but Winter went back outside and returned with a sword, one of the thin, deadly foils I'd seen on the wall over her bed the day I'd visited Edna. The metal gleamed. Its tip looked like a needle.

"Winter is an expert with it. Not adequate or even good, but an expert," Victoria said with pride. "It's a deadly art, and rare. Its very unexpectedness is something of an advantage in, well...

awkward situations. Like when intruders come into your house. I took lessons when she was an infant, then I taught her, in private. She was a quick study. She's considerably better at it than I am, now. It's amazing, the things you can learn while you're young."

Winter ripped the steel through the air with a hissing sound, then held the point at my chest, at my heart, putting enough pressure on it to break the skin. A few drops of blood rolled down my chest. She was balanced on both feet, arm cocked, ready to thrust the slender steel deep into the machinery I hold so dear. For ten seconds she held me poised on the brink of eternity, then she smiled and stepped back, eyes still on mine, full of murky secrets.

So that was what Jeri had seen earlier. If she hadn't surrendered in the hallway, Winter could have killed me in an instant, then her. I didn't know how well Jeri's judo would hold up against an expert swordsman, or woman.

For the first time I noticed the logo on Winter's T-shirt. It said ITHACA across the front, amid pastel renderings of maple leaves that had gone to russet and gold. I must have stared, because she glanced down at it and smiled. "Like it? I bought it there." She pirouetted and showed it to Kayla. "What do you think, girlie? Nice?"

Kayla's face went pale.

Winter turned to me again. "Ithaca's okay, kinda quiet though, and some houses over there have rats."

She pulled her shirt off and dropped it on the floor. Her nipples were erect, looking as hard as rubber erasers. She lifted her breasts an inch. "Like them?" she whispered. There was a faint serpent's hiss in her voice that perfectly matched that cobra image I'd had of her days ago. Her eyes just stared. She had the blink rate of a cobra, too.

"Terrific," I said. "Very Talbot Mundy."

She didn't have any idea what I was talking about. She smiled. "Things don't change, do they? You're still an idiot. You say stupid things."

"You're a real piece of work, kid."

"Go ahead, check me out. You wanted to, that day outside in the yard. And later, inside, after you left Gramma's. I could tell. Do you like my titties?"

I glanced over at Victoria. Amused, she said, "Maybe I should give her a good spanking."

Winter giggled. "She told me what you said. You're so funny." She thrust her chest out and spun in a circle.

"Miranda," I said softly.

For a moment she didn't move, then the smile returned. "You think you know so much, but you don't know anything. Pretty soon you'll be a genius."

"She was your daughter."

"You don't know anything, pops. You'll find out."

She was a living nightmare, a gargoyle of a child. And I could've killed her for calling me pops, the twerp.

She put her shirt back on. She and Victoria left the room, leaving the door open. I wondered if a yell would carry outside the house. Probably not, and making them madder or more psychotic than they already were didn't seem worth the risk. Maybe later.

Kayla gave me a hopeless look.

"We'll get out of this," I said.

She didn't say anything. She didn't believe me. Nothing changed in her eyes.

I heard wood sliding on concrete outside the door. Victoria and Winter backed in dragging one end of a wide plank. Jeri was duct taped to the board with her hands over her head, ankles held together by loops of duct tape around the bottom end of the board. It was an awkward mode of transportation. I doubted they could get her across town that way. I figured Jeri had given them trouble, a reason to have rendered her so helpless. Maybe they'd propped her up somewhere and left her, like in a closet. She was gagged with duct tape over a rag in her mouth, topless like Kayla, wearing only the jade-green panties she'd purchased at the mall in Myrtle Beach.

So much nudity. These two sociopaths were into intimidation, vulnerability, humiliation. Or maybe they liked it for its own sake—I couldn't tell after Winter's little display moments ago. Insanity is its own incomprehensible carnival, but it's probably not a good idea to ask the psychos questions, especially if you think you might not like the answers.

Jeri stared at me with furious eyes as they dragged her to a spot four feet to Kayla's right. They lifted her upright and leaned her against the wall. Winter got a stepladder, climbed up, and looped the center portion of a long nylon rope twice around one of Jeri's wrists, then proceeded to tie neat, solid square knots, one after another, forming an impregnable lattice well beyond the reach of Jeri's fingers. After doing the same to Jeri's other wrist, she ran the free ends of the ropes up through an eye hook, took up the slack and secured the ropes by twisting them and tying it all into a figure eight knot with an extra twist, forming a huge blocky knot that wouldn't pass back through the eye hook. As a final touch, she set fire to the ends of the ropes with a barbecue lighter, allowing the nylon to burn briefly before blowing it out. The liquid nylon cooled, forming tough scabs that would make the knot impossible to untie—if anyone managed to somehow reach them, which wasn't likely. Finally, Winter tied Jeri's wrists together using the same figure eight knot that held my wrists, and Kayla's. The kid was great with knots, just terrific.

When Winter was done, Victoria ripped the gag off Jeri's mouth.

Jeri worked her tongue around for a moment, then spit in Victoria's face. Victoria snarled, "Do that again and I will hack off his balls and feed them to you." She let that sink in, then she put her face six inches from Jeri's. "Or would you like that, honey-bun? Have you ever eaten warm testicles, straight from the sac?"

Jeri turned her face away.

"I thought not," Victoria said. She looked at each of us in turn. "There will be no spitting, kicking, or biting. If there is, you will see intestines. You will wear them like leis."

Ice filled my belly. Kayla appeared sick. Jeri stared at me, still angry, but the previous look of combat was gone from her eyes.

Victoria picked up a wicked, hooked linoleum knife, gave Kayla a look, then me, before cutting the tape that held Jeri's arms and legs to the plank. She stood within kicking distance, daring Jeri to try, allowing her threat to fill the room. Finally, satisfied, she tossed the knife onto the workbench as Winter carried the board back outside. She shut the door behind them, leaving the three of us alone for the time being.

"You okay?" I asked Jeri.

"So far." She looked up at her hands, struggled for a moment to reach the knots, then gave up. "Shit," she said.

"Any idea what time it is?"

"Afternoon, five or six, maybe later, I don't know. It's been daylight for hours."

Christ, I'd been unconscious for at least fifteen hours. That was some hit Victoria had given me upstairs in the hallway. Most likely I had a concussion. "I'm sorry," I said. "Neither of you should be here."

"Or *you*," Jeri retorted. "How's your head?"

"It hurts."

"No wonder. That vicious little bitch dragged you all the way down to the first floor by your feet, down all those stairs. Your head hit every damn one of them on the way down."

Felt like it, too.

Jeri jerked on her ropes, hard. Nothing gave. She chinned herself then came down hard on the ropes with all her weight. Still nothing.

"I want to kill her," she said with the kind of total ferocity she brought to international karate competitions. She glanced to her left. "You're Kayla?"

"Yes."

"I'm Jeri." She looked at me, then managed a faint smile. "Jesus, Mort, she's gorgeous. I didn't know."

Under the circumstances it was an incongruous remark, as if she were as lost as I was. I didn't know how to respond. "Why'd they gag you, Jer?" I asked.

"Probably didn't like what I was calling them. I was making stuff up, things they'd never heard before." Her eyes locked with mine. "Whatever happens, Mort, don't you dare give up, not ever."

I took a little heart in that, the toughness in her voice, then the knob on the door clicked, turned, and Victoria and Winter came back into the room.

CHAPTER TWENTY-THREE

THEY BROUGHT IN a small flat-screen television and a DVD/ CD player. And a video camera that must have cost a thousand dollars.

"Oh, no. Not again!" Kayla cried.

Victoria smiled. "You didn't like it? Maybe these two won't be as critical."

"I can't see that again," Kayla whispered.

"Then don't watch, sister dear."

Victoria positioned the screen where everyone could see it. She said, "I think you'll find this interesting. But first—something of an explanation so you'll understand what you're seeing. Like so much of life, context is everything."

Winter folded her arms and smiled at me, a spooky grin that made her face look skull-like. Something wasn't right about her, other than the obvious, which was that she was a fucking maniac. It was that reptilian blink rate. Eerie goddamn kid. She needed to spend some quality time in the lockdown ward in a mental hospital. Like about fifty years.

"Jonathan Sjorgen raped Jacoba," Victoria began. "He and David Milliken." Her voice was all frost and death. "They took an innocent retarded girl for a ride in Jonnie's shiny new automobile and raped her, thinking they could get away with it because she either wouldn't tell, or couldn't tell. She was too dumb. They could grope her, fondle her, run their engorged cocks into her with impunity, come in her, and no one would ever know.

"Smug bastards, so very rich and smart. They had everything. They'd never wanted for a single thing their entire lives, never known the least privation. To them, the retarded girl down the street was a joke, a toy, just part of what the world owed them, nothing but a warm body, a receptacle, a dumb object without feelings."

Her words shriveled me, the venom in them, the depth of hatred that spilled out into the room. And the madness in her eyes, a live thing, as poisonous as cyanide. I couldn't decide which of them was more demented, Victoria or her spooky kid.

"But they were caught," Victoria went on. "Their fathers had to deal with Edna. She took Wendell Sjorgen's house and large sums of money from both families. She also sent Jacoba away, to live with her sister, Jewel, in South Carolina."

Her eyes softened briefly. "Edna did it for Jacoba. She was very old-fashioned, of course. She was sixty years old. She did what she thought was best. She was born in 1917. It was all she knew—one sends the pregnant child away, removes her from the heat of scandal, protects her. But even if Jacoba had stayed, she couldn't have interpreted the stares or comprehended the words. In that regard, Edna was wrong, but she did what she thought was best.

"In due course, I was born. By the age of six, I was the mother, Jacoba was the daughter. Jewel was never a mother to either of us. She was nothing but a guardian, in the strictest sense of the word. She put a roof over our heads, paid for by Edna. Jewel was a cold woman, bitter and utterly humorless. She did only what she perceived to be her duty, nothing more. Jacoba and I had only each other. I loved her. God, how I loved her."

"Then she died," Jeri said. "In a bathtub."

Victoria looked at her. "Yes. Two months after my fifteenth birthday. I heard her yell, fall. Her neck was broken. It was so sudden, the most terrible moment of my life. I was miserable, and I hated Jewel. I made a lot of trouble. She had to send me away, back to Edna.

"I hated it here too, in Reno. At the time, I'd never heard of Jonathan Sjorgen or David Milliken. But I was"—she turned and gave me an indescribable smile—"relatively normal, whatever that might mean in this day and age."

"Does that mean you know you're not the least bit normal now?" I asked.

She ignored me. "In all the time I'd lived at Jewel's, all my life, no one ever mentioned my father. Jacoba, of course, didn't know. I asked Jewel, once I was old enough to realize people had fathers, but she told me she didn't know, which was absolutely true. She didn't *want* to know. She would never have asked Edna. She told me to hold my tongue, not to ask questions about such nonsense. The subject was utterly taboo.

"It was early summer the year I came to Reno. I roamed this house from top to bottom, with no specific purpose at first, other than boredom and loneliness. I missed Jacoba so very much. But in time it occurred to me that she had once lived in this house, that somewhere in here I might learn the secret of who my father was.

"So I began to look. Down here"—she indicated the room with a wave of her hand—"in all the rooms, every closet, through the dust and spiders and heat of this place. Finally, up in the attic, I found a trunk. It was locked. I broke into it with a hammer when Edna was away and inside I found papers, signed confessions. Sjorgen's and Milliken's, witnessed by attorneys and their fathers and a few others. In the documents I found the concessions and payoffs that had been made to keep it all quiet, every last detail."

And then she'd gone nuts. Snapped. Something in that already unsettled mind had torn loose, frayed bloody neurons whipping in the hurricane force of her fury. Jacoba, her beloved mother, had been raped, and she, Victoria, was the result of that rape.

"Raped!" Victoria said, her voice shrill. "By *savages*!" Spittle flew from her lips. "By vermin, by filth, by sickening, pampered scum." For a moment she lost it completely. Her eyes jittered. Her hands trembled. She looked down at them and curled her fingers into hooks, then slowly, with much effort, she got herself under control again, more or less.

"I found the two of them," she said, and the memory seemed to calm her further. "*Hunted* them. It was the easiest thing in the world. They stayed right here in Reno where they had connections—college educated, untouched by what they'd done. All had been forgotten, buried. Jacoba was dead, but they didn't know, nor would they have cared if they had. I was alive, but they didn't know that either, didn't even know I existed. They'd had their fun, shot their sperm into my mother, and there'd been a moment of trouble, possibly a few days of concern, quietly handled by their daddies, and their lives were perfect again, untainted. Jonathan was a businessman, on the city council. Milliken was a lawyer, a rising star in the district attorney's office.

"Jonathan was my father, I knew. It was obvious the instant I saw him. I decided to kill him. I made plans to kill him, detailed plans. I very nearly carried them out. It was so close. But then—" Something filled her eyes, a memory perhaps, a feeling. Whatever it was, its reflection in her eyes was a thing of perfect evil—or perfect madness.

"I provided him the opportunity to rape *me*," she said. "As he raped my mother."

"Nutso, schizo, whack job," Jeri said.

Victoria whirled on her, then turned and glared at Kayla. "Call it inspiration. It seemed so wonderfully fitting. I made myself available. Do you think your father rejected me, Kayla, dear? Do you think he made the slightest effort to put me off, evade me, walk away, tell me no? Me, every bit as much his own daughter as are you?"

Kayla stared at her, horrified.

"Answer me!" Victoria screeched.

"No," Kayla said.

"No. That is correct. He did *not.*" Her eyes glittered murderously. "He pursued me, in his way. His eyes hungered for me, *swallowed* me. I was fifteen. I looked fifteen. I wore a short skirt and smiled at him, spoke to him, stuck out my chest, and he flirted with me right there on the street in front of the old courthouse on Virginia Street, cautiously perhaps, but he unquestionably knew exactly what he was doing. He was in his mid-thirties at the time. He was an adult. With little more than a word I let him know he could have me. He didn't know who I was, didn't sense it. Would it have mattered to him if he did? I doubt it. It was dusk. I asked him if he'd give me a ride in his nice new car, and he literally jumped at the chance. In the car he touched my thigh, rubbed it. I let him. There were a few words during which we reached a kind of understanding, then he drove me up to Truckee on I-80, then to a motel in Tahoe City. That vile monster practically tore his clothes off in his eagerness, my clothes too, then he fucked me in the darkness in a cheap room, grunting, sweaty, sick with fear for his precious career, afraid for his *life*, knowing *exactly* what he was doing.

"I wanted to tell him who I was right after he climaxed and then kill him—God, how I wanted that! It's what I'd intended all along. No one knew I was in that room with him. I even had a .38 revolver within reach in my purse that I'd found when I searched the house. It belonged to Edna's husband, Herman, my grandfather. I found it in an old trunk with a bunch of his things.

"I could have killed him. I wanted to tell him who I was and gut shoot him while he was inside me, watch him die slowly, miserably, knowing he'd just raped his own daughter, knowing who had killed him, and why. But right then, at that moment, I realized it was exactly the right time of the month for me, that I might become pregnant as my mother had, that without consciously thinking about it, I might have planned it that way all along. And in that instant I knew—if I were to kill him and *then* find out I was pregnant, he could never be confronted with his child who was also his grandchild—Winter."

For how long had I suspected it? Only minutes? Or much longer? Perhaps I'd caught a whiff of it in Myrtle Beach. I wasn't sure. All I knew was that this revelation came as no big surprise. It might have been the dementia circling in Victoria's eyes like smoke, a feeling that nothing she'd ever done had the power to surprise me. She'd captured us, stripped us, tied us up in this dank, modern-day dungeon. She'd killed Jonnie and Milliken and Greg—horribly. Beheaded them all, hacked off sex organs, removed brains. In her madness she was capable of anything.

"Oh, how I wanted that, as soon as the idea came to me," Victoria went on. "I wanted it so much...my God, you wouldn't believe. The rapist and bigshot city councilman knocking up his own daughter! The thought was amazing, fantastic. He came in me three times that night, then drove me back to Reno and let me out a block from the bus station at four in the morning, begging me not to tell, shaking with fear. He gave me three hundred dollars to keep me quiet, the same way he'd treated my mother—the

Sjorgen solution to everything. And it wasn't long before I knew I was pregnant, less than a week. I *knew*. I told Edna. I said I wanted to go back East again, back to Jewel's."

"After murdering Wendell Sjorgen," I said.

She smiled. "Yes. Oh, yes-s-s. Granddad. Another monster. To protect his beloved son, he abandoned my mother—and me. He paid tens of thousands of dollars to rid himself and his son of us. He buried my mother's rape, turned it into something that never happened."

"As did Milliken's father," I reminded her.

"Victor Milliken died when I was ten years old. But David Milliken paid for what he did. You found his head. He got what he deserved. But Wendell was Jonathan's father, my grandfather. He bought Edna's silence like he bought everything that was inconvenient, without so much as a passing thought about Jacoba and me. But he knew who I was at the end, in that alley. He knew exactly who I was, and he very much regretted what he'd done. It wasn't *murder*," she added. "It was an execution. Slower, messier and more painful than the state would have done, I must admit, but nothing he didn't deserve.

"I gave birth to Winter, Jonathan's child...and his grandchild. My daughter, *and* my baby sister." She put an arm around Winter's waist and drew her close.

No wonder they'd looked so much alike when I'd first seen them. Not only were they mother and daughter—they were also sisters.

Kayla stared at them in horror. Jeri, however, was sizing up the walls, the ceiling, the floor, the ropes that held her, everything. She gave me a grim smile, still tough, still searching for a way out. Something in her eyes said don't you dare give up.

In Conway, South Carolina, Victoria raised her daughter-sister, told her who her father was, taught her to hate, to loathe beyond all reason, to want to kill, and finally to want to hold steaming loops of Jonnie's intestines in her hands, to hear him scream as she pushed red hot nails into his eyes. All that by the age of six. By the time she should've started first grade, she was already a monster, destroyed. She couldn't go to school, couldn't be around normal children. If the authorities had found out, they would have locked her in a juvenile detention facility and tried to save her with years of therapy. They would have tossed Victoria in prison. Keys would have been thrown away. In order not to lose Winter, Victoria had to keep her isolated at home, away from the rest of the community, watch her every second while she continued to teach her to hate. With Jonnie in mind right from the start, she taught Winter how to fence, starting at age four. And she taught her all about men, their bodies, their weaknesses, their wicked goatish lusts.

"You came back," Jeri said to Victoria. "You had Winter rape Jonnie, didn't you?" She'd been paying attention, even as her eyes were taking in every detail of the room.

"Jonathan raped *Winter*," Victoria hissed. "His own grandchild."

"Yeah, right," Jeri said.

"Dressed up like a hot little whore, no doubt," I added.

She whirled. "She was his *granddaughter*. That inhuman beast climaxed inside his own grandchild. How she was dressed was of *no* consequence, none at all. She was fifteen years old and looked it."

She paced for half a minute, then fixed her eyes on me. "Jonathan hadn't changed. He was still a vile beast. He was fifty-one years old when Winter approached him in a parking garage downtown. She was a ninety-pound schoolgirl, extremely pretty, but young, obviously too young. She barely spoke to him and he was ready, salivating in his desire to be with her."

Divorced from his first two wives, unaware of the satanic soul burning brightly in the girl sitting next to him in his new Jaguar convertible, Jonnie had driven her not to Lake Tahoe but over Donner Summit and all the way to Auburn, a town in California a hundred miles away. He'd grown more sophisticated over the years, more discreet, or maybe more frightened, more aware of how far off the reservation he'd strayed and what would happen if he were caught. He pulled into a motel off the freeway, paid cash for a room, sneaked Winter inside under the cover of darkness. He stayed with her most of the night and got her pregnant, as he had Jacoba and Victoria.

"Believing she was only fourteen," Victoria said, "which is what she told him as soon as he'd entered her. Knowing it was statutory rape, he kept going, finally coming in her with no thought that his sperm might live on, creating new life."

"Miranda," I said. The story was recycling itself, becoming as tiresome as it was horrible, Jonnie's unwitting multigenerational rape of his own offspring, choreographed by Victoria's insanity.

"Yes," Victoria said. "Yes-s-s-s, Miranda."

"Then the two of you went back to Myrtle Beach again," Jeri said. "Back to your lair, talk about complete raving fucking lunatics, Jesus H. Christ."

"To have Jonathan's great-grandchild," Victoria said.

"Fuckin' loonies," Jeri muttered, scanning the walls, yanking on her ropes.

Victoria's emphasis of the word "great" was an indication of the depth of her psychosis. She'd grown obsessed with Jonnie's rapes and with the awful, tangled lineage he was creating. Miranda was a living, breathing symbol of Jonnie's turpitude. Miranda was his daughter, granddaughter, great-granddaughter, all in one. She was Victoria's sister and her grandchild. In Victoria's deranged mind it was all Jonnie's fault. But the endless layering of Jonnie's genes had finally caught up. Genetically, Miranda was fully seven-eighths

Jonnie. She was retarded, but for a vastly different reason than was Jacoba.

"I waited too long," Victoria said. "We should have come back to Reno sooner, but I'd hoped Miranda would be a little older when we finally went public. At least six years. And Winter was growing more skillful with the foil every day, all the better to deal with Jonnie when the time came, and...well, I simply waited too long."

"So which was it?" I asked. "What was the big plan? Were you going to expose these so-called rapes of his, or kill him?"

"*So-called?*" Victoria screeched. Cords stood out in her neck.

"Actual, then," I said in a caustic tone, fed up with this obscene woman and her sick machinations. "Sure-enough, honest-to-god, boy-howdy rapes, have it your way."

She stared at me, hands clenching and unclenching, as if trying to decide which of my body parts to cut off first. "We were going to crush him publicly," she said at last. "Utterly, thoroughly, *crush* him, the great mayor, so handsome, so admired. DNA tests would have proved what he'd done. Everyone was going to know what kind of an animal he was, and I mean *everyone*. The entire world was going to look at him in disgust, spit on him. People were going to recoil at the sound of his name. And after he'd acclimated to that, as he would in time, we were going to kill him."

"But you didn't do that," I said. "You didn't expose him, you didn't humiliate him. You murdered him right away. And Milliken."

"We couldn't. I found out I couldn't let the world know about him the way I'd intended. The statute of limitations on statutory rape hadn't run out. Not with Miranda. If his rapes were reported, it was all but certain that Jonnie would've gone to prison."

"Out of reach," Jeri said.

Victoria nodded. "Yes. And, well...there were other reasons."

"Like little psycho Winter getting loose one night with a sword and killing a boy not far from where you lived in Conway," Jeri said. "Exposing Jonnie would have focused national attention on you and Winter. Her fencing skill might have been discovered. She might have been found guilty of murder. You couldn't risk that."

"My, aren't we the quickest little genius on the block?" Victoria said, staring at Jeri.

I stared at her, too. She'd picked that up from the little Kennedy had told us? Or had she somehow put two and two together, being an actual PI while I was just a pretend PI?

"We killed him," Victoria replied slowly. "Jonathan. We watched him, hunted him, then captured him, let him know what he'd done, then killed him."

"We didn't *just* kill him," Winter said, speaking for the first time in twenty minutes. Her voice was like arctic wind hissing through old canted tombstones. "And that other guy, Milliken."

"No," Victoria responded. "No, we didn't. It wasn't that easy for them. Killing is what one does to flies. Death will take us all one day. Jonathan owed us much more than that.

"Grabbing them was no trick at all," she went on. "Milliken was still a pig, and he lived alone. I took him myself. Nothing could have been simpler. Later that evening, Winter took Jonathan. He didn't recognize her after all that time, five years, and she wore a wig. She took him to a motel room. He trailed along like a horny ape. I was inside, waiting. He woke up in this room, naked—like you." Her eyes passed over me. "And every bit as unhappy. We drove their cars to a hotel by the airport and left them there, while Reno's honorable mayor and district attorney"—Victoria smiled wickedly—"hung around.

"Jonathan found out who we were, Winter and I. He became terribly eager to please us. After all these years he finally called us what we were—daughter and granddaughter." Victoria paused. "And lover. He called us that too, with a little encouragement." She smiled at the memory. "We had him recount what he'd done to us in great detail. Made it into a little video. A documentary, if you will. Which will be revealed to the public sometime in the future. I'm still thinking about how to do that. Toward the end, Jonathan shared his thoughts with us, what was going on inside his head as he fondled us, groped us, climaxed inside us, mere children, fifteen years old. He watched his good friend David Milliken die, with the knowledge that he would die the same way. And in the end...well..." She held up the digital camera. "These things are amazing, so versatile. We made a fun little movie. Watch."

She hit the play button on the DVD player.

As images jerked to life on the screen, words Fairchild had spoken earlier went through my head again: Family. The ones who know you best...

* * *

Jonnie was barefoot, nude, standing slump-shouldered and wary at one end of the room we were now in. He held a sword awkwardly in one hand—a deadly looking number with an ornate, cuplike guard at the hilt. He was untied, free to move about. He was staring at something in front of him but off camera, eyes wide, hunted.

The camera zoomed back, sliding Winter into frame. She was topless, wearing the black thong she'd been wearing the first day I'd seen her. She was barefoot, a slender waif of a girl holding the twin of Jonnie's sword in one hand, facing him at a forty-five degree angle, nothing the least bit awkward about her stance.

Jonnie coughed once, nervously, facing his murderous daughter-granddaughter. The sound was hollow, echoey, but the picture was clear enough.

Victoria paused the action. "In some countries their swords might be called rapiers, a most appropriate term under the circumstances, wouldn't you say? These were imported from Italy. Unlike a classic foil or epee, the rapier has both a point and a single razor edge. Forty-five hundred dollars apiece. Beautiful weapons, perfectly balanced."

She hit the play button. The action moved forward again.

Winter held her rapier at an angle in front of her face, said, "En garde," then lowered the tip until it was pointed at Jonnie's heart. She took a step forward. The camera was behind her, off to one side. In that thong and nothing else, she looked entirely naked. All I could see was the slender black strap of the thong around her waist.

Jonnie lifted the point of his sword uncertainly. Winter flicked his tip aside with the middle portion of her blade, spun his blade away with a deft circular motion, and stabbed him in the torso, inches from his belly button. The whole thing took less than two seconds. She stepped back as Jonnie stumbled backward and slammed into the wall behind him. He lowered his sword in shock, staring at his stomach, at blood running down into his pubic hair. Winter lunged forward and stuck the tip of her sword half an inch deep into his left biceps.

Jonnie yelled, spun away, almost fell down. Winter gave him a moment to recover, then came at him again, batting the tip of his rapier around, scoring points. In seconds, Jonnie was bleeding from the right thigh, right forearm, left foot, and had a cut beneath his left eye. His wild hair and the blood gave him a ghoulish appearance. Winter danced back, giving him time to think about what had just happened. The camera circled as Victoria sought a better angle.

Winter began to toy with him in earnest, lunging in, batting the tip of his sword aside, sticking him here and there, inflicting pain but no significant injury. Turning Jonnie into a human pincushion.

"The opportunity to practice on a live subject with full contact like this is exceedingly rare," Victoria interjected. "She could have killed him in the first second."

"Yeah, but can she arm wrestle?" I said, figuring I didn't have much to lose at that point.

Jeri lifted an eyebrow at me.

"Hard to arm wrestle with your dick in your mouth, cowboy," Winter said coolly, standing no more than three feet from me.

Okay, so I was wrong about having nothing to lose. I shut up.

On screen, Winter continued to toy with Jonnie. This went on for a while. He'd long since given up any attempt to hide his nakedness, and had begun to try to parry her thrusts and even to attack, thrusting, slashing wildly, but nothing worked. His chest heaved and blood coursed down the front of his body from dozens of puncture wounds. His breathing grew labored, coming hollow and heavy out of the speakers. He slipped and fell a few times. The floor was red, slick with blood. As I'd thought, the drain was a real plus in this place.

Finally Winter paused, then darted forward and stuck the point of her blade an inch deep into Jonnie's left eye. He screamed and dropped his sword. He stumbled against the wall then sank to the floor, writhing, holding his ruined eye, shrieking.

After watching this for a minute or so, Winter stuck the tip of her sword into his rib cage, aimed at his heart. He stared at her through his one good eye. "Just do it," he whispered. His words were slurred. He'd bitten his tongue. Blood was spilling from his mouth.

Winter stared at him. "Say please, Daddy."

"Do it."

She looked down at him, pitiless, silent, as if he were a bug, a roach, a gnat.

"Please," Jonnie whispered. "Please."

Winter backed away and changed swords, trading the rapier for one of the slender foils that had been on the wall above her bed, a quarter inch thick at the hilt, tapering to a needle point. She rested the tip in Jonnie's belly button for a moment, then lowered her center of gravity a few inches for leverage and shoved the foil entirely through his body. The tip exited out his back.

It took several minutes for him to die, writhing with the sword in his guts, keening, then at last he went quiet. His lips worked silently as he gazed up into the camera. Finally he bled out internally and it was over.

* * *

Victoria turned off the DVD player.

I felt sick, down deep. Had Jonnie deserved to die that way? I'd never witnessed anything so deliberate, so terrible and one-sided. He hadn't had a chance. Truth was, I'd never seen anyone die before, other than metaphorically with the IRS. I've led a sheltered life. Victoria and Winter had produced what amounted to their own private snuff film. No doubt they watched it every night before going to bed, then dreamed sweet dreams. Ghouls.

"The whole thing took two hours," Victoria said in a voice so calm it took my breath away. "I edited out the more tedious parts.

And I had to change memory cards in the camera and put in a new battery, but, well...you get the idea.

"I think it's only fitting that at least one of you should die like Jonathan." She looked at each of us in turn. "And I think that someone should be"—she spun in place, considering the available options—"his lovely daughter," she said. "The one whom Jonathan called 'daughter' all these many years."

"No!" Kayla said in a thin voice. "Oh, God, no." She wrenched at the ropes, then sagged on them, crying when her legs gave out.

"The one," Victoria went on calmly, "who didn't have the wits to stay in Ithaca, where death would have been so much faster, relatively painless."

"Please, no," Kayla wailed. "I can't."

"But of *course* you can," Victoria said. "You're a bright girl. You can do anything you set your mind to. Surely your loving father taught you that."

Kayla continued to cry weakly. It was terrible to hear. I tried to close my ears to it, but couldn't.

"I'll do it," I said. "I'll fight her." Tough words, but in fact it was a coward's way out. I wanted this to be over and that was one way to accomplish it.

Victoria turned. She smiled. "Ah, a volunteer. Such bravery. Such chivalry. The world is saved."

It was anything but bravery. I damn well didn't want to die the way Jonnie had, inch by horrible inch, possibly with steel in my eye. But I couldn't watch Kayla die like that. Or Jeri. I couldn't.

"Not him," Jeri said in a hard, tough voice. "Me. I'll take on that anorexic little bitch. I'll chop your psycho slut daughter into pieces the size of scallops."

Slowly, Victoria turned and stared at her. "My God, we are awash in heroic figures."

Jeri's eyes blazed. "If you touch him again, just touch him, I swear in Christ's name that when I die I will curl up in your brain and leave you with gibbering nightmares until the end of time."

"Goodness!" Victoria exclaimed. "That sounds very much like love."

Jeri looked straight at me. "It is."

For an instant I thought my heart had stopped. My vision blurred, fractured into shards of rainbow-colored light.

"Look," Winter said, staring at me. "He's crying. How sweet." Her eyes, however, were volcanic pools of fury.

"You're jealous," I managed to say. "No one gives a fuck about you, kid, including your crazy mama. God, how she must hate you, Jonnie's kid—"

Winter punched me full in the face, bouncing my head off the concrete wall.

My skull throbbed. A wave of nausea returned, but I managed to grin at her anyhow, tasting blood. "Part of you is almost human, isn't it? A very small part."

But already the moment was over. Winter smiled at me, rubbing her knuckles. She arched her back. "When I do you, cowboy, I'll do it topless in that thong like in the video, give you a real nice show."

I glanced indifferently at her chest. "Yeah? What with?"

A murderous look filled her eyes. After a sharp word from Victoria, she grabbed the television and video player and carried them into the other room, pausing at the door to give me a long, lethal stare, like a monitor lizard eyeing a rat.

Victoria tilted her head at me. "Was anything...unusual found in Jonnie's skull? Nothing was mentioned in the news."

I gave her a blank look. "In his skull? Unusual? Like what?" I wasn't about to give the fiendish bitch the satisfaction.

"So you don't...well, I'm not surprised. Winter and I played a little joke."

"Did you?"

"A symbolic gesture, very appropriate. Nothing important." She turned away.

"Where is Jonnie now?" I asked. "His body, I mean."

Victoria shrugged. "Out back with Milliken, buried under newly planted roses beneath a layer of lime and powdered sulfur to keep dogs from showing any interest, not that they would —we put the two of them down deep. The soil digs easily, and we were motivated, Winter and I. By the way, the desert here is alkaline. Sulfur's good for plants."

"I'll keep that in mind," I said. "What about my nephew, Gregory?"

"What about him?"

"Did you...how did he...?"

"Die? A lot quicker than Jonathan, but he was much better with the foil. He had intuition and was surprisingly athletic. The best full-contact sparring partner Winter's ever had, not that he made any contact himself. He was an extremely nosy person, but quite taken with her, the way she was dressed. He came inside for a Coke, and once he regained consciousness from the tap I gave him from behind, she entertained him in this room while I drove his car down to the Peppermill Hotel and walked back. You saw how Winter entertains. In spite of your silly vindictive comments, she has a very nice body."

"You didn't have to kill him."

"We found him on hands and knees at the back of the house, trying to peer through a window into the basement." She waved a hand, indicating the room beyond the door. "How was I to know what he'd seen? Maybe nothing, but I was most annoyed to find him out there snooping around. One look at Winter, though, and, well, you know the rest. We returned him to his office at three in the morning. His head, that is. The rest is under a honeysuckle beside the garage. It's doing very nicely, too. Plants like food as much as the rest of us."

"You're insane," I said.

"Oh, I should think that's perfectly obvious. But at least life is interesting."

Her eyes took in everyone in the room. "Talk it over. Decide which of you will try their hand against Winter first."

Then she was gone.

CHAPTER TWENTY-FOUR

"Me," I said.

"*None* of us," Jeri responded, giving me a savage look. "Let's get the fuck out of here."

Right. Easier said than done.

Jeri lifted herself and let her weight crash down on the eye bolt. And again, and again, with no discernible effect. I hauled down as hard as I could on the ropes that held me. With my ankles tied as they were I was able to generate even more force on the ropes and the eye hook, but nothing gave. Hopeless.

Jeri jangled on her ropes like a ferret on a hook. A sound, almost a growl, came from her throat.

And then I saw something. Or thought I did, an awareness that crept through a gray haze that had kept my thoughts at half speed ever since I'd regained consciousness.

"Jeri!"

She kept at it, violent, possessed, trying to get something to tear loose.

"Jeri, stop!"

She hung there, breathing hard, staring at me. "What?"

"Hold on a minute."

"Screw that, Mort. No way I'm gonna wait around until they—"

"*Hold on a minute.*" I was looking at the beam over her head, at the eye bolt to which her ropes were tied.

"Mort—?"

"See that eye bolt above you?"

Jeri craned her neck upward. "What about it?"

I squinted, trying to focus. The bolt went into the bottom of the beam, an inch from its outer edge. The eye of the bolt wasn't tight against the wood, not even close. It stuck out four inches below the bottom of the beam, as if whoever had put it in hadn't been able to screw it in any farther, or couldn't be bothered. I couldn't tell how deeply it was embedded, but it obviously wasn't in all the way. Two inches of threads were still visible. It was a weakness. I explained it to Jeri. Whether or not she could exploit it, I didn't know.

She stared up at the bolt for a moment, considering, then she turned and faced the wall. A glimmer of life returned to Kayla's eyes. She raised her head and watched.

Hanging from the ropes, Jeri pulled her legs off the floor, planted her feet against the wall and walked them upward, turning herself completely upside down. She looked like a piston again, exhibiting that colossal strength I'd seen in her gym. But what she'd done so far was the least of what she would have to do.

Hanging upside down, she set her feet against the wall at either side of the eye hook, twenty inches apart, toes touching the underside of the beam. Then she did what amounted to a vertical sit-up while hauling on the ropes, reeling them in until she was in a horizontal crouch against the wall with her feet below the bottom of the beam. Her face was almost touching the ceiling.

She grunted softly, playing the ropes out as she slowly extended her body outward from the wall, standing up, but sideways. A sheen of sweat appeared on her body as the forces built up in her, gravity pulling her down, ropes pulling horizontally. Nothing was keeping her up there but the power in her arms and legs, the incredible strength of her torso.

God, she was beautiful!—doing something I couldn't have done on the best day of my life. Tendons stood out in her neck. She was in a partial squat, legs not quite straight, suspended by forces I couldn't begin to calculate. Her thighs looked as if they'd been chiseled out of granite. Muscles in her shoulders bulged with effort, arms corded. Her breasts were compact cambered pads, inches from the ceiling. I felt a sense of wonder, knowing that I had never seen a woman like her before, never would again.

Kayla gaped at her, mouth open in amazement.

Jeri was stretched out almost full length beneath the ceiling. I don't think she took a breath. I doubt that she could have. Her body was rigid. If I felt any occult force radiating off her—and I thought I did, waves of it—it was pure, blinding love.

Then she began to pull in earnest, deadlifting the eye bolt from the side, using the part of the eye bolt below the beam as a short lever, motionless, a statue of stressed stone. She pulled for our lives. She pulled for love. Christ, she could have lifted the front end of a '57 Buick.

The side of the beam exploded with a gunshot sound of rending wood. Jeri flew across the room in an arc, falling nearly ten feet to the concrete floor, landing on her back and shoulders with her chin tucked into her chest. I heard her breath go. Her head bounced off the door in the opposite wall.

She lay utterly still. Seconds passed. I thought she was out cold. She didn't appear to be breathing. Kayla gave me a terrified look, then Jeri's eyes fluttered open and she pulled her knees up to her chest, rolled onto her side, mouth open, trying to suck air into her lungs.

I didn't say anything. Nothing would have helped. I listened for footsteps, sounds of Victoria or Winter, willing Jeri to get up, get moving. I didn't hear anything yet, but I didn't see how they could have missed that sharp crack of tearing wood. They might have felt it, a shock wave jarring the entire house. A fifteen-inch section of the beam had torn out, leaving a splintery gash of exposed wood.

Jeri got her knees under her, then staggered to her feet. The ropes around her wrists were still tied to the eye bolt, and her wrists were still bound by that figure eight of rope between them. She gathered it all up and stood unsteadily, looking around.

I felt a vibration in the wall behind me, sounds, distant footsteps. "They're coming," I said.

Jeri darted past me to the workbench, still trying to breathe. She tucked the unwieldy mass of ropes under her left arm. She got the linoleum knife that Victoria had left on the workbench, then turned and took a few steps toward the door.

The footsteps grew louder.

Suddenly the door burst open. Victoria ran inside, slowing to look around. Jeri took a half step toward her, a little half hop, then kicked her under the chin. Not a sparring kick, but the real thing, knee almost locked, leg extended, everything she had. Her heel connected with the underside of Victoria's chin, bone on bone.

Victoria's head snapped back, way back, impossibly, unnaturally far. There was an ugly sound of bone breaking, a hideous clack of teeth. Blood sprayed from Victoria's mouth. I saw bits of teeth fly through the air, and part of her tongue. Jeri kicked her again in the chest with her other foot before Victoria could fall, sending her crashing back through the door, then Jeri slammed the door shut with a shoulder and held it.

Outside, Winter's voice rose in a hellish scream.

"Get a two-by-four!" I yelled. "Block the door!"

Jeri followed my gaze. She didn't hesitate. She dropped the knife and grabbed a length of two-by-four, wedged it between the door and a leg of the workbench.

Winter rattled the doorknob, then slammed her weight against the door like a hellcat, screaming, *"You killed her! She's dead! You killed her!"*

Easily the best news I'd heard all year.

Jeri got the linoleum knife again and ran to me, pure focused energy, no wasted motion. She couldn't easily cut the ropes around her own wrists, so she cut mine. The knife was razor sharp. In seconds, my right hand was free. Then my left.

My feet were still tied to the wall. I almost fell flat on my face. Jeri caught me and held me up in a crouch while I used the knife to hack frantically at the cords around my ankles, slashing myself as did, drawing blood. I saw it, but didn't feel a thing.

Winter pounded on the door. Not like before. She was using a tool of some kind, yelling the whole time, sobbing and threatening us with death, with the slow removal of body parts. Single-minded damn kid. Tiresome, but she was an orphan now, so I tried to make allowances.

I got my legs free. I staggered into the middle of the room, then got the blade of the knife under the nylon behind Jeri's wrists and cut it away. When she was free, she severed the ropes holding Kayla.

The blade of an axe sliced through the door, sending slivers of wood flying into the room.

I looked around for a weapon. My legs didn't want to obey me. I felt stiff, clumsy, slow. I stumbled over to the workbench hoping to find something that might be useful against a foil, like a crossbow or a hand grenade. No dice. I got the crowbar off the pegboard. Two feet long. With luck I could crush her skull with it, but it was an ungainly weapon and she had the axe.

And, of course, her foil.

I doubted I could out-duel her with the crowbar. If nothing else, I could throw it at her. All three of us could throw things, hammers, screwdrivers. We might be able to hold her off. We might even get lucky and hurt her. Maybe.

Winter missed a beat or two, then the light above us went out. She'd stopped long enough to throw a switch out there. Then she was back at it. Splinters flew. A chunk of the door tore out, then another. She was doing a hell of a job with the axe, working steadily, breathing like a lumberjack, attacking the door with cold fury. I could hear her panting outside, grunting with effort. She'd given up threatening us, at least for the moment.

The room was almost entirely dark, but not quite. Light came through holes in the door that Winter was attacking. I looked around, couldn't see Jeri in the gloom. The other door I'd seen earlier was standing open, an even deeper darkness in the basement. Kayla was holding it, peering in.

"Jeri in there?" I asked.

"Yes."

"What's in there?"

"It's...like a closet, or something."

No good.

"You two better grab something, get ready to throw it at this kid," I said to her. "She's almost got that door licked."

Winter slammed the axe into the door, knocking out more wood. I saw her naked belly through a jagged hole, saw her twisting, tensing, swinging the axe. She stopped and peered through the hole at me. Her eyes were glittery with rage. She started up with the axe again, sending shards of wood flying into the room. Another hit and a big piece tore out leaving a gap she could've crawled through. I lifted the crowbar, prepared to crush her skull if I got the chance.

Behind me, glass broke. Metal, wood, and a lot of other things I couldn't identify clattered down onto concrete. I couldn't figure out what Kayla and Jeri were doing in that closet.

"Mort!" Jeri yelled.

"What?" I yelled back.

No response.

Maybe I could defend the door. I was twice Winter's weight and then some, and I had the crowbar. She couldn't come in without me turning her into a pile of bloody mush. If I got her down, I wouldn't stop pounding till I couldn't lift the crowbar one more time.

Winter swung the axe again. More splinters flew into the room. She picked a new spot, aiming at the lock. After a few hits the bolt popped free of the strike plate. Another hit and the lock assembly clattered out at my feet. The only thing keeping the door from opening was the two-by-four wedged between it and the workbench.

"What're you two doing?" I yelled.

No answer. Shit. I couldn't see Winter. I could have put a big dog through the hole she'd chopped in the door. Before I could react, a broom handle shot through the hole and knocked the two-by-four off to one side. Winter kicked the door. It opened a few inches. I managed to shove it shut. Winter's foot slammed into it again. The shock of it went through my shoulder right into my head. This wasn't going to work. Winter could thrust that foil through the hole in the door and into my calf, my thigh, my stomach.

"There's a way out back here, Mort. Come on!"

A way out? I abandoned the door and ran. I was halfway across the room when Winter kicked the door open and came in with her foil in one hand. She had on shorts and the shirt I'd first seen her in, days ago, hacked off to the underside of her tits.

I made it through the other door three steps ahead of her. Jeri yanked it shut. In that split second I got a brief glimpse of a small storeroom, walls of naked two-by-four studs, shelves, broken glass and piles of junk on the floor, no Kayla, then everything went pitch black.

"The shelves," Jeri said in the dark. "Climb the shelves. There's a trapdoor in the ceiling. Kayla's up there." Winter yanked on the door, but Jeri held it. "There's no lock on the door," she said. "Get going."

"You go," I said. "I'll hold it." I was worried that my weight might rip the shelving down, trapping us both.

"I can do it," Jeri said.

I pulled her hands off the knob and held it myself. I was bigger than she was. Guess I still hadn't learned who was stronger.

"No, Mort!"

"Go, goddamn it! Soon as you're up I'll be right behind you." I hoped.

The axe slammed into the door inches from where my hand was on the knob. One hit, and a wedge of light the width of the blade was visible. I had to hold the knob to keep her out, but another few hits and I was going to lose a hand.

"Go, Jeri! *Now!*"

She went. I heard her scrambling up the shelves.

The axe ripped into the door an inch from my hand. Winter was going for the latch, and I couldn't turn loose of it. More light leaked through. Goddamn doors of theirs weren't worth a shit.

"I'm up," Jeri said. "Come on."

The axe struck again. I looked behind me, then up. Still couldn't see anything. I tried to visualize the shelves I'd glimpsed a moment ago. I let go of the knob and scrambled up the shelving, praying that it would hold my weight. My feet slipped. I grabbed wildly, hands flailing at air, then touching wood. I hauled myself up another foot. With Winter somewhere behind me, it seemed to take forever. I scraped my shins. The climb was dead vertical. I felt like an ox trying to shinny up a rope.

At the top I bumped my head on the edge of the trapdoor, hard, almost losing my grip. Again I felt that nausea, a deadly faintness. Below, Winter yanked the door open and lunged into the room. I saw the gleam of the foil in her hands. Jeri grabbed my wrist and hauled me partway through the trapdoor, into whatever lay beyond. I smelled mold, a kind of leafy rot, couldn't see anything, then a bolt of agony went through my leg as Winter's foil pierced the bottom of my left foot, came out the top between the bones and continued up into my calf, glancing off my tibia.

I screamed. The steel jerked out of me as Winter prepared for another thrust.

"Mort!" Jeri cried.

"Go, go! I'm okay."

I wasn't, but she didn't know that. I crawled away from the trapdoor, visualizing that rapier coming at me again, tearing through my buttocks and deep into me, all the way to my liver.

Cool moist dirt was under my hands. We were under the house somewhere, the part that was supported by concrete piers. To my left I saw diamonds, pale glowing diamonds—latticework—and suddenly I knew where I was. Jeri was ahead of me. I pushed her deeper into the blackness, away from the latticework, then I rolled to my right into darkness, knowing I had no time left, sensing Winter behind me. I hoped the move was unexpected and that she couldn't see me. I slammed into one of the concrete pilings that was supporting the underside of the house, then spun around, facing her.

I heard Winter coming, still breathing hard. The foil hissed blindly in the dark, clattering against a floor joist then whipping down across my nose and cheek. The feel of flesh telegraphed through the blade into her hand and I knew she'd found me. I tried to move off to one side, but the foil came out of the blackness, a straight thrust into my chest, all the way through and out my back, missing my heart by an inch or two, then it jerked away.

The next one would kill me.

I leapt toward her instead of away, scrabbling with outstretched hands, trying to get inside the radius of her foil. She yelled, we butted heads, and then her fingernails were at my eyes, clawing. I tucked my head into my chest and grabbed at her, got hold of her hair and yanked her down, off to one side, then instinctively rolled with her hair in my hands, winding her hair up, twisting her neck. She shrieked, nails ripping into my wrists, and I kept rolling, forcing her to roll too or lose her scrawny neck, seeing those diamonds flickering in the gloom, rolling toward them, getting closer, eight feet, five, then I got her in front of me and kicked her in the belly, hard, sending her sprawling up against the lattice.

I scrabbled away, back into the dark, through tough spiderwebs that hissed and snapped like fine steel wires. I slammed into another support piling. The pain in my chest and back was like a poker, heated to a dull red. I coughed, tasted blood, knew she'd pierced a lung.

I lay still for a moment. Silence, then I heard a murmur of traffic on Virginia Street and the sound of Jeri and Kayla scrambling away on dirt. Suddenly Winter screamed, a full-blooded wail of pure horror that turned me cold. She crashed into something wooden, shrieking insanely, her body drumming and thrashing against earth and pilings.

I crawled away. Jeri plowed into me in the dark.

"It's me," I said quickly. If I hadn't, she might've torn me apart thinking I was Winter.

"What's goin' on?" she asked.

I wasn't sure, but I thought maybe Winter had ended up in the midst of all those black widows I'd seen the other day. My skin crawled at the thought. I imagined them all around, gathering—except that they would be thickest near the latticework where flies came in, not this far under the house. Or so I hoped.

Winter was still screaming, smashing into things, but that didn't mean she wasn't about to pick up that goddamn foil and come after us at any moment.

"Go," I said. "That way." I shoved Jeri back the way she'd come, toward what I thought was the front of the house.

We caught up with Kayla. The three of us crawled across dank earth that hadn't been disturbed in decades. Winter's voice became a eerie sobbing moan, rising and falling. In that sound was madness, despair, bubbling horror. I heard her thud against wood, not as loud as before.

Our way was blocked by horizontal wooden planks, visible only as faint strips of light that came through hairline cracks between the slats. I coughed, felt blood swirl into my mouth. Not good, but now didn't seem the time to mention it to Jeri or Kayla.

Something pounded on wood, a solid, crashing noise, loud like a sledgehammer. And again. Then more of it, splintery sounds. Suddenly light spilled through in a broad band. My vision began to dim. I toppled to one side, feeling faint, too weak to kneel.

Another crash. Jeri was on her back, one bare foot slamming into the clapboards like a battering ram. One was gone; another was loose, flapping at one end. Then a third. Kayla helped her. Winter screamed one more time, weakly. Jeri disappeared through the opening she'd made. More boards were ripped away, torn loose from outside.

Jeri's hand reached in and grabbed mine, and I was dragged out onto Edna Woolley's front lawn on my back, into a crowd of goggling strangers, ten or fifteen of them, more of them coming, jogging across the street from the Golden Goose, drawn by Winter's screams, or maybe by the splintering of clapboards at the front of the house.

Kayla's face appeared above me, crying. Then Jeri's, but she wasn't crying. "Mort," she said. "Oh, Jesus, Mort." She put her hand against my chest and pressed, hard, into my blood. I tried to tell her it probably wasn't doing any good, but I couldn't say anything. I felt blood spill from the corner of my mouth.

Beyond Kayla and Jeri, hot pink wisps stood motionless against a field of sweet, luminous blue. I stared at it, entranced by the sight.

The sky. Clouds at sunset.

The colors slowly faded to gray. Peace settled over me. Nothing hurt.

"They're all like *naked*!" a woman said, a dumb, young-sounding half-giggly voice, and Jeri screamed, "Call 911! Get an ambulance!" her cry coming from far away, the echo of it growing fainter and fainter until it disappeared into a soft eternity of darkness that lay far beyond the clouds, beyond the sky, beyond sight or understanding.

CHAPTER TWENTY-FIVE

THE HOSPITAL WAS alternately cold, warm, then cold again, incomprehensible, visionary. A place of blurred fluorescent lighting, unintelligible urgent voices, scurrying people, hallucinatory half-remembered images and smells. Then they put me under. I remember that—being terrified that Winter would find me and kill me if I lost consciousness.

I awoke sometime during the night, either hours later or days, I had no way of knowing. I didn't say anything, though I tried. My mouth wouldn't work. My body felt unresponsive, a breathing, inanimate thing that was me, but not me, something I lay inside. It was a cocoon of me, not hot or cold, a numbed wrapping out of which I saw Kayla in a chair, staring at nothing. A moment before I drifted off again, I caught a glimpse of Dallas, or thought I did.

* * *

In time, the dreamworld came to an end. As I'd feared, Mortimer Angel, gumshoe extraordinaire, was once again a household name—and Dallas, Kayla, Jeri, Victoria, Winter, the whole damn circus—but I'll get to that in a while.

Sometime before midnight, Winter died. I heard about it the following day, or maybe the day after. She'd been bitten twenty-three times by black widow spiders, possibly a North American record. It was determined that she had rolled and thrashed along that lattice, gathering some, crushing others, pissing them off thoroughly, which is never a good idea. When she arrived at the hospital she had a few smashed and dead in her hair and one missing legs but still gnawing. Black widow envenomation. Technically, it's called latrodectism—the kind of word I'm inclined to forget within minutes, but I would remember this one, and fondly, because it had rid the world of a monster. They gave her calcium gluconate and antivenin among other things, but she didn't make it. Maybe she'd been brought in too late, but I'm inclined to think that at barely a hundred pounds she wouldn't have stood much of a chance if she'd been brought in sooner. She had one bite for every four-and-a-half pounds of girl. It's hard to bounce back from something like that.

She was under the house for over an hour before the paramedics found her and pulled her out—unconscious, breathing with difficulty, cramped, covered in oily sweat. Kayla and Jeri hadn't known what had happened to her, and I couldn't tell anyone. Winter had a broken arm and numerous contusions, all of them self-inflicted except for an enormous bruise where I'd kicked her belly, managing to break two ribs. I was happy about that. May she rest in pieces.

Victoria was found in the basement with a broken neck, broken jaw, ruptured windpipe, teeth shattered. Russell Fairchild told me she was dead before she hit the floor. As far as I was concerned, Jeri had the best damn kick in all of North America, bar none.

Mine were the first fencing wounds anyone at the hospital had ever seen. They'd pretty much gone out of style in the 1700s. Chalk up another one for me. The doctors treated them like .22 caliber gunshot wounds. I was in surgery for five hours, mostly because of that damn punctured lung. The steel had gone in between my second and third ribs, missing the left subclavian artery by a quarter of an inch. By millimeters, I was still alive.

Jeri wandered into intensive care wearing a hospital gown at ten o'clock the morning after—about the time I was starting to come out of it, though I was high as a kite on a very nice morphine derivative. She'd spent the night up on a different floor, under observation. She had a slight concussion after landing on her back on the floor, hitting her head on that door. My concussion was worse. We traded concussion stories like old combat Marines, and she held my hand for ten minutes with Dallas smiling at us—then a gang of nurses chased them both away in order to do terrible things to me, one of which was unmentionable and involved a catheter.

All of this was fine fodder for the media. A news van had pulled up at Sjorgen House before any police or ambulance crews got there, and, later the following day, I saw myself on television— again. It had taken considerable effort on the part of blackout artists to render Jeri, Kayla, and me acceptable for consumption by an alert, eager, news-hungry nation.

I missed Greg's funeral. Catheters, I didn't have to be told, make for awkward, unsightly travel. But my sister, Ellen, came by and we had a good long visit until I lapsed into morphine-derivative unconsciousness right in the middle of a sentence I don't remember starting.

Awake the next day, I decided it would be a good long while before I showed up at the Golden Goose and heard what that sonofabitch O'Roarke had to say about all this. As it turned out, I didn't have to. Five days into my recovery, when I was hours out of intensive care, he wandered into my room with a shit-eating grin on his Irish mug, a bunch of dumb-ass pink-and-white carnations he'd probably swiped from the room next door, and sixty free-drink coupons that wouldn't expire until the end of the year.

In time, of course, the police trooped in, meaning Fairchild. He wasn't happy that we'd solved his case for him, made him and the department look bad on national TV. Before the Sjorgen House Battle, his men had tracked down the bare-bones, sanitized agreement that had given Sjorgen House to Edna Woolley, but not the reason behind it. They'd never heard of Jacoba, Victoria, or Winter. They'd been spinning their wheels while the country's finest gumshoe—okay, gumshoes—had busted the case wide open. Forty years had buried the relevant history too deep, even if it was the police department that had helped to bury it. I tried to cheer Russ up by pointing out that he had been about two years out of diapers at the time Edna took over occupational possession of Sjorgen House, probably tearing around his backyard on a bright yellow Big Wheels and watching *Sesame Street* or *Mr. Ed* reruns on television. That was the first and only time I'd been given the finger in a hospital.

* * *

I went home after eleven interminable days, six days after they removed the drains from my chest, four days after I decided hospital food might be more lethal than being run through with a sword. Dallas was with me when a nurse pushed me out the front door in a wheelchair, through half a dozen video cameras and a flurry of inane questions. She drove me back to my house in a brand-new Mercedes, one in which neither Jonnie nor his head had ever taken a ride. By then, Jeri was away on a case, somewhere in Las Vegas. It had been five days since I'd last seen Kayla.

Ever the note-leaver, she'd left one on a nightstand in the bed-room. It read:

Dear Mort,
She would have died for you.
I've gone back to Ithaca.
Please forgive me.
K.

What was to forgive? Things had gotten pretty hairy down there in that dungeon-basement. I could understand her not wanting to remember any part of it. I set the note down, feeling rotten even though I'd known she was gone, known back at Sjorgen House that terrible afternoon that she and I would never make it even if we survived the ordeal. Not after what had gone down.

"That from Kayla?" Dallas asked, looking at the expression on my face.

"Yeah. She's gone."

"I'm so sorry, Mort."

"Uh-huh."

I was still tired. Dallas hung around a while longer, made me eat a little soup, then she left.

* * *

In time, however, and it didn't take all that long, considering, the entire business took on something of a dreamlike quality. I think that was because it was so weird, the whole thing. The horror of it softened to something resembling a well-remembered nightmare—frightening as hell, but unreal. I could deal with it. At times I could even shut it off, forget it for full minutes at a time. I could even watch Leno and laugh. Jonnie had died very badly, maybe worse than he'd deserved, Milliken too, but people die badly every day and too many of them are innocent children, so I didn't shed a tear for Jonnie, per se, just for the sick horror of it all. Mostly, I tried to forget.

A week went by. I was in the shower and fairly well recovered from my wounds when the doorbell rang. Perfect timing. God must arrange these things to see what'll happen. So, not wanting to disappoint, I got out—dripping—thinking now was my big chance to run some hotshot media buzzard from my doorstep all the way to the sidewalk by the seat of his chinos. The sutures had been removed. It would be a good test of my shoulder and basic arm strength. I wrapped a towel around my waist. One glance at a clock told me it was seven o'clock in the evening.

Rachel was at the door. Rachel. Wow. I had a flashback, a sudden smell of meat and cheese, a vision of Skulstad's bean counters hunched over their desks. She had a paper sack in one hand. She looked good, very statuesque, wearing a clingy sleeveless dress that came to eight inches above her knees, neckline so low it took all I had to keep my eyes from drifting.

At my attire, and the puddle forming at my feet, she gave me an apologetic smile, then took a single step into the house so I could close the door. I caught a whiff of perfume. "It was Iris," she said.

"Huh?"

"Iris Kacsmaryk? She left one day after you gave that menacing little speech of yours, which Betty repeated for me. Betty Pope, if you remember. Lady with the big hair. Since then, things have been fine. We hired a new girl yesterday."

"Oh. That's good."

"I just thought you'd like to know."

I'd solved bigger cases since then, so her news amounted to small potatoes, but I didn't tell her that. "Thanks," I said.

She smiled awkwardly. "I, uh, brought over some food. It's from Sardina's, over on Mira Loma. Rigatoni and lasagna, garlic bread. It's still hot."

Smelled good, too.

Behind me, Jeri said, "Hi, I'm Jeri." She was wearing a towel that matched mine. And, like me, she was dripping all over the floor. I'd told her to stay put, I would handle it, whatever *it* was, but...hell, she never listens.

Rachel said, "Oops, uh, I'm Rachel. A friend."

I said, "Jeri, Rachel. Rachel, Jeri."

"Guess I'll be on my way," Rachel said. She put the bag in my arms, backed out the door, and said, "Enjoy, Mortimer, Jeri."

"Mort," I said.

Rachel left. I shut the door, then turned and looked at Jeri. She smiled, water dripping into her face from sopping hair full of those wonderful deep-red highlights.

"Hey, look," I said. "Food." I held up the bag.

"Delivery girls are getting prettier all the time."

"Uh-huh."

"Uniforms are cut kinda lower, too."

"Uh-huh."

"You never mentioned that one before."

"Uh-huh. It's not my fault that girls flock to me like pigeons to a statue."

Jeri unwound the towel and let it hang from one hand. She stood hipshot and looked me in the eye. "How about you put that stuff in the kitchen. We were interrupted. You're needed in the shower."

"Yes, ma'am...uh, boss," I said. "Right away."